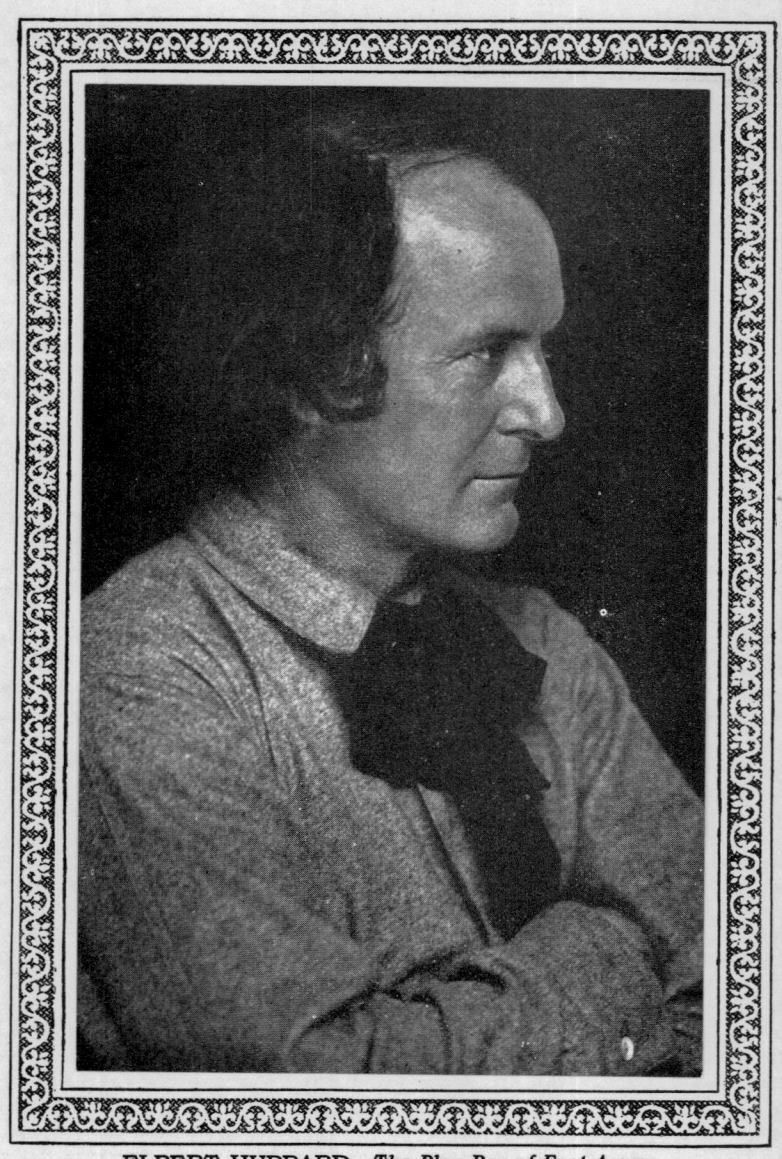

ELBERT HUBBARD—*The Play-Boy of East Aurora*

SHORT STORIES

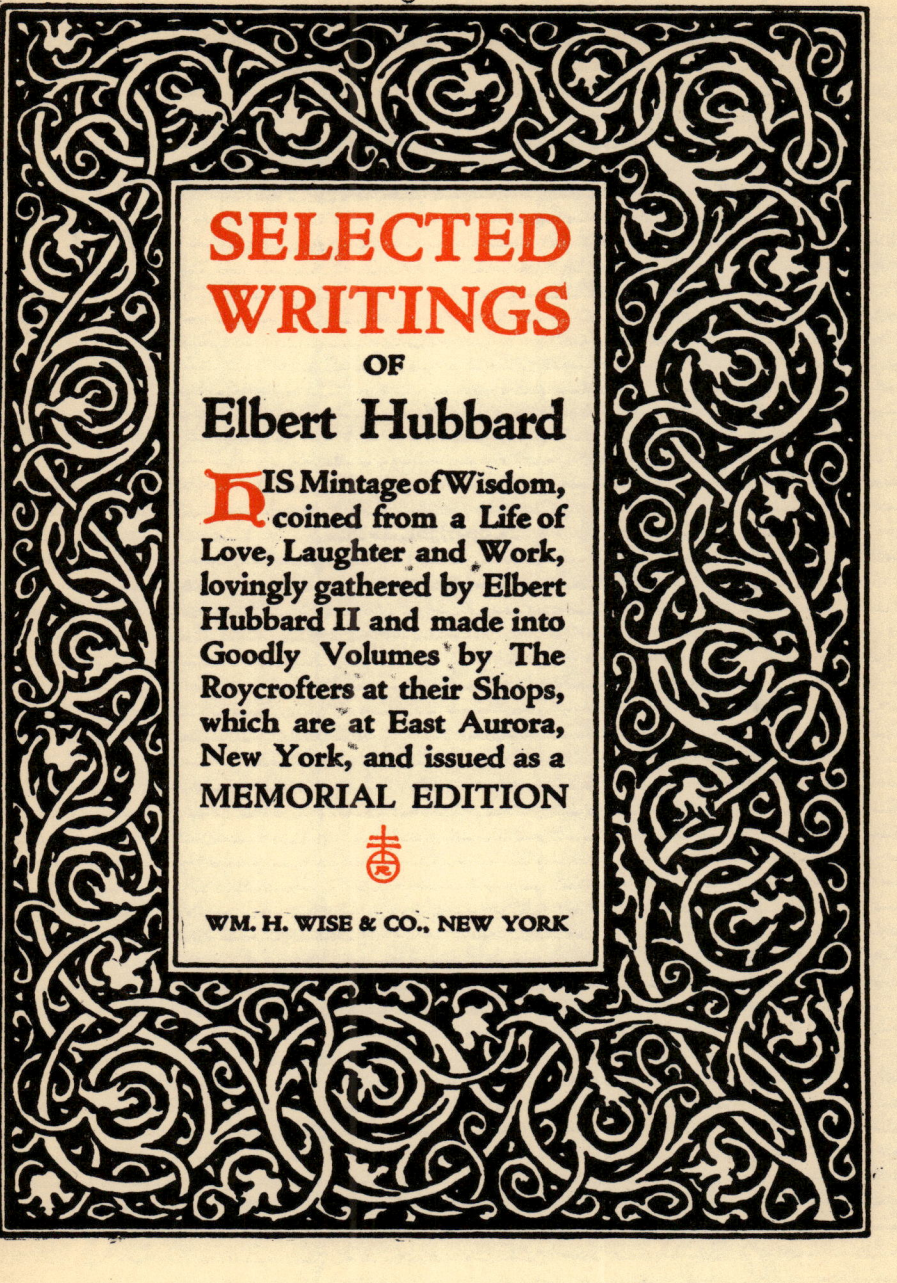

SELECTED WRITINGS
OF
Elbert Hubbard

His Mintage of Wisdom, coined from a Life of Love, Laughter and Work, lovingly gathered by Elbert Hubbard II and made into Goodly Volumes by The Roycrofters at their Shops, which are at East Aurora, New York, and issued as a MEMORIAL EDITION

WM. H. WISE & CO., NEW YORK

**Copyright, 1928
by
The Roycrofters**

CONTENTS

The Silver Arrow	13
How I Found My Brother	27
Sam	38
Please Be Seated	41
Uncle Joe and Aunt Melinda	43
The Fish are Coming	45
"Give It to Him, Tim!"	49
A Roycroft Christening	51
God Save the King	53
The Master Man	57
Louis V. Eytinge	60
Charles S. Whitman	66
Anna A. Malley	70
"Jimmie" Durkin	73
Heinrich Schliemann	78
The Great Raymond	83
"Golightly" Morrill	87
W. D. Wilmot	91
David Bispham	93
William G. Hussey	94
Hon. Thomas Brackett Reed	100
J. W. Jenkins' Sons Music Company	102
Saskatoon	113
A Little History in Tabloid	131
A Notable Achievement	136
A Little Journey to the Home of the Columbia Grafonola	142
Tools of Civilization	152
Venture in Vaudeville	154
Canada and Reciprocity	180
A Top-Notcher	184
Bad Breaks in Business	185
The Winners	188
Business Conditions	196
Who Is Boss?	201

System and Success	204
A Report on Yourself	207
Women Farmers	209
On Making Investments	211
Tyranny of Fashion	212
As to Competition	215
The Quitter	219
Great Inventions	222
Loss and Gain	226
Conspicuous American Success	228
Dr. Jenner's Discovery	230
The Legal Profession	242
The University Militant	248
Justice, Human and Divine	252
The Day of Your Death	256
The Common People	259
The Beautiful Dream of Socialism	262
The Good Fellow	267
Physician's Farewell	269
The Other Side	274
He Used the Synonym	277
J. B. Runs Things	278
His Umps Saves the Day	280
A Fable	281
Good Night	283
Acquired by Antiquarian	284
Every Man to His Job	285
Titanic Survivor	287
"Days are As Grass"	290
One of the Elect	291
In the Wrong Pew	293
Health and Play in North Woods	294
Farming and Railroading	297
Butterflies	304
Index	309

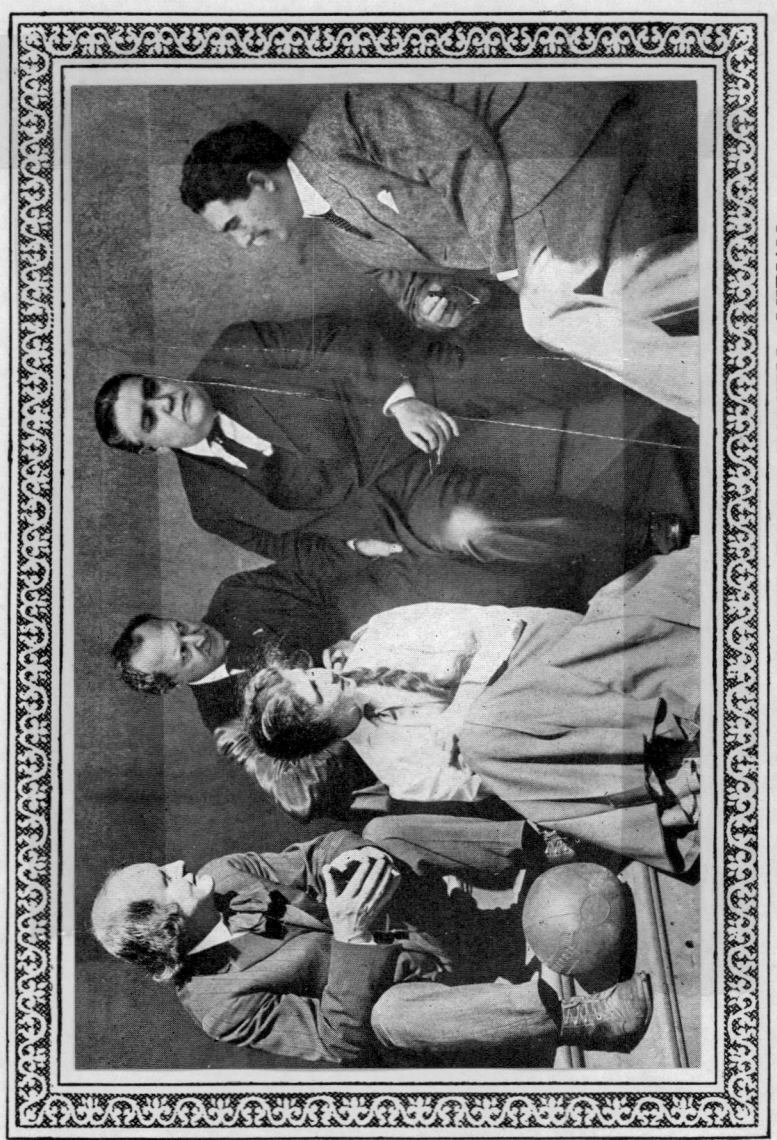

ELBERT HUBBARD—STRAUSS—REEDY—NORVELL—MIRIAM

The Silver Arrow

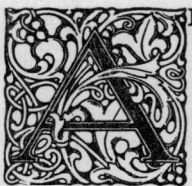AND so it happened that Sir Walter Raleigh, the graceful, the gracious, the generous, had spread his cloak in the pathway of Queen Elizabeth and had been taken into her especial favor.

The Queen was nineteen years older than Sir Walter; that is to say, she was in her fifties, and he was in his thirties.

But Queen Bess hated old age, and swore a halibi for the swift passing years, and always delighted in the title of the "Virgin Queen."

Sir Walter did one great thing for England, and one for Ireland. He taught the English the use of tobacco, and he discovered the "Irish potato"—which is native to America.

They do say that Sir Walter and Queen Elizabeth enjoyed many a quiet smoke with their feet on the table—so as to equalize circulation. Both of them were big folk, with plans and ambitions plus

Sir Walter was contemporary with Shakespeare, and in fact looked like him, acted like him and had a good deal of the same agile, joyous, bubbling fertility of mind.

That is, Sir Walter and William were lovers by nature; and love rightly exercised, and alternately encouraged and thwarted, gives the alternating current, and lo! we have that which the world calls genius. And I am told by those who know, that you can never get genius in any other way.

Good Queen Bess—who was not so very good—fanned the ambitions of Sir Walter and flattered his abilities. And of course any man born in a lowly station, or high, would have been immensely complimented by the gentle love-taps, and sighs, vain or otherwise, not to mention the glimmering glances of the alleged Virgin Queen.

But a good way to throttle love is to spy on it, question it, analyze it, vivisect it. And so Sir Walter's bubbling heart had chills of fear when he discovered that he was being followed wherever he went by the secret emissaries of Elizabeth.

Had he been free to act he would have disposed of these spies, and quickly too; but he was in thrall to a Queen, and was paying for his political power by being deprived of his personality. Oho, and Oho! ⚜ ⚜

The law of compensation acted then as now, and nothing is ever given away; everything is bought with a price—even the favors of royalty.

And behold! In the palace of the Queen, as janitor, gardener, scullion and all-around handy man was one John White, obscure, and yet elevated on account of his lack of wit.

He was so stupid that he was amusing. Sayings bright and clever that courtiers flung off when the wine went around were imputed to John White. Thus he came to have a renown which was not his own; and Sir Walter Raleigh, with his cheery, generous ways, attributed many a quiet quip and quillet to John White which John White had never thought nor said.

Now John White had a daughter, Eleanor by name, tall and fair and gracious, bearing in her veins the blood of Vikings bold; and her yellow hair blew in the breeze as did the yellow hair of those conquerors who discovered America and built the blockhouses along the coast of Rhode Island.

Doubtless in his youth John White had a deal of sturdy worth, but a bump on the sconce at some Donnybrook Fair early in his young manhood had sent his wits a woolgathering.

But the girl was not thus handicapped; her mind was alert and eager ⚜ ⚜

The mother of Eleanor had passed away, and the girl had grown strong and able in spirit through carrying burdens and facing responsibilities. She knew the limitations of her father and she knew his worth; and she also knew that he was a sort of unofficial fool for the court, being duly installed through the clever and heedless tongue of Sir Walter Raleigh.

Who would ever have thought that Sir Walter, the diplomat, the strong, the able, was to be brought low by this fair-haired daughter of John White, the court fool!

" You are Sir Walter Raleigh," said this girl of nineteen one day to Sir Walter when they met squarely face to face in a hallway. It was a bold thing to do to stop this statesman, and she only a daughter to a court fool, and herself a worker below stairs!

◐ Sir Walter smiled, removed his hat in mock gallantry, and said, " I have the honor to be your obedient servant. And who are you? "

The girl, buoyed up by a combination of pride and fear, replied, " I am Eleanor White, the daughter of the man whom your wit has rendered famous." And their eyes met in level, steady look. Fair femininity aroused caught the eye and the ear of Sir Walter.

" Yes," said he; " I think I have seen you. And what can I do for you? "

" Only this," said Eleanor, " that from this day forth you will not attribute any more of your ribaldry to my father."

" Otherwise, what? " asked Sir Walter.

" Otherwise, you will have me to deal with," said the proud Eleanor, and walked past him.

He tried to call her back; he felt humiliated that she did not turn and look, much less listen. He had been snubbed.

The banderilla went home, and the next day Sir Walter felt that he must hunt out this girl with the yellow locks and make peace with her, for surely he of all men did not want to hurt the feeling of any living being, neither did he want his own feelings hurt.

◐ So he sought her out, and that which began in a quarrel soon evolved into something else. There were meetings by moonlight, notes passed, glances given, hand-clasps in the dark, and all of those absurd, foolish, irrelevant and unnecessary things that lovers do ❧ ❧

The girl was not of noble birth. But neither was Sir Walter, for that matter. Love knows nothing of titles and position.

But how could these two ever imagine that they could elude the gimlet eyes of Good Queen Bess, who was n't so very good!

⁋ Queen Elizabeth had ways of punishing that were exquisite, deep, delicate and far-reaching, which touched the very marrow of the soul ❧ ❧

Sir Walter had been presented by the Queen with a title to all the land in America, from Nova Scotia to Florida; and he, in pretty compliment, had officially named this tract of land Virginia.

⁋ The French had taken possession of the New World at the North, and the Spaniards at the South, and along the coast of what is now North Carolina the English had planted a colony.

⁋ It was the intention of Sir Walter to send expeditions over and take the whole land captive, so that Virginia would in fact be the land of the Virgin Queen.

At the center of this tract along the coast was to be the city of Raleigh. The Queen and Sir Walter had worked this out at length, and she had given him a special charter for the great city to be.

⁋ And now, behold! She, with the mind of a man, had perfected her plans for the building of the city of Raleigh. She planned an expedition, and fitted out the ships with sixty men and women from a receiving-ship that lay in the Thames. These people were being sent out of England for England's good. And these were the people who were to found the city of Raleigh; and the Governor of this colony was to be—John White! he was to be the first mayor, Lord Mayor, of the city of Raleigh.   .

Queen Elizabeth had selected a husband for Eleanor White, an unknown youth—a defective, in fact, and one without moral or mental responsibility. She had forced a marriage, or in any event had recorded it as such. The youth was known as Ananias Dare.

Even in the naming of this individual, who had never dared anything, the name " Ananias " carried with it a subtle sting.
John White and his daughter Eleanor, and Ananias Dare, were taken forcibly and put on the ship, which was duly provisioned, and the order given to found the city of Raleigh on the Island of Roanoke in the country called Virginia.
A suitable sailor was selected as navigator, and orders were given him to land the colonists, and come back.
And so the expedition sailed away for the New World; and Sir Walter Raleigh in the secret of his room beat his head in anguish 'gainst the wall and called aloud for death to come and relieve him of his pain.
And thus did Queen Elizabeth dispose of her rival, and punish with fantastic hate and jealousy the man she loved.
John White, Eleanor and Ananias Dare, with the motley group of unskilled men and women, were duly landed in the forest on Roanoke Island. Battle with the elements requires judgment, skill, experience, and these were things that our poor colonists did not possess.
Two weeks after landing on Roanoke Island a daughter was born to Eleanor. The captain of the ship had been given orders that if the babe was a boy it was to be named Walter Raleigh Dare; if a girl the name was to be Virginia.
And they called the child Virginia Dare, and her name was so recorded in the history of the colony. She was duly baptized a week later, and the record of her birth and baptism still exists in the Colonial Archives in London.
This was the first white child born in America.
Very shortly after the baptism of the babe, the captain of the ship sailed away for England, leaving the colonists in their ignorance and helplessness to battle with the elements, wild beasts, and Indians as best they could.
We can imagine with what cruel delight Queen Elizabeth called

Sir Walter Raleigh into her presence and had him read aloud to her and the assembled court the record of the birth of Virginia Dare ༄ ༄

As for the colonists, their days were few and evil. Dissensions and feuds arose, as they naturally would. John White was deposed as Governor, and when he resisted he was killed.

The idea of going to work, tilling the soil, and building a permanent settlement was not in the hearts of those people. They expected to find gold and silver and fountains of youth. They felt they were marooned, robbed and stranded. The Indians, at first fearful, were not jealous of these white intruders. The quarrel came and the Indians fell upon the colonists and killed every one. Every one, did I say? There was one saved; it was the little white baby, Virginia Dare.

She was rescued by a squaw, who but a short time before had lost her own babe, and her hungry mother heart went out to that helpless little white waif. She seized upon the child and carried it away into the forest for safety.

PART TWO

On Thursday, October Twenty-ninth, Sixteen Hundred Eighteen, at the Tower of London, the curtain fell on the fifth act of the life of Sir Walter Raleigh. It was a public holiday for all London. ❡ The morning was cold and foggy.

Sir Walter was kept standing on the scaffold while the headsman ground his axe, the delay being for the amusement and edification of the people assembled.

The High Sheriff approached the man who was so soon to die, and asked if there was not some last message he wished to send to some one. Sir Walter took from his neck a gold chain and locket. He handed them to the Sheriff and said, " Send these by a trusty messenger to Virginia Dare by the first ship that sails for the New World."

Sir Walter's frame shook in the cold, dank fog, and the Sheriff offered to bring a brazier of coals, but the great man proudly drew his cloak about him and said: " It is the ague I contracted in America. I will soon be cured of it!" And he laid his proud head, gray in the service of his country, calmly on the block, as if to say, " There now, take that, it is all I have left to give!"
ℭ Among the crowd that pushed, jostled, leered and looked was one Oliver Cromwell, short, swart and strong, a country youth who had come up to London to make his fortune. And Oliver Cromwell there and then made a vow that he would dedicate his life to the death of tyranny. So died Sir Walter Raleigh.
And Oliver Cromwell went forth to meet Fate as Destiny had willed ֍ ֍

PART THREE

The Indian woman who rescued Virginia Dare was Wahceta, wife of Manteno, the Croatoan chief.
This Indian woman had other children of her own, some almost grown up, and when she brought this little white waif into their midst they gazed in awe and wonderment, and exclaimed, " White Doe!"
And this was the name given by common consent to the little intruder ֍ ֍
Wahceta cared for the babe as if it were her very own.
The helplessness of the little guest made an appeal to Wahceta, and she guarded her charge with jealous eyes, and a love that she had never manifested for her own children. Manteno looked on and shrugged his shoulders in half token of fear, for a white doe was a thing to be feared, since the superstition was that it was sent by the Great Spirit as a warning.
Hunters to this day are familiar with the occasional appearance of a white deer—an albino—one of Nature's sports, like the proverbial black sheep, to be found in every flock of white ones.

The Indians regarded a white doe as invincible to all weapons save a silver arrow alone. A white doe bore a charmed life, and was looked after with especial care by protecting spirits.

And so in wonder, when Wahceta would walk past, bearing on her back the white babe, the Indians silently made way, feeling somehow that they were close to the Great Spirit.

The child grew and learned to speak the Croatoan language with a glibness that made Wahceta laugh aloud in glee.

White Doe had flaxen hair, that glistened with the sheen of the sunshine. Very proud was Wahceta of those yellow locks, and she used to braid them in long strands, while the Indians stood around, looking on, having nothing else to do.

One day, when White Doe was about ten years old, she went away into the forest as she often did; but when night came on she had not returned. Wahceta went out to look for her, and called aloud in shrill soprano, but no reply came.

Manteno was appealed to, to arouse the braves and go search for the lost little girl. But Manteno was tired and sleepy, and he had faith in Providence. He knew that the child would be cared for by the Great Spirit. Wahceta started a bonfire on the hill above the village, and waited away the long hours of the night for her lost baby so so

In the morning, just as the sun peeped over the tree-tops, White Doe appeared, her hair all wet with the dew of the night, and her feet cut and bleeding.

She was leading and half-dragging something—was it a dog or a wolf? Wahceta sprang forward to take the child in her arms. " Get behind, mother, and push," said little White Doe. " It's a white doe, and I've held it all night for fear it would get away! Push hard, mother, dear, and we will get it in the teepee and tie it with green withes, and it will become gentle, and bring us all good luck."

The child had discovered this white fawn with its mother, feeding near a salt-lick. White Doe lay on a rock above the spring, waiting for the deer to come up close. There the girl waited for hours. She knew that at dusk the deer would come to the spring. Sure enough, her patience was suddenly rewarded. She leaped from her rock and pinned the white fawn fast. The old deer disappeared into the forest. The girl held on to her prize. It struck her with its forefeet, but she held it close. By and by, tired out, the fawn lay still and rested entwined in the girl's arms. Now came the test—to get it home! She succeeded.

In the teepee of Wahceta, the animal was fed, caressed and cared for so so

It grew docile, and in a few days followed its little mistress about wherever she went.

The Indians looked on in half-dread, with superstitious awe. ❡ "All the wild animals would be as tame as this if you were not so cruel to them," she said. " You fear the wolves and bears and so you kill them!"

To prove her point she began to hunt the forests for young bears and cub wolves. She found several, and brought them home, making household friends of them. And still more did the Indians marvel so so

So the days went by then, as the days go by now, and White Doe grew into gorgeous, glowing girlhood.

Her ability to run, climb, shoot with bow and arrow, to see, to hear, to revel in Nature, gave her a lithe, strong, tall and beautiful form and an alert mind. Of her birth she knew nothing, save that she was descended from another race—a race of half-gods, the Indians said. White Doe believed it, and her pride of pedigree was supreme.

The other children, dark as smoked copper, stood around clothed in their black hair—and little else—hair as black as the raven's wing so so

Wahceta watched her charge with fear for the future. White Doe had temper, intelligence, wit, ability. She would roam the forests alone, unafraid. She knew where the bee-trees were, for even as a child she saw that the bees would gather at the basswood, and then loaded with honey would fly straight away for their homes. To follow them in their flight required a practised eye, but this White Doe had, and always the white doe followed her. She wove the inner bark of the slippery-elm into baskets, and would supply the teepee of Wahceta and Manteno with more berries, potatoes and goobers than any other teepee enjoyed.

Then she laid out gardens and tilled the soil with a wonderful wooden hoe, carved out of solid hickory with her own hands.

❡ Wahceta was growing old, and as her sight was becoming dim White Doe would lead her about through the forest and care for her as Wahceta once cared for White Doe.

The work of looking after Manteno's tent drifted by degrees into the hands of White Doe. Her industry, her thrift, her intelligence set her apart.

The Indian is like a white man in this: he allows work and responsibility to drift into the hands of those who can manage them. White Doe set about to build stone houses to replace the bark teepees. Where did she get the idea? Prenatal tendencies you say? Possibly.

She drew pictures with a burnt stick on the flat surface of the cliff, and then ornamented these pictures with red and blue chalk which she dug from the ground.

She took the juice of the grape, the elder and the whortleberry, and brewed them together to make wondrous colors for the pictures: and in some of the caves of North Carolina may be seen the pictures, even unto this day, drawn by White Doe.

❡ Wahceta passed away and her form was wrapped in its winding-sheet of deerskins and bark and placed high in the forks of a tree-top, awaiting the pleasure of the Great Spirit.

Manteno also died. And the people did not choose another chief—

they looked to White Doe for counsel and guidance. She was their "medicine-man," in case of sickness or accident, and in health their counselor and Queen. Indians from other towns and distant came to her. She cured the sick and healed the lame.

She lived alone in a stone hut, guarded by a wolf and a bear that she had brought up from their babyhood. They followed her footsteps wherever she went, and also, too, came the white doe, fleet of foot, luminous of eye, sensitive, intelligent, seemingly intent on carrying the messages of her mistress.

White Doe, the Indian Queen, with long yellow hair, and the big, mild, yet searching blue eyes, knew her power and exercised it.

❡ Indian braves, young and handsome, came and sat on the grass cross-legged for hours, at a discreet distance from her hut, making love to her in pantomime. They sent her presents rare and precious, of buckskins, tanned soft as velvet, nuggets of silver strung as beads, and strings of wampum.

These braves she set to work down in the bottom-lands. It is said that no other person was ever able to set the male Indian to work. But for her the braves built stone houses, planted gardens, and laid stepping-stones across the fords, so that she could walk across dry-shod.

The nuggets of silver that they brought her from the mountains she fashioned into an exquisite arrow of silver, sharper at the point than the sharpest flint. For days and weeks and months she worked making the silver arrow.

"What is it for?" the Indians asked.

"It is to help me when all other help is gone," she said.

And the Indians were silent, mystified.

She planted slips of grapes brought from the sunny slopes; these she tended, dug about, trained and trimmed. The wonderful Scuppernong Grape was her own evolution. By care and culture it covered the cabin where she lived, and reached out to an oak a hundred feet beyond.

She showed the Indians how to double their crops of corn, how to grow such melons as the Indian world had never before known. She taught them that it was much better to work and produce flowers, grain, grapes, and make pictures on the rocks than to roam the woods aimlessly, looking for something to kill.

She told them that the Great Spirit loved people who were kind and useful, and temperate in the use of the juice of the grape and in all other good things. So the Croatoans advanced and grew in intelligence quite beyond any of the other Indian tribes on the Atlantic Coast.

One day White Doe sat at the door of her cabin, under the great vine where hung the grapes.

She was intently painting a picture on buckskin.

The white doe was nibbling at the bushes only a few feet away.

¶ The gray wolf that crouched at her feet suddenly snarled, and the hair on his back arose in wrath.

White Doe looked up, and there at a distance of a hundred feet stood a man—a pale-faced man.

He saw the wolf, and stood stock-still.

White Doe looked at the man, and suddenly her heart beat fast. She felt the color mounting to her face. She drew her long, yellow hair over her neck and her buckskin dress up at the shoulder.

The man motioned for her to come to him.

Evidently he saw the wolf and dare not go forward.

She arose, pacified the wolf, and slipped forward.

The man had a dark beard, but his complexion told her that they were of the same race.

He spoke to her in English.

She had never before heard a word of the language spoken.

In amazement she listened, and then shook her head.

The man now resorted to the sign language; he made the motions of paddling a canoe, and pointed toward the sea. And then she knew that he had come from far across the sea in a ship.

He took from one of his pockets a chain of gold; and attached to this chain was a little gold locket.

He opened the locket and showed her a picture inside. On the locket were engraved the words, " To Sir Walter Raleigh, from his Queen, Elizabeth."

White Doe saw the inscription, but she could not read it.

The man offered to put the chain and locket about her neck. She stepped back, and the wolf at her heels snarled. She made a motion that the interview was ended and that the man should go to see the Indians whose houses and cabins were but a short distance away.

The man did not go. Instead, he in the universal sign language took off his hat, pressed his hand on his heart, and fell on one knee ॐ ॐ

He motioned to the East, away—away, away across the sea! ⁋ Would she go with him?

Proudly she shook her head, half-smiled and again ordered him to go ॐ ॐ

Her manner said plainly that this was her home: She was Queen of the Croatoans—was this not enough?

A shade of anger moved across the man's face. He was used to having his orders obeyed. He moved toward her as if he would seize her. Now it was her turn to stand still. The wolf leaped to her side, and across the intervening space from the cabin lumbered a big black bear.

The man now backed slowly away some ten paces, and then he lifted a gun that lay on the grass where he had left it.

Suddenly a score of white men emerged from the bushes.

There was a flash of fire, a loud explosion, a great volume of white smoke. And the wolf, the bear, and the white doe all fell weltering in their blood.

The wolf was not dead, and with fierce snarls tried desperately to crawl toward the white man.

One of the men ran forward and beat its brains out with a club.
℃ The Indians came rushing from their houses.
There was another flash of fire, a cloud of smoke, and the forward Indian fell dead. The rest of the red folks fled in wild alarm.
℃ White Doe stood still, her yellow hair blowing in the sunshine. Again the leader of the white men came forward, a smile of triumph on his face. His manner said more plainly than any words could express: " You are in my power. See! I have killed your protectors, your friends. So I can kill you. You must come with me."
He pressed his hand to his heart in sign of love.
The woman backed away from him, her eyes shooting hatred and defiance.
At her girdle hung the silver arrow. Her hand now reached for it.
℃ The man leaped forward and attempted to seize her. His reach fell short, for the woman was quicker and quite as strong as he. She flung him aside. The silver arrow was in her right hand. She held it aloft like a dagger.
The man retreated.
" Coward," she cried in Croatoan. " Coward! it is not for you. It is my last friend—the friend that has been waiting to save me all these years! "
The arrow flashed in the air, and with a terrific lunge went straight to the woman's heart.
She leaped into the air, reeled and fell across the body of the dying doe. And the blood of the two friends intermingled.

How I Found My Brother

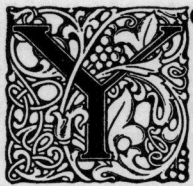OU see, it was about like this: I was 'leven years old, going on twelve. Our folks lived at the village of Hudson, McLean County, ten miles from Bloomington, which is in the state of Illinois. My father was a doctor, and being a country doctor did not roll in wealth any to speak of. In those days every one in Illinois was poor, no matter how much land he owned. However, we owned our farm, had four horses, five cows, a dozen pigs and a flock of hens.

There were always vegetables in the cellar, smoked meat in the wood-shed, and pickled beef in the kitchen. At the back door was a keg of soft soap.

In the garret where I slept, in the winter the snow drifted cheerily in through the cracks and covered the buffalo robes that covered me. But I did n't lie awake nights thinking about it—country boys who work all day begin to pound their ear as soon as they hit the pillow.

I was the only boy, and you know what that is in a family where there are four big sisters! I had to make the garden, milk the cows, bring in the wood and churn. Of course, there was a lot of fun about it all—more than I knew of at the time. In the winter I hunted rabbits with an old army musket, and brought home so much bunny meat that the whole family went on a strike, and declared I should study my books more and not hunt rabbits quite so much.

In the spring and fall when the prairie ponds were full of water, the wild ducks on their regular trips north or south got stop-overs and remained with us a few days—thousands of them—and a few of them neglected to go on. Ducks are harder to kill than rabbits. I used to load the old musket up so heavy that when I would fire it off, if I did not look out sharp, I would get kicked end over end.

Then I would get up and look for ducks, and usually they were flying away on "the far and distant horizon," as the poets say.
⁋ In winter I went to school. We used to play "Anteny Over," with a yarn ball. That is, we chose sides; one gang stood on one side of the school house and the other half on the other. You yelled Anteny Over and threw the ball over the school house. The boy that caught it yelled Anteny Over, but instead of throwing it, he sneaked around the corner and soaked the first fellow he saw, and usually the ball was soaked in water, so when you got hit you knew it. Then the fellow that was hit had to go over on the other side. When the bell rang the side that had the most men was the winner.
Then we played one-old-cat and three-cornered-cat. Saturdays there were boys playing ball on the prairie back of the church all day, and if I could sneak away I was usually one of the players. I was a genuine Son of Swat.
This brought me many scoldings, and a few mild lickings, because I neglected my work.
As a ball player I was a bird—I used to take a piece of a barrel stave and when that yarn ball came anywhere around I gave it a wallop you could have heard a mile. We pitched underhand, and I could certainly do up the town on pitching as well as crossing 'em out. I became a three-cornered-cat fiend.
Everything that came on the first bound, I gathered in; the flies I caught in my hat. When my big sister played, she used to catch 'em in her apron.
Finally, I almost forgot how to curry a horse, and the girls had to milk the cows, carry in the wood and hunt for the eggs, because I was off playing three-cornered-cat.
Our folks took two papers, weeklies: the *Baptist Standard* and the *Weekly Pantagraph*. I read the *Pantagraph*.
Now, one day I saw in the *Weekly Pantagraph* that a man, calling himself the agent of the Children's Aid Society of New

York, was to be in Bloomington the next week with twenty-five children and that respectable farmers and such who wanted to adopt children should be on hand and make their selection.
¶ I spelled out the item four or five times, and then carried it to my mother asking what it meant. And she explained to me that these children were orphans, and there were people who had no children of their own, or not as many as they wanted, who adopted them ⁂ ⁂

And then a great idea came to me—I needed a brother, and here was a chance to get one. The three brothers I once had, died while very young, and although I could remember them but dimly, there were three little mounds in the graveyard that we used to visit on Sunday afternoons, that kept their memory green ⁂ ⁂

When I suggested going to Bloomington and picking out a brother for myself, my mother tried to laugh, but I saw the tears running down her cheeks, and then she threw her apron over her head and went out to bring the clothes in off the line.

The next day I brought up the subject at the table. Everybody smiled—they thought it was a fine joke.

Father concluded that we had all the children he could feed, but I argued that I got fifty cents a day when they were running the Brown cornsheller for driving on the horse-power, and in harvest time I could get a dollar a day. If we had another boy, I could work all the time and the other boy could do the chores. " And give you time to play ball," chimed in my big sister.

I loftily waived her remark, but clung to the argument that I needed a brother.

Sis felt a little sorry for what she had said, so she came over to my side and suggested that these orphan children were sent out for a month first, and then adopted if all parties were willing.

" Sent on suspicion," said father.

" It is better than the other way," I argued, " because if you don't like 'em, you don't have to keep 'em, and the other way you can't send 'em back after they have been used."

"The garden work is behind, you know," I continued, "and I can never do it alone."

There was a little more parley with instances by father where orphan boys had set fire to hay-stacks, turned the cows in the corn, stolen chickens, and cooked them on wire fences by making a fire beneath.

But Sis offset all this by naming three adopted boys who not only worked well, but had joined the Baptist Church and been baptized by cutting a hole in the ice in the creek, only a few months before. That last settled it, I was given permission to go and pick out a boy. Father and mother would make no promises—if I could get him on a month's trial, all well and good.

And right there I ceased all agitation and talked of other things. I was afraid the permission would be revoked. Not a peep did I give forth on the subject of brothers, but I thought about it all day and dreamed of it by night. I wanted a brother who could work, who could fight and who could play ball.

The day arrived when the orphans were to be at the Ashley Tavern in Bloomington.

Did I say anything about it? Not I!

I was up at daylight, without being called. I tried to eat breakfast but had no appetite. So I just made a bluff at it, and then sauntered out into the garden and began to hoe.

Soon father took his saddle-bags and went off to see patients. Mother began baking. The girls started for school.

I ran to the barn, stood in the manger and put a bridle on Ol' Molly and backed her out, first fastening her colt in the box stall. I climbed on her bare back. Instead of taking the road that ran in front of the house, I cut across the fields and struck the creek road a mile out of town. Then I dug my heels into the old mare's sides and gave her the gad.

I rode the ten miles in a little over an hour, jumped off at the court house, tied the horse and made for the Ashley Tavern. I knew what I wanted.

I walked into the office, looked around and asked, "Where are them orphans?"

"Parlor—up-stairs," said the clerk.

I climbed the stairs, two steps at a time and entered the parlor.

❡ It was not yet nine o'clock in the morning, but there the children were—washed, dressed and seated all around the walls of the room.

Several men and women were standing around, looking at the children and talking. Two women in black, and a man with long whiskers and upper lip shaven, seemed to be in charge of the orphans ❧ ❧

"How old are you, sonny," said an old man to me, patting me on the head ❧ ❧

"'Leven, going on twelve," I answered.

"Can you work?"

"I guess so," I answered.

He called his wife over and they both looked at me earnestly. Then the old man said to one of the widow women in black, "We think we will take this one," at the same time giving me another pat on the head.

"I am already took, you'll not get me," I roared. "I'm here to pick out a brother. I want a boy that can work, and who can play ball!" ❧ ❧

This centered attention on me. Most everybody laughed, including several of the orphans.

The boys were dressed in gray and the girls in red. They all seemed quite content—not near as miserable as I thought children should be who had no parents.

I walked twice around the room looking at these orphans, just as I had often looked at pigs at the McLean County Fair.

None of them seemed to answer—all were too yellow, and several of them whispered together and made fun of me. I was in my bare feet and they wore shoes and stockings. All at once I saw in the corner a boy with tow-head and freckles. He had settled down in the corner trying to hide. He was so homely he was attractive.

⁋ I walked over to him, and asked, " Can you work and play ball —I want a brother! "

I did not say anything about fighting for I had suddenly noticed he was a hunchback.

He just looked at me and gulped, scared like, he was that embarrassed ം ം

" I want a brother—will you come with me and be my brother? " I asked. I omitted all qualifications this time—my heart went out to this boy—he seemed so scared and half-sick. I could work, fight and play ball for both.

" Is your name—your name Mudsock? " he whispered.

" No, I 'm Bert Hubbard," I said.

" Are you relation of Si Mudsock? "

" Nobody around us by that name," I answered.

" Then I 'll go with you and be your brudder," he whispered.

⁋ He stood up. He only came to my shoulder. " I 'm fifteen," he said as if in apology. " I 'm fifteen—I 'm not sick—it was spinal complaint—but I 'm all over it now. I am strong—I can work and I can play ball."

I took him by the hand and led him to the nearest widow and said, " If you please, Missus, I 'll take this one! "

Then the woman asked me who I was, where I came from, who sent me and explained that if my parents wished to adopt a boy, or to take one on probation, they must come and sign the papers.

⁋ Just then in walked Uncle Elihu Rogers. I referred to him. Uncle Elihu assured them that I was the son of Doctor Hubbard and that I knew as much as my father, or thought I did. All the time I held my boy tight by the hand.

It was finally agreed that if Uncle Elihu would go out and get Dr. Crothers, and both of them would sign for the boy, I could have him on a month's trial, to be adopted then by my parents if they so desired ❧ ❧

Dr. Crothers came over, smiled, asked me a few questions. He then gave me and my new brother each ten cents, and signed the papers ❧ ❧

I walked out of the parlor rapidly, down the stairs and over to the court house, leading my new found brother. He carried a bundle tied up in a big red handkerchief.

I unfastened Ol' Molly, climbed up on the hitching rail, and jumped on her back. Then I held out my hand, stiffened my foot, and up climbed my brother. He was nimble and strong—I felt better ❧ ❧

As we jogged along I asked, " Why did you ask me if my name was Mudsock? "

" He's the man that had me last—'dopted me—he lives near Peoria. Is that near here? He used me to bat up flies—beat me, starved me, and then when I ran away he tried to get me arrested. He said I stole a horse! "

" Did you? " I asked.

" Never, I just ran away and stole rides on the railroad clear back to New York—it took me six weeks. There they put me in the Home and brought me out West again to be 'dopted. I don't mind being 'dopted by you. I can work, I can—but I want to go to school a little, to read and study and be a man. I like you—but if Mudsock comes for me, what will you do? "

" Kill him," I answered.

Mother was just putting the dinner on when Ol' Molly, Brudder and I reached the front gate.

I led the boy in, holding him by the hand, " I 've got him," I announced ❧ ❧

Mother turned and stared. " Who? "

" My brother! "
" What? "
" I 've found my brother."
" Land sakes, are you crazy! "

She looked at me and then at the boy. It seemed a full minute. Then she walked right over, put her arms around Brudder and kissed him ∂● ∂●

The month of probation past, and father and mother straightway adopted Brudder, all without any coercion from me. It was very funny—at first they thought it a calamity, then they got to telling the neighbors how they sent me after him.

The lad was alert, obedient, willing. He was grateful for everything; whereas I was a Grabheimer from Grabville.

Again and again my sisters would say to me, " Now, why don't you try to be gentlemanly like Brudder, and not hang your hat on the floor and talk back! "

I had intended to select a boy who looked like myself—this being the highest type I could imagine. Instead I picked my opposite. I was tall, slender, and had black hair and brown eyes. Brudder was short, and a genuine blond. I was saucy—he was polite. Instead of picking out the strongest and likeliest boy I could find, I chose the smallest, the sickliest, the homeliest one in the bunch. My judgment was in the ditch, and I was carried away on the back of sympathy. It was head against heart, and heart made a home run ∂● ∂●

In spite of his physical disability Brudder was very strong, and he could do fully as much work as I. In his books he was a bit deficient, but the girls taught him evenings, and in long division I had to call upon him to help me out. He used to hold the hank of yarn for mother to wind and would do this without either snarling the yarn or Mother's temper. Once I heard Mother say that Brudder was just like my brother Charley who died when he was nine years old.

We worked together, got jobs at the station unloading lumber, drove on the horse-power and sold corn-cobs to the section men for fuel. Saturday afternoons we played ball. This was Brudder's passion, as well as mine. We found a big chunk of solid rubber on the railroad, that had served its purpose as a car spring. Or did we work it out of the car with a crow-bar? I really can not say. But anyway Brudder got busy cutting out a solid rubber ball with his knife. Very patiently did he work cutting and paring. At last the ball was done. Oh, it was a daisy! With a round club you could knock it a mile. We then quit playing three-cornered-cat, and my Brudder showed us how to play baseball. He sent away and got the " Rules." He was always sending for catalogs and sample copies of magazines. We made him captain of our team, and when the Bloomington Giants came up to play us we beat them forty-nine to twenty-three. We were making plans to go out as professionals when something terrible happened. It was one Saturday afternoon. Brudder had been with us just six months. He and I had dug potatoes hard all morning, and mother had told us we could have the entire afternoon. We were playing the " Invincibles," from the Normal.

Brudder was pitching, and the way he sent that solid rubber spheroid over the plate and around the plate was marvellous. He could throw a curve that circled the batter's neck—or nearly so. The " Invincibles " were n't in it. They had a cloth ball with a piece of rubber in the center but we kicked on that and insisted on our own or nothing. Things were coming our way. I was catching. The way I picked that ball right off the wood was marvellous.

⁋ All at once I saw a strange man coming across the diamond with a black snake whip in his hand. He was big and had red bushy whiskers. Brudder saw him and turned pale—he was so scared that he just held the ball in his hand and stood first on one foot, then on the other. I was paralyzed.

The big man in his ragged, dirty clothes with his black snake whip was walking right toward Brudder, yelling, "So I've found you at last—I've found you at last!"

Brudder ran across the diamond toward the field. The man followed after him. Suddenly Brudder stopped—his hand with the solid rubber ball shot up, over, around, his knee came up to his chin, and the ball flew forward!

It caught the man square on the mouth. He dropped the whip, threw up his hands, reeled, staggered and fell on his back, the blood streaming from his nose and mouth.

The crowd was around him in a minute. We thought he was dead.

¶ Father was sent for and came with his case of instruments ready to cut off a leg, but before he arrived some one had thrown a bucket of water in the man's face. By this time he was sitting up. He had spit out a mouthful of teeth and was trying to talk, asking for that damn boy who had tried to murder him when he had n't done nothing to nobody.

I began looking around for Brudder. He could not be found. No one had seen him. We searched the house, and the barn. We looked in the wheat bin and under the hay. Then we discovered that our three-year-old bay colt was gone. A scrap of paper in the oats measure told the tale. On it was scrawled:

DEAR BERT: If I killed Mudsock, they will hang me. If I did n't kill him he will kill me, for he says I am his. I have to leave you. When I score I'll pay for the colt. I am not bad—God has forgotten me, that is all.   BRUDDER.

¶ It was a lonely household after Brudder had gone. We thought he would be back in a few days. We put a notice in the *Weekly Pantagraph,* but no one had seen my brother. One of our neighbors at church once said to mother: "So he stole your horse, did he—they are all alike!" And mother said something to the man he did not soon forget. Sunday afternoons we still went up to the graveyard, and I wondered why there were not four mounds instead of three. The graves kind of seemed very near, and dear and close ~ ~

Four years passed, and I secured a job in Chicago. I was as big as a man and did a man's work, even if I was only sixteen years old. I was down home on a visit and a letter came. I hold the letter now in my hand as I write. It is yellow and soiled, but still is legible. Here is what it says:

DEAR BERT: Here is a draft for two hundred dollars to pay for the colt. Give it to your father with my love. The horse was worth the money to me, but I had to sell him. I am secretary to the Manager of the White Sox. I get twenty-five dollars a week. I play shortstop. I got a walk to first, then I stole second, and a small bunt put me on third, and I'll not die here. When I score you will hear from me. The Great Umpire, I guess, has n't entirely forgotten me.   Yours truly,

             BRUDDER.

I am fifty years old. Brudder is fifty-three. I saw him last week when I lectured at the Academy of Music in Philadelphia. He was right in the front row, " rooting," as he expressed it when he came up on the stage after the spiel.

" You look as if the Great Umpire was on your side," I said.

" He is — I am not rich—but I have all I need — I get three thousand dollars a year. Then I have my daughter, and any man with such a daughter is rich. You know I am superintendent for the A. J. Reach Co., the folks who make the baseballs."

Brudder is a trifle bald, but his face is the same that I saw at the Ashley Tavern, only without the pallor.

Men who love baseball seem to keep young, they are always boys: to play is wisdom. With Brudder was his grown-up daughter, a beautiful girl, a head taller than he. She called me Uncle.

Sam

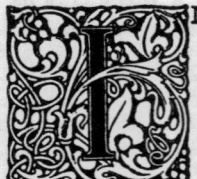IN San Francisco lived a lawyer—age, sixty—rich in money, rich in intellect, a businessman with many and varied interests. Now, this lawyer was a bachelor, and lived in apartments with his Chinese servant, "Sam." ¶ Sam and his master had been together for fifteen years.
The servant knew the wants of his employer as though he were his other self. No orders were necessary. If there was to be a company—one guest or a hundred—Sam was told the number, that was all, and everything was provided.
This servant was cook, valet, watchman, friend. No stray, unwished-for visitor ever got to the master to rob him of his rest when he was at home.
If extra help was wanted, Sam secured it; he bought what was needed; and when the lawyer awakened in the morning, it was to the singing of a tiny music-box with a clock attachment set for seven o'clock ❧ ❧
The bath was ready; a clean shirt was there on the dresser, with studs and buttons in place; collar and scarf were near; the suit of clothes desired hung over a chair; the right pair of shoes, polished like a mirror, was at hand, and on the mantel was a half-blown rose, with the dew still upon it, for a boutonniere. Downstairs, the breakfast, hot and savory, waited.
When the man was ready to go to the office, silent as a shadow stood Sam in the hallway, with overcoat, hat and cane in hand. When the weather was threatening, an umbrella was substituted for the cane. The door was opened, and the master departed. When he returned at nightfall, on his approach the door swung wide. Sam never took a vacation; he seemed not to either eat or sleep. He was always near when needed; he disappeared when he should. He knew nothing and knew everything.

For weeks scarcely a word might pass between these men—they understood each other so well.

The lawyer grew to have a great affection for his servant. He paid him a hundred dollars a month, and tried to devise other ways to show his gratitude; but Sam wanted nothing, not even thanks. All he desired was the privilege to serve.

But one morning as Sam poured his master's coffee, he said quietly, without a shade of emotion on his yellow face, " Next week I leave you."

The lawyer smiled.

" Next week I leave you," repeated the Chinese; " I hire for you better man."

The lawyer set down his cup of coffee. He looked at the white-robed servant. He felt the man was in earnest.

" So you are going to leave me—I do not pay you enough, eh? That Doctor Sanders who was here—he knows what a treasure you are. Don't be a fool, Sam; I 'll make it a hundred and fifty a month—say no more."

" Next week I leave you—I go to China," said the servant impassively

" Oh, I see! You are going back for a wife? All right, bring her here—you will return in two months? I do not object; bring your wife here—there is work for two to keep this place in order. The place is lonely, anyway. I 'll see the Collector of the Port, myself, and arrange your passage-papers."

" I go to China next week: I need no papers—I never come back," said the man with exasperating calmness and persistence.

" By God, you shall not go! " said the lawyer.

" By God, I will! " answered the heathen.

It was the first time in their experience together that the servant had used such language, or such a tone, toward his master. The lawyer pushed his chair back, and after an instant said, quietly: " Sam, you must forgive me; I spoke quickly. I do not own you—but tell me, what have I done—why do you leave me this way—you know I need you!"

"I will not tell you why I go—you laugh."

"No, I shall not laugh."

"You will."

"I say, I will not."

"Very well, I go to China to die!"

"Nonsense! You can die here. Have n't I agreed to send your body back if you die before I do?"

"I die in four weeks, two days!"

"What!"

"My brother, he in prison. He young—twenty-six, I fifty. He have wife and baby. In China they accept any man same family to die. I go to China, give my money to my brother—he live, I die!"

Next day a new Chinaman appeared as servant in the lawyer's household. In a week this servant knew everything, and nothing, just like Sam. And Sam disappeared, without saying good-by.

¶ He went to China and was beheaded, four weeks and two days from the day he broke the news of his intent to go. His brother was set free.

And the lawyer's household goes along about as usual, save when the master calls for "Sam," when he should say, "Charlie." At such times there comes a kind of clutch at his heart, but he says nothing.

Please Be Seated

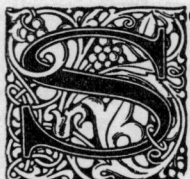SOME years ago one Prof. Jarrett Bendell of Harvard did himself the honor of reading one of my daily themes. Straightway he sent for me, and on being ushered into the Presence I stood first on one foot then on t' other, and rolled my hat in a vain hope of giving an impression of the humility which I did not feel.

Finally the ass opened its mouth and spake: I was told that my work was totally lacking in *tout ensemble,* you know—that I would never make a writer, that I should be a tiller of the soil, an agrarian, an agriculturist, a buckwheat, a farmer.

"But," said I, "I have been a farmer, and having made a success of it I aspire to a higher life. I sold my farm, Kind Sir, to a Natural Son of a Dutch Burgomaster who is now happy in his environment; while I never was. Mine is the experimental life; all we do things for anyway is just for the exercise of our faculties, and I am trying to bring into play as many of my mental muscles as possible. Emerson, you are aware, says, 'I would have every man rich that he might know the worthlessness of riches.' I am convinced of the logic of the remark and have come to college to find out how little a college education is really worth. I do not take my literary aspirations seriously—nor yours—it is just an attempt at expression, for all life is expression. So I pray you waive the advice as to occupation and criticise my theme."

⁋ Prof. Dumbell heard my little speech, and before I had finished was so shocked at my temerity that he looked up at me and his jaw dropped, his cheroot availed itself of Newton's Law of Gravitation and slid down his shirt bosom, inside his vest. In an instant the Professor was dancing dervish steps all over the room, fighting fire ❧ ❧

I asked him if I should turn in an alarm, and he told me to go to hell. But soon composure was restored through my holding firm to the thought that fire is only a belief of mortal mind, anyway, and that a right mental attitude can control all material conditions ॐ ॐ

At last the Professor asked me to be seated. I accepted the invitation and we had a real nice little chat about this and that. In some way this small encounter with the Boyleston Assistant Professor of Rhetoric, and his surprise, made me think of Laurence Sterne who, one stormy evening in Paris, out of the goodness of his heart, picked up a dwarf and carried him, in his arms, across the muddy street. Sterne always felt a kindly interest toward children, and as he set the dwarf down on dry land, he asked pleasantly, " How old are you, my little boy? "

" Forty-seven, last June, Sir," came the answer in a deep bass voice. And the Rev. Laurence Sterne fell backward over an inconvenient hydrant. When he had gotten up, and found his watch gone, and the dwarf, too, he was thoroughly convinced that the wind is sometimes tempered to the shorn lamb and sometimes it is n't ॐ ॐ

Uncle Joe and Aunt Melinda

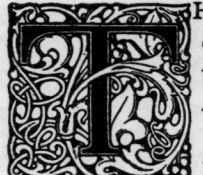THE opinion prevails all through the truly rural districts that the big cities are largely given over to Confidence Men.
And the strange part is that the opinion is correct.
⁋ But it should not be assumed that all the people in say, Buffalo, are moral derelicts—there are many visitors there, most of the time, from other sections.
⁋ And while at all times one should exercise caution, yet to assume that the party who is "fresh" is intent on high crimes and misdemeanors may be hasty and unjust.
For instance, there is Uncle Joe and Aunt Melinda, who live eight miles back from East Aurora, at Wales Hollow. They had been married for forty-seven years, and had never taken a wedding journey. They decided to go to Buffalo and spend two days at a hotel regardless of expense.
Much had been told them about the Confidence Men who hang around the railroad station, and they were prepared.
They arrived at East Aurora where they were to take the train, an hour ahead of time. The Jerk-Water came in and they were duly seated, when all at once Uncle Joe rushed for the door, jumped off and made for the waiting room looking for his carpet bag. It was on the train all right, but he just forgot, and feeling sure he had left it in the station made the grand skirmish as aforesaid ⁂
The result was that the train went off and left your Uncle Joe.
⁋ Aunt Melinda was much exercised, but the train hands pacified her by assurances that her husband would follow on the next train, and she should simply wait for him in the depot at Buffalo ⁂
Now the Flyer was right behind the Jerk-Water, and Uncle Joe took the Flyer and got to Buffalo first. When the Jerk-Water

came in Uncle Joe was on the platform waiting for Aunt Melinda.
⁋ As she disembarked he approached her.
She shied, and passed on.
He persisted in his attentions.
Then it was that she shook her umbrella at him and bade him hike. The eternal feminine in her nature prompted self-preservation. She banked on her reason—woman's reason—not her intuition. She had started first—her husband could only come on a later train.
"Go way and leave me alone," she shouted in falsetto. "You have got yourself up to look like my Joe—and that idiotic grin on your homely face is just like my Joe, but no city sharper can fool me, and if you don't go right along I'll call for the police!"
⁋ She called for the police, and Uncle Joe showed up a strawberry mark that proved his identity.

The Fish are Coming

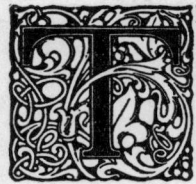HE Northwest reminds you of that man who lived over the Rhine in Cincinnati, who used to remark, " What's the use of being rich when you can only drink forty glasses of beer a day, anyhow! " Puget Sound puts the ichthyological romanticist to the bad.
The fish liar is the one man who stands no chance in this country. His finest efforts fall on dull ears. His choicest creations are flat, stale and unprofitable.
At Bellingham, Washington, is the greatest fish-canning concern in the world. The season is only about six months long, but the way the salmon head toward that cannery paralyzes one's vocabulary and makes language of no avail.
An Englishman I met at Bellingham remarked, " Is n't it singular that the fish come to the exact spot where the cannery is situated, you know—most astounding, you know? "
And it certainly is.
The fish come here with clockwork periodicity. They are due on a certain day of the year. Wind and tide may hold them back a little, but they come with as much certainty as the liners from Japan
In May come the " Springs," in July the " Humpbacks," in August the " Sockeyes," and toward the last of September come the " Silvers."
These are all salmon, and to the novice are about alike, varying only in size and weight. Each school runs almost uniform in size. The weight varies from ten pounds to seventy. To be presented with a seventy-pound salmon, I found to be a bit embarrassing. " It is for your supper," assured my friend, the kind donor. I gave fifty cents to a Chink to carry the fish to my hotel. Before he reached there he staggered under his load and called to another

Celestial for help. The landlord cooked this representative of the finny tribe for me. I did not eat it all. And I could not distribute it among my party, for each had a salmon of his own ✹ When the fish first come in the Spring a thrill goes through the town. The cannery employs over a thousand people—Japs, Chinks, girls, boys, men, women, roustabouts, sailors!

" The fish are coming! "

The news spreads.

It is passed over the telephones and back fences, shouted across gulfs that before were gulfs of misunderstanding.

" The fish are coming! "

The word has been brought by scouts in fast-sailing sloops, who bring in a dozen or so of salmon, which are sold at five dollars each, as the first bale of cotton in the South is sold at a dollar a pound ✹ ✹

" Hurrah! The fish are coming! "

Perhaps they are a hundred miles away, just breaking into the inlets of the Sound from the great Pacific.

The scouts let down their nets, seize a few and sail away, crowding on all canvas, or counting not the cost of gasoline. " The fish are coming! "

Sell fast, ye speculators, for tomorrow salmon will be a glut on the market!

" The fish are coming! "

The fires are already banked in the cannery boilers. Now steam is gotten up, the gauges are tested, knives are sharpened, machinery tried. Orders are given out to the foreman, and Japs, Chinks, girls and boys, men and women, are given cards showing that they are hired. " The fish are coming! "

The traps are set—wide-mouthed gateways, fenced by rope, with a mesh that lets out all fish excepting those of a certain size. The trap may be a hundred feet wide, or two hundred at its mouth, narrowing down to twenty feet, then bellying out again.

Into this trap swim the fish, moving North in a dense mass, all headed one way, intent on reaching the spawning-grounds of fresh water, just beyond, where they themselves were hatched, and from whence they swam, four years before.

During this time they have traveled clear across the broad Pacific, skirted the shores of China, the Indian Ocean, and then drifting into the Japan current, started for home and native land. They either reach this passionately desired spawning-place, or else are caught by the busy fishermen or likewise busy sea-lions who lie in wait.

Those that reach the happy breeding-places get there only after a terrific, frenzied fight. The cosmic urge is upon them. They arrive and then they die. That is their goal and end of life. The females lay their eggs, the males pass over and fertilize them.
¶ Then both relax into a stupor, the nuptial sleep, that knows no waking. They die that the young may live.

They give their lives for the race, and their dead bodies are carried down by the current, and out upon the unforgetting tide.
¶ In gathering these dead fish that line the banks of all these little streams a new industry has sprung up. The fish are used for fertilizer, just as the waste from the canneries is likewise utilized.
¶ When the big runs of fish occur, the traps are often full to bursting, at which times the ropes are cut, and for safety the traps are eased.

The salmon are taken out of the traps by an endless chain, worked by a steam-engine or a tug that steams into the trap. The endless belt carries a loosely drawn net, which simply transfers the fish from the water to big barges. These scows are, say, sixty feet long, twenty feet wide and six feet deep.

A scow will hold about the same as a railroad-car, say forty thousand pounds.

When a scow is loaded, it is towed by a tug to the dock that lines the cannery

At times the barge men bring in more fish than the cannery, running day and night, can use. In which case a bulletin is posted, " Free Fish Today." No special credit need here be given the cannery gentlemen, for the law provides that no one shall catch live fish and use them for fertilizer.

When the sign of free fish is put out, people, old and young, rich and poor, plebeian and aristocrat, pundit and proletariat, go and carry away all the fish which they can manage, and salt them down ෴ ෴

I saw children lugging salmon home that were as big as themselves. Two little girls had a fish that weighed fifty pounds, strung on a pole, between them. They offered to sell me the fish for a quarter. I bought it just to encourage an infant industry; and then gave another youngster twenty-five cents to take it off my hands ෴ ෴

The salmon fisheries at Bellingham are the largest in the world. They do a business of twenty million dollars a year.

No doubt there is a fair profit in the business.

Fish do not have to be housed, fed, curried, herded or cared for. They have no value until they are caught, and to catch them here is a very inexpensive process. Cattle cost money; hogs are high, but fish are free. However, they are perishable and can be handled successfully only by men with big ideas and big capital. The big financial fish fix the price of salmon, and the little packers cut under, just enough to sell their product.

If they would go under too much they might find themselves in a fish-net, just as a sea-lion does, at times. In which case the boys on the tug do not do a thing to that sea-lion.

However, if the price of canned salmon were put too high, the minnow-canneries would all get extremely busy, because the big boys can not really monopolize the supply.

Their advantage lies in the ability to catch, handle and market. And in this they seem quite able to keep the kiotes from the door.

"Give It to Him, Tim!"

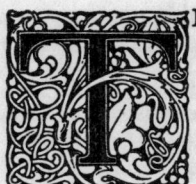THEODORE P. SHONTS of Chicago is regarded as one of the best ink-slingers in this country. His reputation in this line came to him sort o' through accident—that is to say he had greatness thrust upon him. In the year 1895, as President of an Important Railroad, Mr. Shonts was called upon by a tall man who was also large around—also full of bad whiskey. This man was spokesman of a Commit-tay that came in the Interests of the Switchmen's Union, asking that two non-Union Swedes be discharged and their places filled by two men who had been giving Mr. Shonts a deal of trouble.

The request was not so very unreasonable, but the methods of the Committee were unique. They chose what they thought was a short cut in diplomacy, just as Cromwell did when he said to the Keeper of the Mace, " Take away that bauble!"

This Committee awaited a time when Mr. Shonts was alone in his office, and then they sent in their big spokesman, who addressed Mr. Shonts somewhat thus: " Here, you dirty tentacle of a hungry Octopus—sign this order to have them men discharged, and do it quick. No damn palaver, now, or I'll smash your face. I'm goin' to lick hell outer you if you say a word—see?"

" Yes, I observe!" said Mr. Shonts. And as he spoke he stood up and placed his hand upon a quart bottle of Stafford's red ruling ink that was on his desk; and in some way that bottle of ink shot straight at big Tim Driscoll—all in a flash. The bottle struck Tim square on the forehead and exploded into ten thousand and four pieces. Then Shonts closed in on his man and landed short arm blows left and right; upper cuts were sent home, and fancy taps in the solar plexus were quickly interspersed with stiff punches on the beak ∞ ∞

All the time the Committee held the door shut and gleefully

cried through the key-hole, " Give it to him, Tim! Give it to the dirty tintacle of a hungry Oc-to-pus!" Then there was a silence.

⁋ When the Emergency Ambulance came for Tim Driscoll the doctors examined the man, then looked at the floor and the furniture and told the driver to head for the morgue. Tim was not dead, though, but it was six months before he was out of the hospital. In the meantime Shonts looked after Tim's family and when he was able to go to work his place was waiting for him; and today there is no more trustworthy man in the switch-yards of Chicago than Tim Driscoll.

Mr. Shonts kept Tim's hat as a memento of the occasion; or rather Tim accidentally left the hat. So Mr. Shonts one fine day about a month after, just sent the hat over to Rush Medical College with a note asking, " Are the stains on the hat sent herewith caused by the blood of some beast-brute or are they human?"

⁋ After a week a lengthy report came back (with bill for ten dollars) saying the stains were undoubtedly caused by human blood but the blood was of a most peculiar quality, being almost entirely lacking in serum, with small trace of corpuscles either red or white.

A Roycroft Christening

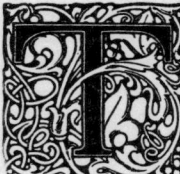HE Pastor of His Flock has often officiated at funerals. And in one instance he was invited to perform a marriage ceremony, but this he was obliged to decline for conscientious reasons. ℭ However, several weddings have occurred in The Roycroft Chapel—with the kindly assistance of the local Baptist clergyman.

But the first christening that has occurred at Roycroft took place recently. On this occasion Mr. and Mrs. George H. Maines of Poughkeepsie, New York, came to Roycroft on pious pilgrimage bent, bringing with them their lovely little boy, aged four months, by name, Elbert Hubbard Maines. Elbert Hubbard Maines is as fine a sample of scientific eugenics as the world has ever seen; dimpled, laughing, kicking, hungry, beautiful, healthy, strong—cooing his way into the hearts of all who see him!

Some one has said that if all rituals were abolished, a new one would be inaugurated very soon, just as good.

Prayers, forms and rituals have their use. They have a reactionary effect on the individual, which under right conditions is beautiful, esthetic, and has a marked survival value.

And so on this occasion the naming ceremony was performed, with Frederick D. Underwood, Frederick N. Finney and Alice Hubbard as sponsors. Fra Elbertus officiated and made the following remarks: "We have gathered here, a little company of friends with like tastes, ambitions and beliefs, to dedicate this beautiful baby to the Good, the Beautiful, the True, and the Useful.

" Born under happy conditions, sponsored by the able, we hope, aye, more, we expect, that this child will grow up into manhood and become a pride to his parents, and an able, efficient worker who will carry his share of the world's burdens and make the earth a better place because he is here.

" This is a solemn, yet glad occasion. This dedication or christening ceremony is always impressive. This child is a manifestation of the Great Intelligence of which we are a part. And being normal, he is essentially divine.

" No one standing here this beautiful morning will forget this day and event.

" We are workers all. Frederick D. Underwood and Frederick N. Finney, who stand here as sponsors, or ' godfathers,' to this beautiful child are world-makers, both.

" They have left their impress on the times. Born in decent poverty, knowing difficulties, trials, hardships, grief, loss, out of it all they have woven a fabric of success, not only for themselves but for millions of other people.

" They have made the desert to blossom like a rose; they have made the waste places green, and in great degree they have made sorrow and sighing to flee away.

" And here in this presence they promise their friendship and their good offices, under every and all conditions, to point this child in the way of industry, economy and efficiency.

" I now baptize this child in pure spring-water, in token of his close kinship to Mother Nature; and I predict for him a life of work, play, study, laughter, health, long life, and power to confer great good on the world.

" So let it be! "

God Save the King!

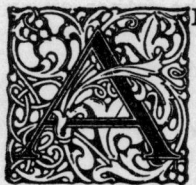ND so, as the midnight bells went ringing out the old, they rang in the new, "The King is dead—long live the King!"

When George V. announced the death of his father, he proclaimed his own accession. And England, Ireland, Scotland and far-off India fired volleys to show their loyalty; and from St. John to Vancouver, Canada called him Sovereign, and sang, "God save the King!"

All those earnest prophets who had foretold that Edward VII. would close the English kingly line were wrong.

The death of Edward Guelph neither retarded nor accelerated the British heart-beat. The men in field and factory were given an hour off, and then worked as usual. The shops opened wide their doors. The busses ran. The railroad-trains started on schedule and arrived on time. The stock-market gave no sign. The sun shone, the winds blew, the birds sang.

The emblems of sorrow were on public buildings, all over the world, but there was no sorrow in the hearts of the people. For sorrow that can be expressed is a subtle form of joy. Read your Burke on the *Sublime!*

Why should there be sorrow?

A worn-out old man had paid the debt for having lived. Life is a lingering disease; it has but one cure—death. As old John Brown said to Governor Wise, "You can pardon me, but you can not make me immortal. You will not pardon me, and so I die tomorrow. But, Governor Wise, I only precede you by a day. Across the River of Death I'll wait for you."

The King had not died, because the King never dies. He is like a corporation with perpetual charter, "a body without death, a mind without decline." Power passes.

A man of sixty-eight had ceased to breathe—that was all. His son aged forty-five, takes the scepter from his stiffening fingers. This son is a respectable country gentleman, the father of six hearty frolicking children.

George V. is a collector of postage-stamps, and raises rabbits. These are his only fads.

He has knock-knees, while sure-enough kings are always bow-legged ⚜ ⚜

Bowlegs means will plus; knock-knees stand for weakness. George V. is commonplace in form and feature. When he asked the man who swore him in, to omit that part of the oath which made him declare his hatred of the Pope, he did as Asquith suggested. This was wise and well. Catholics are numerous in Ireland and plentiful in England—why insult them!

The Archbishop of Canterbury called him " our high and mighty and powerful Prince George." But this is theologico-legal parlance. and means nothing.

However, as King of England he symbols for us certain qualities. That is his business. He symbols each day in three shifts of eight hours each. That he is silent, shy and unknown are points to his advantage in playing this papier-maché, opera-bouffe. He does it better than Francis Wilson ever could hope to do.

¶ Royalty means superiority.

There is something royal in humanity.

Great Britain forms no insignificant part of the human family. We think well of the race—better than ever before in history.

¶ As the people grow strong, kings wane and become weak.

¶ We respect manhood.

All the intellect we know is man's intellect.

If there is a Supreme Being, His highest manifestation is through the minds of men. In all ages it has been taught that He "inspires" us. All the charity we know is man's charity.

All the forgiveness we know is man's forgiveness.

All the justice we know is man's justice, and when we tell of
"God's justice" we mean what we would do if we were God.
The British Lion has no existence as a lion, and his tail has never
been twisted except in literature. He has no more tail than
Halley's Comet.

Uncle Sam has no existence as an uncle, or as a man.

The king of England has no existence as king. The man who
impersonates the ruler is but a symbol of the solidarity of the
English people.

There was once a King George who thought he was a sure-enough
ruler. His arrogance caused a shot to be fired at Concord Bridge,
and thirteen American Colonies were lost to the British crown.
And they were lost simply because this man forgot that he was a
symbol of power, and not a powerful symbol. He would if he
could have oppressed a people grown to a point where they
prized freedom. George III. should have been deposed—and we
should have stayed in the game.

Canada prizes freedom, quite as much as do the States. Also,
she has quite as much commodity as we have. Freedom is not a
gift—it is an achievement.

The amount of a man's freedom is not on the outside—it is in.
Freedom is a condition of mind. And people with slavish, servile
minds are apt to find themselves behind the bars. "Thee shall
build no prisons, for if thee does, thee and thy children shall
occupy them," said Elizabeth Fry.

Freedom implies responsibility. Freedom is bought by loyalty to
duty. To break out of jail is not to be free. You still have yourself
to look after. You are in bonds to your passions, your temper,
your power—or lack of it—wherever you go. Weakness is a
tangible something. It grasps you, grabs you, forces you down
and holds you under.

The citizens of Canada are free to the degree that they are able,
competent, self-reliant and recognize that each man can only

help himself as he helps humanity. ⓒ This idea of mutual service is sanity ᛋ⬤ ᛋ⬤
The lack of this consciousness that one man's rights end where another's begin is what makes a man a criminal, or as one insane. Helpful men are safe men.
Human service—this way freedom lies!
He who would seize and appropriate is seized. To consume or destroy and not produce, is to be enslaved.
The highest achievement of modern thought is this consciousness of the Brotherhood of Man.
The Sovereign is a man who symbols for us solidarity.
Organization is civilization. The word " King " is a rallying-cry.
ⓒ The English are a great and powerful people, and because they are powerful, the death of one man—any man—is to them an insignificant thing. **ENGLAND IS ORGANIZED.**
God save the King!

The Master Man

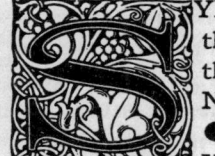YMPATHY, Wisdom and Poise seem to be the three ingredients that are most needed in forming the Master Man.
No man is great who does not possess Sympathy.
❦ Sympathy and Imagination are twin sisters.
Your heart must go out to all men: the high, the low, the rich, the poor, the learned, the unlearned, the good, the bad, the wise and the foolish; it is necessary to be one with them all, else you can never comprehend them.

Sympathy!—it is the touchstone to every secret, the key to all knowledge, the open sesame of all hearts. Put yourself in the other man's place, and then you will know why he thinks certain things and does certain deeds.

Put yourself in his place and your blame will dissolve itself into pity, and your tears will wipe out the record of his misdeeds. The saviors of the world have simply been men with wondrous Sympathy ❧ ❧

But Wisdom must go with Sympathy, else the emotions will become maudlin and pity may be wasted on a poodle instead of a child—on a field-mouse instead of a human soul. Knowledge in use is Wisdom, and Wisdom implies a sense of values—you know a big thing from a little one, a valuable fact from a trivial one. Tragedy and comedy are simply questions of value; a little misfit in life makes us laugh; a great one is tragedy and cause for expression of grief.

Poise is the strength of body and strength of mind to control your Sympathy and your Knowledge. Unless you control your emotions they run over and you stand in the slop.

Sympathy must not run riot, or it tokens weakness instead of strength. In every hospital for nervous disorders are to be found many instances of this loss of control. The individual has Sympathy, but no Poise, and therefore his life is worthless to himself and to the world.

Poise reveals itself more in voice than it does in words; more in thought than in action; more in atmosphere than in conscious life. It is a spiritual quality, and is felt more than it is seen. It is not a matter of bodily size, nor of bodily attitude, nor attire, nor of personal comeliness; it is a state of inward being, and of knowing your cause is just.

I know a man who is deformed in body, but who has such Poise that to enter a room where he is, is to feel his presence and acknowledge his superiority.

To allow Sympathy to waste itself on unworthy objects is to deplete one's life-forces.

To conserve is the part of Wisdom, and reserve is a necessary element in all art, as well as in life.

Poise being the control of our Sympathy and Knowledge, it implies a possession of these attributes, for without Sympathy and Knowledge you will have nothing to control but your physical body. To practise Poise as a mere gymnastic exercise—just as to study etiquette—is to be self-conscious, stiff, preposterous. Poise is a question of spirit controlling flesh, heart controlling attitude ∞ ∞

Get Knowledge by coming close to Nature. That man is the greatest who best serves his kind. Sympathy and knowledge are for use—you acquire that you may give out; you accumulate that you may bestow. And as God has given unto you the sublime blessings of Sympathy and Wisdom, there will come to you the wish to reveal your gratitude by giving them out again; for the wise man is aware that we retain only as we give. Let your light shine. To him that hath shall be given. The exercise of Wisdom brings Wisdom; and at the last the infinitesimal quantity of man's Knowledge, compared with the Infinite, and the smallness of man's Sympathy when compared with the source from which

ours is absorbed, will evolve a humility that will lend a perfect Poise ❧ ❧
The Master Man is one with Sympathy, Wisdom and Poise. And such are always learners, as well as teachers.

Louis V. Eytinge

RECENTLY I lectured in the beautiful and prosperous little city of Phoenix, Arizona.

¶ Just before the curtain went up, one of the stage hands negotiated the peekhole and reported that Governor Hunt was in the audience.

¶ After the chairman had said, "We have one with us tonight," etc., I popped a few oratorical bunts up the Governor's way, and was pleased to see that he did n't muff anything.

When the bout had been pulled off, Governor Hunt came around on the stage and said to me, "I was down at Florence yesterday, and some friends there want to see you."

"Delighted!" I said. "Who are they?"

"Prisoners in the penitentiary," he replied, and then he explained that Tucson, where I was to speak the next night, was two hundred miles from Phoenix, but by going down to Florence forty miles, you can take an automobile across the desert seventy-five miles and reach your destination on time.

"I will have one of the convicts take you across in my auto," added the Governor in a simple, matter-of-fact-way.

I had heard of taking convicts in an auto, but to have a convict take me was different. But I accepted the Governor's invitation. We reached Florence after a two hours' ride through a rich, irrigated, farming country.

There it was—this great walled square on the desert, the golden Arizona sunshine beating upon it. The desert was treeless and devoid of beauty save that peculiar, awful, compelling beauty that the desert possesses. As we went up the mesa toward the prisonwalls I noticed a well-used baseball-diamond.

Down in the valley I could see a vegetable garden where a dozen men or more were busy at work.

"That garden helps feed our family," said my guide with a wave of his hand, "and the men you see there are convicts. You will notice that they have shanties where they live. We aim to give every man in the place all the liberty that he can use to advantage. We used to play baseball inside the walls, but over the fence was out. So one day we just concluded to have our baseball-ground outside, and every man in the institution who behaves himself properly goes to the ball-game on Saturday."

I dined with the prisoners in their dining-room. The old order of silence is not enforced. If you have anything to say to your neighbors you say it. The place was quite as orderly as the average hotel dining-room. The food was simple, but there was plenty of it ∾ ∾

After dinner I talked to the assembled citizens.

Every prison is made up of what you might call three classes. First, there are mental and physical defectives.

Next, sufferers from intoxicants and drugs. Third, those who have energy plus, and who through some unkind antic of Fate have bumped into difficulty. They have quarreled with parents, with sweethearts, or employers and they go "Out West," and do the wrong thing and are some day landed behind the bars.

There is no "criminal class," or, if there is, we all belong to it. The things we have done in imagination would certainly put us behind prison-bars if they had ever broken through thought into action ∾ ∾

The prison at Florence has a few things to recommend it which no other prison in the United States has.

All State Prisons nowadays have libraries, a brass band, and a school ∾ ∾

A prison, like a corporation, has a soul. As a school is keyed by the principal, so is a prison keyed by the warden and the men in charge ∾ ∾

Robert B. Sims, the warden at Florence, is a schoolteacher, an economist a workingman, and reminded me very much of that very able man, Governor Ferris of Michigan.

Then comes J. J. Sanders, parole-clerk, who makes it his business to know every prisoner and to use his influence constantly and in every possible way for the betterment of the boys under his charge ∽ ∽

The third important man in the prison happens to be a "lifer." His name is Louis V. Eytinge. Eytinge has taken the vow of chastity, poverty and obedience, and prison has given him opportunity ∽ ∽

He is a very good-looking soul, intelligent, frank, friendly. He wears citizen's clothes. His cell is an office where the door is never locked. He has a roll-top desk, and on the wall are pictures of many of America's important literary men, writers, orators, inventors, businessmen.

Eytinge has a filing-cabinet for his correspondence. He also has two private secretaries. Fortunately, Eytinge does n't have to pay his secretaries, neither does he have to pay room-rent or board ∽ ∽

He is the most systematic, methodical individual you ever saw in your life. Also, he has the biggest private correspondence I believe, of any man in America.

In most prisons prisoners are allowed to write one letter a month and no more. In Florence there is no such limit, thanks to the sensible regulation inaugurated by Warden Sims, with the consent of Governor Hunt. When a man is sent to prison, there is no reason why his relatives, friends and family should be punished by not being allowed to hear from him. That is where the wrong individual is penalized.

Why should n't a prisoner be allowed to write to his folks, telling whether he is alive or dead, well or sick, miserable or fairly content? Who suffers? You know—it is the folks at home.

It is a great privilege to write letters, and it is a still greater privilege to receive them. Any one who has ever felt the abject misery of looking for a letter that never comes will understand me ෴ ෴

There is no reason under the blue sky why a convict should not be allowed to send out as many letters of a social nature as he cares to buy postage-stamps for.

The object of putting a man in prison is twofold: first, to protect society, and second, to make the convict a better man.

And certainly, breaking off all connections with the outside world does not make for human evolution.

This is what Governor Hunt thinks, and that is what I think, and that is what a great many other sane and sensible people think ෴ ෴

And so I say that every prisoner in every prison in America should be allowed the full, free privileges of the United States mail, under exactly the same conditions that men outside enjoy.

The mail service is a privilege, and it should not be abused— that's all. There is nothing in any law in the land that says that imprisoned men shall be denied mail privileges.

The forbidding of prisoners to send out mail is a foolish, vain, unnecessary rule that has come down to us from the Dark Ages. When a prisoner is sentenced, it should be for a term of sunshine, fresh air, simple and abundant food, and honest work.

All this with the intent that when the man is given back to society he will be an asset and not a liability.

Louis V. Eytinge started a business in prison—a mail-order business ෴ ෴

This business was to manufacture and sell Mexican hair-goods and curios—things made in the prison. He had a force of men that he taught to do this work, and the business is still carried on.

⁋ Eytinge, however, discovered that in selling his products, he had something else in stock which was valuable, and that was brains. The man is a wizard of words, and he is supplying selling letters and advertisements to a great number of businessmen throughout the United States.

Also, he has a school of advertising literature, and is teaching convicts how to write good English.

Whether it will ever come about that most of the good literature of America is produced in prisons or not I can not say. Go ask the shades of John Bunyan and the Apostle Paul!

To say that Eytinge's ideas of education and the teaching of literature and business methods in prison are hot air, does not quite dispose of the subject. It is a deal better that Eytinge should wax enthusiastic and ebulliate at low temperature about uplift and betterment than that he should eat his heart out in sullen silence, wearing the stripes of disgrace.

Eytinge is saving money. He is getting an education, and in the main he is just as happy as a great many people who have their sweet liberty. We are all more or less in bonds, and the things that we are in bonds to most are our own limitations.

And so I talked to the boys in the prison.

Afterward there was a lot of handshaking; then a little batting up of flies on the diamond; and I climbed into a "Packard" and the driver headed for the desert.

As we slipped past the last shack on the street my chauffeur waved a hand and said, " That is the last house you will see for twenty-one miles."

The road was Nature's own, winding in and out through sagebrush past the giant cactus, occasionally going down through a gulley and seemingly heading for a great mountain-peak, snow-covered, a hundred miles away. And so the hours went by.

Strapped firmly to the automobile, on either side, was a keg of water, ominous reminder of the danger of the desert.

The distance we had to traverse from Florence to Tucson was seventy-five miles. It was a wonderful, wild, romantic, unique ride ✎ ✎

For thirty miles we did not see a human—prairie-dogs, a few coyotes, owls and rattlers!

Just one automobile we met on the way. We sighted them five miles across the desert.

We began tooting our horn when we got within a half-mile. They responded.

When we met we got out and shook hands with our friends. They drank out of our canteen and we drank out of theirs.

We met as long-lost brothers.

I had told the warden that I would keep the chauffeur over night, as the ride back was somewhat dangerous on account of the gulleys ⁂ ⁂

And so I registered for myself and my convict friend. We were given adjoining rooms.

We washed up, brushed our clothes, and dined together.

Then we went to the theater, and the management gave my partner a box seat.

I had to catch a train out at three-thirty in the morning. I did not expect my friend would get up and go to the train with me but he was up before I was.

"Could n't you sleep?" I said.

"No," was the reply; "these rooms are too confining."

And then he explained, "you know, at home I sleep on the roof!"

And it was so, for no man is locked in a cell at Florence except those who have failed to show a proper degree of respect for the liberties allowed.

We got into the auto just as the first flush of pink came into the East ⁂ ⁂

We had an early breakfast at the railroad lunch-counter, and then I bade my friend good-by. He climbed in behind the wheel, and headed for the desert and his prison home, seventy-five miles away.

Charles S. Whitman

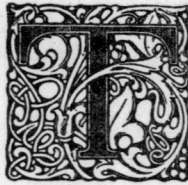THE Governor of the State of New York is **Charles** Seymour Whitman.

He is the son of a clergyman—passing rich on forty pounds a year.

Whitman was born in August, Eighteen Hundred Sixty-eight ॐ ॐ

Consequently, the Governor of New York at this writing is forty-seven years of age.

In two years he will be forty-nine years of age!—if my arithmetic does not fail me.

From fifty to sixty a man who has lived rightly is at his best. Charles Seymour Whitman has lived rightly.

At fifty, time has tamed a man, and he has molted a good many of his illusions.

Governor Whitman has ripened slowly.

He has come by the thorn road, fighting the way step by step.

He has also been in the trenches, and any victories that have come to him have been hard-earned.

Fate has decreed that in these modern days no man can be President of the United States, unless he be a college graduate ॐ ॐ

This in spite of the fact that the principal advantage of going to college lies in the discovery that there is nothing in it.

If a man goes through college and does not ascertain that a college degree has no value as collateral, he has had his trouble for his pains.

Governor Whitman is a graduate of Amherst. He also has degrees from " Williams," the University of New York, and the University of Hard Knocks.

Nobody ever referred to Governor Whitman either as a genius or as a good fellow.

He is earnest, honest, intelligent. He has a saving sense of humor, without trespassing on the preserve of the cut-up.
He can talk well on occasion, but his strong point is that of being a good listener.
He has memorized that wonderful book, *The Essay on Silence,* and has a habit of repeating passages to himself.
He belongs to many clubs, but seldom attends any of them— which is beautiful and right. Governor Whitman is persistent and patient, but he is n't brilliant, scintillating, nor yet handsome. He is n't quite safe from old Doctor Johnson's interrogation, " Sir, are you anybody in particular? "
Governor Whitman can fade into the landscape and look like a piece of the drop-curtain.
He is a man of commonsense, and I once heard a woman say he was " good-looking," because anybody is good-looking who looks good. He was not born under the sign of Taurus, nor yet Capricornus. He deals not in rant, cant and fustian.
Governor Whitman carries his own grips, rides on the street-car, takes an upper on the Pullman without protest.
He is an average man, focused and concentrated. He has grown strong by doing.
Governor Whitman owes much to his wife. Mentally she is geared to a higher speed than her liege. She is a kindly woman, gentle, capable—earnest, with positive ideas on the subject of woman's work.
A good deal of the Governor's education is in his wife's name. While Mrs. Whitman is neither fussy nor frivolous, she is never dowdy and indifferent. Yet people who know the Governor can not think of him apart from her.
They are an eminently commonsense couple, and represent all of the old-fashioned virtues for which science has never found a substitute: industry, economy, truthfulness, self-reliance, self-respect—helpfulness.

They are good neighbors, and have a habit of speaking well of other people. They have the virtues of the people who go forth to their labors until the evening.

These are the folks who make the world go round, for without them there would be neither literature, science, art, nor any such thing as civilization.

Whitman's instincts are for peace.

Militarism exists in his cosmos only as a chemical trace. But if you backed him into a corner you would probably find that you had subscribed for a large block of assessable stock, and had taken on a liability.

Whitman fits in. He does not brag, boast nor bluster. He does his work and holds his peace.

He would be a good pilot, even in stormy weather, and on a rockbound coast.

And if disaster came, he, like Jim Bludsoe, would " hold her nozzle ag'in the bank 'til the last galoot 's ashore."

A good pilot, yes, Hezekiah — that's what I said, "A good pilot!" The staunch ship " America " needs no captain except our Uncle Samuel, and it will be a sorry day for this country when we fire him.

Whitman could take out a locomotive on the Twentieth Century Limited, and hit 'er up eighty-five miles an hour, and never wink an eyebrow—nor mention the fact afterward. He could climb telegraph-poles in Winter and hang on the cross-arms until he made all snug and secure.

He is as poised as Old Walt, his distant relative, but he is without Old Walt's eccentricities.

He is n't rich; yet he never will be poor.

He can not be stampeded, coerced or bribed.

You can not surprise him by jumping out of a corner and shouting, " Booh," or " Bah," or " Pooh! "

He is at home with all sorts and conditions of people.

Whitman has enemies and is going to make more—but we will love him for these.

The man who does not make enemies isn't doing anything.

℆ Whitman is not so very wise nor so awfully good. But he is wiser than he knows and better than the men who berate him.

℆ His name is Cummings, not Goings.

Anna A. Malley

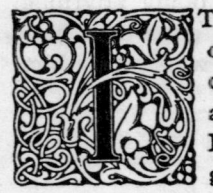IT will be remembered that Mrs. Marilla Ricker of Dover, New Hampshire, made a spirited campaign for the governorship in that State a few years ago.

For a time it looked as if Mrs. Ricker stood a good chance of being elected.

The matter, however, was referred to the Attorney-General of the State for a legal opinion as to whether Mrs. Ricker would be allowed to serve if she were the people's choice.

After due deliberation, the Attorney-General gave it as his opinion that a woman could not legally be inaugurated Governor of the State of New Hampshire, even if a majority of the citizens voted for her.

The decision of the Attorney-General rested on the dictum that no person could serve as Governor who was not a legal voter.

◧ If it were otherwise, he argued, we might elect a foreigner, a minor, an alien, a detective, a criminal, to the office. Only a legal voter could be elected legally and allowed to serve, and the law did not recognize such a thing as a qualified female voter.

◧ This sort of put a damper on the Marilla Ricker campaign, and the only thing then was to fall back on the good old fight of Votes for Women.

Now, however, in the State of Washington, Miss Anna A. Malley has been nominated on a referendum for Governor on the Socialist ticket.

Miss Malley is a schoolteacher, a lecturer and a writer. She is a woman of a good deal of ability, and withal, she is a working-woman—a wage earner—and has had considerable experience in the world of business and in practical affairs.

The Northwest is n't afraid of initiative. Rather do they pride themselves on doing things that have never been done before.

The Northwest is really the home of the initiative, the referendum and the recall. And the women of Washington have done all three. If you do not believe it, ask ex-Mayor McGill of Seattle. Miss Malley seems to be acceptable not only to her own party, but also to a great number of men and women in the Republican and Democratic parties.

The best thing, some say, that the Democrats and Republicans can now do is to put up a woman candidate in opposition to Miss Malley. If Miss Malley is elected, she will be the first woman Governor in America. And this time there are no legal disabilities in the way.

Abraham Lincoln said that the object of government was to do for the people what the people could not do, so well, for themselves.

¶ In degree, government is a sort of corporation—a body without death, a mind without decline. It is a matter of business, and relates to matters of the education of the young; the care of the old, decrepit and infirm; the keeping of public records; the question of good roads, public parks, pure water and fresh air.

Government gives opportunity and protects the individual in his rights. The hand of the government should touch the people very lightly.

For the most part we know enough to do right, because right conduct brings good results and is a part of the great law of self-preservation ∾ ∾

Government is a business proposition. It is a matter of wise economics ∾ ∾

Woman is a natural conservator. I never in all my life heard of a woman who played the part of a Coal-Oil Johnny and flung money to the English sparrows. If a woman were allowed to pay the bills, there would be no lobster-palaces. The after-theater supper would be cut out. We would get three square meals a day with just what we needed, and no more.

Women who have their own money in their own pockets, and

know where their pockets are, never say, " Keep the change," with a lofty flourish. If there is any money coming back to them, they sweep it into their reticule, be it five cents or five dollars. Tips are tabu. It is only male man who is intent on impressing the head waiter or the floorwalker.

My opinion is that women are better financiers than men. They are not so much given to bounding and exploitation. A woman is a safer cashier than a man.

Taking it all in all, I do not see why women should not occupy high positions in the State. And apart from party lines, I am inclined to think the people of the State of Washington might do well to elect Miss Malley Governor—provided it was fixed by special enactment that no one should ever refer to her as " Governess."

"Jimmie" Durkin

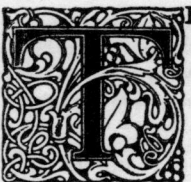THE best man in the worst business in America is the Honorable James McGillicuddy Durkin, of Spokane, Washington, known to the great Northwest as simply " Jimmie."
Nobody ever thinks of calling him " Mr. Durkin" or " Colonel Durkin." He is always plain Jimmie.
⁋ A few years ago Jimmie stood as a candidate, and also ran for Governor. He made a rather spectacular sprint, adding to the zest of the contest and giving great joy to the proletariat.
Jimmie runs a booze-bazaar. Not one of your high-class bar-rooms; just a joint that appeals to the middle class—"A Poor Man's Club," he calls it.
There is little style and no art about Jimmie's studio. It stands on a corner in the center of the business district, with big show-windows running along both streets.
These windows are filled with jugs, bottles, barrels, flagons, kegs and all of the impedimenta and props of damnation that the temperance orators refer to. It is as bad as " Shoomaker's " in Washington.
Jimmie claims to sell the best quality of wares in his own line that are offered anywhere in the round world. He says he has standardized the business to a point where only a fair profit is expected ❧ ❧
Like many others in the same line, none of his bartenders ever touch a drop of anything stronger than water, either on the premises or elsewhere.
Jimmie never allows any one to treat his bartenders. Neither does he accept a treat from any one on his own premises, any more than he would ask a street-car conductor to " have a ride with me." ❧ ❧
He, however, upholds the idea of treating, as a matter of good-

fellowship, and he makes the argument, based on Paul's advice to Timothy, that we should all, at times, take a little wine for our stomach's sake.

And when preachers make long lists of the dire results of alcoholic drinks, Jimmie, over against this, says that for every case where men suffer through strong drink, a thousand men are uplifted and benefited, inspired and made able to " forget it."

Most of our troubles never happen, but when trouble comes and sits on a man's chest, Jimmie's advice is to drown it out, but be sure to go to the right place, where the goods are guaranteed and the price is moderate, and where no minor, woman or drunkard is ever allowed to enter, much less loiter. Jimmie says this is hard on the women, but he can't help it.

Very seldom do you ever find a man that deals in strong drink who dares put up the argument in favor of it. Usually, they say it is a necessary evil, and " if I do not sell it somebody else will."

¶ Jimmie says he sells liquor in order to keep the trade from falling into disreputable hands. What he wants is to keep the holy enterprise on a high ethical basis.

His advertisements breathe forth a fine literary spirit, and are of a kind that makes most ad-writers jealous.

Jimmie takes a page, often, in every paper in the town, and sends forth his message of love, hope, good-cheer and rot-gut.

Of course, the ministers abominate him, but Spokane without Jimmie would not be what it is.

The banks in Washington close at noon on Saturday. So Jimmie, for the accommodation of his friends, advertises that he will cash checks for everybody to any amount.

And on Saturdays he piles into one of his front windows gold and silver—a half-bushel of it, seemingly—and there he stands and accepts the checks Saturday afternoon and evening until midnight ᴈ❦ ᴈ❦

These checks are thrown over into another window, and outside

around these windows, crowd and cling and push the sightseers.
⁋ Not long ago, about noon, on a certain Saturday Jimmie went to his bank and, as usual, drew fifteen thousand dollars in gold and silver, assorted.
With him was a boy, who carried half the money in a bag on his shoulder. Jimmie carried the other bag. Each of these bags weighed about forty pounds.
In the midst of the crowded throng Jimmie slipped—or pretended he did. He made an effort to recover himself. His heels went from under him and he pitched the bag twenty feet onto the asphalt.
⁋ The bag burst with a loud R. G. Dun report.
The money rolled in every direction. Cartwheel dollars, true to their name, rolled under the street-cars and beneath the automobiles. Twenty-dollar gold pieces chased after them. Quarters, dimes, nickels, five-dollar gold pieces—away they flew through the street.
The crowd, without taking a second thought, flew for the money. Everybody grabbed a handful, and Jimmie stood on the curb laughing, his hat in his hand, and yelled: " Hey, neighbors, help me pick up my money. God knows none of it is tainted! "
Newsboys shouted, " Stand where you are, Jimmie, we 'll get it for you." And so they went after the money, and Jimmie loaded it into his overcoat-pockets and then into his hat and finally a little newsy held out his hat, too, and got it full.
And then Jimmie, after fifteen minutes' time, seeing there was no more money coming back, started for his gin-mill, the newsy after him, the other lad holding fast to his bag of money to see that he did not do the same thing. Arriving at the budge emporium, Jimmie telephoned for a bank clerk to come up and count the cash. The man came. And how much do you think was short? Not a blessed cent! All the money was picked up and returned; and Jimmie argues from this that the people from Spokane are eminently honest.

Also—please note the fact—Jimmie got his advertisement. A few years ago when Evangelist Torrey and his singer Alexander were in Spokane, they put forth a special offer to get Jimmie to come to Jesus. Prayer-meetings were held, and finally, on Jimmie's failure to go to church, the church moved down and the Evangelists asked permission to hold services in the barroom. Jimmie told them that the next evening he would close down and give them the whole place. They agreed to this, and so on this single evening Jimmie quit business and advertised a column in every paper, where the services would be held.

Of course, there was a vast crowd of people in attendance. Jimmie himself took up the collection for the dominies, and started it off with a twenty-dollar gold piece. The bar was draped with the Stars and Stripes, and it looked really as if Jimmie had quit the business. And he let the idea get out that he had, which, of course, added to the general buzz.

The clergymen asked permission to redecorate the windows and also to put a sign on the outside of the building.

This Jimmie generously allowed them to do. So, having obtained permission, they secured the services of several men who were expert in lettering, and banners were hung all over the building, calling sinners to repentance in words like these:

Where will you spend your eternity?

God abominates a drunkard.

Strong drink leads straight to Hell.

Where is your wandering boy tonight?

Turn ye! Turn ye! Why will ye die?

Keep away from here—it is the Gateway of Hell!

Cards of similar nature were printed in big letters, and filled the windows ❧ ❧

The next day after the meeting in the saloon, Jimmie opened as usual, but refused to allow any one to remove a single card, banner or sign.

These remained for many months, and it is hinted openly that Jimmie replaced them from time to time when they seemed a trifle worn.

These emblems of earnest religious feeling decorating this pizen palace were one of the sights that every traveler to Spokane insisted on seeing.

If the churches could secure Jimmie Durkin as advertising agent, their success in Spokane would be much greater than it is.

Jimmie is a staunch Bryanite. He says that when Bill becomes President—as Jimmie declares he surely will—he intends to sell out his business, and accept a Cabinet Portfolio, as Secretary of War, which the same has been offered him.

Heinrich Schliemann

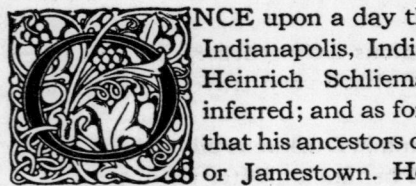NCE upon a day there was a grocer who lived in Indianapolis, Indiana. The grocer's name being Heinrich Schliemann, his nationality can be inferred; and as for pedigree, it is enough to state that his ancestors did not land either at Plymouth or Jamestown. However, he was an American citizen. ⁋ Now this grocer made much monies, for he sold groceries as were, and had a feed barn, a hay scales, a summer garden and a lunch counter. In fact, his place of business was just the kind you would expect a strenuous man by the name of Schliemann to keep.

Soon Schliemann had men on the road, and they sold groceries as far west as Peoria and east as far as Xenia.

Schliemann grew rich: and the gentle reader, being clairvoyant, now sees Schliemann weighed on his own hay scales—and wanting everything in sight—tipping the beam at part of a ton. The expectation is, that Schliemann will evolve into a large oval satrap, grow beautifully boastful and sublimely reminiscent, representing his Ward in the Common Council until pudge plus prunes him off in his prime.

But this time the reader is wrong: Schliemann was tall, slender and reserved, also taciturn. Groceries were not the goal. In fact, he had interests outside of Indianapolis, that few knew anything about. When Schliemann was thirty-eight years old he was worth half a million dollars; and instead of making his big business still bigger, he was studying Greek. Schliemann studied the history of Hellas.

About the year Eighteen Hundred Sixty-eight Schliemann turned all of his Indiana property into cash; and in April, Eighteen Hundred Seventy, he was digging in the hill of Hissarlik, Troy. The same faculty of thoroughness, and the ability to captain a large business—managing men to his own advantage and theirs—made his work in Greece a success. Schliemann's discoveries at Mt. Athos, Mycenae, Ithaca and Tiryns turned a search-light upon prehistoric Hellas and revolutionized prevailing ideas concerning the rise and development of Greek Art.

His Trojan treasures were presented to the city of Berlin. Had Schliemann given his priceless findings to Indianapolis, it would have made that city a Sacred Mecca for all the western world—set it apart, and caused James Whitcomb Riley to be a mere sideshow, inept, inconsequent, immaterial and insignificant. But alas! Indianapolis never knew Schliemann when he lived there—they thought he was a Dutch grocer! And all the honors went to **Benjamin Harrison, Governor Morton** and **Thomas A. Hendricks**. If the Indiana novelists would cease their dalliance with Dame Fiction and turn to Truth, writing a simple record of the life of Schliemann, it would eclipse in strangeness all the Knighthoods that ever were in flower, and Ben Hur would get the flag in his Crawfordsville chariot race for fame.

Berlin gave the freedom of the city to Schliemann; the Emperor of Germany bestowed on him a Knighthood; the University voted him a Ph. D.; Heidelberg made him a D. C. L.; and St. Petersburg followed with an LL. D.

The value of the treasure, now in the Berlin Museum, found by Schliemann, exceeds by far the value of the Elgin Marbles in the British Museum. We know, and have always known, who built the Parthenon and crowned the Acropolis; but not until Schliemann had by faith and good works removed the mountain of Hissarlik, did we know that the Troy of which blind Homer sang was not a figment of the poet's brain.

Schliemann showed us that a thousand years before the age of Phidias there was a civilization almost as great. Aye! more than this—he showed us that the ancient city of Troy was built upon the ruins of a city that throve and pulsed with life and pride, a thousand years or more before Thetis, the mother of Achilles, held her baby by the heel and dipped him in the River Styx. Schliemann passed to the realm of Shade in Eighteen Hundred Ninety, and is buried at Athens, in the Ceramicus, in a grave excavated by his own hands in a search for the grave of Socrates.

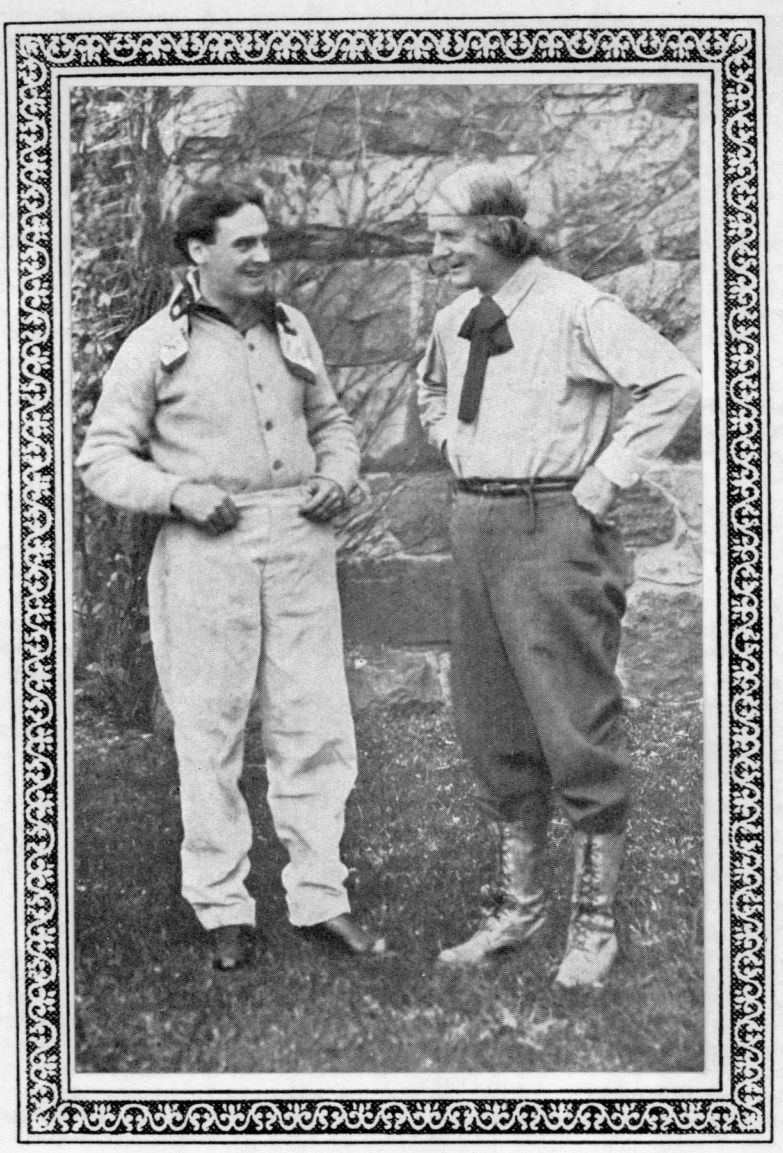

ELBERT HUBBARD AND THE GREAT RAYMOND

The Great Raymond

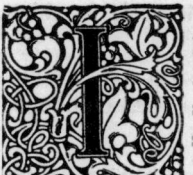I WAS in Chicago the other day and went to see Raymond—"The Great Raymond."
I went Saturday afternoon, Saturday evening, and again Sunday evening. In truth, I liked the show so well that I went Monday night.

It was the same performance, but never exactly the same, because good men never duplicate themselves. They never give the same show exactly alike. Nothing but a machine is automatic ✒ ✒

The good health, the good cheer, the grace, the strength and the intellect that the Great Raymond puts into his performance are very beautiful and very wonderful.

And yet the innocence and simplicity of it all!

It is a great thing to relax and laugh and be a child again, when you get the chance.

Raymond helps you turn the dial back. He takes dozens of eggs out of an empty derby hat, transfers a few of these eggs to a basket, then shows you the basket. It is perfectly empty. And now, behold, out of the basket he lifts chickens, guinea-hens, ducks, geese, turkeys—and then a rabbit—just as fast as they are hatched.

Raymond is a profound Bible student. The story of Noah's Ark interests him much.

He has a wonderful Noah's Ark, of his own, on wheels. In fact, it is a great big lifeboat with a deck.

On the stage, in order to get up a storm, you must have the co-operation of the orchestra.

And so the musicians play storm music, and there not being any water, the stage-hands have to fetch in a few buckets, and Raymond pours it into the Ark.

The Ark is perfectly empty; you see that, all right. But when the storm comes they have to fasten down the hatches and close the portholes. It is a terrible storm—the orchestra whoops it up, every man for himself. And finally, the whole boat is in shipshape, ready to weather the blast.

As the storm subsides, for no storm lasts forever, Raymond opens a porthole, reaches in and pulls out a duck—then chickens, guinea-hens, geese, turkeys.

Then come sheep, goats, dogs, cats and wonderful Teddy bears.
⁋ It occurred to me that a couple of nice pigs, Roycroft Reds, would add to the joy of the occasion.

So I telegraphed home to Ali Baba to send us a pair of pigs.
⁋ He picked out the reddest pair of little pigs you ever saw in your life, and sent them to Raymond by Parcel Post.

They were healthy, good-natured pigs, with no special excess baggage. They arrived in good order and I went to the theater to see their first performance. Raymond named one pig Fra Elbertus and the other Emmiline Pankhurst.

Of course, not being used to the stage, they were a bit nervous before they went on, especially in view of the fact that this was a critical Chicago audience—of course, 'way up on the subject of pigs.

When Raymond reached into Noah's Ark and yanked one of the pigs out by the ear, it set up a terrible squeal. The magician set it down gently on the stage and reached for its mate. But the little pig on the stage felt lonesome, and began to look around for his partner.

Finally, both pigs were placed out on the stage, and the supers in the wings were given the cue to round up the animals.

They caught everything, all right, except the little pigs. The pigs showed a fine capacity for speed.

They eluded the supers, and all hands were piped to catch the pigs ✌ ✌

But alas and alack! Emmiline Pankhurst made one mad dash

and went over the footlights on to the bald pate of the leader of the orchestra, caromed off into the big bass-drum, busted it, slid under the seats and wrigleyed among the feet of the Spearmint audience.

The house was in an uproar. Women stood on the seats. Brave men reached for the pigs, but failed to catch them. The stagehands came down in the audience and finally the porkers were secured and carried squealingly to their dressing-room.

At the next performance, on my advice, Raymond got a poodle-dog harness for each, one of those arrangements that go over the back and then around the neck, with jingling little bells.

One of the Raymond girls contributed a great big blue bow for Fra Elbertus, and Raymond got a green ribbon for Emmiline Pankhurst. Then a strap was attached to the ring on the back of each, as a safety precaution.

And now, would you believe it, those pigs are so trained that they will trot along on the street, anywhere, with their attendants. Two of the beautiful Raymond girls are making it their business to take care of these little homeless pigs—sort o chaperoning them, as 't were.

I met them the other day on Michigan Avenue, leading their pets like poodles.

And do you know, they attracted so much attention that a crowd gathered and the police had to call a taxi and take the girls and their pets back to the Hotel Sherman.

When Moses placed his ban on pork, of course he did n't know anything about the intelligence, the beauty and the affection of a sure-enough Roycroft pig. The pigs in the Orient were scavengers; Roycroft Reds are vegetarians and have a college education *⁕* *⁕*

The evolution of humanity is no more wonderful than the evolution of the pig.

Of course, in time, a pig grows up into just a plain hog. But there is this advantage, that if hard times come, a pig has a tangible value as collateral, which a poodle does n't possess.

It is probable that next year at this time, eugenics will have had its way; and instead of pulling simply two pigs out of an Ark, Raymond will have to liberate a dozen or more, all in the interests of the Higher Criticism according to the law of Poetic Unities, and the Economic Dictum that the ratio of pigs keeps pace with the price of corn.

The Great Raymond is not only a man of brains, but he is a poet, full of tender sentiment. He declares that, come what may, no matter what Mrs. Grundy says, he will never part with Fra Elbertus and Emmiline Pankhurst.

Great is the Great Raymond!

"Golightly" Morrill

UP in Minneapolis there is a preacher who is the only one of his kind. After God had made the Reverend George L. Morrill, he broke the mold. Perhaps one preacher of this kind is enough, although I am not so sure about that.

He is the only preacher in the world that I know of who makes religion absolutely funny. When I am in Minneapolis on Sunday, I always go to hear him preach, and I nearly roll out of my seat with laughter. Morrill is as funny as a box of monkeys ॐ ॐ

He is also a good sport. He works eternally for the Now and the Here. He wants everybody to have a good time in order that we may acquire the habit so we will be happy when we get to heaven.

⁋ He is orthodox; and yet he gives you permission to believe anything that you are able to believe; and most certainly he will never put you out of the church for anything you do or say.

⁋ The worse you are, the more you need him. And so "Golightly" is the Father Confessor to every sinner, every lawbreaker, every rogue. He is bishop of all bastards—theological and otherwise.

⁋ Of course I hear you gently murmur that this is why I like him. But never mind the persiflage! The other day Golightly preached a sermon on dancing. And the curious thing is that Golightly himself is a great Terpsichorean artist. There isn't one of the steps in the new-fangled dances that he can not take with grace. He is as light as a feather on his feet. When he preaches he wiggles, jiggles, jigs, jumps, and at the same time passes out the divine jolly and the sacred josh. He makes you laugh.

Life is full of difficulties and sorrows. We need some one who can flash good, wholesome rays of sunshine across our path.

Golightly manipulates a divine spotlight of his own. He illumines everything he touches.

So here is a sample from a recent sermon put over the footlights by the Reverend George L. Morrill, of Minneapolis, alias **Golightly, Skypilot to all Outsiders:**

Praise Him in the Dance.—Psalm, Cl : 4

The world has danced since the dawn of creation, when the morning stars sang together and the sons of men shouted for joy. ¶ Nature dances in sunbeam and shadow, wave and rivulet, leaf and flower. Animal life capers, gambols and dances to and fro with no definite object but happiness.

There have been religious, military and festal dances which have been healthful to the body, pleasant to the eye and harmless to the soul. Homer says that Merion was distinguished by his dancing. Hesiod declared that the gods had bestowed fortitude on some men and on others a disposition for dancing. Socrates, the wisest man, not only admired dancing, but learned to dance when he was an old man.

The old Bacchanalian dance was more intoxicating than wine—there was a confusion of sexes; their ivy garlands were emblems of clinging and cleaving; they imitated the satyrs and were attended by goats.

The modern " bunny hug " is the Dionysian orgy, or ancient can-can, portrayed on old bas-reliefs. It was conducted in the depths of a lonely forest, where Bacchus, the Savior of Sensuousness, led the triumphal march with wild abandon, while fauns, satyrs and bacchantes listened to music soft and sweet that burned into their very souls, keeping time with lewd gesture and loathsome grace.

So depraved was the dance in Rome that the senate made a decree to expel all dancing and dancers from the city.

The Church Fathers said, " As many passes as man makes in dancing, so many passes doth he make to hell."

" Everybody's doin' it," may be applied to dancing.

I have seen the dances of the Old World and the Orient, the contortions of Egypt, the suggestion of Naples, the excitement of the " hula hula " in Hawaii, the houchee-couchee, the unspiritual dance in Indian temples, but they are all tame, modest or decent compared with some of these " rags " where the " G " string of modesty is all that is left of Virtue's robe.

" Rags " are as wild as Tam O'Shanter saw when witches old and young reeled fast and furious until they sweat and threw off their clothes, and tripped in their " sarks " while the Devil played the music and the dead in their coffins held a light in their cold hands.

Erotic feeling has characterized many dances ancient and modern, while the " Grizzly Bear " and the " Tango " of today would make the Devil blush and hesitate to introduce them into hell ❧ ❧

Salome danced John's head off, and many have gone to their death since. There was a time when statues were made of graceful dancers—today there is a demand for statutes against disgraceful dancing.

The next thing in order is the naked dance proposed by Plato in his Ideal Republic.

Children are post-graduates in rag-time tunes and dances before they can sing a hymn or repeat the Lord's Prayer.

The " Turkey " has trotted over the Ten Commandments, and the " Grizzly Bear " has hugged the life out of Gospel ideals ❧ ❧

The animal world is libeled. Mr. Bear and Mrs. Turkey were never guilty of such antics, and must look with surprise and shame on the dances which bear their names.

These rag dances are animal in name and nature, and as much more passionate than the Oriental dance as Vesuvius is warmer than an iceberg. The dance has degenerated from devotion and diversion to dissipation and debauchery.

Rag-dancers listen to sensuous rag music, and often gaze with goatish eyes upon each other.

"On with the dance," though the waist be dislocated, the floor mopped, the partner half-pulled out of clothes.

"Hot from the hands promiscuously applied,
Round the slight waist, or down the glowing side."

Holbein's *Dance of Death* should be painted over the entrance of many dance-halls. The " Turkey Trot " ought to be relegated to the barnyard, the " Bunny Hug " to the alfalfa-patch, the " Crab Crawl " under the waves, and the " Grizzly Bear " to the tall timbers ⁂ ⁂

The " rag " dance is a Delilah that has shorn many a Samson of his physical, mental and spiritual strength, put out his eyes, and made him grind in the mill-prison of despair.

Woman in the dance has fallen furthest from the gate of heaven and nearest to the door of hell.

Dancing is called " fashionable " in society; so are cigarettes, drinking and gambling; but that does n't make them right. The dancing whirlpool of society is drawing into its drowning depths many of the best craft that sail Life's sea. There are enough safe pastimes and pleasures without taking risks.

Instead of asking, " What 's the harm? " say, " What 's the good? " and give your better self and God the benefit of it.

¶ Poets and painters have described Sin as a dark devil with horns and hoofs. Paint her a dancing Venus with sunny hair, bright eyes, sweet voice, polite manners, white arms and soft hands, but with a poisonous breath that blights, blisters and blackens into death.

Life is a masquerade-ball, and the time comes when we throw off our disguises. Lights grow dim, music moans, flowers fade, speech gives way to sighs, the scarf is exchanged for a shroud, and the painted musk-scented skeletons in the dance of death glide into the grave.

W. D. Wilmot

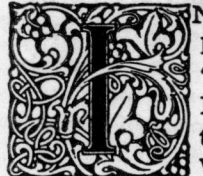IN Fall River, Massachusetts, lives W. D. Wilmot, known throughout New England, and more, as "The Uplifter."

It is a wonderful compliment to be given such a title by the people in a man's own town. And Wilmot is not exactly the man either, that some folks would pick to uplift a whole town, as he certainly has done. Wilmot is a sportsman, an athlete, who for ten years or more barnstormed this country and abroad doing bicycle trick-riding on a high wheel.

But while Wilmot is a sportsman, he is the right kind of a sport. He is like Muldoon, in that he has always respected his body. He has never gone the pace that leads to Bedlam. Incidentally, he has always had an eye for a good book, a choice picture, and his ear is attuned to beautiful music.

Wilmot runs a sporting-goods store, where he sells athletic goods of any kind and description.

Would you expect this man to write one article a day for a newspaper on " What can we do to make this town a better place? "

❧ Well, that is just what Wilmot has done—one column a day for three months in the Fall River *News*. Wilmot signs himself "Secretary of the Uplift Club."

He is the club, all of the officers, and the membership.

He has asked for no subscriptions, and received no salary.

He has done the thing for fun. Now they say a movement is on foot among the citizens to print Wilmot's Uplift articles in a book for a world-wide distribution.

The argument of all the articles is, stand by your town, stand by your neighbors, stand by your better self.

If you live in a bum place, why not make it better? Are your neighbors stupid and selfish? Well, perhaps you have helped make them so. But before we disparage, let us take an inventory of our advantages and blessings.

There is a play called *The Passing of the Third Floor Back*. A boarder in a second-class boarding-house redeems the whole beanery. Gradually, by his courtesy, intelligence and unselfishness, he introduces a new spirit, the spirit of good-will and mutual service. But it is all a play—an airy, fairy figment of a poet's pigment ॐ ॐ

And it is a splendid play, too. No sermon ever preached teaches so fine and vivid a lesson. But Wilmot and Fall River are facts. And the strange part is that Wilmot is not aware that he has done anything. Yet, this he acknowledges—his business has been doubled. And not by trying to, but just as a natural result. Wilmot has siphoned the love of bootblacks, newsboys, working-girls, laborers, and big men of big brain capacity in his direction.

He has made friends, not because he went in search of them, but as a result.

The Dreadnought Policy will never redeem the world from its sin and sorrow. A Dreadnought dries no eyes, mitigates no pain, relieves no heartache, turns no bitterness to kindness, makes no man more generous and gentle. It does not replace fear with courage, nor love with hate.

But an Uplift Club can. An Uplift Club is a club stuffed with good will and affection.

In uplifting his town, Wilmot has uplifted himself. In educating others, he has evolved and educated one man above all others, and that man is Wilmot. Look at his face! It mirrors gentleness, truth, purpose and noble endeavor.

David Bispham

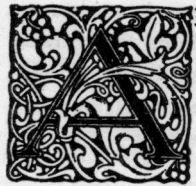BOUT the Wireless Boys who know things without being told, and who have grown rich by giving, I have often had something to say. There are a good many of 'em, dotted here and there over the world, but there is no better representative of the type than David Bispham, Royal-Roycrofter-at-Large.

The last Song Recital Bispham gave in America, just before he sailed to sing at the Coronation, was at the Roycroft Shop, without money and without price. He came to us with that magnificent physical health that runs over and inundates everything, with his generous sympathy and the Bispham laugh that is infectious. He gave us an hour and a half of pure delight— just the same program he gave the week before at Carnegie Hall to two thousand people

Most of those who heard him sing at the Shop, could never have heard him otherwise, but there was no condescension, no patronage, he met all as equals. Emerson has said, " Every sentence must have a man behind it." The song that sings itself right into our lives must be backed up by soul. The secret of the art of Sol Smith Russell lay in a great and tender heart; Francis Wilson is something more than a mime; Joe Jefferson carries with him the lavish heart of youth; Henry Clay Barnabee is a big man off the stage as well as on; and David Bispham is one of God's Great Singers, not merely because he can sing well, but because he believes in himself, believes in humanity, is in love with life, and has a heart that goes out to everybody and every living thing.

❡ It is all right to practise music, but music is something more than music, and David who sang for Saul had it.

William G. Hussey

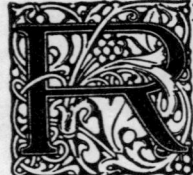HODE ISLAND has already distinguished herself in many ways. Here Roger Williams first raised the flag of liberty in America; and here it still waves. Free thought and free speech for America were first recognized as God-given rights in Rhode Island.

I had the great privilege of speaking in the Roger Williams Church and as I did so, the proud history of Rhode Island came to me. Here Anne Hutchinson—America's first suffragette—found a home and friends. The mother of fifteen children, Anne Hutchinson still had time to lift up her voice for human rights. A very great, able and influential personality was Anne Hutchinson, much of whose thought we are reflecting now consciously or unconsciously.

℃ The City of Providence is one of the most beautiful municipalities in America. The elms that line the streets in every direction, waving their branches in defiance to the breeze, seem like giant sentinels. Many of these trees were here in the days of Roger Williams, and some of them he planted with his own hands, for he was a working-man as well as a preacher.

The day after I had spoken in the Roger Williams Church, having a few hours to spare, I made a Little Journey to the beautiful workshop of Baird-North Co. It is two miles out from the center of Providence, and occupies a city block.

The great, gnarled, rugged elms were there on the lawn to greet me. There are tennis-courts, shrubbery, and a commodious garage. A general air of solidity and comfort surrounds this massive, ivy-covered workshop, where so many busy hands make precious things.

Five years ago, the Baird-North shop was in Salem, Massachusetts. Salem also lives in history, as well as Providence. Nathaniel Hawthorne gives some wonderful glimpses of Old Salem, written when he was a Customs Collector there, and lived where the witches once rode their broomsticks, and cultivated black-cat proclivities as a pastime.

In Salem, ten years ago, I first met Mr. A. W. Holmes, who was then a teacher with pedagogic ideals, and now behold, on my visit to the Baird-North people, I found my old teacher-friend from Salem, serving as Treasurer and General Manager of this great institution. Time works wondrous hurdy-gurdy changes, and this time it seems to have been all for the good.

There are men and institutions that can never be kept down, and the Baird-North people seem to be just that kind. When I first knew the Baird-North folks in Salem, they occupied a shop about thirty feet wide by seventy feet deep.

The business of the Baird-North Co. was manufacturing jewelry and selling it direct to the user through the mails. The innovation interested me greatly, but little did I imagine the extent to which the business would grow. I should have prophesied, and thus have been able to say, " I told you so!"

Said Napoleon Bonaparte, " Get your principles right, and the rest is a mere matter of detail."

The business of the Baird-North Co. evolved from a mere local jewelry-shop. Its interest for us dates from the time when William G. Hussey became the owner of a little business and a big idea. In fact, the idea was so big and the business so little, that nobody wanted to join him in it.

The idea was this, that the United States mails could carry jewelry direct from the workshop to the user at a trifling cost, and thus could be saved to the customer the many expenses involved in the old method of selling through the middlemen. The old method simply added cost to the article, without adding value. Mr. Hussey's idea was to save the consumer the intermediate profits.

⁋ This was seventeen years ago. Mr. Hussey was then thirty-eight years of age. He was a workingman—a graduate of the

University of Hard Knocks. Mr. Hussey came of rugged New England parentage—Mayflower stock. He was born on a rocky farm in Augusta, Maine, where we are told there is six months of winter, and six months of cold weather. Maine produces two great crops—able men and good potatoes. Maine is the land of granite, and much of its temper filters into the blood of the people.

⁋ William G. Hussey became a stone-cutter. Like Socrates he mastered the trade, and became an expert. Examples of his ability along this line can now be seen in the State Capitol at Albany, New York, and in many other public buildings of lesser note ☙ ☙

Mr. Hussey next became interested in pastel art, and in photography. His first studio was located at Lewiston, Maine. From Lewiston he moved to Salem, Massachusetts, and for some seasons his studio there was second to none in New England.

⁋ It was there that he became interested in the jewelry business, and in catalog-making, and it was there that he evolved the big idea of saving to the consumer the unnecessary profits that accrue to the middlemen.

From the cumbersome toil of making buildings of enduring granite, and from his beautiful art-work in the studio, we find the young man interesting himself in exquisite ornaments made from gold, silver and precious stones.

The boy, by nature and prenatal tendency, was a geologist. He knew the quartz, the granite, the feldspar, by sight and by touch. From these things to jasper, onyx, turquoise, the ruby, the emerald, the diamond—crystallized carbon—was but a step.

⁋ He made head and he made money: not as we count wealth today; but when he was thirty-eight years of age, he had, through New England thrift, saved ten thousand dollars or so in ready cash. So in the fall of Eighteen Hundred Ninety-five, he got out a little sixteen-page catalog, in which he pictured the precious things he had to offer. His idea was to sell these at the bare cost

—plus the small expense of packing and shipping—plus his one modest profit.

He sent out his catalogs, and wrote a letter to each person with his own hand, explaining what he was trying to do and asking them for their Christmas orders.

Mr. Hussey endeavored to surprise his customers on the right side. He decided to give them a little better value than he had advertised. A few orders came, mostly small ones, from buyers with caution plus.

Great care was taken in filling these orders, especially in the packing, so as to insure the safe arrival of the article, and to give the receiver a thrill of delight upon opening the package. Again, great care was taken in the shipping, because he had guaranteed satisfaction, and he had also guaranteed the safe delivery of each piece. ❡ Jewelry to the extent of thirteen hundred dollars was sold during November and December of that year.

The next fall preparations were made for a bigger trade. The Baird-North catalog was advertised in the various magazines. Mr. Hussey won the confidence of his customers—he began to receive larger orders, and for goods of the highest quality.

Many of the best people in the United States, instead of making personal shopping-tours at Christmas-time, enduring the waits, the jostle, and the germ-laden air, entrusted their orders to the Baird-North people.

In October, Nineteen Hundred Seven, the Baird-North people moved from Salem to Providence, Rhode Island. The business had grown to such an extent that Salem no longer offered facilities for expanding—the labor problem was the principal difficulty. In Providence live the sixth generation, jewelry-bred, of workers in precious metals. Providence is the home and the center of the jewelry business of America, if not of the world. The gold, the silver, the gems, and all of the materials used in manufacturing, are handled in Providence.

And so, if you want to do business, you have to go where business is being done. ¶ The great manufacturing centers of England, Germany and America are places where men have specialized on certain things.

Sheffield stands for cutlery.

And Manchester stands for steel and machinery.

Etruria recalls art pottery.

Liverpool, mirrors, jugs and queen's ware.

When I say South Bend, you think of plows and wagons; Detroit, stoves; Lynn means shoes.

There is more jewelry manufactured in Providence and the surrounding towns than in all the rest of America.

When your business grows, you would better grow with it. There is no such thing as putting the brakes on an expanding enterprise. Safety lies in moving with the tide. You must expand—become—you must grow or go. So William G. Hussey and his faithful band of executives packed up stock, tools, furniture, and on a special train of express cars moved in one day from Salem to Providence ❧ ❧

Orders were filled in Salem up to noon of Thursday. On Friday the trip was made, and on the following Monday morning, orders were filled in Providence. This one achievement is expressive of the great energy, the co-operation, the efficiency, and the executive ability of the organization.

William G. Hussey was a man big in brain, big in body—he was an athlete. He was the first man on the job in the morning, and the last one to leave it at night. Full of animation—good-cheer—ambition, he never seemed to know what it was to be tired or depressed. He accepted life in its every form, and found it good. ¶ In just nine weeks after the Baird-North people had moved to Providence, in the first week of January, William G. Hussey, founder of the business, was dead. " A clot in the heart-valve," the doctor said. Just a few moments' struggle in the middle of the

night, and that strong, earnest mind had gone out like a candle blown upon by the breath of the North.
The loyal, loving and faithful helpers that he had trained in the business were shocked—stunned. But behold, after the first spasm of grief, these men faced the day, as we all must. Life was here; it was for them to live it. ⁋ The corporation was promptly reorganized. Mr. George R. Hussey, the son of William G., a young man of twenty-three, was elected President. My friend Holmes was made Treasurer; and Harry R. Wheeler, Secretary.
⁋ Since his death, the young men whom Mr. Hussey called his "boys"—have more than doubled the business.
When I saw the army of Baird-North workers come trooping out of the factory at noontime, I was amazed, surprised and delighted to see what a well-dressed, intelligent, happy throng they were. Flowers are in the windows of this modern workshop, pictures are on the walls, and a flood of light comes streaming in from every side through the many windows.
The attractive boxes, the care exercised in packing and in rechecking orders was a revelation to me. I said to myself, "The people who receive these beautiful things must at times run short of words to express their feelings of surprise and satisfaction."
⁋ A serious concern for the interest of each customer pervades every department—then and there I was made to feel the full import of the word service. The good-will of the customers of this marvelous concern, as has been so feelingly expressed in their many letters of commendation, was no longer a mystery to me. So here we find a concern that manufactures and distributes direct to the user at the lowest possible expense of handling the order. The goods sold are artistic, beautiful, exquisite in design, and of the latest pattern and style of workmanship.
The endeavor is not only to satisfy, but to please every customer, and to make of him a firm and lasting friend. In very truth, this business is built upon friendship.

Hon. Thomas Brackett Reed

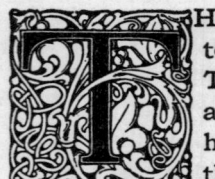HE Hon. Thomas Brackett Reed was "Tom" to three-fourths of the people who knew him. The first time I met Mr. Reed I called him "Tom" and it never occurred to me until the next day how presumptuous my action was. Perhaps the reason I addressed him as "Tom" was because he called me "John." "Say John," said Tom as he approached me at the Transportation Club. "I see you have been making a few pleasant remarks about a man by the name of Gould; now if you do not mind I want to give you a list of about half a dozen friends of mine, and if you will write about them in your own familiar vein, I will be very grateful!"
"Don't you give Colonel Littlejourneys the list, Tom," interposed Edward Lauterbach, "for he'll surely head it with your name." so so
"In which case I withdraw the commission," solemnly answered the ex-Speaker.
When half a nation calls a man by a nickname, it is a title of greatness far beyond what kings can bestow.
Tom Reed was one of the big men of the world, too big, far, to ever be president of the United States. "I'd rather be right than president," once shouted a disgruntled member at the Speaker, who was supposed to have presidential aspirations. "The gentleman will never be either," answered the Speaker, and the gavel hit the desk with a bang. Tom Reed was usually right, but he could never be president—he was too well known. There has been but one great man in the White House, and he was elected only because he was unknown to the nation at large. Only second-rate men secure a first prize at anything, excepting on a fluke. A man who is great enough to be himself, evolves enemies who hang upon his coat-tails and eternally cry, "whoa!"

Theirs is a death clutch, and not until he is dead and they are dead does the yelping of the pack cease.

The enemies of Tom Reed were of two classes: those who could not understand the man, and those whose tricky games were blocked by his unswerving personality. Neither class could ever forgive him. The stupid could never pardon him for not being as stupid as they, and the rogues, intent on roguery, called him a rogue until they really believed he was one.

Tom Reed was an absolutely honest man.

My belief is that much of his brusqueness and sweeping sword play was merely nature's plan of protecting the inmost recesses of a very great and tender soul.

In this man there was nothing cheap nor tawdry—he was a man. In his conversation he neither discussed the weather, nor his ills, nor the scandal of the town. He was big enough to hold his peace when he had nothing to say. In his speeches he was forceful, direct, convincing, and kept expectancy on tip-toe by a subtle play of wit, and a use of similes and epigrams that were the delight of every man who loves our English tongue. His writings have a distinct style that marks the man who does not write to fill space, but who has a message for the world.

In his spirit mingled the qualities of Charles Lamb and Tom Hood; his wit was as keen as that of Sidney Smith; his insight was that of Burke and the younger Pitt; and in his own life he disproved his oft quoted epigram, " A statesman is a politician who is dead." And if he was right when he said, " An honest politician is one who stays bought," then he was not one, for he could never either be bought, bribed, nor intimidated.

J. W. Jenkins' Sons Music Company

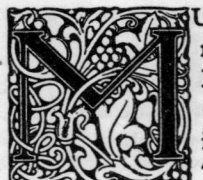USIC is the youngest of the arts. ⁋ Modern music dates back only about four hundred years. It is not so old as the invention of printing. ⁋ As an art it began with the work of the Church in endeavoring to arrange a liturgy.
The medieval chant and the popular folk-song fused, and the result was our modern science of music.
Sculpture reached perfection in Greece, painting in Italy, portraiture in Holland; but Germany, the land of thought, has given us nearly all the great musicians and nine-tenths of all our valuable musical compositions.
Art follows in the wake of commerce, for without commerce there is neither surplus wealth nor leisure. The artist is paid from what is left after men have bought food and clothing; and the time to enjoy comes only after the struggle for existence.
When Venice was not only Queen of the Adriatic but of the maritime world as well, Art came and established there her Court of Beauty. It was Venice mothered Giorgione, Titian, the Bellinis, and those masterful book-makers, and the men who wrought in iron and silver and gold; and it was beautiful Venice that gave sustenance and encouragement to Stradivarius (who made violins to the glory of God) up at Cremona, only a few miles away.
⁋ But there came a day when all those seventy book-makers of Venice ceased to print, and the music of the anvils was stilled, and all the painters were dead, and Venice became but a monument of things that were, as she is today; for commerce is King, and his capital has been moved far away. So Venice sits sad and solitary, a pale and beautiful ruin, pathetic beyond speech, existing on the sale of souvenir postal-cards and by taking in boarders, patroled by petty pilferers, degenerate sons of the robbers who once roamed the sea and enthroned her on her hundred isles.

All that Venice knew was absorbed by Holland. The Elzevirs and the Plantins took over the business of the seventy book-makers, and the art schools of Amsterdam, Leyden and Antwerp reproduced every picture of note that had been done in Venice. The great churches of Holland are replicas of the churches of Venice. And the Cathedral at Antwerp, where the sweet bells have chimed each quarter of an hour for three centuries, through peace and plenty, through lurid war and sudden death—there where hangs Rubens' masterpiece—that cathedral is but an enlarged Santa Maria dei Frari, where for two hundred years hung the *Assumption* by Titian.

In these churches of Holland were placed splendid organs, and the priests formed choirs and offered prizes for the best singers and the best composition. Music and painting developed hand in hand, for, at the last, all of the arts are one—each being but a division of labor. The world owes a great debt to the Dutch. It was Holland taught England how to paint and how to print, and England taught us; so printing, painting and music came to us by way of the Dutch.

The march of civilization follows a simple trail, well defined beyond dispute. Viewed in retrospect it begins in retrospect. It begins in a haze thread stretching from Assyria into Egypt, from Egypt into Greece, from Greece to Rome, widening throughout Italy and Spain, then centering in Venice and tracing clear and deep to Amsterdam, widening again into Germany and across to England, thence carried in "Mayflowers" to America.

That remark of Grover Cleveland that there is no culture west of Buffalo was indelicate if not unkind; and residents of Kansas City aver that it is open to argument. But the fact stands beyond cavil that commerce and art have traveled westward.

From the rocky shores of New England civilization moved toward the setting sun.

The march was slow until the railroad arrived.

In older time all great cities were on the seashore, because to and fro from thence came and went ships to the markets of the world. Now, the railroad brings the world to your door.

Transportation is the second most important thing in the world; food comes first, and Kansas City is the world's metropolis for both. Kansas City, Missouri, is situated in almost the exact geographical center of the United States. It is noted as the greatest distributing plant for agricultural implements in the world. Possibly it is not necessary for me to state that agricultural implements are used by agriculturists—also by farmers.

The farmers who get their supplies from Kanses City are eminently prosperous, otherwise this growing municipality could not have attained its present proud position.

Cities do not produce wealth—they only manipulate it. Swing a circle around Kansas City and within a radius of five hundred miles will be found an agricultural district big enough and rich enough to feed the world.

Plows, cultivators, traction engines, self-binding reapers, threshing machines, seeders, diskers, mowers, farm wagons, automobiles—these are the things in which Kansas City stands preeminently and undeniably first as a distributing point.

Education is a thing that is not overlooked in the vicinity of Kansas City. Many of the boys and girls born on the farms gravitate to the towns and cities.

All through Missouri, Kansas, Nebraska, Texas, you will find at the county seat and in all of the thousand of thriving, growing prosperous towns, colleges, schools, universities, musical conservatories patronized and built up by farmers.

Art is born after food, clothing and shelter are provided. Art is the result of a surplus.

A happy, growing, prosperous people naturally evolve art.

Music is the most universal form of art which we possess.

Sweet sounds minister to us in a thousand forms.

A multitude of people appreciate music who have small thought of painting or sculpture or literature. Music is the great civilizer. It appeals to the young and the old alike. It rests, benefits, inspires, and under its beneficent spell we are different people and better people.

The old-time traveling agent who "canvassed" organs, twenty-five, thirty or forty years ago was really a missionary in disguise. He may have been more or less of a rogue in heart, but he did good just the same. His musical instruments possibly were indifferent in quality, and he had a shading, sliding scale of prices. He charged all the traffic could bear. He got an instrument in the house, and then he collected for it as long as the family would pay and as much as they would pay.

Nevertheless, the sweet sounds of the Cottage Organ inspired the owners to something better.

The organ was parent to the piano.

As prosperity came other musical instruments were desired. Towns sprang into being. Theaters were built. Halls were devised. A band stand was erected in the village square, and a band was evolved into being by the process of natural selection. Most everywhere you go there are one or two men with a musical bias. Usually these men are of Germanic extraction, for Germany is still the home of music, philanthropy and education.

The Germans of the southwest have played a wonderful part in the promulgation of musical education. Good things are catching as well as bad.

The greatest Choral Society in America is at the little town of Lindsborg, Kansas. Lindsborg is a rival of Bayreuth, a competitor of Weimar, and in some things leads even East Aurora. Art here has found a voice. People travel from all over the world to attend the musical festival held annually at Lindsborg. But in all of the growing towns and cities of the southwest in degree there are musical festivals held from time to time.

The prosperity of the farmer allows him to supply his family things which to the pioneers of twenty-five, thirty or forty years ago were barren idealities.

In my boyhood I spent a considerable time in the vicinity of Kansas City. In the year 1876, the year of the Centennial Exposition, Kansas City was a straggling village of a few thousand inhabitants. Down on the flats there were stockyards, and a few warehouses from which agricultural implements were shipped up on the hillside on the bluffs overlooking the river. Main street stretched its length up and down between the ravines.

The man who remembers Kansas City as it was in 1876 would not recognize it now.

The hills have been leveled, the streets widened. Beautiful cluster lights have been installed. The grades have been reduced; and from a village of shacks, with a few flashy houses, we find a city, modern, beautiful, prosperous, with architecture complete and satisfying. The latest buildings erected in Kansas City are the best; and concrete, steel, glass, bronze, marble, enter into their making ∞ ∞

Kansas City is a municipality of homes. In Kansas City there is "A Backyard Society," devoted to the beautifying of the backyard ∞ ∞

Pure air, fresh water, trees, parks, flower gardens, are to be found here, unequaled by any city in America.

A home without music is something we can not imagine. The growing girls wish to entertain their company. The mother sings and plays for her children. All the household enjoy and are benefited by a musical atmosphere. Music has played a big part in the evolution of Kansas City.

In the year 1878, an Illinois Musician, J. W. Jenkins, founded a little music store in Kansas City. It was a daring thing for a man to devote his entire time and attention to selling musical instruments to this pioneer people. But Jenkins himself was a lover of music, a fair performer, a good singer, and an able critic. He sympathized with musical people, knew the history of music, was on good terms with the great composers, dead and living, had a working knowledge of all musical instruments, and the great performers he thought of as his personal friends. Schubert, Mozart, Beethoven, Wagner, Liszt, Paganini— all these were known to Jenkins. What booted it perchance he had never met them face to face! Had not the mintage of their minds been written out in musical terms? And was not the net result of their toil of love there on his shelves!

The store of J. W. Jenkins became the headquarters for all the music-loving people in Kansas City.

He sold cottage organs, pianos, harmonicas, violins, guitars, accordeons, band instruments, and when he ordered out from New York a Grand Piano, it was prophesied that the referee in bankruptcy would be along that way pretty soon.

Jenkins was a lover of music—also he was a lover of humanity. He realized the benefits and advantages that music was playing in his own education.

I remember Jenkins when he used to hold singing classes in the little Red School House in Illinois, and set the whole township doing, " do, fa, sol, mi, si, do."

People who wanted a church organ came to consult with Jenkins.

⁋ When bands were organized Jenkins made out a list of the instruments that were required. He encouraged, inspired, and assisted in a practical way in getting hundreds of bands and orchestras on their musical feet. He carried in stock the new and popular pieces that were being produced from time to time.

Gradually Kansas City ceased to be a pioneer town. The " wild and wooly " was disappearing. The wealth plowed out of the prairies was finding concrete form in better buildings, in street railways, in elevators, banks, shops, hotels, stores, factories, libraries ❦ ❦

As the town increased in size and prosperity, so grew the business of J. W. Jenkins.

The man made friends, and when you make friends you have potential customers. We make our money out of our friends—our enemies will not trade with us.

"When I make a sale I make a friend," said Jenkins.

His neighbors believed in him. This plain, simple, unpretentious man did not overstate, he did not brag nor boast. When he made a promise it was his business to keep it.

His word was as good as his bond.

If he had his doubts about a musical instrument he explained the matter to the customer, and when the customer was disappointed it was always on the right side, for Jenkins made it his business to give a little more and a little better value than the buyer expected.

⁋ When he placed a piano in a home it was with the hope and the fervent expectation that this home would be a sweeter, happier, better place for the fact that it contained one of the Jenkins musical instruments.

Jenkins had a reverent regard for music, and a great respect for music loving people.

He looked upon music as a necessary factor in the education of the young ∽ ∽

To him music was a sort of sacred thing.

Stradivarius said he made violins to the glory of God.

Jenkins might have said that he sold pianos with a similar idea in mind ∽ ∽

Jenkins loved his work. He was proud of his business. It was n't moil and toil. His heart was in his daily duties. "It is all play," he used to say, and to please and benefit and bless his customers was his earnest desire.

Jenkins told the truth about his instruments. He always felt that he was dealing with a neighbor and a friend. Nothing was concealed. Simple, honest, direct in all of his dealings, he attracted to him the best musical buyers of the entire southwest. The business grew step by step.

Jenkins had three sons who were brought up practically in the business. They were taught to interest themselves and take a hand in every department of the work. With J. W. Jenkins there were no menial tasks. The necessary was the sacred, and the useful to him was the divine.

His sons were not above sweeping off the sidewalk, cleaning windows, opening up cases, polishing pianos, and seeing that the whole store was kept properly cleaned, lighted, ventilated. These boys welcomed customers, ran errands, made themselves useful in a thousand ways, and through carrying responsibility they grew strong and self-reliant.

The business in due time gravitated to these young men. A corporation was formed. John W. Jenkins, Jr., is now president of the company; Fred B. Jenkins is Vice President, Clifford W. Jenkins is Secretary and Treasurer.

Many of the helpers and clerks in the store of J. W. Jenkins Sons' Music Company have been here upwards of two decades, and the best helpers in the business came along as youngsters and have grown up and been educated in the business as the business grew and evolved.

Today the J. W. Jenkins Sons' Music Company occupies the proud position of being the largest dealers in musical merchandise between Chicago and San Francisco.

An accurate knowledge concerning the value of musical instruments is the work of an expert.

In no line of business is deception so easy.

Only time proves the value and enduring qualities of musical instruments ✺ ✺

It is easy to palm off something "just as good," and to deceive the buyer with a beautifully polished case. Few people, comparatively, know values when it comes to musical instruments.

In buying, wise are they who do business only with men whose veracity is unquestioned.

The house of Jenkins ministers to a territory one thousand miles square. Not a town, village, hamlet or city in all of the great and growing southwest but that there are customers who buy musical merchandise from the house of Jenkins.

Theaters, churches, societies, bands, orchestras, individuals, look to the house of Jenkins for advice that is reliable and goods that are exactly what they are guaranteed to be, or better.

¶ There is no music store in America that is run on a higher ethical policy.

The other day I met a man who asked me this question: " Why are all the rogues in the world in the piano business? "

And I answered, " I do not think all of the rogues in the world are in the piano business, it only seems as if they are."

The piano business, nevertheless, has been good picking for the bashibazouks ✍ ✍

But there are not quite as many confidence men in the piano business as there were a few months ago—some of them have been forced out for violation of the Postal Laws in working confidence games.

Not long ago I received a check for $113.00, from an unknown company. It was a beautiful check on water-mark paper. It was printed in two colors, and a protectograph had been used to prevent my raising the check. It was a beautiful, wrinkly, crinkly bit of paper. It came in a No. 10 envelope, and the whole thing had at first glance a look of genuine business.

I soon discovered, however, that the letter that came with the check was signed with a rubber stamp.

The check was signed in the same way.

The letter had been printed by machine process in typewriting ink, and then my name had been added in on the typewriter. Nevertheless, the check commanded my attention.

The letter explained that on account of my prominence as a teacher the Company had decided to present me this check which would be as part payment on a piano.
The Company signing the letter I had never heard of, but on a little investigation I found that the concern was actually supplying pianos of a certain kind and quality.
Probably they would stand together and the glue would not give way until after full payment was made. The piano might have been worth a hundred dollars.
The concern charged me $400.00 and gave me credit then for the check that they had sent me.
Of course, I did not bite, but I have since learned that thousands of these checks were sent out, and that a few people bought poor pianos at fabulous prices.
Another firm advertised a guessing contest with a list of cash prizes. You were to state who it was said, " With malice toward none but charity for all." Of course, every school girl knows who used these words, and the youngsters did certainly write in. Then back came a letter with a beautiful check, and the youngster was told that this check was good only as part payment on a piano. In a good many instances people were deceived into buying these practically worthless pianos through the lure of the check so so
Lottery, guessing contests and bunco games in many forms have been used to palm off pianos.
It looks, however, as if people were getting wise to these silly schemes, but through it all, in fair weather or foul, the house of J. W. Jenkins Sons' Company has followed its one plan.
A spot cash price, no preferences.
One price and no more.
The J. W. Jenkins Sons' Company are agents for the Victrola. They carry in stock perhaps the biggest and most complete collection of records of any one institution in the world.

A few years ago the Victrola was looked upon as more or less of a toy or plaything. The machine, however, has been improved and bettered, and today is recognized as a practical educational instrument ॐ ॐ

It introduces us to the best players, performers, singers and artists in the world. To know these, to be on friendly terms with them, to hear them over and over again, is to increase your horizon and give you an outlook into the realm of art otherwise impossible.

¶ Every home should have a Victrola; it is an educational force not to be overlooked. Not only will it interest and please the children, and add to the joy of life, but it will educate, refine and better those who have lived longer. We are all children in the kindergarten of God.

Life is a school, and good music is too important a factor to overlook ॐ ॐ

As the farmers have prospered, so have prospered the towns and villages of the Southwest. Kansas City is a great distributing point. For the better accommodation of their thousands of customers the Jenkins folks have inaugurated branches at Joplin, St. Joseph, Independence, Bartlesville, Oklahoma City, Salina, Fort Smith, Hutchinson and Muskogee.

Each of these towns and cities represents a radiating center that ministers to a happy, intelligent, prosperous and appreciative community ॐ ॐ

The people of the Southwest prize the best.

Also, they have the money to buy the best, but they are not throwing any money to the English sparrows.

They want their money's worth.

Value is demanded and expected, and the business of Jenkins has been to couple up the entire Southwest as one great musical family ॐ ॐ

Saskatoon

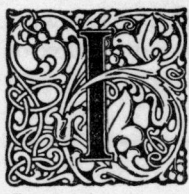I ONCE heard Canada described by a high-school sophomore as "that tract of land just opposite Buffalo, New York."
Mention Canada to most Americans, and delightful remembrances spring up of a good square meal at Saint Thomas, on the line of the Michigan Central ∞ ∞

"They little know of England who only England know," sings Rudyard Kipling. Also, they little know of the world who only the United States know.

If the Honorable Champ Clark had ever visited Canada he would not have made that indiscreet remark about annexation, which was taken seriously by a great political party and blazoned to the world as a sample of Yankee intent.

The average American is too busy with his own affairs, too thoroughly immersed in his own interests, to take a good look to the North ∞ ∞

When he thinks of the North, he thinks of Doctor Cook, and before his gaze spring visions of the Ananias Club. In order that the world shall not longer wander in Egyptian darkness concerning Canada, I want to set down a few facts.

Mark Twain says, "Truth is such a precious article; let 's all economize in its use!"

Anyway, we grow as we give. So here goes—starting with a bromide: Canada occupies that part of the North American Continent exactly North of the territory owned and duly occupied by the United States of America.

Canada extends from the Atlantic Ocean to the Pacific, a distance of, say, four thousand miles, East and West.

The Dominion of Canada covers 3,745,574 square miles. The United States, exclusive of Alaska, covers 3,026,789 square miles.

⁌ Canada has only one-tenth the population of the States; that is, the United States has ninety million, Canada has nine million.
⁌ It is estimated that one million of the people in Canada were born in the United States. There is a constant, steady influx of Americans into Western Canada, gradually increasing month by month ❧ ❧

The reason of this is easy to understand: Americans in Western Canada are making more money than they could make at home. Their exodus has been no error in judgment. If it were otherwise, you would find a tide of Americans going back to the States. But this is not the case.

People who prophesy what Western Canada will be fifty years from now are bold to the point of rashness.

The men on the ground who have been here longest dare not make an estimate.

The growth of the country has exceeded the wildest dreams even of the railroad-promoter.

Canada has a greater extent of wheat-producing land than the United States has; a greater grazing-ground; greater potential mineral wealth; greater development possibilities as yet untouched; greater potential electric water-power; greater fisheries, perhaps ten to one.

Ontario and Quebec will always be interesting, but not exciting. The future of Canada practically lies in the territory West and Northwest of Winnipeg.

In the year Eighteen Hundred Seventy-six, there was no wheat produced North of Saint Paul and Minneapolis.

When the first steamboat was carried across to the Red River of the North, in parts—pieces put together—and sent up to Fort Gary, the idea was that there would be a traffic for the boat, because Fort Gary had to be fed with supplies brought from the South.

The wheat-belt gradually moved North until it was discovered that wheat could be grown clear to Fort Gary, which is now the city of Winnipeg.

But now great crops of wheat, oats and flax are produced five hundred miles North of Winnipeg. Here is a tract of a thousand miles East and West, and five hundred miles North and South, where the soil is a black loam—practically the soil of Iowa and Illinois, evolved and produced by the same geologic conditions.

℃ The mighty currents which once flowed over Illinois, Iowa, Indiana and the entire Mississippi Valley covered the territory North as far as Hudson Bay.

Manitoba, Saskatchewan, Alberta and British Columbia have just as many hours of old Sol's beneficent rays as the people have in Wisconsin, this for the simple reason that as you go North the length of the Summer day increases. The season is short, but the days are long.

At Saskatoon they play baseball in the evening, calling the game at seven o'clock. You can read a newspaper on the veranda at ten o'clock at night, and at two-thirty in the morning the day dawns ∾ ∾

Nature is a great economist. Also, she is an opportunist, and where the season is short and the day is long, she improves the time ∾ ∾

The Missions of California were placed forty miles apart, from San Francisco to San Diego. Forty miles was a day's travel. Now the distance between stopping-places is a night's ride, as you sleep warmly, safely and securely in your Pullman.

From New York City you go to Buffalo in a night. From Buffalo to Chicago is a night's ride.

Nobody goes through Chicago. Everybody stops and spends a day there, at least. No trains pass through Chicago. Number One and Number Two not only hesitate, but absolutely stop.

You leave Chicago in a beautiful electric-lighted train in the evening and land at Saint Paul or Minneapolis in the morning.

⁋ In the evening you embark on another beautiful, complete, luxurious train, and reach Winnipeg in time for breakfast.

No one goes through Winnipeg. Every one stops here. You might stop longer, if you could get hotel accommodations. But while Winnipeg has various beautiful hotels, they are filled until the walls bulge ❦ ❦

Business booms and bustles at Winnipeg. Skyscrapers go up over night. You remain away from Winnipeg six months, and when you come back you have to hire somebody to conduct you around the town.

The one thing that has made Winnipeg is Number One Hard.

⁋ Wheat is the world's staple food-product. It is the one thing that has an intrinsic value—something which gold has not. Value lies in things that will sustain life. When you think of life-sustaining products, just put wheat down as the first item on the list.

Wheat was once a weed, growing wild in the mountains of India. It was carried down into the valleys, where the sunshine was warm and friendly. The soil was pulverized, water applied, and the happy weed bloomed and blossomed and produced six or ten kernels where there was only one before.

"All wealth comes from labor applied to land," says Adam Smith. We add one word, and say, all wealth comes from *intelligent* labor applied to land.

Wheat was first grown successfully as a business in the valley of the Nile, where the water overflowed and not only irrigated, but fertilized the land.

The story of Joseph and his brethren going down into Egypt in order to get food to fight off starvation is no fairy tale. It is history, and tokens the struggle of the nations to live.

Then wheat was raised on the plains of Assyria, and the example of the Nile was repeated along the banks of the Tigris and Euphrates ❦ ❦

Civilization moved on to Greece, and wealth was computed in measures of wheat.

Rome ruled the world as long as she maintained a close and constant sympathy with the interests of the farmers. And when the farming-land was devastated and the agrarians grew sick and tired and despondent, the rule of Rome languished and the borders of the Empire contracted until population was driven in by the barbarians on the Eternal City, and starvation, pestilence and death followed.

Civilization moved on, and Constantinople, the city of Constantine arose ❧ ❧

Little by little Europe increased in population, and always and forever the cities grew and prospered only in that territory where the wheat was brought to market.

Fifty years ago the Genesee Valley, in New York, was the great wheat-producing district in America. The city of Rochester was called the "Flour City," because there at the Genesee Falls where Sam Patch launched the unforgetable epigram, "Some things can be done as well as others," gristmills grew great, grinding the grain up into flour and then sending it out and down the Erie Canal.

The wheat district moved gradually to the west—Southern Michigan, Ohio, Indiana.

Then from Illinois the wheat-belt moved gradually North into Wisconsin. And by Eighteen Hundred Seventy-six, it reached nearly to Saint Paul and Minneapolis, but not quite. The Sacramento and San Joaquin Valleys were once great wheat-producers, but the land languished and now is being used for diversified farming ❧ ❧

A grain of wheat contains a wonderful intelligence. In its hard kernel life lies sleeping.

Wheat was used as the symbol of immortality by the Egyptians. They worshiped it as the token of life, and well they might, since it was the one thing that sustained life and made Egypt supreme in her day and generation.

The land that produces wheat holds the key to the situation. Wheat-raisers rule the world. If you have the thing that sustains life you are master of life itself.

When the Canadian Pacific reached Manitoba in Eighteen Hundred Eighty-eight, and Winnipeg became a market for wheat, it ceased to be a trading-post, and became a city.

The C. P. R. carried the people out on to the prairies. They built homes, and tickled the soil with the plow that it might laugh a harvest. The land produced twenty, thirty, forty bushels of wheat to the acre; of oats there grew forty, fifty, sixty, seventy, perhaps a hundred bushels to the acre.

The C. P. R., heavily subsidized by the Government, given alternate sections of land across the Continent—the whole thing built at a venture and as a kind of gamble—soon found that it had a paying business.

And yet the railroadmen, who knew most about the country, never anticipated the extent to which this country would evolve.

❡ Wheat was carried from Winnipeg to Port Arthur, the shipping-port on Lake Superior.

Here elevators were built and grain stored, and ships with wooden bottoms carried the grain to tidewater.

Soon larger ships were demanded, and finally we got "whalebacks," which carried ten times as many bushels of wheat as the old-time wooden steamboats did.

On May First, Nineteen Hundred Thirteen, I saw the thrilling sight at Port Arthur of sixty steamships laden with wheat, starting Southward, as the ice broke up. If these ships had been placed end to end they would have measured four miles of solid iron and sheet steel.

They carried a cargo valued at twenty-seven million dollars.

❡ The railroads so far have not been able to carry the crop out of Canada during the time when the farmer wanted to ship. The wheat-producing country has grown faster than transportation facilities.

But if one wants to realize the prosperity of the Canadian Pacific, let him remember that the net earnings of the Canadian Pacific in Nineteen Hundred Three were eight million dollars. In Nineteen Hundred Twelve, they were forty-five million dollars—and this figure does not include receipts derived from the sale of land and the natural increase in valuations.

In a single year the C. P. R. will be able to pay four per cent on its bonds and preferred stock and have a balance left of more than forty million dollars, for double-tracking, and making various other improvements.

For let it here be stated that it is the policy of the Canadian railroads to put back into the roads every dollar that is earned. Even the dividends paid come back, and more, too, because the roads are offering, from time to time, opportunities for its stockholders to reinvest.

Just here one might preach a little sermon to the lawmakers of the United States. There seems to be a general fear among politicians and the genus demagogue that some one individual will make too much money out of railroad-building and railroad-operating ৯ ৯

The fact is that so-called rich men are simply trustees. All they have, at best, is a life-lease on the property.

If these men are producing wealth—digging it out of the soil, cutting it out of the forest, fishing it out of the sea, digging it out of the mines, manufacturing it into forms of use and beauty—this wealth is the heritage of society. You will remember the question, "How much did the gentleman leave?" And the answer was, "All he had."

The idea of curtailing the production of wealth through vexatious, hampering legislation is something that the United States of

America has got to abandon as a financial and economic policy.
⁋ Canada knights her big businessmen; the United States indicts hers.

The provincial policy of guaranteeing railroad bonds and thus securing a big influx of money is a very wise policy; and on this policy, practically, the prosperity of Western Canada has turned.

⁋ One can readily understand, on visiting this growing and evolving country, why Canada sustains a great sentimental regard for the Mother Country. Granting that the king is a mere figurehead, symboling the power of the British Empire, there is yet a very positive reason why Canada's heart should beat loyally and lovingly for Great Britain.

The Mother Land is true to her children. There is a continual tide of British gold coming into Western Canada. And while the country itself is producing vast wealth from the soil, say in Saskatchewan, Alberta and Manitoba—upwards of five hundred millions a year from the products of the grain-fields—yet British gold is helping build these marvelous cities, extending from Winnipeg to Vancouver.

Business is now based on friendship, and the most valuable asset in the world is good-will.

It is necessary that Canada should have the good-will of the Mother Country; and Canada, without thinking it out, perhaps, or analyzing it, is true to her instincts, and is carefully guarding her national credit.

She is adding to her good-will. And so here come British investors making permanent investments, which are bound to bring them returns on their money, with ample security, and dividends beyond the dreams of avarice.

In twenty-five years from now, Winnipeg will have a population of a million people.

The cities of Saskatoon, Edmonton, Moose Jaw, Medicine Hat, Calgary; all prosperous, growing municipalities, each ministering to a vast territory—will have populations varying, say, from a hundred thousand to five hundred thousand.

These estimates are conservative, and are based on the rate of growth in the Middle States, say Minnesota, the Dakotas, Wisconsin, Illinois, Indiana, Iowa, Missouri, Nebraska and Colorado.

¶ Fold the map of Canada back on the States and you will find that Manitoba, Saskatchewan and Alberta will take in all of the states mentioned, and more. And the rate of production of wealth plowed from these prairies of Western Canada is fully equal to the rate of production in the past from the farming districts in the sections just enumerated.

It is not necessary that Western Canada shall increase in the same ratio that she has in the past ten years to meet this prophecy, but her power to produce food forms a basis for prosperity that can not be discredited.

Less than fifteen per cent of the arable land in Alberta, Saskatchewan and Manitoba is under cultivation; yet sufficient wealth is now being produced to give every man, woman and child in this district an annual income of five hundred dollars, or, say, two thousand dollars per annum per family. In New York State the average income per family is under six hundred dollars.

¶ Wheat-growing has been likened to placer-mining. It gets the gold that is on top of the ground.

For ten years the C. P. R. sold land at the fixed rate of three dollars and fifty cents an acre, and five dollars for specially selected quarter-sections.

Land that was sold at these prices eight years ago, say in the vicinity of Saskatoon, is now worth, for farming purposes, anywhere from forty to seventy-five dollars an acre.

Now just a word of warning. For while it is a fact that Canada is immensely prosperous, and that the great fertility of the soil and the right conditions have evolved wealth, yet at the same time there is no place in the world where you can make foolish

investments with a greater degree of ease than you can here.
⁋ Western Canada affords the real-estate boomer his paradise. He is laying out town lots in every direction, staking out the prairie, and he will continue to stake out just as far as buyers will go ॐ ॐ

Most of these real-estate boomers are Yankees—some of them Damyankees. Granting that all of them are honest in their hopes and expectations, yet it is a fact that men are ever prejudiced in the direction of their own interests. The boomer has his use up to a certain point. What that point is, has not yet been decided.
⁋ If you are going to buy real estate in Canada, deal with a man you know, or make sure by going and seeing the property yourself before putting a dollar into it.

Town-sites, ports, terminals, are mostly too good to be true.
⁋ A bellhop may give out the information that the Grand Trunk Pacific is going to lay out a town and build carshops at a certain place. A boomer picks up the information, passes it along, and it is published to the world as a fact.

The plot looks very beautiful on paper; but the actual fact that certain men have bought land for five dollars an acre and sold it in a year at a thousand dollars an acre does n't prove that you can do the same. Such financial deals are the exception, and are taken care of by men on the spot.

Long-distance buyers are apt to get absent treatment. This is no criticism on Canada. It is n't even a comment on the prosperity of Western Canada. It is a comment on the high hopes, the exuberance, the effervescence of the real-estate boomer and humanity in general.

Punch's advice to the man about to wed will fitly apply to the individual who sends his money into a country that he has never seen, and to men whom he has never met.

Having thus given due warning concerning the necessity of keeping one's feet on the ground, although your head may be in the sky, I wish to tell the simple truth, without varnish or hand polish, of one Canadian city that I visited.

In August, Nineteen Hundred Twelve, five Englishmen, representing a financial syndicate in London, came over to visit the city of Saskatoon.

They were introduced by a committee of local businessmen.

⁋ These Englishmen were loaning money to the municipality for the building of street-railways, putting in a water-supply, taking care of sewerage, supplying electric lights. While in Saskatoon, they were taken out to the farm of my old friend Fred Engen who came here eight years ago from the Dakotas.

Fred had been a homesteader, one of those freckled, fair-haired Scandinavians, born in Norway, North of the Arctic Circle. When four years old he induced his parents to migrate. They came over steerage, their chief assets being a generous brood of youngsters, of which Fred was one, but who made noise enough for several ✌ ✌

Fred became a farmhand in Dakota. He saved enough money to land him in Saskatoon, where he heard that men who could hitch up and drive six horses could get forty dollars a month and board ✌ ✌

Instead of getting a job he took up a homestead of one hundred sixty acres. He ran in debt for seed and agricultural implements. The next year he raised ninety acres of wheat at the rate of thirty bushels to the acre, and sold it at seventy-two cents a bushel ✌ ✌

With the money he bought land at five dollars an acre. He became the owner of two thousand acres. He owns this land now. It is one of the fairest farms I ever saw—just about three miles out of the beautiful, restless, growing city of Saskatoon.

And so to this farm of Fred Engen, the merry Englishmen were taken, a year ago. The wheat was just ripening, waving yellow and lustrous, kissed by the Autumn sun.

The Englishmen had never seen such a sight. Fred Engen had a tractor pulling five self-binders. This tractor walked across the fair acres, cutting a swath forty feet wide. " Do you call this much of a farm? " asked Fred, as he struck a match on the seat of his overalls.

And the Englishmen said, " We certainly do."

" Well," said Fred, " this is just Mrs. Engen's gardenpatch—simply a place where she raises stuff for the family, and from which she carries butter and eggs into town when she wants clothes for the children. If you want to see a farm, you should go over to the Goose Lake district, where I have a sure-enough."

¶ And so the Englishmen stayed over a day, and the next morning two automobiles lined up in front of the King George Hotel at Saskatoon, and they started for the Goose Lake district, a hundred miles away.

This Goose Lake country Engen had discovered six years before, while riding over it on horseback, and he at once entered into negotiations with the Government and the railroad-company and secured fourteen thousand acres at a cost of something like three dollars an acre, paying what he could, the rest on mortgage, payable in twenty years' time.

At that time the railroad did not run through the district. Engen, however, with prophetic eye, saw the future, but not as big a future as it turned out to be.

The business of the automobile is to annihilate distance. These prairie roads are natural trails which form an ideal automobile-track. You can run thirty miles an hour with perfect safety. There is just enough resiliency in the ground to get a good hold for the rubber and to make your tires last. I know of no track in the world with less jar and jolt and friction than these natural trails that Saskatchewan possesses. A hundred miles before dinner—sure, Terese, sure—dead easy!

Fred had telephoned ahead to his foremen to have a good prairie-

chicken dinner for the Englishmen. This meant one whole prairie-chicken on every plate. And for those who didn't exactly care for prairie-chicken there was a wild duck, roasted whole. For be it known that this is a land of small game—prairie-chickens, wild ducks, wild geese, cranes and rabbits galore.
⁋ The party brought up at Fred Engen's ranch at eleven-fifteen o'clock.

Out across the prairie, half a mile away, they saw a sight such as they had never seen before. Eight traction-engines, one behind another diagonally, each pulling five self-binders, a straight run of a mile across the prairie before a turn was made, and the wheat was ready to thresh out, revealing a yield of thirty-six bushels to the acre.

Then close at hand were oats, showing a yield of sixty bushels an acre ✺ ✺

Just to add to the interest of the occasion, Fred had started a threshing-machine going so as to show up the yield. The grain was being cut, harvested, sacked.

After dinner the visitors went out again to see the machines turning out the golden grain.

Fred explained to them that if it were necessary he could run the reaping-machines until eleven o'clock at night; then take a lay-off of three hours, and start again at two o'clock in the morning, when daylight came looming up and jocund day stood tiptoe on the wheat-fields, and the prairie-fowls strutted and boomed a welcome.

These Englishmen gathered in a knot, and talked in undertone, "You know, by Jove, really, old chappie, I sy, wonderful, marvelous, really!"

Then they separated and walked in twos.

Then they talked with Fred Engen.

This was no matter of boast and brag. There was the land; there was the grain; there were the traction-engines; there were the reapers; there was the threshing-machine, and there were the sacks piled on the wagons.

And the railroad ran right through the farm. Then the Englishmen got together and talked some more. Then they said to Fred, " What will you take for the fourteen thousand acres, you know? "

" Well," said Fred, " I don't want to sell it all. I have got to have a place to live. But I'll sell you ten sections at sixty dollars an acre."

The Englishmen walked off fifty yards and entered into confidences. Soon they came back and said to Fred Engen, " Let's go over to the ranch-house and have a cup of tea, you know, and some marmalade and toast, and we'll draw you a check for the first payment."

And so they went over to the ranch-house, and the Japanese cook make them toast and tea, and these Englishmen drew a draft on London for fifteen thousand pounds, as advance payment and to them the title of the property in due time passed, on a total payment of three hundred eighty-four thousand dollars.

⁋ The total cost of the property to Fred Engen was less than thirty thousand dollars, including improvements.

These Englishmen made no mistake in their purchase. They were representing a syndicate of capitalists who had money to invest. They will clean up and pay for the entire tract within five years' time, and have a surplus beside—this as a straight business deal. If they build a town on the property, of course no one then can say how much their profits will be.

Saskatoon is a city of thirty thousand people—a city without a pauper—a town of tireless workers! The pioneer of old was a whipped-out party who left home because he could not stand competition. The men you meet in Western Canada are the opposite type.

The reason of the evolution of Saskatoon seems to have turned on the fact that here a little company of strong men have worked together. It is a beehive, with one animating purpose, and that the success of Saskatoon.

The Saskatoon Spirit accounts for Saskatoon.

Ten years ago Saskatoon had a population of one hundred thirteen. Now it has thirty thousand.

Saskatoon has sixteen banks. It has three railroads.

Saskatoon is halfway between Winnipeg and Edmonton—a night's ride from either place. For five hundred miles in every direction the land is rich black loam, mingled with just enough sand to keep it mellow.

Saskatoon is in the exact geographical center of the arable land of Saskatchewan Province. I visited Saskatoon, on invitation of my old college chum, Harold M. Weir—all-round cosmopolitan and citizen of the world, plus.

Harold was born in Australia; spent his boyhood in California; went to college in England; studied art in France; circled the globe for English investors; has been connected with big and successful enterprises in the States, and has the confidence of the financial world.

His father was Colonel John Weir, President of the Nevada and Utah Mining and Smelting Company. Harold is the worthy son of a worthy father, who went down gloriously on the *Titanic*, dying like a gentleman.

Harold organized the Industrial League for the Promotion of Saskatoon enterprises. It is a Civic League, and its quality is revealed when I tell you that under Weir's persuasive personality the citizens of Saskatoon subscribed a million dollars within four and a half days for bringing here manufacturing and commercial enterprises.

Cities are only possible where they minister to the needs of a great agricultural district. We get our wealth out of the soil.

ℂ Saskatoon is the natural distributing-point for seventeen thousand square miles of richly producing farmland.

Saskatoon is situated on the Saskatchewan River. Unlike most prairie towns, here is a diversity of scene that lends surpassing beauty to this growing young city.

The Saskatchewan is a rapid-running river with high banks on one side, and on the other, stretching away for miles, is a great, happy, smiling, undulating plain.

On this high upland, diversified with its hills and valleys, is situated most of the city of Saskatoon. No flood can ever reach it, and no financial blizzard blow it away.

Here are railway-terminals, great railroad-shops, employing upward of five thousand men. Here are grist-mills, lumber-mills; the chief Western plant of the Quaker Oats Company; shops, stores, factories, and more than two hundred concerns dealing in a wholesale way in the necessities of life.

Saskatoon ranks third as the greatest distributing-point for agricultural implements on the North American Continent. No city in Canada does so large a business in agricultural implements as does Saskatoon.

Here are big warehouses, built and owned by the International Harvester Company, the Fairbanks-Morse Company, the John Deere Plow Company, and by various other manufacturers of agricultural implements and appliances.

I saw the goodly sight of a trainload of thirty-nine flat cars, each carrying a traction-engine.

In Saskatoon are owned more than seven hundred automobiles.

⁋ The city, although only ten years of age, has gotten past the shanty stage. Brick, stone, concrete, steel, are the materials used in the construction of its houses.

The Fire Department is equipped with motor vehicles. The pavements cover forty-two miles of cement. There are upwards of five hundred cluster tungsten electric lights, fifteen modern hotels, and on banks of the river, overlooking the city, are the Saskatchewan Provincial University and the Saskatchewan

Agricultural College. Upwards of two million dollars have already been spent on these buildings.

The College Farm covers an area of thirteen hundred acres. And most beautiful of all, the entire spirit of this University and Agricultural College is to train and fit young men and women for actual workaday life. The New Education, the education for usefulness, has arrived.

Scientific farming, scientific stock-raising, domestic science and economics of every kind and nature are here taught as they are taught, say, at Cornell, Ames and Manhattan.

Saskatoon has built on the basic bedrock of commonsense. The big men here are graduates of the University of Hard Knocks. They know everything that will not work.

For instance, the natural thing would be to run the sewage into the river, because there is a perfect gravitation. Instead of this, the sewage is taken care of by a disposal-plant, and the waters of the beautiful Saskatchewan are left unpolluted.

Then there are depressed streets, so that at the principal thoroughfares there are no grade-crossings. The streets either run over the railroads or under them.

Saskatoon has a friendliness and a degree of order, decency, thrift, courtesy, kindness and deliberation which one does not expect to see in what is usually regarded as a " pioneer country."

⁋ The great Cairns Department-Store, standing four sides solid to the wind and sun, is flooded with light from every side, fitted entirely with brand-new fixtures. Here the stock is all new, bright, clean, fresh, everything old being cleaned out at some price or any price after sixty days, mirroring the stability and giving a keynote to the entire city.

The Cairns Store is headquarters for every newcomer. The man arriving in Saskatoon finds himself among friends.

The promoter who overstates and can not back up his proposition with a guarantee has been eliminated.

The man who invests in Saskatoon must feel that he is on safe footing and is investing with men whose interests are his. These people are here to stay. The buildings they are now building will be here long after their builders have turned to dust. All the money they make goes back into Saskatoon. What did Fred Engen do with that three hundred twenty-five thousand dollars those Englishmen paid him? I'll tell you: he deposited it in Saskatoon banks.

I was delighted to see that the railroads have faith in the country. In all of the big towns and cities in Canada you will find that the C. P. R. and the Grand Trunk are building hotels and business blocks after the most improved modern standards.

The principal men of Saskatoon came here as homesteaders—that is, farmers. As luck would have it, they located in the right place. Call it good judgment, if you prefer, but time and chance still hold their place in life just as they did in the days of Ecclesiastes ೂ ೂ

In Saskatoon you find the Norwegian, the Swede, the Dane, the Scot, with all of the primal virtues of industry, economy, integrity, which go into the making of a man and into the making of a nation—the simple primal virtues—the things for which there are no substitutes.

These are the things—combined with geography and opportunity—that have made Saskatoon the most remarkable city of its size on the North American Continent.

A Little History in Tabloid

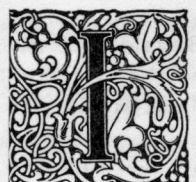FIRST arrived in Buffalo on May 10, 1875. I was nineteen years of age, and had been earning my own living since I was twelve.

In my own mind I was considerable of a man. I wore spring bottom pants, a warm vest, a dinky derby and had a fairly good opinion of myself. Looking at myself as I then existed I can perceive that I might have been something worse. I did not use tobacco. I never touched strong drink, and my Baptist environment had made the pasteboard proclivity strictly tabu. I had lived in the out-of-doors, and I prized my health.

I came to Buffalo with a man who was eleven years my senior. He was born in Canada, had shifted to Chicago, learned to make soap, keep books and do business. He was an active, energetic, simple, unpretentious, honest man, with a firm hold on the Scottish virtues, the virtues of industry, economy, truthfulness. He did not have much money, but he knew what he wanted to do and he did it.

We rented an old brick building down on Chicago Street near Louisiana and started a soap factory, just the two of us, with two boys as helpers.

At the end of a year we saw that we were on the right track and the boss bought a lot on Seneca Street with a one-story blacksmith shop on it. This lot was thirty by one hundred and twenty feet, as I remember it, and cost something like Three Thousand Dollars ❧ ❧

We built a frame building back of the blacksmith shop. We worked nights, days and Sundays, and I went out on the road and sold the product.

It was the famous year 1876, and I pulled all the door bells in Philadelphia to a purpose. In the fall of 1876, I left the selling to other young men whom I had trained, and came back to Buffalo to help enlarge the plant. There were eleven names on the pay roll ∾ ∾

At that time there were two horse car lines in Buffalo. One ran from the foot of Main Street to Cold Springs and the other ran from the foot of Main Street, out Niagara, to Black Rock. The fare was eight cents.

Buffalo at that time had a population of about one hundred thousand ∾ ∾

At the Central Railroad Station, Charley Miller was always on hand to greet the passengers and speed them on their way. He had only one good lamp, but he saw as much with that Mazda as most of us see with two. He had three 'buses and six carriages.

¶ Charley was the first man in America to go out and meet incoming railroad trains, and check your baggage. This is where he put one over on the hackman. He surely has taught the world a few things in the line of local transportation, and he is still on the job.

¶ About that time I saw Grover Cleveland, who was pointed out to me as a very great man—also a large man. He had been Sheriff of Erie County, and had studied law to a purpose and the intent was to elect him Mayor of Buffalo.

Taking more or less of an interest in public affairs I busied myself in this campaign carrying a leaky torch in sundry parades.

¶ Cleveland was elected Mayor of Buffalo in the year 1881. He set himself against graft and the abuses of the ward heeler and got the ill will of his own party.

The howls of his enemies lifted him into a national prominence.

¶ In 1882, he was nominated for Governor of New York and elected by the unprecedented majority of 192,000 votes.

As Governor, his policy was exactly the same as when he was Mayor. He worked for all the people all of the time.

In 1884, he was nominated for President of the United States and resigned the Governorship to accept the office.

I remember meeting Cleveland in the Public Library, and the man who had practical charge of the library then was our old friend Ives, who has just turned his ninety-seventh birthday.
℄ The biggest business in Buffalo then was the Hamlin Grape Sugar Factory, and next to this was the stove foundry of Jewett and Root ❧ ❧
The West Shore Railroad, The Nickel Plate, the Lackawanna, the Lehigh Valley, and the Grand Trunk have all entered Buffalo within my recollection.
The fastest train to Chicago in 1882, left Buffalo at one o'clock in the afternoon and reached Chicago the next morning.
Buffalo was a transfer point for the mails, and all of the mail that arrived was hauled up to the post-office, redistributed, rebagged, hauled back to the railroad station and placed again on the cars.
℄ Our soap business gradually, slowly, surely increased, and the Chief grew with the business. We got to making perfumes, soap-powders and various toilet articles.
In 1888, I evolved an idea, sitting at a table eating a twenty-five cent meal in a restaurant which was under the building now occupied by the People's Bank.
The idea came to me with a great big thrill, and I wrote out the proposition on a sheet of paper and forgot to eat my dinner.
℄ I hope I paid the check. I laid the idea before the Chief and he was not very long in accepting it and having just as much faith in it as I. How big an idea it was neither one of us knew or guessed ❧ ❧
"Get your principles right," said Napoleon, "and the rest is a matter of detail."
And that business down on Seneca Street, founded with a few thousand dollars, and which at one time was owing more money than it had assets, is now the biggest business of its kind in the world. And it is big simply because it has moved in the line of the tides that play through the human heart.

The big man at the last is the man who takes an idea and makes of it a genuine success—the man who brings the ship into port.
⁋ If I were to state the number of millions of dollars actual profit that this concern has made, and if I would state the amount of mazuma that it is now worth, I would be promptly placed in the Ananias Club, because no man is in such danger of the Ananias Club as he who tells the truth. The institution is manned by big, strong, able, patient, persistent individuals of right intent, who do not cultivate the spot light, who do their work and hold their peace.

The men and women in that institution, stockholders and employees, I am told, represent an ownership of upwards of fifteen hundred houses in the City of Buffalo.

Naturally, I take a pardonable pride in the evolution of that great concern, just as I take a pride and an interest in the prosperous city of Buffalo.

Since 1875, when I landed in Buffalo, to this tenth day of May, 1914, I have never been sick a day, never consulted a physician, never lost a meal, and life on the whole has been one delightful little journey. Erie County has been good to me.

In fact Erie County is good to every one who will get out and hustle ✺ ✺

In Buffalo there are over a thousand factories representing over two hundred lines of manufacture—peculiar, separate, useful commodities. Soap, linseed oil, automobiles, railroad cars, furniture, paper, the packing industries, the biggest horse market in the world, a great grain market, railroad industries magnus and steamboating superbus. Look 'em up in the Encyclopedia.

⁋ One point is that with such a diversity of industries, business in Buffalo never suffers a slump. If things are a little dull in one line, the others are booming, so the money flows and the Pay Envelope is pink and pudgy.

And this means progress and prosperity.

In 1890, 1891 and 1892, Buffalo had a real estate boom. Town lots were laid out sufficient to make a city of two million people. We all went land fluffy in the alfalfa.

Since then things have been normal. Buffalo real estate now is right down to the limestone. The moisture is all out of it. Buffalo is ripe for a boom.

I've watched Buffalo grow for thirty-nine years. I've seen big fortunes made by men who bought and held on. And it seems to me that, of all times, now is the time for Buffalo folks to hold on to their real estate holdings, and if convenient add a little to them ∾ ∾

Buffalo can never go back.

A Notable Achievement

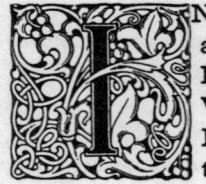IN November, Nineteen Hundred Eight, I gave a lecture at the Oliver Opera-House, South Bend, which is in the State of Indiana.
Very naturally, I stopped at the Oliver Hotel. Now, no one can visit the Oliver Hotel without thinking better of himself and the whole human race. The only objection to the place is that it exhausts one's stock of adjectives in attempting to describe it.

In this frame of mind, sitting there in the lobby of the Oliver, bathed in the soft, cathedral lights, a young fellow seated near looked at me, tipped his derby over one eye, and said, " Great —eh? "

I nodded assent.

He continued, " Plow men—that's the bust of the old man, over there. That loving cup in the case is eighteen-karat gold—cost about seven thousand dollars. Given by the people of the town. Gr-r-r-reat! "

Now, I had held the handles, for many a long week, of an " Oliver Forty " in my boyhood, and this was before the " Chalmers-Detroit Forty " was imagined.

It all kind of came back to me as I gazed on the heroic face pictured in bronze. The indrawn chin, the tousled hair, the bold features of a man who feared no man, and of whom no man was afraid!

That afternoon I walked out to the Oliver Plow-Works, pushed in the big gate and wandered over the hundred acres of manufacturing plant at my own sweet will.

And about the time I expected to be fired as an intruder, I bumped into Gail Davis, royal, loyal Roycroft Rooter, daffy as an owl on all things Philistinic, gulping Roycroft philosophy without fletcherizing. I had forgotten he was an Oliver man.

But here he was, the trusted confidential man of this great institution. He introduced me to James Oliver, the grandson of the picturesque and heroic Chief.

I rather liked the youth on sight. He was simple, modest, direct, athletic, and not too deuced clever, you know. He was quite unaware of his proud pedigree or of the fact that he was the heir to millions. Evidently he was mindful that wealth is a responsibility, and I saw he was getting under the burden. His face was smudged with foundry dirt, and his hands were the hands of Esau. He seemed to have in him a trace of Hamiltonian Ten, and a look of the Oliver Forty. And I said to myself, " Give him time and work enough, and a dash of trouble, and he will acquire that martial Highland look of his grandfather, the look of the Scotchman, with whom you will have to agree, or kill."

The grand old man who loved the snow and ice, the wind and rain, feeling in the elements something close kin to himself, had passed out but a few months before, and the whole place was sort of subdued with the sense of loss.

Gail Davis gave me a photograph of the Chief, and an envelope of clippings concerning his passing.

The man who had invented and perfected the Oliver Forty of my boyhood was dead. It came to me with a sense of personal loss.

¶ To live a big, busy life, and pack the swift-passing days with the plain, homely, manly virtues, for which modernity has found no substitute—the virtues of industry, truth, economy and an ambition to benefit every farmer who walks in a fresh furrow—to succeed, and then to sleep—well, dammit, Terese, I say, I'm no moping mollycoddle, but superior men are not so plentiful that Clio can afford to give their memories the hook.

And so I gave my spiel, and went the route of the barnstormer who works the one-night stands with the fond anticipation of a whole week at home, just ahead.

The first week in December was my Pippa Passes holiday. I

started in by helping the boys cut down some trees that were blocking the path of progress. I succeeded so well that one tree in falling got caught in another. This is the way trees get even with men. I cut down the second tree, to liberate the first, and both trees went after me.

When two trees combine, no one can say what they will do. They smashed me to the ground with their branches, and one grabbed my right foot. Had I been alone, that tree would have held me for ninety-nine years. As it was the boys cut me loose, Mr Johnsing.

I was n't really injured, but my feet were not mates, and I knew that I could n't wear a shoe or put my foot to the ground for a month and a day.

It is a fine thing to get laid up. You do not realize how sweet it is to be waited on, and have loving hands and feet run and fetch and carry for you, until then. " To be blind and to be loved, what happier fate," says Victor Hugo.

I was happy, happy to think it was only my foot and not my sky-piece, and also I was feeling enough pain to key me up and keep my mental molecules in motion.

And as gentle, loving hands—beautiful, helping hands—bandaged my sick and broken foot, I reached over to the table and took up the envelope of clippings that Gail Davis had given me about my dear, dead friend.

Straightway, I wrote the *Little Journey to the Home of James Oliver*. The next day I finished it.

It was born of love and pain. And I think yet that it is one of the best things I ever penned.

The Oliver folks, down at South Bend, liked it, too. They showed their appreciation in a very tangible way, Terese, the only kind of compliment that really counts. In fact, they sent out Quite—Some—Few of that 'ere " Oliver Little Journey."

Almost every really good thing a fellow fishes out of the literary

ink-pot is regarded by a few people as rot, rubbish, hogwash and drivel, and they write and tell you so.
This gives Pro Bono Publico and Old Subscriber a chance.
But that Oliver booklet is an exception—it has brought The Roycrofters a whole little army of loyal, loving friends—an army of men who have held the handles of an " Oliver " and of women whose hands have been held by the hands that held the handles of " Oliver." Blessed be brotherhood!
Especially did it please the Scotch—that redheaded, thistle-topped clannish bunch, with a hoot-mon bias. They bought it by the hundred. Andy Himself bought a thousand in de luxe covers and sent them to the land of fen and heather, of oatmeal and haggis, just to show how the Scotch are getting along in America ❧ ❧
I understand from reports put out from Ellis Island that more Scotch are arriving on these friendly shores than ever before. Charlie Post says, " There 's a reason," and Charlie is a man who decides quickly and is sometimes right.
But of all the hundreds of letters I have received about that " Oliver Little Journey," the one from Robert Collyer I prize most ❧ ❧
It is a long letter, written by the Prophet's own hand, the big, honest hand that used to swing a blacksmith's sledge. And Robert Collyer has been making the sparks fly for over eighty years ❧ ❧
Now in this " Oliver Little Journey " I tell of the striking resemblance between Robert Collyer and James Oliver, and of how, when traveling, Oliver was often congratulated on his sermons by kindly old ladies who insisted that they had heard him preach ❧ ❧
In his letter to me Dr. Collyer says:
" When I look on the noble face of James Oliver and think of his long and useful life as you have so truthfully pictured both, I am

complimented and also abashed to remember that we were sometimes taken for each other. However, as I admit I am abashed, I will now muzzle my modesty and tell you a story on your solemn promise never to repeat it. It is this: On request of a good woman who used to hear me preach in Edinburgh, I presented her my photograph ☙ ☙

" This picture she thought enough of to have framed and hung on the wall of her library.

" One day, Constable, the great publisher, came along. Constable looked at the picture, and finally said, 'Mrs. MacDonald, I want to borrow this picture for a few days.'

" ' Why, ah—er, Mr. Constable, really what do you want to do with it? ' ☙ ☙

" ' I want to send it to Jove, just to show him what kind of men we can produce here on Earth! '

" You see this story puts me in a most ridiculous light, and I would not have told it to you, save for the fact that I was just now looking on the picture of James Oliver, and you, with your eyes of love—which are always out of focus—say that we looked alike." ☙ ☙

It is curious how far a little candle will throw its beams. Clear from the other side of the world comes a letter from Sir Robert Stout, Chief Justice of New Zealand, to say that, to him, James Oliver is not only the typical Scotchman, but the ideal, universal citizen, who reforms the world by minding his own business, and does it superbly well. It is over a year since we printed the first "Oliver Little Journey." I have just been back to South Bend. Again I enjoyed the quiet luxury of the Oliver Hotel. Again I roamed through the great plow-works. Never were they so busy, working in double shifts, with orders way ahead, and telegrams coming, " When may I expect those plows? " A new building to cost half a million dollars is in course of construction.

I rubbed my hands in glee. I congratulated everybody.

Battle Creek with its breakfast tumbo timber is surely correct, "There's a reason!"

"What do you think is the reason?" asked Nip, the Watchdog of the Oliver Treasury, with a Number-Forty grin.

"Nip," said I, in a voice filled with gentle rebuke, "Nip, you know why this business has nearly doubled in a year. Everybody knows—the case isn't open to argument. However, we will let Gail Davis tell. Speak up, Gail!"

And Gail spoke up, thuswise: "You can search me. All I know is that while the whole country shows an increase in orders, yet the greatest increase has come from South America, where we didn't send a single *Little Journey*."

And far across the moor, borne on the night winds, a cuckoo called plaintively to its mate.

A Little Journey to the Home of the Columbia Grafonola

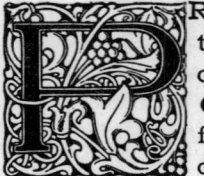PRINTING has been called the "Art Preservative," because by its use we duplicate the record of a thought and pass it down the centuries. ❡ David Garrick once regretted that the vibrant, far-reaching voice of Edmund Burke must some day falter and be heard no more by men.
And nobody then, or for a hundred years after, ever imagined that song and speech and music's sweet sounds could be recorded, duplicated, and given to millions, thereby making them wiser, happier, better.
Personally, the Columbia Grafonola has given me more inspiration, more rest and recreation than anything else of a mechanical nature that has ever come into my life.
When my nerves seem overtaxed and my mind has dwelt long on one subject, I turn to the Columbia Grafonola for rest and relief. I play some of the selections of the great composers, dead and gone, some of whom I knew in their lifetimes.
And although these men may have passed out from this earth-life, their work still endures, and here, without any disturbing personal presence to interpret and intervene, I hear and enjoy their wondrous melodies.
With the great living artists I am also familiar. They abide with me. They sing and play for me when I wish. They are never tired —they never obtrude—my pleasure is theirs.
Music is the most universal form of harmony. It makes a quick appeal to the human heart, and through the aid of the Columbia Grafonola we are brought into touch with the world's greatest artists ∽ ∽
Singers, players, famous orchestras, great bands—popular songs,

amusing sketches—these are all yours for the asking. They wait so patiently for you. When you need them, they respond.

As a plan for driving away the Glooms, and an invitation for the Joys to enter, there is nothing on earth to equal this Columbia miracle ﻼ ﻼ

In all sanitariums and hospitals, the pathological value of music is fully understood and appreciated, and there the Columbia plays its part.

However, there is something better than to go to a hospital and be cared for, and that is to care for yourself and not go to a hospital ﻼ ﻼ

The proposition of keeping well and strong and efficient—finding our rest in change and allowing harmony to creep into our lives through the sweet influences of divine music—surely this is the art of arts.

No one can say to what extent the Columbia Grafonola will add to our length of days and our usefulness as well.

When I want to concentrate on some particular bit of writing, I make use of the Columbia and call on my old friend Zenatello, good and great, to minister to me.

There is no stimulant for the imagination equal to good music.

⁌ Thus do I get my mental molecules in motion. The Columbia serves as my cosmic starter.

There are just two kinds of musical instruments. One had its rise in the hollow reed, or the pipes of Pan, and the other began with the hunter's bow, which some hunter on a march noticed " sang " when struck and was made to vibrate.

Then another hunter discovered that no two bows sang just alike, owing to different degrees of length, structure and tautness. Where it was, or when, that a hunter took one bow and with it agitated the strings of another, and thus suggested the " fiddle," we do not know. Also, we can only guess when it was and where that a soldier sitting near a campfire surprised his fellows by putting four strings on a bow and making music on that progenitor of all 'cellos. To add many strings and make a harp played with the fingers was a natural and easy evolution.

We hear of how, a thousand years before Christ, the Israelites " hanged their harps upon the willows." The harp was the symbol of joy and gladness, and when a supreme sorrow came it was laid aside, and grief was expressed by singing or wailing.

In Ireland, the wail of the professional " keener," or mourner, is still heard, and once heard is never forgotten.

Then comes the cithern, or zither, played by " plucking " the strings. Next we have the dulcimers, instruments with rows of strings, which are struck by little hammers in the hands of the player ❧ ❧

The clavicord was played by striking keys which released little hammers, which, in turn, struck strings. This was an adaptation from the pipe-organ, which by pressing keys released the pressure of air in the pipes and made music.

Organ music reached perfection with Sebastian Bach.

The violin reached its height with Stradivarius, and the piano—but that is another story.

And the Columbia records give you the quintessence of the ages: players, performers, singers—all are yours!

What is holding you back? Lack of soul fluidity—not quite enough harmony in your cosmic ensemble—you take things too serious—nerves sort of outside of your clothes—you are forgetting how to enjoy. What you need is more Music!

All Art is harmonious expression. Painting appeals to us through the sense of sight; Literature through the understanding; Sculpture through the sense of proportion; Music through the hearing. " I would bathe me in sweet sounds," said Ralph Waldo Emerson. And again he says, " The world is being held back on account of a lack of music."

The Columbia Grafonola supplies exquisite music composed by

the master minds of all time, and places this music within reach of those who love harmony, but are unskilled in its production. The people who make the Columbia Grafonola are a happy, animated and prosperous people. Good-cheer and courtesy prevail. Cleanliness, order, organization, are on every hand. Each helper is doing his own appointed task, doing it quietly, surely and well ❧ ❧

In it all there seems to be no hot haste, no hurry, no anxiety. A sureness of purpose is everywhere evident. Only a well-paid people, whose services are duly appreciated, could produce these marvelous machines.

Workers in gold, silver, brass and wood are here. Engineers, inventors, machinists—each has his own particular work. The manufacture of the various parts of the Columbia is often done by special machines, invented on the premises for this particular purpose, and none other. And then the man must be found who can run the machine. Practically the best men here were educated at their work, by their work. Emerson says that ten men saved Kansas for the Union. He might have said one.

Fourteen men made Athens the wonder of the world; but without Pericles, probably the beauty of Athens would have been intangible, and the Cupids would have remained forever locked in their blocks of marble. Within a hundred years, a city the equal of Athens will be reproduced, and better possibly, in America.

¶ Where this ideal city will be, no man can say. But this holds: We have in America a growing hunger for beauty, a reaching out for the ideal, a great desire to express harmony. And through this desire will be created cities that will surpass anything the world has as yet seen.

The prophecy is safe, for while the world has always had individual artists, yet it has not had the material wealth nor the practical men to re-create the poet's dreams in stone, iron or enduring bronze.

But now we are evolving men who are both artists and businessmen—dreamers and doers—men whose heads are in the clouds, but whose feet are upon earth.

Big things in the way of innovation can be accomplished only when backed by public opinion and public patronage. And now everywhere, in a degree never before known, is there a tendency to hold up the hands of the man who has the creative faculty. Not long ago, instead of holding up his hands, we made him hold up his hands—there is a difference.

The American People welcome the Columbia Grafonola with open arms ∾ ∾

Here is a brand-new business, born in our own time. ⁋ Literature is reproduced over and over through the printed page. It can never die. Why should sweet sounds perish and be gone, and gone forever?

Every good thing in the world, when it is first introduced, has to fight for its life. We distrust an idea or an invention just as we distrust a new dish.

Every innovation has to pass through this period of suspicion, when ridicule, denial and accusation are rife.

"Truth," said Huxley, "passes through three stages: First, we say it is contrary to commonsense. Second, we say it does not make any difference, one way or the other. Third, we say we always believed it."

It is easily understood how many simple souls would be greatly interested in a talking-machine. The mere novelty of the thing would cause us to stop, look and listen.

When it came, however, to reproducing classic music, naturally the artists of the world were opposed to the Phonograph.

A mechanical thing is supposed to be inartistic. Mechanism breaks away from individuality. A machine is opposed to personality. Art is a matter of individuality. Ah, ha, and oh, ho! You will please excuse this smile!

The Columbia Grafonola has gone through this period of doubt, distrust and patronage that damn with faint praise.

Great artists now do not have to be importuned to play or sing and make records for the Columbia. In fact, they come and offer their services, and a special department has been organized to fight off the near-artists, the would-be and the has-been. This because the Columbia policy is to produce only that which is supremely excellent in its particular line.

Not only do they feel that they are highly honored in having their performance reproduced, but incidentally they make a vast amount of money out of it.

So, too, with the critics and connoisseurs. At first they smiled complacently. Now they listen with attention, for the actual fact is that not only does the Columbia reproduce the technique, but the spirit and the soul of the musician are apparent as manifested in his work. If this is not so, the world never hears the record ✧ ✧

Very few of us have the time and the money to travel so we can hear the great artists of the world. But with the aid of the Columbia, the artist comes to us.

Many of our best music-teachers, everywhere, are making use of the Columbia in giving lessons. A great singing-master of my acquaintance inspires his pupils by giving them reproductions from the masters with the aid of the Columbia. Teacher and pupil listen together and enjoy. With the aid of the Columbia a standard is set, and to approach it is the thing desired.

In my little experiences on the stage I noticed that very often on Monday morning the musical headliner, instead of being present in person and rehearsing with the orchestra, would simply supply a Columbia record and thus save his own strength. And the orchestra would work with the Columbia until the spirit of the act was taken captive.

In one particular theater in San Francisco, I saw in the hallway of the dressing-rooms a printed card reading thus: " Do not operate your Grafonola while the performance is on."

This was no mere pleasantry, because I found that quite a number of people in our company carried Columbia Grafonolas with them for their own amusement, instruction and edification. And almost always, in the morning, the Columbia could be heard, operated in some one of the dressing-rooms, where some performer was studying his part or endeavoring to improve upon it.

In all of the many beautiful homes of America, in all of the great towns and cities of the world, the Columbia Grafonola can be found. It entertains the family, supplies amusement and recreation for the guests, and benefits, pleases and inspires all who hear, as sweet sounds always do, and must, and will.

I stood in that wonderful room at the Columbia Shop where the records are made—a high-vaulted, monastic chamber, beautiful in its simplicity.

The Columbia Band was making a record. This is the only band that is never applauded, and the only one that I know of that plays to so small and select an audience, and yet is heard by millions. There is no clack and nobody ever shows a sign of approval—or disapproval. In this room you almost hold your breath ❧ ❧

One well-known singer I heard go over the record five times, because at the end of certain pauses he breathed so deeply that the conductor said the sound would mar the record, and, therefore, he had to do it all over.

The man paced the room three times, stood at the window, breathed deeply, spat on his hands, and tackled the job again.

⁌ My old pal David Bispham once spent three days in this room on one record.

Dave is a hard man to manage. In fact, he could not manage himself before the Columbia, for he kept up a fusillade of talk, explosion and asides, to the effect: " Oh, my God! I never can do that! To think of my standing before this thing, talking into a brass horn! What would my friends think of me now!"

And then he would begin to laugh.

And so it was that the particular gentleman who has charge of this room had to take Dave out and explain to him that grimaces, attitudes and fun were of no avail. These things could only be taken care of by the moving pictures.

And Dave said: " Why! Why! Why! I thought the whole thing was a moving picture. What else is it? "

But at last some wonderful records were secured.

Dave afterward told me that this experience of singing into the horn was the hardest job he had ever undertaken, and the only thing that made it possible for him to continue, and try again and again, was the thought, constantly repeated to him by the manager, that on every record sold he would get a big royalty.

¶ Germany excels in philosophy and in music—a seeming paradox.

¶ Music is supposed to be a compound of the stuff that dreams are made of—hazy, misty, dim, intangible feelings set to sounds —we close our eyes and they take us captive and carry us away on the wings of melody.

And so it may be true that music is born of moonshine, and fragrant memories, and hopes too great for earth, and loves unrealized; yet its expression is the most exacting of sciences.

¶ A great musician has not only to be a poet and a dreamer, but he must also be a mathematician, cold as chilled steel, and a philosopher who can follow a reason to its lair and grapple it to the death.

And that is why Great Musicians are so rare, and that is also why, perhaps, there are no great woman composers. " Women of genius are men," said de Goncourts.

A great Musician is a paradox, a miracle, a multiple-sided man —stern, firm, selfish, proud and unyielding; sensuous as the ether, tender as a woman, innocent as a child, and as plastic as potter's clay. And with most of them, let us frankly admit it, the hands of the Potter shook.

When people write about musicians, they seldom write moderately. The man is either a selfish rogue or an angel of light—it all depends upon your point of view. And the curious part is, both sides are right.

The father of Clara Schumann was a philosopher, but he had a notion that the blood of woman is thinner than that of man— that it contains more white and fewer red corpuscles, and that Nature has designed the body of Woman to nourish her offspring, but that man's energy goes to feed his brain. Yet his two girls were so much beyond the average mortals—and beyond himself —that they set men a pace in spite of the handicap of sex.

¶ Fortunate it is for me that I do not have to act as the court of last appeal on this genius business. The man who decides against woman will forfeit his popularity, have his reputation ripped into carpet-rags, and his good name worked up into crazy-quilts by a thousand Woman's Clubs.

But certain it is, women are the inspirers of music. As critics they are more judicial and more appreciative. Without women there would be no Symphony Concerts, any more than there would be churches. Women take men to the Grand Opera and to Musical Festivals—and I am glad.

But the Columbia Grafonola appeals to men, women and children alike. By its use, especially is the taste of children evolved so that they appreciate the best music.

Through the Columbia you can hear the greatest company of singers the world has ever known—Lillian Nordica, Olive Fremstad, Mary Garden, Emmy Destinn, Alice Nielsen, Zenatello, David Bispham, Maria Gay and other Immortals!

And so in schools, churches, hospitals, prisons, and countless rich and beautiful homes, where only the highest art is allowed, the Columbia carries its sweet message of harmony, distributing without limit the wonderful work of artists—great, distinguished, splendid—who otherwise could never come to the millions who now hear their voices.

But living, yet do we join the Choir Invisible, whose music is the gladness of the world.

Tools of Civilization

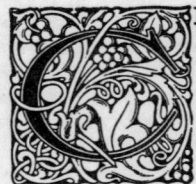CIVILIZATION is a way of doing things. Civilization turns on organization, and every man's success is a matter of rendering service for other people ❧ ❧

The savage succeeds by looking after Number One ❧ ❧

He grabs, appropriates and fights for the particular thing that he wants. If he succeeds in getting away without being killed, he calls it " success."

No man is ever fired from a factory. He fires himself when he no longer serves the institution. ⁋ So, in one sense, every man is an instrument of civilization. He is one of the tools with which the Deity works ❧ ❧

God operates through man, and man's business is to be a good conductor of the divine current which we call Life.

Civilization is the efficient way of doing things.

Art is a beautiful way of doing things.

Economy is the cheapest way of doing things; and in order to do things rightly we must combine efficiency, industry, art and economy, and cement all with love.

All modern efforts of commerce are in the line of making life pleasant, safe, agreeable and beautiful.

The first tool was a rock in the mitt of a baboon.

The second tool was the hammer, and this is a tool that is very much in vogue even as a matter of symbol. The Anvil Chorus is a very popular organization. It is so numerous that many of the men who play in it are not aware of its existence. So let it go at that ❧ ❧

The third is the stone hatchet.

The next is the arrow, which is an extension of the knife or the dagger ❧ ❧

The first tool in art is the stylus, a sharp, pointed instrument to engrave on wood, leather, wax.

The next is the pen. Quill-pens were in use in the time of Homer. ¶ Every country boy knows that he can take a hollow reed and point it like a pen and split the point and get an instrument with which he can write.

The early scrolls produced in Egypt and afterward in Babylon, Nineveh and Athens were undoubtedly written with this sort of a pen

No brushes are found in the remains of those early cities, Pompeii and Herculaneum, or in the tombs of Egypt.

However, we see the result of brushes in the pictures and on the walls. At Pompeii I have been able to trace distinctly the mark of what was evidently a brush.

What the form of this brush was we do not know.

In any event, it was not a brush of the kind and quality that we now use. It may have been simply a little bundle of fiber in the hands of the artist.

The first brushes were doubtless made from feathers: and from writing with the quill point of the feather the man could easily turn the feather the other way, and by dipping the feather in ink could leave his mark on the annals of time.

Just one step further, and he took a bunch of little feathers and tied them around with a piece of slippery-elm bark, and he had a sure-enough brush.

All of the early brushes used by the Romans, Greeks, Assyrians and Egyptians were of such a transient and fragile quality, being made of reeds, or simply feathers or bristles tied around with bark, that they have not endured.

The making of the modern brush comes to us with the Italian Renaissance, which centers around the unforgetable year Fourteen Hundred Ninety-two.

Michelangelo made brushes of bristles. He discovered that a

bunch of bristles tied around with a string would hold paint or other liquid pigment and pay it out as an artist's needs required.

❡ Brushes are now made of a kind and quality and variety the equal of which the world has never before seen.

Sanitation, cleanliness, order, decency, as well as our progress in the arts, have demanded the brush. New needs of civilization have come to us within a few years that make more brushes necessary ∽ ∽

The brush, for instance, for the use of manicures has come in within a few years, as well as the manicure herself.

Well has it been said that the consumption of brushes mirrors the advance of civilization.

So we have very costly brushes finished in silver, specially embossed or engraved, and in gold, as well. And, in a few instances, I have seen brushes that were set with diamonds or precious stones, as individual gifts.

The cost of these hair-brushes or clothes-brushes runs into hundreds of dollars, and represents prices such as were absolutely unguessed a few years ago.

It is well worth noting that, although the high cost of living is with us yet, brushes for the use of the plain people of the world, as used in the arts, in housekeeping, in the handicrafts, are cheaper today than they were twenty-five years ago.

This is on account of the improved machinery used in making them, although the material that enters into brushes is much more costly than it ever was before.

On account of the difficulties in making effective brushes, selecting and assembling material, using the exact style of bristles required to carry any certain medium or to bring about any certain result, special machinery had to be invented.

No novice or amateur can make as good a brush now as those made by the big manufacturers.

The natural trend of things has been to center the work in the hands of those who are skilled and who were brought up in the business, who do one thing and nothing else.

The disappointment naturally encountered in the use of an imperfect brush has sent the trade into the hands of men who put their names on brushes.

Thus it happens that the John L. Whiting-J. J. Adams Company manufacture most of the brushes used in America, if not in the round world ❧ ❧

They have given better service and produced better brushes at lower prices, and as a natural result trade has gravitated in their direction ❧ ❧

Not only have they manufactured the brushes that the people required, but they have invented new uses for brushes and educated the world into using certain brushes for certain purposes.

⁋ Brushes made by John L. Whiting-J. J. Adams Company can be used until they are worn out. Their brushes do not go into bankruptcy and dissolution.

Lincoln died only forty-seven years ago, and to realize how fast the world has progressed we have but to stop and think that Lincoln never rode in a sleeping-car, never dined in a dining-car, never saw an electric light, a trolley-car, a cash-register, a telephone, a sky-scraper, an automobile, an aeroplane, a concrete building.

Practically, toothbrushes have come into general use only since Eighteen Hundred Sixty. The method of cleaning the teeth, if employed at all before that time, was simply to gargle the mouth and spit out of the window. Finicky folks used a soft pine stick with pumice-stone or some other gentle abrasive. ⁋ The perfection of brushmaking is one of the achievements of civilization. No concern in the wide world equals the John L. Whiting-J. J. Adams Company as makers of brushes.

The big men in this institution were born in the business, have invented the machinery for making the brushes, have gone the round world over to assemble the materials. They know everything about brushes, and how to make them.

For any brush for any possible work, for artisans, artists, mechanics, housekeepers, all of the professions, the world goes to this great institution.

Their prices are lower than all others, the goods superb.

There is no instrument in such common use now as the brush. Every civilized person starts the day with the use of a brush. Tooth-brushes, nail-brushes, hair-brushes, clothes-brushes, all come into use before we eat breakfast, and there is n't an article on our tables in which the use of a brush has not been evident in the preparation of the commodity.

Not a manufactory, not a store, not a shop, not a bank, not an office where brushes are not in use every day in every room. If the pen is mightier than the sword, then the brush has the cannon skun a mile.

All the guns in the world might be melted up and no more made, but brushes we must have.

Venture in Vaudeville

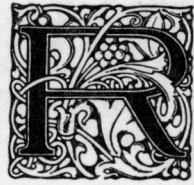RECENTLY, at the Majestic Theater, Chicago, I made a venture in art, via Vaudeville. I did two turns each day, of twenty minutes each, and one day three, making in all fifteen appearances ❧ ❧ Why did I do this?

Softly, Clarice, one reason was, because I could.

And anyway, your question, girlie, is not unique or peculiar. It has been asked me orally, by mail and by telegraph—in all, nine hundred and fifty-seven times—but never once by a person who had the ability to take the Vaudeville stage and hold it down.

¶ Go call up Samson and ask him why he carried off the gates of Gaza; let the terrapin interrogate the bird as to why it flies; have the mollusk pooh-pooh the moose because it runs, or let Mustapha the monk write in scorn of love—we will none of these ❧ ❧

This looks, I know, as if I had fatty enlargement of the ego; but the fact is, Vaudeville demands the very life's blood of the performer. If one could only do it commonplace! But that is impossible. You might as well shoot off a cannon easy.

Happiness lies in self-forgetfulness.

Art supplies you this complete abandonment—this exquisite solace—this divine nepenthe.

Life without absorbing employment is hell: joy consists in forgetting yourself.

The art of the actor is the most intense form of art that exists. It must be done on the instant—it is now or never. No erasures are allowed; a false move is inexcusable; one bad intonation and your cake is dough; a cough or a sneeze, and it is you for a flounder in the mulligatawny.

The difference between the Lecture Platform and the Vaudeville

Stage is this: On the Lecture Platform the lecturer comes out and says, " I am here! "

On the Vaudeville Stage when the performer walks out of the wings the audience says, " Here we are! "

On a certain Amateur Night at an East Side theater the manager appeared before the curtain and announced, " Miss Wiolet Cummings will now do us an original sketch of her own, by herself." ∾ ∾

Out upon the stage lightly pranced Miss Violet Cummings, aged say, forty-seven, tall, spare, smiling, smirking, with spit curls and such ∾ ∾

She started to sing with a raucous tone, when from the gallery came a foghorn voice, " This is n't Miss Cummings; this is Miss Goings! Back to the garden, Wiolet, back to the garden! "

I greatly enjoyed my experiment. Fra Martinbeck, Impressario Extraordinary, Fra Edkohl the Proprietor, and Fra Glover the Manager are splendid gentlemen. Always I was treated with great courtesy. Everything was given me that I asked for, and more. " Abe, " the stage-manager, helped me with various, valuable, professional suggestions.

My competitors, the performers, were all lavish in words of encouragement. The audiences were most responsive. Not a single unpleasant thing of any kind or shape occurred to mar the unforgetable memory of the week. Bill Reedy's suggestion that the high price of eggs was prohibitive, is only obvious persiflage by a man who means well.

But the Vaudeville pace is terrific. To meet that great audience twice a day with smiling abandon—to play upon their emotions, to weld them into a whole, wiping the talented performers who have preceded you off the cosmic slate—this is a tremendous undertaking ∾ ∾

There are two big things to do in Vaudeville—interest and amuse the audience and keep yourself in shape to do it again tomorrow.

Don't talk to me about the immoralities of the stage! The player booked to go on at eight forty-seven is an absolutely moral man if there is one alive. His work absorbs him: he can think of nothing else, even if he would.

The Majestic Theater is run like a battleship. It has the discipline of the German Army. It combines order, system, regularity, cleanliness and effectiveness in rare degree. Nothing is ever slighted or overlooked. There are no loafers behind the scenes nor in the offices.

The beauty of the place seems to react on the audience, so it's hats off, and be a gentleman! from the moment you enter the lobby so so

Never a match is struck on the stage or behind the scenes unless it is a part of the play—and then an eagle-eyed fireman watches that match. There is no smoking or chewing tobacco in dressing-rooms or elsewhere.

The halls and aisles are either carpeted with rubber matting or deep velvet, so you never hear a footfall, save it is a dancer before the footlights.

The seats are on ball bearings and rubber-tired, so it is possible for the whole audience to leave—a thing which fortunately did not happen to me—and yet the performance would not be disturbed. The sanitation and accommodation for public, performers and stagehands reveal a world of loving care. Courtesy and consideration are for all; but behind the scenes the discipline is that of Admiral Evans. Things go by clockwork and on the instant. Apologies and excuses would have no more place there than if you were charging up San Juan Hill in the face of the enemy.

Silence, sobriety, sincerity are supreme.

I have been a public speaker for twenty-five years. I have spieled at schoolhouses; lectured at colleges, universities, chautauquas, banquets; preached in churches and camp meetings; made addresses in opera-houses; reeled off arguments at court; tore a passion to tatters in a play; barked on the street corners; sawed the winds in the woods—literally on the stump; lambasted the ether from the platform of a rear coach; and spellbinded the proletariat—but never until last week did I ever experience anything like the intense pressure of Vaudeville. The sophisticated, cosmopolitan audiences; the blinding lights; the competition—coming before and after your work—of actors of rare skill, talent and long experience, form a combination that might quell, and does, many a man of iron nerves.

In talking with Fra Martinbeck of the Orpheum Circuit, I discovered that the Literary Feller was in bad repute with Vaudeville ∾ ∾

The authors, writers and wits who have been passed up include about all who have ever tried standing in the glare of the spotlight. And the reason they failed was not because they were not interesting, but simply because they were not consecutive. They could do it once—usually braced by booze and bromide; but to do two turns a day for a week was beyond their power. When the Jersey lightning died in the man's epidermis he was shaky as an aspen and a has-been.

This does not mean that all writers are boozers, but the fact is, the rule has been that no writer has tackled Vaudeville until he was on the blink, and he then made the move as a hazard to retrieve lost fortunes.

The man who fortifies with anything stronger than Hyson is already a dead one. Let him stick to his stylus. If he tries to go on the Vaudeville circuit, he will probably flat, falter, forget his lines and sneak for the wings. In which case, the orchestra picks up the tattered thread where he left it, and in two minutes the portieres part on the next act.

The audience does n't much mind, but your Poet is now a member of the Down-and-Out Club.

Usually, though, he does one fairly good stunt, then his nerve fails him and the watchman at the stage-door sees him no more, forever. This for the management is a calamity. The attraction has been widely billed, the programs printed, and if a number is dropped out, that is the very one the people want to see.

In advertising an attraction the house makes a contract with the public, and not to produce the goods is to jiujit its reputation.

⁋ I am sorry to say it, but the literary fraternity boys are not apt to prize fresh air, sound sleep, exercise and cold water. Your writer works when the mood is on, and if he works himself to a frazzle, no one cares. All the public sees is the poem.

But the actor writes his poem in the presence of the passengaire. A man may have wheezy bellows, weak eyes, a flabby mouth and a wobbly chin, and yet write great stuff. But the actor must have glowing health, a vibrant voice, an easy step, a calm eye and good teeth, because teeth mean tone.

The drama reached its height in Greece in the time of Pericles. Also, sculpture reached perfection then, if ever. Let the further fact be noted that the arts of the drama and sculpture both sprang out of the love of the human form. Had Greece not gloried in contemplation of the human body, her art would have been a minus quantity and died a-borning.

All genuine art had its rise in love, laughter, joy and exuberant health. The art that is sick is unspeakable. Vaudeville is vital only as it has the spontaneity which springs from health.

A goodly dash of the Spartan spirit was necessary to the Dorian soul of the drama. That glowing health—the processions of naked youths—the singing of songs as they went into battle, all these found favor in peaceful days in the Greek Chorus and in the measured, stately plays of Æschylus.

When by the division of labor you separate literature from life, you get a weak and degenerate thing—a thing of cigarettes, patchouli, absinthe, dyspepsia and nerves that lead adown the ways to dusty death.

No man who does not breathe deeply and well and eat moderately can hope for recognition on the stage.

Literature does not make this physical exaction of her candidate; and so you see why the man of letters on the stage does not spell his name "Cummings," but "Goings." For him it is not Banzai, but a bas!

No people on earth are so true to their art as the actors.

The stage is to life what sparkling wine is to water.

The stage says, "Thou shalt have no other gods before me."

⁋ Every living person does the thing he can do—the thing that is in his nature to do. And strangely enough, the things a man can not do, he does n't. And often the thing he is not up on, he is down on ∾ ∾

Life is expression. He lives most who expresses most. Not to express is not to live. Every person expresses as he can, each in his own way. Some carry small voltage, others more. The way to replenish your dynamo is to pay out your voltage and Vaudeville is one way of turning the current of your life through ten thousand other lives.

A man is a storage-battery of divine energy.

Vaudeville is a form of entertainment, incidentally of instruction. As such, it is as legitimate as letters, or the art of the painter, illustrator or sculptor.

For instance, I am writing this article on Vaudeville, and you are reading it. Had I not played in Vaudeville I would not have written on the subject. Literature is a confession—he knows most who has seen most, and experienced most. My knowledge of Vaudeville, and busting broncos, was not gained through a correspondence course. Vaudeville is a system or plan for vividly presenting art to the people. All art is liable to misuse and abuse.

⁋ Ask Fra Antonius Comstock, he knows—or thinks he does!

⁋ The written word is not always sweetly innocent of shame; often in the past it has carried a color that borders on gamboge,

and a flavor that is Neuchatel. Pictorial art is not always chaste as the Ice Trust—pure as snow.
To all the poor all things are poor. Let it go at that.
Modesty being only egotism turned wrong side out, let me here say that I am an orator. It does not have to be proven before the University of Copenhagen—I acknowledge it myself. What I lack in shape I make up in nerve.
I am an orator.
I have health, gesture, imagination, voice, vocabulary, taste, ideas. These combined, vitalized by ambition and in right proportion, give us oratory.
Do they?
Not exactly! Oratory requires an audience. Of course, this is not quite all of oratory—there is ever the undissolved residuum. The whole fabric is shot through by the actinic ray of pulsing personality—that thing which forever eludes the analyst.
Now, oratory is a collaboration between the speaker and the auditor, just as music is collaboration between the listener and the performer.
Delsarte refers to the orator as the masculine or active agent; the audience is the feminine or passive principle, and these two harmonizing generate the art of oratory.
About the best time for an orator to orate is when he has an audience. For only then do we get three needful things—the time, the place, the listener. These three spell opportunity. " Master of human destinies am I." Fate in a Mother Hubbard wrapper is at the door ∾ ∾
On reading the newspapers I see I was paid from one thousand to five thousand dollars for that week's work, so take your choice. But I say to you this, money is a secondary feature—it is simply a result, an incident, and no man who puts money first can ever win a place in Vaudeville, or anything else.
The vital thing in Vaudeville is the play—the play's the thing.

I had two audiences a day, of an average of over two thousand people each. And every time a new audience—for people seldom go to a Vaudeville show more than once a week.

The matinee gathering was a totally different audience from the evening. It took me several days to comprehend this fact and key the warm stuff accordingly. An afternoon audience is made up of children, idlers, convalescents, elderly people—folks who do not venture out o' nights.

You hold them on your lap—poetically—and it is a ponderous weight, with gravitation plus and levitation minus. They squash, squash and smother you, until you gauge the range and know enough to pass them out mush interspersed with your shrapnel.

❧ In the evening it was different. In the audience was always a goodly number of business men—acute, bright, alert, rapid. These lifted the whole atmosphere, and the lassies with their laddies forgot their gum-chewing as the gladsome giggles gurgled gleefully under their lee scuppers, and they rolled in the wash of forgetfulness ∞ ∞

To show you our quality, let me explain that one night I saw Judge Peter S. Grosscup, Sam Alschuler, Max Pam and Colonel Foreman, with a dozen other legal lights filling three of the boxes. The next night we had fifty or more men from a convention of railroad managers. Later came a delegation of Equitable Life boys, who had met here from all over the West.

Here were men coming in a body from life's forum of fight to a finish, the hairsplitting of law or the scuffle of business, to gain an hour's relaxation. To interest them, and not lose the laddies and the lassies, and the boys in the balcony, was the problem. Things must not be keyed too high, not too low.

Your stories must not be too long, nor too broad. But into them all must go the jolly, joyous jamake.

Above all, heroics will not go in Vaudeville—you must not pose as a candidate for Carnegie medals. If you tell a good story on some one else, you must tell, also, as good a one on yourself. You build up a house of cards—and then by a breath blow it to the four corners. The laugh turned on yourself is always a good stroke—and you had better do it yourself, or the audience may do it for you.

The earnest word is all right, but it can not be dragged in by the scruff. Always I managed to get in three or four body blows against shams and superstition—serious, sober words, and always, even at the matinees, I got a " hand."

Did I know a month ago what I now know about Vaudeville, I would never have ventured my argosies between the Scylla and Charybdis of professional Vaudeville, but having made the voyage, and in degree charted the channel, I see I must go back—in another incarnation.

The siren song of the stage has a wondrous lure. To stand in the glare, unarmed save for your wit and gesture, before two thousand indifferent people, to play upon them, to sound their stops, to appeal to that great common heart-throb of humanity, which ebbs and flows through us all, to get their response—that breathless silence, followed by a roar and rumble of prolonged applause —to bow yourself off the stage and be called back, and yet again called back, until the orchestra with a bang and a smash and a biff and a bing chops off the tumult—this is a gratification—a wild, weird intoxication—which once tasted is never forgotten.

⁋ I hear the call of the wild!

And if at the Last Great Day, Gabriel wants a response from me, let him lay aside his B Flat horn, and use the stage-manager's call-bell, and I'll pull myself together, though all hell yawns, and as the heavenly orchestra blares at it, with boom of the big drum and crash of cymbals, through my veins will again run the ruby wine of life, and I will shout under my breath, " Coming up! Aha, aha! Let 'er go, flash those lights—let the curtain part, here we are again! "

"Be at the Majestic Theater at nine-thirty Monday morning," the order said. I turned the corner of State Street at nine twenty-five, and was a bit shocked to see my name spelled out, ten feet across, with the electric lights.

In the lobby were three gigantic pictures of myself—one in the center and one on each side. I stood in the throng, but no one knew or noticed me.

I started to enter and a giant colored man told me it was the stage-door for me. I mosied up the alley, entered at an iron door that swung out, and upon which was the single word in big white letters—STAGE! At the bottom of the stairway, I saw an iron-grated door, and behind this sat a watchman. He asked me my name, examined a list he had, and said " All right! " as he opened the wicket of angle iron.

It looks easy to get on the stage. The fact is, it is n't. You require an artistic jimmy. That watchman was armed, and his business was to repel boarders. I found out later that there is a fine of a hundred dollars for any employee or performer who allows an unauthorized person to enter the theater.

The watchman took a key from a keyboard and led the way to my dressing-room ॐ ॐ

" Have your trunks arrived? " he asked.

" I have neither trunks nor tights, " I answered.

The joke did n't go, and soon I perceived that joking was tabu ॐ ॐ

" No baggage? " asked the man in surprise.

" None, positively none! "

" Why, I thought you did an aerial," he said.

I went up on the stage.

Everything was in a bustle of confusion. The scene-shifters were bringing up " props " and getting them together in groups.

⁋ A little man in shirt-sleeves and straw hat, with a big card in his hand, was in charge. He was checking off a list of the stunts.

He nodded to me in a businesslike way, and said, " I'll see you in five minutes."

It was Abe, the Omnipresent.

A woman in street clothes stood on the stage, singing and leading the orchestra. " Try that again," she said.

The orchestra was endeavoring to meet her wishes. " Once more!" she called.

" That is Lillian Herlein," said Abe. " When she is through, the leader of the orchestra will look at your music score."

" But I have no music."

" None? "

" No, only chin music," I ventured.

Abe did not smile — stage-managers never do — that is the business of the audience.

I could scarcely believe that this fine, modestly-dressed demure and motherly woman leading the orchestra was the smashing, dashing opera bouffe, " Miss Manhattan."

That afternoon I saw her again and she was transformed — nerved to meet the ordeal — and clothed like Cleopatra when she went out to meet Mark Antony.

" Can you play flush? " Abe asked.

" Sure," I said, " sure — I have, but perhaps you'd better explain."

" Can you play against a flush curtain? " And he let down a great, dark-green velvet drapery.

It was just what I wanted, and with a Roycroft chair, a table, a dozen Roycroft books and a copy of *The Fra*, I was satisfied.

❡ " I wish everybody was as easy to please as you," said Abe.

❡ He gave me a card marked with the time I was to go on — three forty-seven and eight fifty-three. " But you must always be here fifteen minutes before. See you this afternoon!"

And he turned to Zethro and his wonderful collection of educated dogs. I made my way out into the alley with the time three forty-seven seared into my thinkery.

It was ten o'clock, and I figured it out that it would be five hours and forty-seven minutes before I would seek to rival the canines.
¶ Would the time ever pass?
The time passed, even in spite of the Hepburn Bill.
At three-thirty I was again before the iron bars. " You will play to capacity! " said the watchman, in a friendly, encouraging way as I entered.
" Beg pardon! "
" The house is sold out—has n't happened before at a Monday matinee since Marshall Wilder was here."
" Indeed! " I said; " that rogue who makes two grins grow where there was only a grouch before! "
" We all love him here, " said the man.
" Of course you know the reason today for the big audience, " I ventured
" Yes; those trained dogs are very good." I went on through to my dressing-room. It was the " Star's Room." There were mirrors on every side, transportable electric lights, hot and cold water, a lounge, a table and five chairs.
On the table was a half-bushel of American Beauty roses, some one had sent me.
On the wall I saw an electric bell and beneath it a card printed in bold black-face—WHEN THIS BELL RINGS, REPORT TO THE STAGE-MANAGER IN FIVE MINUTES.
It was a grim and awful sign. Suppose I did n't hear the bell! And what if I should beat it for the street now and let the bell ring and be damned!
I sat down and again read the sign. And as I did so that bell broke loose. It buzzed, banged, surged, echoed and vibrated through the room like the crack of doom.
Then it ceased, and left an awful hole of silence.
I could hear the orchestra, and the sound of dancing feet over my head. Now and then there was a prolonged rumble of applause.

⁌ I made my way upstairs over the deep, soft carpet, holding one hand on the brass rail. "What if I'd fall downstairs and sprain my ankle!" I thought.

Abe was at the top of the stairs, serious and a bit anxious. The reputation of the house was at stake. He looked me over from shoes to bald spot. He said nothing, but seemed satisfied. He led me around to the left entrance.

"When the curtain goes down on this sketch, the music starts, and when they stop that is your cue—see!" he said in a stage whisper ⁌ ⁌

He left me and ran around and climbed up in a little balcony in the right wing, out of sight of the audience, but where he could see everything on the stage.

I looked across and saw him staring intently at me over the void of light ⁌ ⁌

Up went the curtain—the orchestra stopped with a bang.

I walked out on the stage as if I were going to The Roycroft Farm on a Sunday morning in June. To my great surprise my voice came easy, true and vibrant from the first word. The footlights were intense and in the gallery was a spotlight that followed me, wherever I went.

I could not distinguish individuals in the audience, but I knew that they were there.

They were just men and women after all. They listened and then they responded. They applauded and they laughed.

I talked of the folly of enjoying poor health; the excellence of getting our happiness out of our work; the wisdom of a little play-spell like going to the Majestic Theater; the joy of a laugh in which there was no bitterness, and I told just four stories. Simply the good old lecture stuff, filed down and sandpapered Roycroftie ⁌ ⁌

I bowed myself off, amid a thunder of applause, acknowledged the appreciation three times, the curtain dropped, the orchestra was at it, and out of the wings came Dan Burke, and his dancing girls, to wipe out all memories of me.

As I made my way downstairs, Ray Royce who was to follow Dan was coming up. " I heard you, old man, " he said; " I heard you, and you are making it awful hard for the rest of us."

" Am I?—I'm sorry, but how—what shall I do? " I did not get the drift of his compliment.

" Do nothing," he said, " but what you have done—that's the business of a performer in Vaudeville—to set a pace! "

Ray sets a pace, himself—he is a man of brains, and his words were balm

At my dressing room stood Fra Glover, the Manager. He held out his hand.

" I hope you liked your audience," he said.

The only thing that I had thought of was " Will the audience like me? " And here was a new view.

" I never spoke to a finer, more appreciative and intelligent body of people," I answered, the glow of success in staying the limit still upon me.

And so it went, twice each day at three forty-seven and eight fifty-three

The week crawled slowly but surely away. On Friday there was the Actors' Annual Benefit at the Auditorium, and the house sold at two dollars a seat.

Every theater in Chicago sent representatives to take part. The Majestic sent me. It was Vaudeville as was. It began at one-thirty and ran until six. John Drew, Louis Mann, Tommy Ross, Frank Daniels, Grace George, Frances Starr, Elsie Ferguson, Grace Van Studdiford, Sam Bernard, and fifty other good ones took part. Behind the scenes, they paced like caged lions, chewing gum for God's sake! I was delighted to see that these old stagers were scared stiff—scared fully as badly as I—and this gave me courage

One actor of more than national reputation said to me in a husky, shaky, just-going-on voice, " I 'm damn glad I 'm not in your place! "

" Why? " I asked.

" You have to make a speech, while all we have to do is to play our parts. "

When I went on, these old war-horses crowded the wings each in his own peculiar make-up and watched me with awe and things. To walk out to the center of the stage and make a speech for ten minutes to five thousand people they considered a tremendous stunt. It 's all a point of view. And courage is simply a matter of having done the thing before.

A man in Cincinnati once called on me at the theater, just before I was to " go on." He was a nice man with chin-whiskers and a bias for Socialism.

He addressed me as " Comrade."

But I failed to respond as I should. He found me cold, absent-minded, preoccupied. I did not gush over his presence, and he went away muttering. He did n't know, and does n't yet, that I was carrying a hundrd and fifty pounds pressure to the inch on my psychic boiler, and was in no mood for friendships.

He went away and proclaimed me an overgrown this and that.

⁋ Poor man! Also, poor me! I lost his friendship through his failure to understand a bit of simple psychology which every man knows who has stood before an audience.

Do not try to visit with a party who is up against gooseflesh.

⁋ The greenroom of the olden time must have been prolific in an awful lot of bad acting. If Sir Harry Vane lived now, he would have the run of the alley, but never would he get past the guard at the stage-door. He could only see Peg Woffington on the stage by walking up to the box-office and laying down the good coin.

⁋ At one of the Douglas debates a friend found Mr. Lincoln all of a tremble just before the speechifying began.

"Is it possible, Mr. Lincoln, that you—a practised speaker, a lawyer—are nervous about this coming speech?"

"Look here, young man," said Lincoln, "I have spoken well." It isn't the audience you are afraid of—it is yourself. Will your voice come clear, full and vibrant, or will you begin with a squeak and a squawk?

The man with a record for good work labors at an awful disadvantage. The better he has done in the past, the more the audience expects. The work of a big lawyer grows more difficult after every success. And if he is really big enough he gets only the cases that others have discarded.

The reward for good work is not rest and rust: it is more work and harder work. I have noticed that racehorses on the day they are to be raced are often all a-tremble with excitement. They refuse to eat—appetite is gone—the coming struggle is upon them. How do they know it is coming? Ask the horse—I only know that he knows. Perhaps he catches the idea from the hostlers, for I have noticed that a horse is seldom scared until his master is.

If I had a spiel on hand, I wouldn't go across the street even to see Teddy Da Roose, unless he was on this side of the street.

Nothing tastes—nothing interests—your work takes possession and consumes you.

The absolute absorption of the actor in his act is apt to give us a man who is very innocent of a vast number of things which the pragmatist knows. That is, the actor is a specialist, and as such must pay the price.

"Did you write your own monologue?" asked a fine young acrobat of me.

And a stage-hand seated near me came to my rescue by saying, "Why, he just makes it up as he goes along. He don't commit the lines—see! He can give a fresh monologue right off the reel every night."

And the young tumbler said, "I wish you would write me one; I

want to do a swell single like you, instead of just being a flip-flopper." ✏ ✏
And surely he could have done my part easier than I could have done his. The lecturer meets his audience as individuals after his effort, but the actor labors at the great disadvantage of never exchanging ideas with his auditors, and receiving their personal congratulation and thanks. They go their way, and he his. He is apt to mix only with those of his profession, and in time life to him is simply a stunt; all things in the world are only props, and all the men and women merely players.
" He acts, I believe," said a woman to Whistler of a certain man. " Madam," said Jimmy, " he does nothing else."
¶ The hunger of the actor for a word of praise is almost pathetic. I made it a point to see the whole show, and see it from every part of the house, and to tell every one of our company that he was good stuff, as they all certainly were.
All were intense workers, and straining every nerve to make it better. They invited criticism, and were eager to profit by it.
¶ Altogether, they were a superior lot of people, these actors. Never a smell of strong drink did I detect, and what is more, I know, and they knew, that to play well your part you have to have perfect nerves and a good digestion.
There was good old Dan Burke, whom every night I saw out of the tail of my eye as I did my stunt, there in the wings. As he moved about I could hear the merry music of his dancing-shoes.
¶ " It's the only life—my boy," he used to say to me, " the only life—and the thing most folks call life is but a cheap and tawdry imitation of the stage! "
Dan was with Harrigan and Hart for ten years in the old days. He is a sort of rudimentary survival of a former age. The stage demands youth, but here is a man who has carried with him the perfume of the morning, and the lavish heart of youth. His body is lean, lithe, graceful. He is as fine physically as Muldoon. Only

by eternal vigilance could he have preserved this bounding enthusiasm, this matchless agility, this effervescent fun and frolic. He plays the part of an old dancing-master, and his six beautiful Wonder Girls are his pupils.

This is the play and also the fact. They rehearse in the morning and play afternoon and evening. Their work is done with an abandon that is absolute. Do you think they have any time to be "bad?"

It was on my third appearance that Abe came to my dressing-room door. He wore his coat as if making a party call, and his hat was in his hand. He coughed, apologized and said, "Er—ah—Mr. Glover wants to know if you would n't just as leave stick to that electricity story and the one about the horseshoes? You see they are sure-shot and when you have made a knockout you'd better not experiment—see!"

I held out my hand and assured him that what he and Mr. Glover said was holy writ.

The next day at the same hour Abe again appeared. His face was white and anxious. "Well, Abe, what is it this time!"

"Say, you must excuse me—but is it true that you have a new suit of clothes? The watchman said you had!"

"Yes—Hart, Schaffner & Marx—see! Are n't they all right!"

"Of course, they are all right—for the street, but for God's sake, man, don't wear that suit on the stage! Stick to the long, black Prince Albert. In it you are such a perfect gent. You will not change—please, tell me, you will not!" And I assured him.

Then Abe explained technique. "Vaudeville works in weekly stunts. The people who come expect the same bill, done in exactly the same way. They go away and describe the acts. The new people who come expect to see things of which their neighbors have told them. To change an act is a dead admission that it was n't right. So when you 've got 'em on the run—change nothing—not even your sox—or your mind—see!"

Thus we behold how Vaudeville is standardized by men who study the public as a microscopist studies the amœba.

Behind this Orpheum Circuit is a capital of ten millions or more. It is the art of amusing the people reduced and refined by the statistics of the actuary. Chance and accident are eliminated—the public get their money's worth, and the performers get their pay ❧ ❧

Acting is a most exacting business, and the man who gets the big money must give an undivided service.

Such men as Fra Martinbeck, Fra Edkohl and Lyman Glover are constantly planning to give the public a little better show—a little more phosphorus in their fun. But they know better than to get beyond the public and be martyred for their pains.

"A merry laugh doeth good like a medicine," said Solomon a thousand years before Christ. And today if we laughed more we would need medicine less. Aye, if we mixed laughter, love and work in right proportion, medicine would be but a dream of things that once were.

Vaudeville is today setting the church a pace. And the church will meet the competition by putting in Vaudeville attractions, as it is now doing—and some of them very bad.

Also, Vaudeville is trying to make itself attractive to church people ❧ ❧

Henry Ward Beecher once said that laughter would yet become a legitimate feature in religion. Why not?

No one ever saw a church where the auditors were more orderly, decent, well behaved, better dressed and revealed a higher average of intelligence than at the Majestic Theater. No one ever saw a church more beautiful, hygienic, safe and sanitary than the Majestic Theater. The whole place stands for human service. The commodity offered is amusement, with instruction on the side, all presented on a business basis, the basis of a complete organization, and a vigilant service to the public.

The theater and church have been in competition since the days when Theodora danced her way into the heart of Justinian. History has been written by clerics, and this has given the church its chance to defame the stage—an opportunity which has not gone unimproved ॐ ॐ

Sing-Sing has thirty-seven preachers and forty bankers, but not one theater-manager, and only five actors—bad actors.

Had history been written by actors, we might have gotten a few facts about the church and churchmen which Clio has overlooked.

ℭ Both the stage and the church cater to the public. One has its offertory, and the other its box-office. In East Aurora we "pass the hat" and soak the deacon with plugged dimes and brass buttons ॐ ॐ

But it will hardly do to call a "collection" a free will offering, when a proffer of an endless life of ease and bliss is held out for believing and paying, and a threat of hell is yours if you don't ॐ

Let it be said to the credit of the stage that it has never promised perdition to those who failed to file up to the box-office and secure reserved seats. The stage has lived on its merits.

In Vaudeville there is no voodooism. In catering to a depraved public, the stage has, occasionally, come tardy off, but the fact is, it has usually been a little better than the public it has served. And always, virtue, loyalty and honesty are applauded. Shakespeare was incomparably beyond his time; and as actor, manager and playwright has added to the wealth of literature more than any other name we can conjure forth. No cleric is in his class.

ℭ When the church can not meet the logic of the situation, all is not lost, she can still call vile names.

Actresses have been defamed by priests and preachers from the golden days of Greece to the time of Gypsy Smith and Torrey the Tricky. The muftis rip the reputations of players up the back and revile and defame the stage whenever there comes a rumble in their mental tumbos.

No one who has witnessed the gyrations of the modern evangelist can doubt for a moment why he hates the stage.

The Vaudeville of Fra Martinbeck is a refined, pleasing, innocent and effective form of recreation, with which the preacher finds it hard to compete.

But gradually the Fates move towards their destined end. Evolution is the law of nature. The church and the stage will yet clasp hands in Vaudeville.

Indeed, what is the "service" of the fashionable Protestant church now, but a series of pleasing stunts by the organist, preacher, soprano, bass, violinist and cornetist!

Many churches use stereopticons and moving pictures; and Billy Sunday calling strikes on sinners from a trapeze would complete the program. That most gentle and charming gentleman, David Belasco, archbishop of all histrions, wears a semi-evangelic garb, and when William Morris begins to button his collar behind, Orpheus and St. Peter will join hands, the Muses will dance with the Saints, and the merger will be a fact.

Those awful specific times and places—three forty-seven and eight fifty-three—sort of get on one's nerves, and you wonder if you can last the week.

A single omission would spell disgrace.

Suppose sciatica should compel you to limp out on the stage! And how about a nice cold in the head, or stomach on a strike!

But twice a day you mark off the spiels, and finally Sunday comes, and there are only two more. As I walked up the alley towards the stage-door for the last performance, the old soldier selling chewing-gum called out, " Good boy, Fra; this is your last, and we are all with you!"

I turned back and gave him a dollar bill. " Keep the change," I said; but he insisted on emptying his whole box into my overcoat pockets so so

To finish strong—better than ever—is now your ambition.

To my surprise all my fellow players seemed filled with the same desire. Naturally, one might suppose that at the last performance there would be a sort of tendency to slur things, walk through your parts, get your money and hike.

Not so. Dan Burke and his girls finished the week in a burst of Terpsichorean glory; Zertho and his dogs were funnier than ever; Lillian Herlein sang with an abandon that put Nordica to the bad, and Little Billy was more little than ever before.

As fast as we had played our parts we began to pack up, and say good-bye. We shook hands, exchanged photographs, gave out autographs and promised to write often.

I distributed my roses—they had been arriving all the week—among the girls, and I gave gum to everybody. I shook hands with Abe, all the stage-hands, the scrub-women, and down at the foot of the stairs stood the Housekeeper, a grim woman with whitened hair, intelligent, kindly and helpful to everybody—mother to all the Majestic girls who played, sang and danced ∞ I gave her a package of gum and a big rose. She looked at me in silence; a half-stare of surprise came to her face, and then she held out her hand—a big, red, calloused, honest hand. I took the hand and pressed it to my lips.

For the moment she was Queen Elizabeth and I was Sir Philip Sidney ∞ ∞

Two big tears were chasing each other down her cheeks. Stage tears, you say. Well, have your way, but they were sincere and honest tears. " God bless you—we all, all—love you—next year you will be back!" she stammered.

I went up the iron stairway and out into the alley.

The week had passed and not a hitch had occurred. Not a player had missed his part, not a cog had slipped. Personally, I had faced the glare fifteen times, and on a vegetable diet, without a drop of stimulants. I felt fresh and strong, light of heart and clear of brain. The task was behind.

It was a week of new, curious and intense experiences. Thirty thousand people had heard my voice. A few will remember me. Many experiences come and go, and are lost in the dust-bin of forgetfulness. This one will never pass. I made new friendships and for a week I was one with a strange world, separate and divorced from the world of trade—the world of mimicry and mimes; of players to whom "The play 's the thing!"—loving, tender, intense, innocent, loyal to their art, living in dreams, grips, boarding-houses, steamer-trunks and emotions, the Children of the Stage! After life's fitful play may they sleep well— God bless them all!

Canada and Reciprocity

EMERSON says that the honest person can not accept a favor without giving one.

Gifts not backed up by the proper spirit are insults ❧ ❧

We want love, but only on certain terms.

¶ Reciprocity, when it is reciprocal, is beautiful. But reciprocity passed out with a guffaw or a grouch we decline. Reciprocity is a matter of spirit. Reciprocity can not be voted in any more than virtue can be a matter of legislation, of edict, mandate, injunction and interdict.

Canada voted against reciprocity, if the papers have correctly informed us. Also, the overwhelming vote against reciprocity was a surprise to both Liberals and Conservatives. Also, it was a surprise and a shock to the United States of America.

For twenty years Canada had been suggesting reciprocity with us. McKinley scorned the thought. In fact, the whole District of Columbia did the same, and all the time population in our cities was increasing faster than the rural districts.

Twenty-five years ago, half of our population were farmers. It is not so now. The population of Iowa, for instance—the greatest farming State in the Union that is, the State with the least amount of waste land—had decreased during the last decade. Illinois shows an increase of a million people, but this increase is all in the cities and towns, and especially in the city of Chicago.

¶ Food is the primal need. We dig our sustenance out of the soil. Cities have to be fed by and through the efforts of the people who live in the country. This is a fact so patent that it seems foolish to say it, and yet wise people very often know everything but the obvious ❧ ❧

High prices of living are owing to this steady increase in city population ❧ ❧

And so it comes about that we need Canada's farm-products to feed our people.

Pinched by the growing and increasing prices of foodstuffs, shocked at our grocery-bills, grieved at the independence of the grangers, and the American buckwheat ceasing to be a joke, we suddenly look to Canada for relief and offer her the reciprocity which she has been offering us.

In the meantime, Canada has found a market elsewhere for her growing things. She has awakened a distinctly national spirit. Moreover, her values have vastly increased and the tide of empire has turned in her direction. The world has not only discovered Canada, but Canada has looked out of the window and discovered herself.

Love from a discarded suitor, who wears his derby over one eye and neglects to remove his cigar when he approaches, is not a gracious figure, especially when he comes from Missouri, his flag a-fluttering in the breeze, and on his banner the slogan, "Show Me!"

A becoming curiosity is always beautiful. A desire to learn is most excellent, but the attitude of asking to be shown should be balanced with a desire and ability to show. And so Canada replied to Colonel Missouri with a shibboleth of her own to this effect, "I'll Show You!" And she did.

The question of economics was not even remotely considered. ⁋ Material prosperity is beautiful, but it must come only on certain terms. Sentiment speaks louder than soup, especially if you are not hungry.

We should have talked reciprocity with Canada soft and low, in the moonlight, years and years ago.

Even the Scotch turned reciprocity down, good and hard.

The word "annexation" is always an insulting word. No individual wants to be annexed. We want to give ourselves, not to be grabbed

The Romans annexed the Sabines—and every one else. In fact, the wealth of Rome came through exploitation and annexation.
⁋ Nowadays, no gentleman wants to annex anybody unless the other party is perfectly willing.

The talk about annexing Canada was an absolute insult—if it were not silly—because Canada is supposed to be the weaker party, and for a country of a hundred million people to annex a country of ten million people, without even saying by your leave, comes with a slam and a bang and a biff.

The man who used the word annexation, even as a joke, lacked humor. Humor implies a certain knowledge of psychology. When this joker followed up his joke with remarks to the effect that the Stars and Stripes would soon be unfurled over Parliament House in Ottawa, he caused a revulsion to spread through the Dominion, and the Conservative party were not slow in making use of the turn things took.

The Liberals in Canada were in the right, but the attitude of certain talkative men in the United States brought about their downfall ∾ ∾

It will not do to say a majority of the people in the States sympathized with this talk of annexation, but we were too slow in condemning it. But the sentiment swept on and tinted the Canadian *Zeitgeist*, and naturally, and very properly, Canada declined the soft impeachment.

The rebuke was coming to us. In one sense, it did not come through the Canadian people; it was a part of the great law of compensation ∾ ∾

When we passed retaliatory laws against Canada, issuing a prohibitory tariff because Canada kept our property that reached the Dominion by the Underground Route, we built a Spite Fence.

⁋ And every Spite Fence has a line of spikes on top. In the course of time the builder of this Spite Fence is surely going to find it necessary to climb over; and when he does, God and Destiny can't keep his trousers from getting ripped. ⁋ Uncle Sam got caught on the Spite Fence that he built.

The sentiment of Canada now, I believe, is one of greater respect for the States than ever before existed. And this I say positively, that we have a better comprehension of Canada than ever before. We have taken this matter home to ourselves. How would we feel to have the English people talk about annexing us? Wrath and revulsion would fill our souls and virginal hate would take possession of us. The people in Canada are just such folks as we. We trace a common ancestry. We have a common language, a common literature, and the things that move us are identical.

The love that comes after a good healthy spat, I am told by a widow who knows, is the best kind.

The next time reciprocity comes up for discussion Canada will vote it in, because it will be offered in a due spirit of respect. Uncle Sam will leave his overshoes on the veranda, he will throw away his cigar, and he will hang his hat and overcoat in the hallway. He will not stick his head in the window and shout his protestations of love. Everything must be done rightly and " the artistic way," says Ruskin, " is the beautiful way." Also, when the question of reciprocity again comes up, any gentleman or gent from beyond the Mississippi who jibbers the word annexation will be passed the frappé, and if he repeats it he will be thrown, poetically speaking, into the raging Kaw.

A Top-Notcher

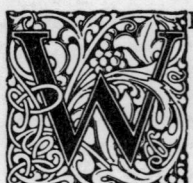HY not be a top-notcher?
A top-notcher is simply an individual who works for the institution of which he is a part, not against it.
He does not wear rubber boots and stand on glass when he gets orders from the boss. He is a good conductor, and through him plays the policy of the house. The interests of the house are his—he is the business and he never separates himself from the concern, swabbing the greased shute, by knocking on the place or management.

A top-notcher never says inwardly, or outwardly, " I was n't hired to do that," nor does he figure to work exactly eight hours, and wear the face off the clock.

He works until the work is done and does not leave his desk looking like a map of San Francisco after the shake-up.

As a general proposition, I would say that top-notchers and cigarettists are different persons. A top-notcher prizes his health more than a good time, so he has a good time all the time. Sore heads and belliakers are usually suffering from overeating, lack of oxygen and loss of sleep.

If you want to be a top-notcher beware of the poker proclivity and the pool-room habit—otherwise destiny has you on his list ∞ ∞

Bad Breaks In Business

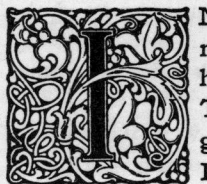I NOTICE that almost every man who is the manager of an office thinks that his helpers have a monopoly on stupidity.

The real fact is, however, that the thing is very generally distributed.

It is one of the facts that we have to face. If our helpers were as smart as we are, or a little smarter—which we expect them to be—they would own the office, and we would be hustling around delivering bundles and taking their grump and grouch as part of our duties. It is no proof of the man's insight to hear him relate his sad tale of woe about the stupidity of his helpers and the inappreciation of the public. Everybody gets it where the millionaire's wife wears her pearls.

There are firms who pride themselves on having such a perfect system that a crack out of the box can not occur; but one of the managers of Sears, Roebuck and Company—who have a wonderful organization, by the way—told me this story the other day:

It seems a certain man in Iowa sent in five dollars for a patent churn ➳ ➳

The churn was duly shipped.

After about ten days the man wrote in, explaining that his churn had not arrived.

The firm then according to the usual custom, intent on having every customer pleased, no matter at what cost, wrote the man saying they had sent a tracer after the churn, but if it was not received within the next week to advise and they would send another ➳ ➳

A week went by, and the churn not appearing, the man wrote in, stating the fact; whereupon, Sears, Roebuck and Company sent the man another churn, with orders to ship the first one back, when it arrived.

Now it seems that both churns arrived at about the same time, and the man was so much pleased with the working of the churn that he just sold the extra one to a neighbor, and remitted the five dollars to the concern in Chicago.

On receipt of the five dollars, Sears, Roebuck and Company immediately sent the man another churn.

On receipt of this churn, the gentleman—who was of Teutonic proclivities and very busy with his farm-work, having no time to write letters—just sold this churn to a neighbor and sent in the five dollars.

Whereupon, Sears, Roebuck and Company sent him still another churn.

Five churns in all were sent, and four were paid for; but in order to stop correspondence, the Dutchman, when the fifth churn arrived, drove ten miles across country to a post-office where the postmaster did not know him, and sent the money under an assumed name, with a fictitious address.

The truth of the matter only came out accidentally, when Sears, Roebuck and Company traced the last remittance, which was sent under an alias; and by use of some Sherlock Holmes methods the wily farmer was located and the facts deduced.

One of the most curious breaks that ever occurred to me was several years ago when I had charge of a manufactory in a distant city.

I wrote a form letter, somewhat as follows:" Smith and Jones—Gentlemen: We want you to take an interest in our goods, and if you will do so and make a special effort on them, pushing the sale, we will give you exclusive agency in your town."

This letter was given to a girl who was told to write the letter to a large number of names, a list of which was handed her.

She called in several other girls to assist her, and the next day the form letters which the girls were writing read as follows: " Smith and Jones—Gentlemen: We want you to take an interest in our goods, making a special effort on them, and if you will accept exclusive agency we will push you in your town."

A few weeks ago I received from a New York firm, all in one mail, a thousand letters, all written by typewriter and signed with a rubber stamp, every letter exactly alike.

I cast around in the vacuum I call my mind and thought it out in this way: This firm decided to write one thousand letters, to as many printers, offering this particular invention which they had.

¶ They wrote the first letter to me; then they gave a girl the list of one thousand names and told her to write this letter a thousand times, all exactly alike.

The girl, being intent on the ball-game, or the dress ball, or something else like that, and taking no special interest in business—not being able to understand it anyway—wrote a thousand letters to me, instead of writing one to each of the printers, and just held the list over for future reference—probably assuming the head of firm was bughouse, anyway.

I knew the firm slightly, and so wrote them that I had received the one thousand letters, outlining my guess as to how the break occurred, and it seems I was right in the proposition.

Bad cracks in business are bound to occur: the thing is simply to minimize them; and as long as we are making headway every day, if a few blunders are made, don't pull out your hair and swear up the elevator. Keep cool—most of our work is well done.

The Winners

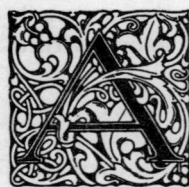AND so, Hezekiah, you say there is no chance today for a good, single-handed fight in the commercial mix-up! ❧ ❧
Soloists in the industrial symphony are not wanted, eh? ⁋ Cut out that apologetic guff while I elucidate.

Now listen to me, Hez—
But say, let's begin with a bromide. In order to win you have to serve. In order to help yourself you must help others.
Lubricate the wheels of existence and the world will pay you. Also, throw sand in the bearings and society will put the skids under your prospects.
Life is a vast system of transfers; each man does the thing he can do best, and if he can do it without supervision he need not throw fits at the thought of the high C of L.
There are men who can serve well in one capacity who are strictly mox-nix in another.
There are men who can become cogs in the wheel, links in the chain, and do good service in teamwork, but now and again there is a fellow who seems to be a rank outsider, and he assists society by flocking by himself.
Suppose we see how it is in the new science of advertising. In a big agency a large number of men are employed under a competent leader. And the fact is, as you have gently hinted, in every big organization there is a conspiracy against the individual.
⁋ It is true that Michelangelo worked in the Garden School of Lorenzo the Magnificent, and there he got his start; but he did not carve the *David* until he had started a shop of his own.
Paul Bartlett never modeled that wonderful statue of Michelangelo until he was the whole show.
Make room for individuality! This is the cry, and yet, strange

enough, we live in a world of organization, and there is going to be more organization in the future than there ever has been in the past ∽ ∽

But in order that great organizations may prosper, I have an idea that the strong individual will never go out of vogue. Big Business is run by big men. Things do not run on momentum for long. And when we cease to have big men, we'll have no big business ∽ ∽

An organization is one thing, and business is another. Business is selling goods, delivering them and getting the money.

Organization is a preparation for doing business—a scheme for taking care of details. Organization without business is a team of horses and a wagon with nothing to haul.

Horses require oats; organization requires men.

Organization is "overhead," and your rating as a businessman is the pro-rata sum of your overhead to the business done.

An Advertising Agency has three problems to face. The first one is to get business. The second is to take care of the business to the profit and satisfaction of the client. The third is to be so organized as to make money for the agency.

An organization can exist, for a time at least, and not make money for either its clients or its owners.

Behind big organizations must exist big men, or your organization is an organism that will eat into the business bowels like a cancer ∽ ∽

The John Lee Mahin Agency makes money for its clients, because at its head is a man who works nights, days and Sundays, and never, even as an hypothesis, separates his client's interests from his own.

He is a salesman who has surrounded himself with young men who reflect his own spirit.

The Frank Presbrey Company is a big and hustling concern, because Frank Presbrey himself is on the job.

Then there is the George Batten Agency, which is only the lengthened shadow of George Batten.

Batten is a worker, restless, eager, always planning. He has the salesman's eczema. He likes to see others make money.

"Big" and "Little" are only comparative terms, and the point is that big agencies are such only because big men are eternally pumping steam into them It is n't the organization—it is the man. An organization without the man is a liability, not an asset, just as non-productive property is not wealth. It may mean a deficiency judgment. My opinion is that there is a bigger demand today for men of initiative, who can be loyal to a trust, than ever before, and that the reward is in proportion. Also, I believe that this demand will continue indefinitely.

No one can place an estimate on the potential wealth of the world, and to keep this wealth in successful circulation is a task, not for average men, but for convex-lens, German giants.

Also, the one-man agency will not evaporate. The big advertising man is an artist, and William Morris said, "Art is not a thing: art is a way."

Art is a matter of imagination—you have to see the thing before you materialize it.

Advertising is publicity plus salesmanship. Now where is the commercial scout to come from?

Will the big advertising agencies, the corporations that employ an army of men, give this service, or will it come from individuals? Will we never see in the ad-field a Leonardo, a Michelangelo, an Edwin Abbey, a Whistler, a Millais?

On the horizon I see the individualist in advertising. In fact, he is here ❧ ❧

The courageous, cautious man who runs a shebang of his own with just half a dozen clients at the most, giving each one in turn an individual attention, thinking out the problem from every possible standpoint, is going to be a winner.

Every advertising man knows that there is no way in the world quite so easy to waste money in as in advertising. Whirlwind campaigns are a gamble. They may have been all right in the days of Vinegar Bitters, but they will not go today.

As I write, I think of an individualist by the name of R. B. Wrigley of Chicago—slim, slender, smiling, pale as a barkeep—who runs an advertising agency.

This man has just one clerk—a girl who is a stenographer: there is n't even an office boy or an office-cat. Every letter is written by that girl or by Wrigley himself.

Wrigley prepares his copy, thinks out his scheme, places his contracts, does all of his bookkeeping. All of his charge-accounts and bills are on a spindle within reach of his hand.

Wrigley has three customers. One of these is John R. Thompson. Wrigley's advertising for Thompson has been so conservative that it would please Harry Lauder.

And yet, to the outsider it looks as if John R. Thompson is plunging in space. But every ad that Wrigley writes for Thompson brings returns. Results are shown in receipts next day, and for the next week, and for the next month. The money all comes back, and when you have discovered how to expend money so that every dollar will come back with five or more, you have pretty nearly solved the problem. That's Wrigley!

Then there is Glen Buck, big, artistic, prophetic, poetic and practical

Glen Buck did business for himself. And he had, at the most, a half-dozen clients. One of these was the Ford Motor Company.

⁋ Glen Buck's advertising was so satisfactory to Ford that Ford insisted Buck should give up the advertising business and move down to Detroit so as to be close up to the throne.

Glen Buck does not "belong," and he went to Wayne County under protest.

Glen could never fit into an organization—he is no spoke in a wheel, no cog in a gearing. He has to be by himself, and as long as Henry Ford was in Detroit and Glen Buck in Chicago they loved each other like David and Jonathan.

But when they got together there was an immediate argument as to who was David and who was Jonathan.

No one was to blame; it was a matter of temperament. Glen Buck has to work by himself and think out the problem at a distance from the dictation of the boss.

Working for me once upon a day was Felix O'Shea. We gave the "O" a rabbinical clip and shivered the "Shea," and the world knows Felix as Felix.

Felix came to me out of the navy. I paid him five dollars a week and board, because he was a good baseball-player and had a most interesting twist to his Irish tongue.

He wore his hair long, and annexed a Stetson that had a wider brim than mine.

He wrote just like me, only better.

Felix could produce more schemes than a salmon can lay eggs, but like a salmon Felix let others hatch the fry.

Felix felicitated, evolved and grew; he ate up my library without Fletcherizing; he seized my pet phrases and framed and flapjacked them into fairish Class B copy.

He did me good service, and when a certain Wisenheimer from Baltimore came along and offered Felix ten thousand dollars a year I lost my laddybuck.

But the man who hired Felix did n't get exactly what he expected. He wanted Felix to fit in and be an individualistic nobody.

⁋ He ran the Willopus-Wallopus over the Milesian, and the result was his butterfly was a grub.

Now Felix is running a shop of his own and doing good service for just four big concerns. Felix has found his niche. He is young, but Time will attend to that. When Fate kicks and cuffs Felix, and the crow's-feet come into his cherubic mug, and his black firbolg hair is frosted with silver, then perhaps he'll put a lever under the world and list it to larboard.

Down in New York ten years ago I met a gazabo by the name of Guenther, son of a German professor, and a pen-pusher by prenatal tendency.

Young Guenther, Rudolph by name, never had any other teacher than his father. The boy was baptized in the classics, fed on mathematics and dosed with history.

Rudolph Guenther has a voice that kicks high C; he has no lilacs, and looks like a differential calculus.

Rudolph Guenther is himself. He doesn't resemble Edwin Booth, and no one ever mistook him for Paderewski.

Guenther wears double-convex lens glasses, as a German student should, and with these he looks right through any proposition that is presented to him, in a sort of uncanny way, just as Doctor Steinmetz blows smoke through a newly invented electric apparatus and tells you what is the matter with it.

Guenther would be absolutely lost in an organization.

Let him work by himself, and he is the keenest advertising man, some say, on this terrestrial. I know of one account that Guenther took on where he raised a necessary million dollars in three weeks, to launch a forlorn hope.

And the strange thing is that this million dollars which this advertising campaign produced was wisely invested and every stockholder secured velvet.

Then I know of Guenther taking on the account of a manufacturer of women's togs, where the party was up against it, and transforming the whole business into a mail-order plan that worked and is still working.

When all the world is howling about fakers and grafters, just make a note that there are some schemes that are genuine, and a few schemers who are honest. All that glitters is not brass.

I am not sure that Guenther could put it over on every occasion —in fact, I am quite sure that he could not—but working separate and apart from any organization he takes up a problem, analyzes it, dissects it, works by elimination, throws away the bad, preserves the good and out of the elements he constructs a complete working policy.

Guenther is more than an advertising man: he is a business counselor, a creator of business.

Rudolph Guenther forgets nothing but the bad. He slights nothing. He plays the game for the game's sake and plays to win. His clients' interests are his own. He says "us," and never "them." And the big point is he has the salesman's itch. His desire is to get the name on the dotted line—not for himself, but for his client.

Any money he makes for himself comes incidentally, for he never chases the elusive rolling disk, any more than he follows the hobbledehoy feminino.

Guenther has had his bumps all right, but he has taken them with a smile. He exudes optimisn, and puts the Syracuse product on the terminal feathers of Success. How old Guenther is nobody knows. He looks like a boy of twenty. He must, however, be forty or fifty when one thinks of what he has done. He is an individualist in a world of organizations and he has made a place for himself from which he can not be dislodged.

And the summing up is this: Do not be afraid that big business is going to kill out individuality, destroy initiative, and reduce everything to a dead mediocrity called a policy.

Whirling worlds throw off nebulæ, and these in turn whirl themselves into planets.

He who acts as his own attorney has a fool for a client, says the old saw ๑● ๑●

And the man who writes his own ads produces bad ones.

But the fact is that no man can write a proper advertisement for his own goods. He is too vitally interested. He views the whole thing from the point of a producer.

The good advertisement must be written largely from the consumer's point of view.

In strictest truth, the advertising man must be both producer and consumer, and must feel a little of the disinterestedness that a big lawyer feels when he plays skittles with a jury, and stands the judge on his head—poetically.

Up and at them, Hez, the world is ours!

Business Conditions

THE true index of business is the face of your banker ∞ ∞

Bankers are now rotund, smiling and chipper—almost needlessly so. They have an even pulse, a remarkably good digestion, a clear eye, and they sit back in their chairs and smile at you when you ask for a little increase in credit.

Money is in demand. It always is when business is good. Business now is normal, and a trifle better. Never in any Presidential year for the last forty years has business been so good as it is today ∞ ∞

The talk of the politicians is mostly in the line of caloric. Politicians live in a make-believe world of their own, and their antics are a sort of stage-play.

And as a matter of fact, let it be stated that politicians and demagogues play smaller parts in the world's cast today than ever before in history.

If you want ethics, philosophy or money, you will find these things in the possession of businessmen, if anywhere.

Honesty as a business asset is being prized.

The United States Steel Company is at present running on ninety per cent of its capacity. The principal items in demand are wire fencing, nails, and building materials.

Prices are lower for steel than they have been for five years.

⁋ The steel folks are putting up a poor mouth and talking about decreasing dividends. But for that, they will have to stand the decrease. The business is now standardized; also publicized. Twenty or thirty per cent profit in staple products is wrong.

⁋ Big business in the future—while it will, of course, be profitable—will not produce any such crops of melons as we have sliced in days agone.

When steel is in demand, it means that farmers are fencing their fields, the people are building homes, and businessmen are erecting sky-scrapers.

Also, the railroads, in spite of low rates and increased wages, are putting down heavier steel.

It is a pity that in the United States today there are practically no new lines of railroad being built. The reason is that the people have been given gooseflesh by the muckrakers. And so England and Holland are sending their money to the Argentine; also into Canada, where the government is friendly toward big business, and has no fear of monopolies oppressing the people.

Both South America and Canada realize the stern fact that it is big business that maintains payrolls.

Actors who can act, no longer count the ties. Instead they count the doubloons. The thing that has changed the time for the histrions is thorough organization and scientific management.

⁋ What is true in the world of amusement is also true in the world of commerce.

There was a time when railroads went bust, and big business blew up, like bubbles, at inopportune times.

Organization is civilization. Also, it is security. Big business is going to be supervised, but it will be supervised by kindly, intelligent, sympathetic, far-reaching men, and not by demagogues and politicians.

Lloyd George has said: " Trade throughout the world appears to be in an exceptionally healthy condition. This is certainly true of the United States, and from this time on we may certainly expect to have a steady trade-wind from America."

Lloyd George is probably the most level-headed man in Great Britain. And then he went on to explain that the reason the trade-winds would blow steadily, and cyclones would not be in evidence, was because he realized that the bounder and the hot-air artist are very little in evidence.

People now have means and methods whereby any business venture can be pretty thoroughly tested out before investing. We call up the world by telephone.

The man intent on blowing a South Sea Bubble will probably have his pipe taken away from him by the Government, or the newspapers, or both, before he really draws a deep breath.

⁋ The law of compensation never rests. And after every great calamity there is an active intent to see that the thing does not occur again.

For instance, every passenger-ship that now sails from New York or from any European port carries enough lifeboats, dories, collapsible boats and rafts to take care of all of its passengers and crew, in case the ship goes to the bottom.

We had to have the Iroquois fire in Chicago in order to get a fireman placed on every stage by the municipality. And the business of this fireman is, among other things, to see that every exit is open before the performance begins.

Every great gain has to be paid for in blood and tears.

Fire losses in America have been atrocious and seemingly unpardonable ෴ ෴

But now all modern buildings, thanks to the use of concrete and steel, are being constructed with especial care to avoid disasters by fire ෴ ෴

The Utah Hotel, for instance, in Salt Lake City, is so thoroughly protected on every side, and outside and in, that no insurance is carried.

A few months ago the world was considerably alarmed by the thought of coal-strikes and consequent coal-famine. The result of this talk, flashed round the world and worked overtime by the press and by zealous individuals, was that every manufacturer filled his bins. Coal-cars were in tremendous demand. Not only did we fill our bins, but we also had a mountain of coal piled up against the day of famine.

Of course, this coal was paid for, mostly spot-cash, but it was paid for at an advance of ten per cent of the former price.

There was no coal-strike to speak of. The miners took a much-needed vacation, and many of the boss miners, and especially various good men and true in the councils of labor organizations, dined high and ordered hot birds and cold bottles; afterward touring in high-powered automobiles in order to get their full supply of oxygen.

Viewed with a proper perspective, neither the miner nor the mine-owner nor coal-dealers were very much cast down or depressed at any time.

It really looks as if most of the lions were plaster-of-Paris, and chained. Our troubles are very largely the things that never come to pass ❧ ❧

Of course we are a great people in America. This we admit. But we have a lot of things to learn about farming and things.

We get our food out of the ground. I hope there will be no argument on that particular point. In America we are going to get more food and better food than we have ever had before, simply because we are bringing science to bear in this matter of agriculture ❧ ❧

Best of all, however, we are teaching the young that farming is an eminently respectable business.

The farmer, above all people should be respected. He is in partnership, if any man is, with the Creator of the world. He is brother to the winds, the sunshine, the showers, and the stars that watch over his work.

All of us pay tribute to the farmer three times a day.

There was a time when if you called on a farmer and listened closely you could hear the mortgage gnaw.

Now the music you hear in a farmer's house is that of the pianola, the cranking up of an automobile, and the gentle singing of the Joys ❧ ❧

Viewed from every side, considering the health of the people, the matter of education, the question of work for the many, the opportunities for progress and advancement to every man who renders an intelligent and hearty service, and the prospects of a bumper crop in cotton, corn and wheat, all these things show that we have much to be thankful for.

Who Is Boss?

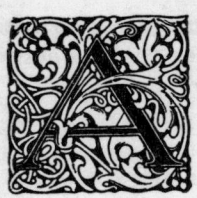A BUSINESSMAN once bought a farm for a diversion, to help balance the day of work.
❡ It was a great joy to him to jump on his saddle-mare and ride through the farm in order to think out a problem that might be puzzling him ❧ ❧
It was a small tract of land and the investment was not great, so how the farm was carried on gave him no serious thought.
❡ However, one day the man who owned the farm adjoining offered the businessman his farm at a price that was reasonable. The farm was worth the money. It was bought.
The land began to be of interest to its owner. Besides, there was quite an investment and it must bring some returns. It must be supervised ❧ ❧
Riding across the farm at an unexpected hour one morning, the businessman found several men sitting down by the roadside, eating their lunch. He took out his watch. It was eleven o'clock. One of the men sprang to his feet when he saw the "Boss" arriving. The owner thought he would be filled with consternation. But no, the hired man, Bennie, made a gesture which meant, Stop. Then, in a piping voice, he said, " I want to be farm-boss!"
❡ " What's that you say? " shouted the proprietor.
" I want to be farm-boss," repeated Bennie, all undaunted.
❡ " Who's hindering you? " ❡ Bennie did not understand.
❡ " Why don't you be farm-boss? Nobody has hindered you. You have every opportunity." ❡ " You just tell the men, now," persisted Bennie, " that I am the farm-boss, won't you? "
❡ It was foolish to try to explain to this clown the fact that farm-bosses, and any other kind of bosses, evolve.
Shakespeare said, "Some men are born great, some achieve greatness, and some have greatness thrust upon them."

He was wrong. There is only one kind of great men: it is the kind that achieve.

The farm-boss evolves. So does the superintendent. So does the manager. So does the man who is responsible for the business. Bennie's ignorance seems ridiculous, but in every factory, shop and place of industry where many people are employed, the majority of the workers are named Bennie.

Bennie thinks that if the owner would only announce to these " underlings " that he is Boss, all he would have to do would be to sit in the Boss's chair, with his feet on the table, smoking infinite cigarettes; that heaven would be his, and he would be really Boss: that the " underlings " would file past him, doing him honor and glory daily; that all matters of great importance would be brought by some trembling vassal for his sublime judgment, and that he would decide. Then no man, woman or child in the vicinity would do anything but just what the Boss wanted to have them do, and that infinite ease, joy and gladness would be his.

Bennie thinks that a rich man has nothing to do but ride around with a multitude of servants to come and go at his call; that the rich man has a great big cave full of money, some King Midas keeping it perpetually full.

Bennie thinks that all there is to being Boss is to have somebody say he is; if he can only get into the " Front Office " and sit in the manager's chair, that he is " It."

You can not explain to Bennie that, "Where MacGregor sits is the head of the table."

You can never explain to Bennie, had you all the gifts of the gods, that the Boss is he who does the most work, who carries a burden that would crush any man but him. Bennie will never know that with every command that the Boss gives, there goes responsibility that he may be wrong, and that the Boss must have the power within himself of making good every one of his own mistakes and the mistakes of all who work for him. The Boss never resigns, and in the darkest hour that can come has only one thought, and that is to stay with the ship.

The Boss is he who can carry off the Gates of Gaza. The Boss is he who is big enough to say, " The mistake is mine; I am wrong—I will make this right," and does.

The Boss is he who is big enough to take any criticism, and takes the criticism that he does not deserve with as good grace as he does the criticism which is deserved.

The Boss is he who is willing to start things, stand by them through their entire making, finish and complete them.

The Boss is he who is capable of saying, as did Napoleon, " The finances, I will arrange them."

The Boss is he who is willing to pay the price of success, no matter what it is.

The Boss is he who finds his completest joy in playing the game, seeing the finish, and being ready for a new job.

The Boss is he who demands of himself more than he demands of all the rest of his people.

The Boss is the one who makes good.

System and Success

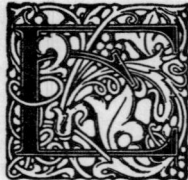EXPANSION without system spells failure. Organization means that a man shall grow with his business.

I used to work in a country store where a ten-year-old boy stole eggs from us at the back door and brought them around in front and sold us our own property. He kept this up for a year, and he might have kept it up indefinitely had he not taken in a partner and tried to do wholesale business.

Success did much for him, too!

Dead stock, bad accounts, pilfering clerks, pinching setters, and lime in the bones of the boss work the certain ruin of every country store.

If the business is so small that the proprietor and his wife can remember everything they have in stock, and then sell for cash, and can not get or will not accept credit, then the business is safe until the sons grow up and take the management. A thousand mice nibble at every business concern.

In order to avoid leaks there must be a system that will locate them. The department store, where there is a system that tells every day, every week, or every month just what every department pays is the safest business that exists. If any one department does not pay it is reformed and made to pay or else is eliminated ܀ ܀

No big business can possibly pay unless it is divided up into departments ܀ ܀

A non-paying department is never allowed to continue and drag the whole concern down to bankruptcy as in the good old general store, where jumble and guess work audit the accounts.

¶ The successful country store is an easy mark for every petty thief and little poker-player in town. The village Smart Aleck hires out as clerk and supplies his friends the things they need, just as a sneakerino reads the postal cards and hands out the news, if he or she clerks in the post-office.

Success in business nowadays turns on your ability to systematize.

No business long remains greater than the man who runs it. And the size of the business is limited only by the size of the man. Our limitations say to our business, " Thus far and no farther." We ourselves fix the limit. Without system the most solid commercial structure will dissipate into the thin air.

The Gould System, the Vanderbilt System, the Hill System, the Harriman System, the Pennsylvania System—they are all rightly named. It is system that makes a great business possible. When Jay Gould gathered up a dozen warring, struggling streaks of rust and rights of way and organized them into a railroad system, he revealed the master mind. The measure of your success is your ability to organize, and if you can not bring system to bear, your very success will work your ruin. The average life of a successful general store is twenty years—then it fails. And it fails through its lack of system—the man does not grow with his business. An army unorganized is a mob. Napoleon's power lay in his genius for system, and he whipped the Austrians, one against three, but only because he had the ability to systematize. " But the finances? " asked his secretary. " I will arrange them," was the reply.

The character of the man at the head mirrors itself in every department of every enterprise. A certain kind of landlord can care for a certain number of " guests "—and the quality of the guests attracted is according to the quality of the landlord. Increase the number of people to be fed and housed, and usually your hotelkeeper quickly gets into very hot water. Fifty extra people upset his system, and either his guests leave or his "help" steal him to a standstill. A new and better manager must then come in, or the referee in bankruptcy awaits around the corner with a stuffed club.

The measure of a man's success in business is his ability to organize ↣ ↢

The measure of a man's success in literature is his ability to organize his ideas and reduce the use of the twenty-six letters of the alphabet to a system so as to express the most in the least space. The writer does not necessarily know more than the reader, but he must organize his facts and march truth in a phalanx ↣ ↢

In painting, your success hinges on your ability to organize colors and place them in the right relation to give a picture of the scene that is in your mind.

Oratory demands an orderly procession of words, phrases and sentences to present an argument that can be understood by an average person.

Music is the selection and systematization of the sounds of Nature ↣ ↢

Science is the organization of the common knowledge of the common people.

In life everything lies in the mass—materials are a mob—a man's measure is his ability to select, reject, organize.

A Report On Yourself

THE service rendered by commercial agencies is well understood and appreciated.

But here is a use for them that is, I believe, brand new.

The scheme was explained to me by Henry L. Doherty, who owns or manages upward of a hundred public utilities in the United States, approximating an investment of, say, two hundred fifty million dollars. The business of a public utility is to serve the people in the town. In fact, it has to be in partnership with the people. The public utility thrives as the people thrive.

There is no such thing as a successful public utility aside from the prosperity of the people it serves.

A public utility does for the people in a town the things they would do for themselves if they were able, only it serves them better, and this is its one excuse for being.

And so in every town where there is a Doherty Public Utility the Doherty boys get out special reports on themselves from time to time, and the way they do it is this:

They arrange with a commercial agency to supply them one hundred reports on themselves, each report to be issued by some particular big businessman or individual of importance in the town where a utility is located.

The agency writes, say, from Seattle, a personal, kindly, confidential, friendly letter, to some man in town, asking him about the Doherty public utility, as to the quality of service rendered, the treatment given to patrons, and especially inviting criticisms and complaints ⇒ ⇒

The same letter is written to practically all the big people in the town ⇒ ⇒

These are not all sent in one mail.

They may stretch along over several months, but finally the reports are all gotten together, and the general manager sits down and takes a look at himself in the cosmic mirror.

Some of the reports, of course, will be fault-finding and trivial, but in the main they will tell the truth, and the manager will get a line on himself that he could never get in any other way. People like to be pleasant to their neighbors, and many hesitate about telling the plain, unvarnished truth straight at a man's head, for usually he will not appreciate it, and you only add one more to your list of enemies. But a report through a third party is different ❧ ❧

Often a commercial agency will arrange with some banker or lawyer to write the letters for them. These letters may come from various cities and towns, and may even come from across the sea so as to divert suspicion of the whole thing being part of a system. The idea is to throw the man who gives the report off his guard, making him think that he is presenting an individual, private, confidential opinion concerning a service rendered by his neighbor ❧ ❧

Surely we live in an age of publicity, and it behooves every man who has not a yearly contract with his barber to shave himself at least a part of the time—this not so much for sanitary reasons as to get a good look at his face in a mirror, in order to prevent fatty degeneration of the ego.

Women Farmers

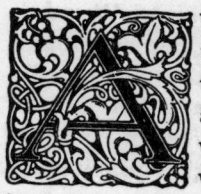A VAST number of businessmen are buying farms. The automobile makes it easy to get out of town. The country invites. Beside that, there is a belief that an investment in real estate is a wise one. The number of women in America who own farms and successfully manage them is on the increase. Women have always raised the " garden sass " and poultry. She succeeded with these when often the men failed with the big things. And now she is taking a hand all along the line ༄ ༄

Many of the men who are buying farms put the property in their wives' names. Woman is the natural farmer. The word " wife " means weaver. Woman furnishes the home. She cooks, prepares and serves the food. Her business is to minister.

This, of course, is more or less poetical among the newly rich, who never do anything that they can hire any one else to do.
⁋ But the third generation, if it exists at all, seems to realize that work is a privilege, not a curse. So we find the most democratic among our people are often recruits from the so-called " Four Hundred."

In England the most democratic people are those with titles. At the stock shows you will find dukes, earls, lords, wearing corduroys, flannel shirts, slouch hats, intent on living the simple life ༄ ༄

In Texas there are upwards of a hundred women who own ranches of ten thousand acres and more each. These women ride horses like men. They help at the round-ups, they market their cattle, they improve the breeds, they are familiar with the cattleman's vocabulary.

They have their own bank-accounts and hire their helpers.
⁋ In a similar way, all over America, women are managing

farms and carrying the work to a degree of success which their husbands and brothers very often do not reach.

It is easy to say that woman's place is the home. Woman's sphere is anything that she can do, and do well; just as a man's work is the thing that he can do best. The mother-heart easily extends itself to the care of pets—their poultry, their horses, hogs and cattle. To raise grain to feed these animals is easy and natural. " Civilization began with the domestication of animals," says Alfred Russel Wallace.

Also, it might be said that women farmers put the kibosh on the ether-cone so far as they themselves are concerned. Women who care for animals and live close to the soil keep well!

On Making Investments

IN making investments in companies or corporations formed to launch new inventions, do not be influenced by the fact that the invention is useful and much needed. This is a secondary consideration ❧ ❧

For while it is true that only a useful invention or appliance can at last succeed, yet the further fact remains that because it is good is no sign it will go. It will not necessarily succeed any more than moral virtue and spiritual beauty will increase in popularity next year at Atlantic City.

Good things go only when captained by big men. It is a question of generalship or salesmanship Sheldon would say, and Sheldon is right. It is a matter of marketing your wares. The superior man is not the one who thinks great thoughts, but he who expresses them so as to give humanity a "vibe." Success is voltage under control.

So to the argument: Excellent inventions, and mines with pay-gravel are nil and nit and mox nix ouse, until a man with phosphorescent oxaline in his ego takes the management and transforms chaos into cosmos.

We all see big pictures in our cosmic mirror, when drunk on art, love, dope or religion, but the fellow who puts his picture on the canvas and sells it to Pierpont Morgan—he is the only one who is really It.

So when you tell me of your wonderful invention and want to sell me stock in your company, just bring me a snap-shot of the man who is going to manage your concern, as well as a list of what he eats and drinks, the hours he sleeps, and how he exercises both his body and sky-piece.

Then I'll talk with you about taking stock.

Tyranny of Fashion

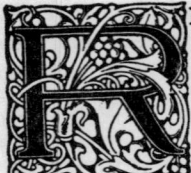RECENTLY there has been a very serious strike of the garment-makers in the city of Cleveland. Many thousands of dollars have been lost through the disruption of trade, through the loss of time, and, worst of all, the engendering of hate, suspicion, the desire for revenge, and all the disease and misery that follow idleness and broken business ties. At least three deaths have followed through violence, and how many more through the evolution of the gloom germs no man can say.

My heart goes out to the striker in sympathy, because if any man needs a friend he is the particular one, for often he has failed to be a friend to himself.

The striking policy very seldom, indeed, leads anywhere except to defeat ॐ ॐ

Even if a transient victory is achieved, it is charged up on the books, and the striker pays for his victory dearly a little later on. Just what the immediate cause of this Cleveland strike was I can not say, but I know the original culminating cause was the tyranny of fashion.

The people who make women's garments are idle about one-half the time, and the other half of the time they are worked like galley-slaves. The speeding up, the rush, the push, the crush, the worry, the excitement, the depression, all this hurly-burly is caused by this one thing of fashion alone.

Dealers will not buy until they know positively what the fashions for the coming season are to be. They wait for the vogue. Then they buy, and they want the things by Saturday night. Then comes the lash, the crack of the whip, and the workers bend to their tasks to a point reaching the breaking strain; and when their nerves can stand it no more, the strike follows.

To be out of fashion is to be in misery. Fashion decrees that a woman's cloak, say, should take the form of a jacket like unto that worn by the bull-fighters.

Next year this jacket falls to the knees in the form of a cloak. The next year it may be to the hips. Two rows of buttons, or one, mean social position or out of the swim. Then follows dire waste, through the necessity of a woman throwing away a garment that might be worn for several years were it not for the fact that it is out of fashion.

I speak here of the fashion of woman's clothes; but the same sad condition, in degree, exists in man's apparel also, and causes the sweatshop methods to prevail for six months of the year.

Then follows idleness, and plenty of time to waste all the money that has been saved. Imagine, too, the people of moderate incomes where the wife must have the new dress or the new cloak in order to be in fashion; the gentle protest, and finally the quibble which evolves into a quarrel between man and woman over the matter of how much a wife shall spend.

There is no other existing cause, I believe, that leads to so much marital misery as this thing of fashion.

The average woman feels that she can not go out in society unless she is clothed in fashionable attire. She does not realize that her acceding to the demands of fashion may cause the murder of a garment-worker in Cleveland—seemingly so separated are causes from events! But the murders in Cleveland can be traced directly by the psychologists to the dictates of the people who launch the fashions in Paris, London and New York.

Another fearful form of waste is manifested just now in the fashion of automobiles. The difference between the Nineteen Hundred Ten and the Nineteen Hundred Eleven model consisted practically in just one thing, and that is the fore doors.

Any man who bought an automobile in Nineteen Hundred Eleven without the fore doors advertised himself as a cheap

skate—or at least he thought he was so advertising himself.
⁋ For all practical purposes the automobile without the fore doors is preferable to the one with. I have automobiles of both types, and find a decided objection to the fore doors, which need not here be stated. Let the men that want the fore doors have them, but why should we all be socially ostracized because we ride in an automobile without the fore doors!

I visited the great and splendid automobile factories of the Willys-Overland Company at Toledo last week. There I was shown an actual acre of Automobile bodies, made with open doors, in anticipation of the trade of Nineteen Hundred Eleven. Beautiful workmanship, grace of lines, strength and efficiency were in these automobile bodies. But, unfortunately, they were built without the fore-door idea. ⁋ When the fact became fixed in the popular mind that only the fore-door automobile would go, Mr. Willys, knowing the futility of fighting a popular fetish, carried these automobile bodies into the open, and there made a bonfire of them.

Here was a terrific economic waste forced upon a manufacturer by the tyranny of fashion. This loss was charged to profit and loss; but I note that Mr. Willys is now agitating a plan whereby the big automobile-manufacturers shall get together and stand out against this iniquitous dictating of an arbitrary fashion. Recently we have heard much about combines in restraint of trade and for selfish and personal reasons, but the real fact is that combines for mutual good are what the country now needs and must have.

I wish the great garment-manufacturers would get together and stifle the arbiters of fashion; just as the automobile-makers are surely going to rise to the level of events, and let commonsense have its way, and cease this senseless, crawling, cringing, catering to the fetish of fashion.

As to Competition

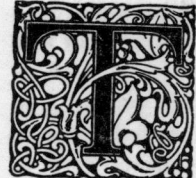THERE is a widespread idea held by the man in the street that competition is a beautiful and beneficent condition.
It was this influence that was brought to bear on the Supreme Court of the United States that caused the court to dissolve the Standard Oil Company and the Tobacco Trust.
The order was that the various subsidiaries should resolve themselves into individual concerns and compete. That is, the big corporations were torn asunder and divided up into the little companies from which they were formed, and ordered to go at it and fight the thing all over again.
Courts give decisions that are in the minds of the people.
⁋ All any court can do is to reflect the popular will.
Judicial opinions that are in line with public sentiment can be enforced, and no others can.
Every good judge has one ear close to the ground, and his success on the woolsack consists in closely interpreting public opinion.
⁋ Unrestrained competition often works to the great disadvantage of a community.
Any traveling man will tell you of little towns where a dozen antiquated village hacks meet each incoming train. The drivers compete vociferously, always vigorously, and sometimes violently ∽ ∽
This grows to a point where the police are called upon to erect barriers and hold the competing merchants in restraint.
⁋ These hackmen sell just one thing, and that is transportation.
⁋ Where you get too many of them they are unreliable and untruthful ∽ ∽
Robberies often occur with the help of these bashi-bazouks of transportation ∽ ∽

They are unregulated, and for the most part make merely a bare living ֍ ֍

Towns can often be found where the driver owns his own particular rig. And in all such cases his anxiety to succeed is very apt to get the start of his conscience. He takes counsel of his ambitions and undoes the unwary client who trusts his person and property to his ramshackle vehicle and sawdust-fed equine.

¶ In such towns there are also found a half-dozen or more hotels where one good one would suffice.

Dust, microbes, dirt, discourtesy, discouragement are met on the threshold and found in every room.

The whole place is run on a haphazard plan, and the traveler makes hot haste to get on to the next stop.

Such towns usually have merchants whose business is very much on a par with that of the hackman who greets you at the station, and of the hotel where you alight.

These hotels are of a kind described as the sort that no matter which one you go to you will wish you had gone to the other.

¶ And also, without exception, in these towns where competition is complete and replete and free, you will find seven churches, with the clergyman in each on half-rations.

These churches are founded on social feuds. Lines of cleavage are sharply drawn. One denomination has nothing to do with the rest, and instead of the town existing as a social unit and working together for the common good, each and everybody in town is doing all he can to circumvent somebody else.

The tactics of the hackmen at the station are in use by the clergy, slightly glossed.

As opposed to this condition of strife, ill-will, incompetency, and competition unconfined, will be found towns where there are one or more big industries, properly organized, and run by some big man on a paying basis.

This man who represents the factory or institution that maintains a payroll, will eventually build a modern hotel and instead of relying on the half-fed hackmen, will inaugurate an automobile service that runs between his hotel and the station.

On his autos there is a taximeter, and the patron will know exactly what he is to pay. There are no quarrels, no quibbles, no upbraidings, no strife.

In the hotel you will find system, order, courtesy, regularity, good-cheer and all that makes for civilization.

Occasionally, we hear criticisms and complaints and threats, dark and dank, about monopolies in transportation or handling of baggage in certain towns or cities.

For instance, in New York City, Westcott Express has a practical monopoly on the railroad business.

In Buffalo it is our old friend Charley Miller.

In Chicago, Frank Parmalee.

Frank Parmalee was born in the little town of Holley, Orleans County, not far from Buffalo.

He and Charley Miller served apprenticeships together as rival hackmen. With the growing spirit of the times they came to an understanding and had a gentleman's agreement with the railroad companies.

Frank Parmalee moved to Chicago and founded what was at the time, the most complete service in its particular line in America. His drivers worked under definite instructions. There were inspectors who saw that no traveller was overcharged and baggage and passengers were promptly and safely transported to their respective destinations or sped on their way.

No one with any knowledge of the subject at all would say that the old condition of unrestrained competition was preferable to this service given by Westcott, Charley Miller or Frank Parmalee.

⁋ The days went by and mechanical power replaced horsepower. The automobile came, and to get rid of thousands of horses and hundreds of vehicles and a vast amount of harness, and to educate horse-drivers into competent chauffeurs, became the task of these men ❧ ❧

They met the changing times and adapted themselves to the new spirit of the age, and the horses were replaced.

And the autos have come to stay.

Single and individual hackmen and cabbies can not transform themselves into automobilists. They have n't the power and they have n't the will. The change can only come about by men with big decision and financial resources back of them so as to give them a surety.

Civilization with competition free and untrammeled, and monopolies forbidden, would leave progress stranded in the mud on the village-hack basis. ⁋ Competition is only a form of legalized warfare and we had better face the fact that the regulated monopoly is the instrument of civilization and is here to stay.

There is no use beating back the eternal tide and crying to the waves, " Thus far and no farther."

A new order of things is here, and wise is the man who recognizes the spirit of the times and is able to avail himself of the blessing which civilization provides.

Progress means moving men, replacing them, displacing them; and it is the business of man to keep himself in a pliable condition and not let sediment get set.

All of these hackmen, a dozen of them fighting for two or three passengers, would do well to consign their rowdy old barouches to the scrap-heap and hitch their horses to a plow.

There are jobs enough for everybody, and what men must do is accommodate themselves to the work, and not ask the work to accommodate itself to them.

The Quitter

IF all the world loves a lover, it is equally true that all the world hates a quitter.

Stand by the ship! If necessary, go down with it, and go down gloriously, as did Captain Smith on the *Titanic*.

Or, if you leave the ship, leave it as did those survivors on the *Jeannette* in the Arctic Sea. When their gallant little craft was crushed by the overwhelming ice, they took the few effects they could carry out on the ice.

Then they went back and ran up the Stars and Stripes to the highest tip of the mainmast. And as the ship slowly settled in the sea, and the flag disappeared in the crevasse, they lifted three ringing cheers for the Red, White and Blue.

And they were alone on the ice, and unafraid, three thousand miles from civilization.

What shall we say of the soldier who deserts on the eve of battle; of the sailor who abandons the ship at sea; of the cook who quits on the day of the banquet; of the waiters who walk out when the guests are coming; of the farm-hands who throw up their jobs at harvest-time; of the employee in business, who, having made a bad break and caused a loss to his firm of thousands, thinks to make all good by sitting down and calmly writing: " I hereby tender my resignation," etc., etc.!

When the captain of a ship has put out from Singapore bound for Boston, we have only one question to ask. And this question does not refer to typhoons, hurricanes, pirates, shoals, shallows or icebergs. The one question we ask is, " Did you bring the ship into port? "

If you make a mistake, acknowledge the fact, and show you can make good, even in spite of the blunders you have made.

Don't run away from a difficulty. If you do, you'll find the difficulty, like a polar bear, will follow you. Besides, you can't run away from a fault, because you carry the cause of the fault with you ∾ ∾

There is a man who has a farm near mine, at the village of East Aurora. On this farm is a flock of South-Down sheep, quite the finest bunch you ever saw.

One day the man and his foreman decided that the sheep should be " dipped." ∾ ∾

The next day the foreman ordered one of his helpers to prepare the mixture.

The sheep were dipped, twenty of them—and behold the effect! The wool came off in patches. The poor things were scalded, scorched and blistered. ❡ The helper had used carbolic acid diluted one-half, when it should have been used as one to one hundred ∾ ∾

Of course, the foreman was to blame—he should have prepared the " dip " himself. But after the damage was done, the average man would have sat down and written a letter to the owner saying " I hereby tender my resignation," etc., etc.

This man did n't. He wrote his employer, stating the plain fact, and asked that his pay be cut one-half as punishment.

The owner accepted the man's offer to work at the reduced wage and never once after referred to the mishap.

The foreman went to work nursing those injured sheep. He looked after them night and day, as a mother does her children.

At the end of the year the owner sent the foreman a check for the difference in wages.

The man had made good!

Both men were of the right quality. If faults were met in this straightforward way, instead of trying to run away from them, the mistake would prove a source of strength, rather than a disadvantage. ❡ The employer has a duty to perform, too, when a helper errs ∾ ∾

Employers used to "fire" men who had done the wrong thing. I find now that the tendency is to keep the man on and try him out elsewhere, in the hope that he will learn by his accidents.
¶ Says John Ruskin: " It is nothing to give pension and cottage to the widow who has lost her son; it is nothing to give food and medicine to the workman who has broken his arm, or the decrepit woman wasting in sickness. But it is something to use your time and strength to war with the waywardness and thoughtlessness of mankind; to keep the erring workman in your service till you have made him an unerring one, and to direct your fellow-merchant to the opportunity which his judgment would have lost." ~ ~
One thing sure, that young farm foreman who dipped sheep in a mixture, without knowing exactly what the mixture was, was a better man after that mistake than he ever had been before.
¶ The fool is not the man who merely does foolish things. The fool is the man who does not know enough to cash in on his foolishness ~ ~

Great Inventions.

AN epoch is a pivotal point, something that changes old methods, cleans up the slate, and starts the game of life afresh.

Epoch-making men are those who render old ideas obsolete.

In history we read of seven decisive battles, turning times in history, when maps were made anew and national lines were wiped out and new ones supplied.

In the lives of individuals there are pivotal points. We meet a person, read a book, hear a lecture, go on a journey, and the course of our entire career thereafter is changed.

Loss, calamity, grief, may be pivotal points—times when an issue bravely met adds cubits to our stature.

Great successes are usually those where victory is snatched from the jaws of defeat. And the old idea of the Indians that when they killed an enemy they absorbed his strength into their own, is poetically true.

It is universally conceded that the greatest invention of modern times is the steam-engine.

The principle of the expansive power of water, when heat was applied, was unknown to Pythagoras, who lived six hundred years before Christ. Other men down the centuries showed that they too knew that when heat was applied to water it would expand ❧ ❧

However, the value of steam as a producer of power was of no avail until we had a receptacle that would contain it. The rolling of iron plates was the thing that made the steam-engine practicable. It was the steamboiler and not the steam-engine that ushered in the Age of Steam. Robert Fulton said his job was to make a boiler to hold the steam—the engine was easy.

Then from making things in the home, we began to make them

in factories, and the modern manufacturing system was built. The factory is the thing that made England mistress of the seas. She manufactured things cheaply and well, and supplied them to the nations of the world. Birmingham and Sheffield made Liverpool possible.

Stephenson rigged up an engine and a boiler on a wagon, ran a chain over the hub, and this chain ran around the flywheel of his engine. With this steam-wagon he could travel on a good roadway at the rate of four miles an hour. Four miles an hour is a good, easy, swinging, walking gait. It is the speed of a traction-engine.

¶ Stephenson found that when he increased the speed of his wagon it jarred his engine so that it was impossible to manipulate it. The wheels of the wagon hit the ground and every inequality caused a shock.

Driving horses on a stone pavement faster than five miles an hour is not practicable.

I once rode to a fire with Chief Hale in Kansas City at the rate of ten miles an hour. We certainly did make the sparks fly. We swung from curb to curb, and the racket, the friction, the pounding was terrific. I vowed that if I ever got out of that red wagon, I would never climb into such a vehicle again.

Emerson says that the first man who made a pair of shoes carpeted the earth with leather.

The invention of the rubber tire made the automobile possible.

¶ And if rubber tires had been invented before iron wheels were utilized, the railroads would never have existed.

When Stephenson discovered that it was impossible to make speed on a roadway with an iron-wheeled vehicle, he laid wooden rails and covered them with strips of iron, thus getting a comparatively smooth surface. When I used to jog horses with my neighbor, Ed Geers, the Silent Man, I realized, in driving a single block over a macadam pavement from the barn to the track, how impossible speed was on any road except one especially prepared.

⁋ The racetrack was made up of dirt loam mixed with pulverized bark from the tannery. And a good, big, hard shower always put our racetrack out of commission.
Here was a soft footing for the iron-shod feet of the horses and a yielding pavement for the iron tires of our sulkies.
One fine day some one sent Ed Geers a present of a little low-wheeled sulky. The wheels were evidently those taken from a bicycle—at least, we thought so. And when we looked at that little low-wheeled sulky, we laughed aloud. We knew that those little wheels could never keep up with our high six-foot wheels.
⁋ At that time I had never heard of ball bearings. But I soon understood that the ball bearings shift the friction from one place to a great many.
There is a little machine made for sharpening lead-pencils that will never break the lead off, no matter how delicate, because the knives are arranged so as to cover a great surface at one time, and the pressure is equalized all over the point of the lead-pencil, and never upon one particular point.
It is somewhat the same with the ball-bearing axle.
The little low-wheeled sulky was laughed at, then admired. Finally Ed Geers hitched a horse to it, and I, driving a high-wheeled sulky, drove by his side. Two turns around the half-mile track, and his horse was used to the contrivance.
It ran as silently as Ed Geers himself, and with so little friction that it seemed to be chasing the horse and pushing him along. And I do know positively that the horse was drawing the sulky by the reins, and not by the traces.
And so we came down the homestretch, with these two horses evenly matched, neck and neck. And then Ed Geers drew out in front of me very easily, and went under the wire three lengths ahead. We tried it again, and the Silent Man delivered himself thus: " It means about ten seconds on the mile." Then he dived into silence and pulled the silence in after him.

A few days later Ed Geers drove a horse hitched to this little low-wheeled, ball-bearing sulky in a race at Buffalo. When he drove out to warm up, he got the laugh from the grandstand. But he walked away with the race, just the same. He had just ten seconds' leeway over the bunch; in other words, they were handicapped ten seconds.

The next year on the Grand Circuit not a single high-wheeled sulky was seen. The bicycle-tire and the ball-bearing axles were here to stay.

As Emerson's shoemaker carpeted the earth with leather, so has the pneumatic tire paved the roadway with rubber.

Fifteen years ago the principal use for rubber was in making gum-shoes for politicians. The gum-shoe is not now so much in demand as it was then. ⁋ Never in the history of the world was there so much demand for rubber as there is today, this on account of the necessity of rubber for paving purposes—that is to say, for automobile-tires.

It is often stated that Dunlop of England was the inventor of the rubber tire. He invented one, all right, but great inventions are usually invented in different parts of the world at the same time—and so it was this time.

Loss and Gain

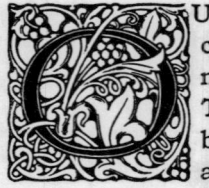OUT of the waste and woe of war across the seas, comes to us a grain of gain. And I do not have most in mind the gain in trade—that is assured. The immediate effect is a loss of our export trade, but gradually our manufacturers and merchants are seeing that this war means America's opportunity. It will be for us largely to feed and clothe a starving and shivering Europe.

Many of the things we have depended upon Europe for we will now make for ourselves.

Chemicals, dyes, perfumes, and a multitude of toilet and household articles, fabrics and textiles, we will find way to make, and in the making we will evolve men and women, and therein will lie our chief gain. ⁋ For as a boy grows when thrown upon his own resources, so does a nation. *Made in America* is a slogan that is swelling into a chorus, and will pass into the current coin of commerce ✌ ✌

Why should we look to Europe for our fashions, when often these fashions symbol ineptitude, inconvenience, inefficiency and immorality? ✌ ✌

American fashions will mirror the mind of its honest American women, rather than the lisping, limping, tortured creature of the pave of foreign capitals.

Why must we look to "European Culture" (how ironical, now, the phrase!) for our art and our artists? Have n't we the soil, the sunshine, the summer showers, and the winter's snow, that produce people of quality and character? Not only will we now " see America first," but we will hear America. And this disposition to discover America and what America offers will develop and bring to the fore the things for which we search. " Seek and ye shall find," is a saying freighted with a meaning wide as the world.

¶ But the great gain from this war is in the heroic attitude of mind which forgets to complain and declines to whimper. The weather has ceased to be a topic for conversation. We have discovered that all weather is good, and stormy weather glorious.
¶ Things are comparative.
When we think of the " Army of Bleeding Feet "—that army of homeless women and tired, hungry children—of the aged, stricken with grief too great for tears, and the woes that are beyond words—will we complain of a social slight, a toothache or a loss in trade?
¶ The high cost of living becomes trivial when we think of bloody wounds and crushed bones and starving widows and outcast orphans. Out upon the faultfinder! Our every hour is jeweled with a joy, and blessings are at our doors beyond that of any people in the whole wide world.
And while our hearts go out in sympathy to our brothers and sisters across the sea, it is for us to face each day with courage and with faith, and we will indeed make America " the land of the free and the home of the brave."

Conspicuous American Success

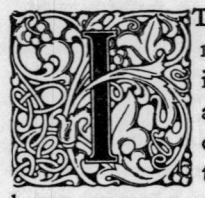T is not the attainment of knowledge which marks the superior person—the Master Man—it is the possession of certain qualities. ⁋ There are three traits of character, or habits, or personal qualities, which once attained, mean money in the bank, friends at court, honor and peace at home—power, purpose, poise.

These qualities are Industry, Concentration and Self-reliance. ⁋ The man who has these three qualities is in possession of the key that unlocks the coffers of the world and the libraries of Christendom. All doors fly open at his touch. " Oh, he 's a lucky dog," they say—and he is.

And the strange part of it is, there is no mystery about the acquirement of these three things; no legerdemain; no rites nor ritual; you do not have to memorize this or that, nor ride a goat; the secret of these qualities is not locked up in dead languages; no college can impart them, and the university men who fail, fail for lack of them.

On the other hand, no man succeeded beyond the average who did not possess them. And it is an indictment of our colleges and universities when we consider the fact that the men who have these qualities plus, usually acquired them at " The University of Hard Knocks "—and in spite of parents, guardians, teachers and next of friends.

Let us take three great Americans and see what made them supremely great: Washington, Jefferson, Franklin.

Let a certain quality stand for each man: Washington (Self-reliance); Jefferson (Concentration); Franklin (Industry).

But each of these men had all three of these qualities, and without these qualities the world would never have heard of them, and without these three men, America today would not be known as a Nation.

It was only the Self-reliance of Washington at Valley Forge which saved independence from being "a lost hope." Washington was hooted and denounced for preferring starvation to defeat, but the persistence of the man never faltered. It was a losing fight for most of those long, dragging, dread, nine years—a fight against great odds—poverty against wealth, farmers against trained troops, barracks against the wind-swept open. But Washington believed in his cause and best of all he believed in himself ❧ ❧

"It is only a question of which side gets discouraged first. I know we will outlast them. Give in? Never! This fight is mine."

You can't whip a man who talks like that.

And as time went by, George the Third had brains enough to sense it, Cornwallis felt it, all England began to acknowledge it, and best of all America knew it.

It was n't fighting that won the independence of the Colonies: it was the generalship and the Self-reliance of George Washington. And this Self-reliance shaped his actions, and finally spread over the land. Our political blessings, as a people, come to us through the unrelenting, unrelaxing Self-reliance of Washington.

Dr. Jenner's Discovery

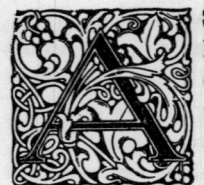A SHORT time ago I spent a week in Saint Louis. During the week there were three deaths of children from tetanus (lockjaw), all the direct result of vaccination.

The Board of Health had been very busy, and all children that could not show a scar were vaccinated, this without consent of the parents or of the child. For each vaccination the city paid the kind doctors delegated to do the work the sum of fifty cents.

That is to say, these physicians operated on healthy children, introducing a poison into their systems, thus giving them a disease, in order to prevent them from having one—all for half a dollar per child.

The three children that died netted the doctors a dollar and a half.

¶ As before stated, these children died, and scores of others were made seriously ill. How many were poisoned for life no one knows.

¶ Children know all that the parents know, and the report that vaccination had killed several struck panic to the hearts of those not yet vaccinated. Many children refused to go to school for fear of the doctors.

And such was the alarm through non-attendance at school that the School Board called a meeting and passed a resolution asking the Board of Health to desist from these fifty-cent operations until the question of the quality of the virus used could be passed upon ✒ ✒

Now, there is no such thing as a "pure virus." Vaccine virus is a poison in itself. And vaccination, if it "takes," always reduces the resiliency or resisting power of the patient, laying him open to any germ that may be flying around that way.

The President of the Board of Health took refuge behind the law, which required him to vaccinate the school-children. But personally he said he thought the whole system was founded on a superstition, and on a very barren assumption. Said the physician: "Many people who are vaccinated never have smallpox. A few who are vaccinated have smallpox. To assume that those who are vaccinated would have smallpox if they were not vaccinated is childish reasoning, fit only for those who are willing to accept a tainted plea, because they are already convinced.

"I must admit that the logic of vaccination is no reason at all, and could only appeal to prejudiced, ignorant and unthinking people ﺽ ﺽ

"I wish we were rid of the whole thing, but I am not strong enough to stem the tide. Doctors get paid for vaccination, the books and colleges uphold it, and this thing will go on until the people revolt, which I hope they will do soon."

Here we get the expression of an honest man—an Allopath physician—caught in the toils of Custom.

Physicians are instructed from books, colleges, by professors we were taught from books in colleges.

This is not knowledge; it is the memorizing of things evolved many years ago by men who knew much less than we do.

Very few physicians know how to live. Everywhere you find doctors who are soaked in tobacco, booze and dope, breathing foul air, thinking vile thoughts, resorting to stimulants as a pick-me-up ﺽ ﺽ

These are the men who uphold vaccination—these are the men who assaulted the school-children of Saint Louis, and forced a poison into their healthy bodies for fifty cents a body.

Oh, the shame of it!

Immunity from disease comes from fresh air, pure water, clean surroundings, an active, useful life, and kind thoughts.

The fear wrought in a school by one of these bewhiskered rogues, with his outfit of scalpels, scarifiers and poison, is a cause of disease in itself. The plan of vaccinating the mind with the virus of fear is in itself a crime, and a most common cause of disease. Doctor J. H. Tilden says that the fear of disease spread abroad by doctors is the cause of more deaths than the White Plague.

⁋ People who live rightly are well. It is right living and sanitary surroundings that have banished smallpox. Just good sanitation has banished the " plague," that mysterious disease which swept Europe again and again, and which killed one-third of the inhabitants of London in Sixteen Hundred Sixty-five.

I believe, with Tilden, that the so-called Science of Medicine has been a positive curse to mankind, just as Christianity has, with its bogus " Plan of Salvation."

Salvation lies in work, play, study, right living and right thinking, and not in belief in the death of a good man in Asia two thousand years ago ∾ ∾

As a cure for our physical pains we have looked to a poison doctor instead of studying the case ourselves and ascertaining why we suffered ∾ ∾

We must learn to rely on ourselves, and not put either our souls or our bodies in jeopardy by turning them over to a " cure of souls " with collar buttoned behind, or to a hirsute gent who will give you a disease for fifty cents, in the interest of happiness, health and long life.

The idea of inoculating the human body with a poison in anticipation that otherwise the person may contract a disease, was first introduced into England from India in the latter part of the Eighteenth Century.

In the year 1796 Dr. Jenner heard a milkmaid say, " I can never have smallpox, because I have already caught it from a cow." ∾

⁋ Upon investigation Dr. Jenner found that cows occasionally had a disease of the udder marked by an eruption that very closely resembled in appearance the smallpox pustule. If the hands of the milkers were chapped they occasionally caught the disease from the cow, and their hands and arms would break out in sores.

⁋ It was a legend held as a fact by the peasantry that such persons were immune from smallpox, having already had the disease, it being believed that you could have smallpox only once.
⁋ And so Dr. Jenner's "discovery" came from the chance remark of an unthinking, unscientific country wench.

Dr. Jenner made investigation and found that no person who had had cowpox had contracted smallpox. Or, more properly, he could not discover that any person who had had cowpox ever had smallpox. It was also the belief that cross-eyed persons and hunchbacks were immune from smallpox, but Dr. Jenner says nothing about this.

Dr. Jenner announced his discovery to the Royal Society and he also informed them that he had inoculated several people who had had cowpox with smallpox virus and there were no ill effects.

⁋ No doubt Dr. Jenner believed there was a direct relationship between cowpox and smallpox, the only difference to him being that cows had cowpox and man smallpox; and if a man had smallpox once he could not have it again. These two things were to him actual, vital, true. We believe things first, and prove them afterward, or not at all.

And so to prove his case Dr. Jenner declared that he had inoculated his cowpox friends with genuine smallpox and there were no ill effects ∽ ∽

It is much more likely that in his excess of zeal Dr. Jenner lied, than that he deliberately ran the risk of laying himself open to the charge of committing murder.

Doctors deal with the sick, the weak, the nervous, the fearful, and that there is a constant temptation to a physician to prevaricate is a fact no doctor will deny. Also—the soft pedal there, professor, please—it is a fact that doctors occasionally overcome the temptation by succumbing to it. Doctor Tilden says that the average practising physician lies all day long, but Tilden lives in Denver, the home of heresy.

However, to me, it is much more to the credit of Jenner that he lied than that he did the thing he said he did. Those good men who confess murder, simply in order to secure transportation, are not so bad as men who actually have killed their kind.

That Dr. Jenner could very easily have made a pretense of inoculating a person with smallpox virus is certain, but that he should have actually done so is doubtful.

Professor Waterhouse, of Harvard University, who introduced vaccine into the United States in the year 1800, vaccinated his children, and then to prove his faith took them to a house where there was smallpox. Afterward, it was admitted that he only took them into the yard, or past the house where the patient lay. As the children did not contract the disease, Doctor Waterhouse jubilantly announced the scientific fact of their immunity.

❡ So persistently did Dr. Jenner plead his cause that he got permission to vaccinate several thousand soldiers in the British army. The number of smallpox cases the next year was much reduced ॐ ॐ

Thereupon the Government voted Dr. Jenner one hundred pounds and a life pension, and pinned to the breast of his coat several medals. That confirmed it—a folk-lore superstition became a scientific fact. And the falsehood went spinning down the centuries to continue indefinitely, or until some heroic person should risk his life and reputation by challenging it.

And fortunately they did challenge it. At first we smiled and called the challengers infidels. Then we hissed them as fools. next we got busy and passed laws making vaccination compulsory, forbidding school advantages to all who did not participate in the medical fetich.

But within three years a change has come about and laws making vaccination compulsory are inoperative, simply because they are not backed up by public opinion.

Vaccination has got to go along with black cat salve for itch, sheep-nanny tea for mumps and that gentle assumption that we must all take sulphur and molasses in the spring.

Forty years ago doctors were a deal more sure of their position than now. They would give a sick man Glauber Salts, calomel, iron, and quinine, and the man got well—or did n't. If he recovered they would say he got well on account of the medicine, when perhaps he recovered in spite of it. In any event, since then the entire scheme of medicine, as it then existed, has been abandoned and we have a new materia medica. Doctors now know, and admit, that most people who are ailing would recover without medicine, quite as quickly as with.

The plan of deliberately acquiring one disease in order to become immune from another, is founded on a medical superstition and belongs to an age when the best educated men in the world believed, and all the colleges taught, that most of mankind were made to be damned, and that a man who had but one parent was necessarily better than those who had two.

Vaccination was the invention of men who thought you had to be very miserable in this life in order to be happy hereafter; and in order to be happy hereafter you must be idle, have all the things that had been withheld from you and which bad people here enjoy, including the idleness.

Inoculation by cowpox virus as an immunity for smallpox causes a disease called vaccinea. That vaccinea is a reduced or mild form of smallpox is a barren assumption—the germ of smallpox, unlike the typhoid germ, never having been discovered.

The immunity is an assumption, absolutely unproved. Those who have been vaccinated occasionally have smallpox, and then we say the vaccination " never took," or " it had run out," two terms without meaning and without sense, save in the dusky feline gibberish ∞ ∞

The Jenner fallacy owes its vogue to being endorsed by the English Government, thus being given a legal standing.

Next, it was fostered by the men who were paid for doing the vaccinating, and the thing that carries honors and money will be stoutly and honestly, too, upheld, for we stand by the thing that is to our interest.

Next, vaccination having been accepted and recognized by the army surgeons, it got into the text book and was explained and taught in the medical schools

Now, to uproot the fallacy, it was required and necessary that the books which taught it, the schools that endorsed it, and the doctors who practised it, should all admit they had blundered. That was too much to expect and hence the fight, for it is the nature of man that he would rather protect a lie than be embarrassed by the acknowledgment of the fact that he did not know the truth. Vaccination has not as much in its favor as the belief in witches, nor is it as reasonable, for witchcraft has the endorsement of Scripture.

The degree of M. D. is given on the pupil's proficiency in memorizing things told him by lecturers and printed in books. These lecturers get their knowledge from books and the men who wrote the books got their information from lecturers and books. Very rarely is any new or commonsense idea advocated in colleges, because to do so is to lose caste. New ideas are forced in by barbarians, who have no reputations to lose, and then are adopted by the school-men when they have to. Any pupil who introduces his own ideas in opposition to the text books is refused his diploma. And any man who does not have his diploma is not allowed by the State to practise medicine. So you see how the tendency is to make ignorance and superstition perpetual in medicine, exactly the same as in theology.

To the average mind sequence is proof. For instance: Plug hats are worn in all civilized countries. In barbaric countries there are no plug hats. Therefore, it is impossible to have civilization without plug hats.

Tuberculosis kills one person out of seven; and between the ages of fifteen and forty-five, one-third of all deaths in America are caused by consumption.

Out of twelve hundred deaths but one is caused by smallpox. Yet there are years when smallpox is much more frequent than in others. For instance: In 1871 there were over five thousand cases of smallpox in the German Army, and in 1873, less than three hundred. Why this is no man can say, but since vaccination was adopted in the German Army many years before, vaccination had nothing to do either with the epidemic or its disappearance, yet, it was exactly upon such an unguessed phenomenon that Jenner secured his reputation.

The danger of having smallpox is infinitesimal where people pay proper attention to sanitation, but the risks from vaccination are considerable. To poison the body of a healthy child with pus taken from the sores on a sick cow in order that this child shall not catch smallpox, admitting for the sake of argument that vaccination causes immunity, is a very foolish operation. There is no general practitioner but who can recall cases where vaccination has caused dangerous illness and occasionally death. Loss of an arm through blood poisoning is not so infrequent but that all doctors know of such. Syphilis, consumption and loss of eyesight and hearing are common results of vaccination.

There is no debasing practice, nor loathsome putrid thing, but that has been used and recommended by doctors as a cure for disease. So anxious have the specialists been that they could not wait for people to get sick, but, like Dr. Jenner, have operated on the well.

A most excellent doctor told me last week that a few years ago he vaccinated a beautiful little girl, three years old. She was the very picture of happiness and health, and as he rolled up the sleeve of her little dress, preparatory to scarifying her arm, she looked at him trustingly out of her bright blue eyes and laughed.

The doctor turned away and a something seemed to clutch at his heart. ¶ "Hurry up, doctor, I can't keep her quiet much longer," said the mother nervously.

"I am not going to vaccinate that child, unless—unless you demand that I shall," said the doctor.

"Well, vaccinate her—that is why I brought her here."

The doctor performed the operation. The child cried a little as children do, but soon forgot her hurt, and laughed out of her bright blue eyes as her mother led her away.

In six days the doctor was sent for. He found the little girl with a violent fever, her arm swollen to an enormous size, and in great pain ~ ~

A week later the fever subsided, but the whole arm was covered with sores, and her eyes were so affected that she had to be kept in a dark room.

Two years have passed; the child's body is covered with an eruption that comes and goes. She has scarcely grown an inch in height and her weight is not as much as on that fateful morning when she looked innocently into the face of the doctor and laughed in glee.

"I often drive around the block to keep from running the risk of seeing her. She is the last person I vaccinated, and the last person I will ever vaccinate," said the doctor. ¶ "What will become of the little girl?" I asked. "Will she outgrow the poison in her system?"

"I know what the end will be," said the doctor, "she will die of tuberculosis when she is sixteen—provided, of course, that she lives that long."

There is no prophylactic so powerful as the happy, healthy resiliency of Nature. Life is a fight against disease, and Nature has provided that life shall win if given about half a chance.

¶ Health is natural; disease is abnormal.

To introduce disease into a healthy body under the plea that you are fortifying the individual against disease, is the very acme of scientific stupidity.

There is nothing resists disease equal to health—keep it, prize it, work for it, pray for it!

And when a doctor, or anybody else talks to you about inoculating the beautiful body of your child with dead matter from a diseased cow, in the interest of health, tell him to go to—India, where dried grasshoppers and snake tongues are considered a cure for cholera.

The cure for consumption is—and there is only one cure for consumption—living out-of-doors. There may be an absolute breaking down of living tissue, yet if the patient can bring will to bear, and live out-of-doors day and night and laugh and play and work, he will probably live to attend the wake of most of his relatives. Conditions that breed consumption and typhoid fever are favorable to smallpox. The so-called "plague" has been banished by proper sewerage systems and good water, not by goat lymph, and the dangers of smallpox have been reduced in the same way.

⁋ The cleanly, sanitary, moderate and useful life as a guard against disease costs effort; but a dirty, disgusting operation like vaccination is soon over, and hence its popularity among the rabble. The books taught it and the doctors being but men, accepted what was taught as true.

But the world is moving, and moving towards the light. Fully one-half of all physicians now know, in spite of text books and colleges, that vaccination is a fallacy, and moreover a dangerous fallacy, unlike black cat salve.

So today the best doctors decline to vaccinate; they may not say much about it, but they refuse to mix up in it any more than they take to blood letting and bee-stings for bronchitis.

A few there be, say like Dr. Z. T. Miller, an eminent physician of Pittsburgh, who come out strong against it, and stand ready to give their reasons and challenge to demonstration and debate.

A few years ago Dr. Miller stood almost alone, but now there are hundreds who are with him.

Dr. Miller writes me as follows;

"Vaccination is a crime, not that it kills everybody vaccinated, but because it kills some of them and maims others. I could show you a woman, the right half of whose face was destroyed as a direct result of blood poisoning from vaccination. The sight of this unquestionable disfigurement should shame every vaccinist in the land. A boy named Gross, in Olean, N. Y., lost his arm from the same cause. Those of you who saw *Ben Hur* when it was here will remember the handsome young man who played Ben Hur. When the play was taken to London that man was vaccinated and lost his arm as a result. In 1898, two soldiers of the Twelfth New York Regiment were compelled to have their arms amputated as a result of vaccination. Within the past month a child living near me died, the cause of death given by the two physicians and the coroner, was blood poison from vaccination. I have received a number of letters giving accounts of deaths from lockjaw from vaccination wounds. These facts could be multiplied thousands of times.

"It has been shown that vaccination does not prevent smallpox; it has been shown that it maims and kills; it is also claimed, with sufficient evidence for official decision, that it disseminates other diseases, all of which is sufficient to bring it under the condemnation of all fair-minded people. Winterburn, in his book on vaccination, relates an outrageous instance, whereby a young women's school in the State of New York was closed because the inmates were inoculated with syphilis through vaccination. The pro-vaccinists have arrayed a stupendous amount of evidence in favor of vaccination; they point to the decrease in the number of cases and claim that vaccination modifies smallpox. To begin with, every vestige of their evidence is inferential and circumstantial. No one can ever tell whether vaccination ever prevented a case of smallpox, for the simple reason no one can assert that any one particular or collective individual is going to take it. That it has been modified as regards numbers and recurrences is true, but it is in spite of vaccination, and not on account of it. Why do I claim this? Because all other contagions have equally, if not to a greater extent, been modified.

"The principle involved in this question is that of self-protection. We are called upon to combat the aggressiveness of the irresponsible. We must defeat the effort of the man who would make sick an entire community of well people in the fear that a small portion of it may get sick. We must denounce the idea that a healthy person is a menace to anybody. We must see that our children's education is not predicated on the point of the poisoned quill. We must see to it that subcutaneous injection of an absolute poison does not take the place of sanitation and hygiene. We must declare against superstition as practised by the State. We must not surrender the right of personal privilege in the selection of our food, our religion, our politics, or our medicine. What does it profit you, if by your efforts you have gained perfect health when your government comes to you, vaccinates you, and you are rendered a cripple? Why should you study the laws of health, attain it and then have yourselves made invalids by your officious officials? Why should you tune yourselves to the principles of right living only to make a field for the propagation of the variolous filth that has been run through a heifer, to protect you, against a disease that kills fewer people than almost any other disease in the calendar?"

The Legal Profession

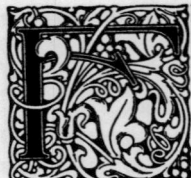IFTY thousand people cross London Bridge every day—mostly fools," said Carlyle. Six thousand lawyers live in New York City—mostly rogues. Old Commodore Trunion was very sure that all attorneys were rogues, and you remember that once when he caught a lawyer in his castle-yard, he gave him a generous taste of the cat, on general principles. And who is the carping quibbler that dare say the castigation was not deserved? ❧ ❧
Still, it does seem hard to declare all lawyers are rogues; and so, to estop all argument and put the case where none can gainsay it, I will simply say that one-half of all attorneys are rogues. Of course it will be easy for the attorneys to cry, " You're another," and to declare that they are just as good as the doctors and preachers or editors, but this does not dispose of the case ❧ The theme is lawyers, and I propose to discuss it briefly.
One-half of all lawyers are rogues.
All lawyers admit it; and I give no offense to any one by making this statement, as every lawyer who reads this will instantly place himself, in imagination, on the side of the virtuous and run over in his mind the lawyers who he knows are sure-enough rascals. The glib plea of every lawyer in behalf of his kind is, " If you had secured the advice of a good lawyer, he would have kept you out of the difficulty." But since it is a lawyer on the other side who has gotten you into the trouble, my proposition that one-half of all attorneys are rogues is proven and acknowledged by the lawyers themselves. When I say that just as many cases are lost in court as are won, I trust no bumbailiff or jaybird lawyer will arise and contradict me. Just as many cases are lost as are won. And in every case, the lawyers get a goodly grab into the pockets of all litigants. The litigants not only lose their money, but wreck

their peace of mind. Every man should have a certain knowledge of law, that he might conduct his affairs so as to keep away from lawyers, and to this end I would have the principles of law taught in all High Schools and Colleges.

Judge Albion W. Tourgee once said in public that no man could enforce a just claim in New York State, where it was litigated, without inviting financial and mental bankruptcy. For instance, here is the simple case of a man loaning two thousand dollars on a first mortgage on real estate. The money comes due, and has not been paid, but a technical flaw is alleged in the papers and the foreclosure is contested. Because why? A lawyer advised it.

Case is tried. Judgment for plaintiff. Case is taken to Appellate Division and after a year, is ordered reprinted—because the rogue lawyer confused it.

Finally, after a year, judgment is affirmed. Case is taken to Court of Appeals, and after three years is sent back for a new trial.

Four years have gone by, and the case is exactly where it began. Again it is tried, and after three years, Court of Appeals confirms judgment. In the meantime, no interest, taxes or insurance have been paid, and property has been allowed by defendant to deteriorate sadly.

Plaintiff secures judgment and finds title of property passed to city on tax sale, and deficiency judgment worthless because the defendant has a year before turned over all his assets to his Uncle, and bondsmen have skipped the country.

Result: Plaintiff loses original amount of loan, twenty-five hundred dollars paid out for costs, and much sleep. Note, the rogue attorney for defense received rent of property, twenty dollars a month, as fee, during the time.

This is not an extraordinary case, neither does it prove that all attorneys are rogues, but it merely shows that the law, to a great extent, is framed for lawyers and roguery.

Dead-beats among lawyers are too common to mention. If you do not know them, it is only because you do not know the world of men ॐ ॐ

Collection Agencies supply lists of "reputable lawyers" throughout the country to whom you are invited to send claims. Send along your claims for collection, and I'll lay you fifty to five that of the claims collected, one-fourth of the attorneys will pocket the whole amount and refuse to reply; and another fourth will reply, denying the claim has been paid, and ask you to advance ten dollars for costs. If you are very foolish you will then send one attorney after another; and if you ever knew one lawyer to enforce a claim against another and remit proceeds to his client, your experience has been different from mine.

In every large city of the land, there are rooting lawyers who chase Emergency Ambulances so as to secure the poor wretch, or his family, as a client. These rogues bring actions against the employer or whoever can be pounced upon, for damages, and take one-half of the swag, or all, if possible. And it was recently shown that in Chicago, a regular conspiracy of lawyers and witnesses prevailed so as to prove any point desired.

If a man is injured, another man is brought forward who happened to be right on the spot, and testifies as to how it all happened. The testimony shows some rich employer or corporation sadly at fault. These witnesses were trained in moot-courts and the same gang that served as witnesses on one occasion, on the next come up smiling as jurymen—declaring glibly that they neither read the papers nor have any thoughts on any subject. Railroad companies are constantly preyed upon by these conspiracies concocted by the rogue attorney. The big lawyers who work for railroads were usually retained on account of their skill in prosecuting railroads.

Having espoused a cause, a lawyer allows his feelings to lead him in the direction of his interests; but the fact is that the practice of law is largely an evasion of law, and a lawyer speedily becomes morally myopic.

The average lawyer is in no sense a producer—he preys upon the business community, and seizes everything that is n't fastened to the floor. An inventor, a creator, a producer is to him legitimate game ∾ ∾

And so have lawyers multiplied, out of all keeping with population, that they have become ravenous, and no man coming within their reach is safe. The booming of real estate has developed a whole round of exercise for their roguery, and has even brought to the surface the religio-lacrimose lawyer who robs schoolteachers, preachers and small tradesmen by getting them to buy gilt-edge mortgages on swamp-land, or " bonds " that represent nothing but driftwood contracts.

Schopenhauer says that clergymen and doctors are necessary evils—there being a kink in the minds of most people to which the professions named minister. No such excuse, however, can be made for an attorney. The only reason ever put forward for his existence by anybody is that he prevents men from wronging other men. But since men do now steal from other men, and attorneys tell them how—every lawyer's office being a kindergarten for crooks—it seems that their excuse for existence is poorly taken. No gigantic theft ever occurred, such as stealing a railroad or a town-site or a monopolizing franchise, but that lawyers had both hands in the rake-off up to their elbows. Were lawyers abolished to limbo, stealing would then be limited to lifting portable things, but now men wrest from other men the rights of generations unborn.

I never yet knew a lawyer who had any real respect for the law, or the judicial ermine, although, of course, there is a whole round of cant phrases and hypocritical mumble about " the learned judge," " the majesty of the law," and the " impartial jury." A lawyer sells his services to whoever will buy; and Daniel Webster once said that if an attorney lacked faith in the righteousness of a cause, a retainer would always animate his zeal. And the extent of his zeal is usually regulated by the size of the check. The biggest fools in the way of clients are, I suppose, those who go into litigation for revenge. The revenge gotten out of law is very costly. Even to maintain a perfectly just claim, your action is unwise if your time is worth anything, and you have any useful work to do. Any good businessman, nowadays, will compromise —accept ten per cent—anything, rather than scramble his brains in court, at the elbow of an attorney. Tolstoy's doctrine of non-resistance is the highest wisdom—you'd better be robbed direct than litigate and be deprived of your property by what is ironically called " due process of law."

The best lawyers now are businessmen. The big successes of the future will not be in either of the three learned professions. Neither the doctor, the lawyer nor the clergyman is now the intellectual leader in his community. The professions are just tolerated—that's all. The old-time lawyer, with his wide culture and fine sense of honor, is gone, and gone forever—granting the hypothesis that he ever existed outside of the brain of a novelist. The transaction that is not mutual is immoral. Both sides must be benefited. Reciprocity must be the rule.

If a property once gets into the lawyer's hands, let no client expect to get off easy.

Judges, courts and lawyers dissolve, destroy, dissipate—divide. According to this test of mutuality, does the lawyer give an equivalent? Let us evade the question, and say with Chief Justice Tawney that lawyers are men who punish their clients for being so foolish as to go to them.

Also this, the rogue lawyer is punished by his roguery, and in time evolves into something less than a man. A man's acts and thoughts etch themselves into his soul, and print his history on his face ∞ ∞

Sensible parents no longer encourage their growing sons to enter the professions. Success lies in human service, in teaching, creating and building for the future, not in bamboozlement, or the godless game of graft and grab.

Blackstone was a lawyer, and he knew the rogue barrister who absolved himself when he kept beyond the nip of law.

Blackstone says, " The man who takes everything which the law allows him to take, is a scoundrel at heart. To limit morality to that which is legal is base; for the extreme of the law is the extreme of injustice. The administration of law requires mercy, and above all it demands the admixture of good commonsense."

⁋ There is something beyond the legal requirements. It was stated two thousand years ago in these words: A NEW COMMANDMENT I GIVE UNTO YOU—THAT YOU LOVE ONE ANOTHER ✸ ✸

The University Militant

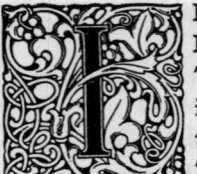HAVE been reading a little book by Charles Ferguson, entitled *The University Militant* ❧ The book is issued by Mitchell Kennerley, which is a guarantee that the volume has enough of the saltness of time to save it.

This book makes a demand upon your Cosmic Kilowatts. It is no substitute for a box of cigarettes and a popular magazine. In fact, it pays the reader a very great compliment in assuming that he knows a good many things that Ferguson leaves unsaid.

Ferguson has been a lawyer, a clergyman and a journalist. I believe, however, he has abandoned the law, theology has abandoned him, and while he used to be a journalist, he is now only a newspaper man.

The first time I saw Charles Ferguson was in Buffalo in the year Eighteen Hundred Eighty-eight. Samuel Richard Fuller was Rector of Saint John's Episcopal Church. This church was downtown, and the tide of fashionable humanity had forsaken the district and ebbed out toward the Park.

This stranded church Doctor Fuller was endeavoring to make into an institutional concern, being impressed with the popular fallacy that the world was to be saved by its churches and preachers ❧ ❧

The swirl of eloquence introduced by Doctor Fuller caught all of the Great Unchurched, especially the young, the restless, the ambitious—what has been called the stewedless prunes.

Charles Ferguson and I attended for the same reason: we were under the spell of Doctor Fuller's eloquence; we wanted to do something to redeem the world.

Charles Ferguson was impressed by Fuller, and Fuller was impressed by Ferguson, and Ferguson duly became curate and preached on Sunday afternoons, and also on Thursdays at noon, the whole affair being a gentle, non-punishable and reasonable imitation of the work then being done by the Reverend Doctor Rainsford in New York.

Ferguson had the most beautiful and mellifluous voice for intoning the service that I ever heard. He could have intoned an auction-bill so as to bring tears to the eyes of a brass monkey. A wonderful man is Ferguson! He has run the gamut of theological esthetics to industrial ethics, and been pooh-poohed all along the line, because he is much in advance of any courthouse, church or newspaper, until now he has evolved into a big, generous and able philosopher who wants little and gives much.

⁋ The Law of Arrested Development has never caught Ferguson; therefore, I say he is a most extraordinary individual. He can neither be bought, bribed nor coerced.

Being a college graduate, he knows the futility, folly and foolishness of calling a man educated simply because he has a college degree. ⁋ What Ferguson pleads for now is a University of the World, and not a University Lim., that is, in a certain locality, managed by villagers, and animated by a belief in exclusion and caste ∽ ∽

Ferguson wants us all to be teachers, all to be scholars, all to be learners. His university is the University of the World, and when we graduate we are shifted to another planet, or, possibly, sent back here for a post-graduate course, all according to the law of the transmigration of souls which Ferguson does not attempt to explain ∽ ∽

In this little book, *The University Militant,* the author asks: What is government for? What is the church's mission? What is the school? And then he answers all these questions, seemingly talking to himself.

And it is our delight to overhear him. His voice has a little of the minor key and is quite subdued from the bully bishop's bazoo that I often heard at Saint John's Church, when he used to say, "And there is no health in us," and, "He slew many mighty kings, for His mercy endureth from everla-a-a-a-sting to everla-a-a-a-sting." ∞ ∞

Charles Ferguson now has pretty nearly caught up with Thomas Jefferson, who was the only Democrat this country has ever seen. Ferguson wants to organize an army: not an army of collegiates, politicians, doctors, lawyers, preachers, and pedagogues, but an army of men and women who earn their own living; who go forth to their labors until the evening; people who realize somewhat of the conditions under which they live and who prize life and its opportunities; and who would be self-governing—a conscious, confident army marching upon the strongholds of superstition, theological and political, intent on honesty, industry, utility and beauty. In every town, village and city ward, Ferguson would have a scientific and artistic recruiting-station.

The world should be one vast university, and we should all be recorded as students.

This being so, an order would be created whereby public opinion would be formed, and we would not be at the mercy of grab-erinos, and self-seeking politicians, and theological grafters.

❡ Ferguson believes that any man who is enslaved deserves to be, and that safety lies in a communism of intellect.

We get the governments that we want; in fact, we get anything that we want.

America is not a Democracy. At best, it is a Federated Republic ruled by representatives of the people. But the demos being very busy making money, each one looking out for himself and his spare time being filled in with suspicions of others, the plunder-bund is given opportunity to evolve in Church, State, Schools and Business; and instead of being a government of the people, by the people, for the people, we have a government of graft, for grafters and by grafters.

The fact, however, that we are awakening to the truth of the situation gives Ferguson great hope; and so, while his diagnosis seems more or less pessimistic, the man is really an optimist, plus.
⁋ He believes that there must and will come a day when the people of America, and of the world as well, will conclude that their safety and happiness lie in organizing a University of Ideas, making it possible for everybody to be educated, and all to have enough money so that poverty, disease, woe, crime and graft will be things that live only in the memory of Clio whose moving pen writes and having writ moves on, nor all your tears shall blot a line of it.

This book, *The University Militant,* is good reading for any kind of weather. I do not know of a better book for you to put into your grip; if you do not have a good time on your trip, you will have a good time with the book, and having taken much with you, you will be enriched by bringing much back.

Justice, Human and Divine

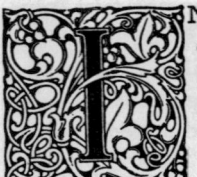IN the olden time the king was the court of "last conjecture." From his words there was no appeal.
¶ King Arthur listened to the pleas and decided questions in person.
The theory of justice was that the king could do no wrong; that his judgments were absolutely right, proper and just.
The king was supposed to be the vicegerent of God, the representative of Deity; and as the justice of God was absolute and right, so were the rulings of the king.
"The divine right of kings" was not successfully challenged until the year Seventeen Hundred Seventy-six.
And in degree, a superstitious taint still lingers in reference thereto, and we expect our courts to be something more than human.
¶ The modern judicial machinery has no method by which it can reverse itself and do justice to an individual that it has wronged ∾ ∾
However, it is good to see that the public conscience is becoming awakened; and this is manifest in Senate Bill Number 974, introduced by Senator Southerland, of Utah.
Senator Southerland has presented to the Senate a strong argument in behalf of the proposition. In addition, is a brief by Edward M. Borchard, Law Librarian of Congress; and a further argument is appended by Professor John H. Wigmore, Dean of the Northwestern School of Law, at Evanston, Illinois.
The bill seeks to remedy certain cases of injustice. It does not seek to grant relief to all and every person who is legally innocent, or whose conviction is reversed on appeal.
All Senator Sutherland's bill seeks to do is two things: to give relief to a man charged with crime, when it is shown beyond question that the crime was not committed at all; and, second,

when it is shown by competent proof that the crime was not committed by this man.

If Congress passes this bill, as it doubtless will, its example will be followed by similar legislation in all of the States.

An incident leading up to this bill is the case of a man who had served ten years for murder and who was released only when the man he was supposed to have murdered presented himself at the penitentiary and asked to see the man who had murdered him.

All of the circumstances pointed in the direction of guilt for the accused man. There had been a fight, which was the culmination of a grudge long entertained. Thus motive was proved. The *corpus delicti* was found buried in a shallow grave. The body was much decomposed, but it was identified by relatives.

Who the actual dead man was made no difference. It was n't the man the relatives thought it was. The other man had got out of the country, thinking he had killed the man who subsequently served ten years for killing him.

The man was convicted and was sentenced, escaping the gallows by a hair.

Now comes the case of John Boehman, committed to Sing Sing for life on account of a murder. It turns out, however, that the murder was committed by another person, and the facts are presented beyond dispute.

Andrew Toth spent twenty years in a prison in Pennsylvania before the authorities discovered, of their own accord, that they had the wrong man.

Relief in the bill is fixed at a sum not to exceed five thousand dollars. Of course, five thousand dollars is a very insignificant sum, say for twenty years of a man's life; but the idea is to prepare a bill that will be acceptable even to the most captious.

The State holds its citizens responsible for their mistakes or their crimes; but the State is not responsible for its blunders. It can not be sued nor arrested. It takes refuge behind its claim of sovereignty and that gets us back to the old superstition that the king can do no wrong.

However, the State may take the property of an individual for public use, and make recompense to the owner. This same proposition holds in all civilized countries, under the plea that it is an exercise of the necessary right of eminent domain for the State to take the thing it needs. Property-rights have always been considered by English-speaking people as more precious than rights of the person. Professor Wigmore says: " The State, in the past, has committed many crimes against liberty. When the State commits a wrong against property there is a redress; but when it commits a crime against a person, no redress, under present conditions, is possible. We say all men are entitled to life, liberty and the pursuit of happiness. This we assume as a fundamental principle.

" Courts are created on the grounds of public good. Their purpose is to do justice between man and man, so that peace and good order may prevail. The duty of courts is public. Truth is on the scaffold. Wrong is on the throne.

" Certainly, as a democratic people, we have slipped a cog somewhere. Our government takes account of property, but it does not take account of human rights and human life. The happiness of the individual is something which the State does not officially recognize. The State can do no wrong, except when it comes to property."

In Switzerland and New Zealand, the individual has a claim for money damages for illegal arrest and punishment, and in case of hanging the wrong man, the heirs can make claim.

The question now before us is, should the State be held responsible for its mistakes, and is it possible for the State to be guilty of a crime against the individual?

The law says " No," but in the human heart there is something that says " Yes."

The Federal Government prosecuted E. G. Lewis of Saint Louis for ten years. Lewis spent one hundred thousand dollars in defending himself. The Government ruined his business, but never convicted him. Then a Committee, appointed by Congress, after taking ten thousand pages of testimony, declared that Lewis had always conducted his affairs in a legal manner, and the State never had a cause for complaint. But that did not reimburse Lewis ∾ ∾

This bill introduced by Senator Sutherland, is an opening wedge. Senator Sutherland has presented a measure absolutely without objection; one that itself answers every argument and is so simple that even the critical and captious can not protest against it. It is the beginning of a great and necessary reform.

The Day of Your Death

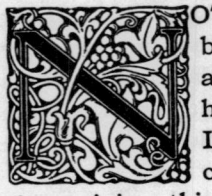OT long ago, in a Western town, I was invited by a district judge to sit on the bench with him and listen to the evidence in a certain case that he was sure would interest me.

It was a divorce suit, and everything had been conceded except the question of alimony. In determining this, the value of certain property held by the parties jointly was under consideration.

The Northampton Tables of Mortality had been cited as authority. To back up these tables an insurance actuary had been called in. Sure enough, the evidence of this actuary struck a cosmic chord in my consciousness.

In the preliminary examination, to show his fitness as an expert witness, the actuary was asked this question:

" Can you make a close estimate on the average length of human life? "

And the answer was, " Yes, if numbers are taken into consideration. "

" Can you tell the probable length of the life of an individual? "

⁋ And the answer was, " No."

When asked why, the witness said, " The element of chance enters into single lives, and where large numbers are considered chance is eliminated, so we get the law of average."

The next question was, " But suppose we bar the element of accident, can you then tell how long an individual will live? "

⁋ And the answer was, " No."

Being pressed for a reason, the actuary expressed himself in a little speech that impressed every one in the courtroom. I can not recall the exact words, but the gist of it was as follows:

⁋ There is an element in longevity that can not be ascertained or passed upon by any one except the man himself.

My opinion is that every man should be his own physician, and he should be wise enough and sane enough to make a diagnosis of his own case—spiritually, mentally, physically—much closer than any one else ever possibly could.

The one thing in human life that no one but the man himself knows, is, how long does he expect to live.

It is a pretty good general rule that, barring accident, the man will live as long as he expects to, or, if you please, as long as he wants to, or hopes to.

Many people are obsessed with the fallacy that the age of man is fixed at the limit of threescore and ten; and so, with a vast number of people, when they are around sixty-five they begin to prepare to shuffle off. They quit business, retire from active work, close up their affairs, and when they do these things, death and dissolution are at the door. There are other men who work on until they are eighty, and then they do exactly what the other man did at seventy, with a like result.

Great numbers of very strong, active, earnest men, reach the age of eighty, and die at eighty-two, eighty-three, eighty-four. And the reason for this passing is not so much a physical one as it is a mental. These men have fixed this age limit in their minds, and their entire life and death conform to the idea.

As a general proposition I would say the way to live to be one hundred is, not to consider the question of time, but simply to continue an active, earnest interest in human affairs, and not overeat ∞ ∞

The individual who looks for ease and rest, and bodily gratification, be he young or old, is in a dangerous position. To eliminate the toxins which accrue in the human body, activity is positively necessary. The activity of the mind reacts on the organs of the body. So thought is a physical process, and to gain this elimination which insures health, no man should ever think of retiring from business and quitting the game.

If you retire from one thing you must take up something else that is more difficult.

Change of occupation is a great factor in human health; but the one thing that makes a man live long is an earnest vow early in life, well kept, to " never say die! "

Only such a one can make a century run, and the death of the centenarian is almost without exception a painless process.

⁋ And no physical examination can probe these inner facts and attitude of the man's mind.

The individual himself knows and can determine how long he will live, better than any one else possibly can; and I believe he can himself, if he is honest with himself, size up his case, and, barring accidents, figure the day of his death, as Moses did on Mount Horeb ❧ ❧

The Common People

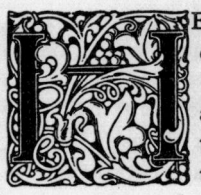E who can make two grins grow where there was only a grouch before is a benefactor of the race.
¶ Nevertheless, I want to enter a demurrer against Brother Opper, the clever cartoonist of the New York *American*. It is this: He portrays the Common People as a half-fed, dead-serious, apologetic and unnecessarily innocent little shrimp with sidewhiskers ॐ ॐ

It's too bad to analyze a joke and put a pleasantry on the microscopic slide, but in the interest of truth it is well to say that the Common People of America do not belong to the shrimp variety.
¶ The Common People are the people who are interested in common things.

If you want commonsense you will find it among the Common People, and not among the patricians or the peons.

The trouble with Mexico is that she has no Common People, and until she can evolve these there is no hope for her. Uncommon people belong to the leisure class, and the leisure class is made up of hoboes and remittance-men.

Ninety per cent of the population of Mexico is illiterate.

Less than ten per cent of the population of the United States is illiterate ॐ ॐ

The Common People work, study, think, laugh—accomplish. There has never been a civilization in all history where the Common People did not hold the balance of power. I am one of the Common People. I do not wear side-whiskers or a look of wild alarm. I am one of the Common People, because I can shoulder a trunk and carry it upstairs. I can sift ashes, shovel coal, drive four horses or six. I can swing a pick, an ax, a baseball-club, feed a furnace, use a paint brush, climb ladders, tend mason, juggle mail-sacks, run a motor-truck, follow a plow, pitch hay, dig postholes, milk cows, slop pigs, curry horses, lead the bull to water, and do five hundred common, plain, simple, every-day things that people in moderate circumstances, in city, town or country, do, and which some one has to do—otherwise there would be no civilization ❧ ❧

I have just been reading a most interesting book entitled, *The Common People of Ancient Rome,* by Frank Frost Abbott, Kennedy Professor of the Latin Language and Literature in Princeton University.

As long as the Common People in Rome were in the ascendent, Rome ruled the world. When they became pauperized through paternalism, weakness, degeneration, disease and dissolution were at the door.

I recommend very few books—beside my own—but this book by Professor Abbott on the Common People of Rome should be read by all of the Common People of America. There is one chapter especially that is worth the price of admission, and that is the chapter on the Emperor Diocletian, who lived in the Fourth Century after Christ.

This man had a deal to do with ushering in the Dark Ages. His intent and desires were right, but he had a wonderful itch for butting in and taking charge of everything.

The people were not allowed either to choose their own religion or to do business in their own way.

Diocletian knew nothing about natural law, that is, spiritual law ❧ ❧

High prices then prevailed. Diocletian devised a scheme for keeping then down—this, in the interests of the Common People, for politicians, propagandists, reformers, rulers, who live off the Common People, have ever been anxious to show the Common People what to do.

So comes Diocletian, solicitous on account of high prices. He sends his secretaries through the market-places, makes a list of seven hundred commodities, and the secretaries fix maximum prices at which things should be sold.

The penalty for charging more than the established price was death ❧ ❧

In order that there could be no misunderstanding, Diocletian had the names of the articles and the prices above which they should not be sold, cut in stone and placed on the walls around the markets.

What was the result? Simply this, that the Common People who had been busy producing all of the commodities that ministered to human life became panic-stricken. Animation flagged. Inspiration died. Laughter ceased. No such thing as joyous labor longer existed ❧ ❧

The threat hanging over them of what the government proposed to do killed spontaneity, and creation, development, production, died ❧ ❧

And behold, there came the Dark Ages, when for a thousand years night prevailed; when for a thousand years the world did not produce a poet, an orator, an inventor, an artist, a navigator, a mathematician; when fear was supreme, and hope stood far away in the shadow, shivering and cold, a finger to her lips.

⁋ Our friends in Washington should read this book on the Common People of Rome, and learn the lesson, which is: the less rulers mix in, dictate and try to regulate economic activities, the better it is for the Common People.

Well did Thomas Jefferson say, " That country is governed best that is governed least."

The Beautiful Dream of Socialism

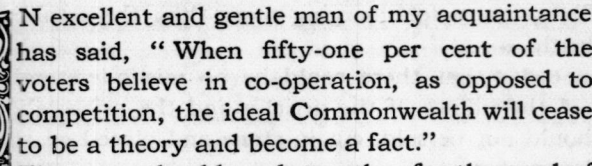AN excellent and gentle man of my acquaintance has said, "When fifty-one per cent of the voters believe in co-operation, as opposed to competition, the ideal Commonwealth will cease to be a theory and become a fact."

That men should work together for the good of all is very beautiful, and I believe the day will come when these things will be, but fifty-one per cent of the voters casting ballots for Socialism will not bring the thing about.

Well, hardly, dearie, hardly!

The matter of voting is simply the expression of a sentiment, and after the ballots are counted there yet remains the work to be done so so

A man might vote right and act the rest of the year like a fool.

⁋ The man who blew breezily into the Roycroft Shop from Cleveland—on a free pass—and asked the first thing, "Well, I hope I'm in time for the semi-annual dividend!" always votes the Socialist ticket.

He's a talking proletariat. And while some of the noblest and finest souls I ever met are Socialists, we all know there is the other kind that wants something for nothing and their grievance against society is a sure indictment against themselves.

The Socialist who is full of fight, faction, jealousy and bitterness is creating an opposition that will hold him and all others like him in check. And this opposition is well, for even a very imperfect society must protect itself against dissolution and a condition which is worse.

To take over the monopolies and operate them for the good of society is not enough, and not desirable either, so long as the idea of rivalry is rife.

As long as self is uppermost in the minds of men, they will fear and hate other men, and under Socialism there would be the same scramble for place and power that we see in politics now.

Society can never be reconstructed until its individual members are reconstructed. Man must be born again. When fifty-one per cent of the voters rule their own spirits, and have put fifty-one per cent of their present jealousy, bitterness, envy, hate, fear and foolish pride out of their hearts, then Christian Socialism will be at hand, and not until then.

This subject is entirely too big to dispose of in a paragraph, and so I am just going to content myself here with mention of one thing, that so far as I know has never been mentioned in print—the danger to society of exclusive friendships between man and man, woman and woman.

Of the love of a man for a woman, I shall not here speak—it is right, natural, beautiful and beneficent. But in passing I wish to say this: The love of man for woman and woman for man, in order to attract the smile of God, must center upon something else—the man and woman must unite their love in a love of art, music, truth, children or work—thus forming a trinity. To love each other is not enough—they must love some third thing. Further than this, I believe that in marriage the strangle hold should be barred. Let sex love go, for this time, at that.

A love that is apt to be full of folly is the exclusive affection of one girl for another. These bonds are apt to be unnatural, maudlin, absurd and the precursor of mental, moral and nervous maladies. The sight of a young woman piking gleefully across the lawn with a nightgown rolled up in a Sunday newspaper is a common sight. She is going to stay overnight with her chum— which is all right, too, but it simply betokens a tendency.

This particular phase of friendship has been treated at length by Dr. Charcot in a book entitled *The Danger of Exclusive Friendships among Young Women*. I will not review Dr. Charcot's essay here. This is not my theme, and I only mention it by way of suggestion so the reader can follow the topic out for himself. The idea I wish to bring up has no taint of vice upon it any more than has the girl friendships to which I have just alluded—it is only tinged with absurdity. The subject is the close and exclusive friendship of two men or two women.

No two persons of the same sex can complement each other, neither can they long uplift or benefit one another. Usually they weaken and deform the mental and spiritual estate. We should have many acquaintances or none. When two men begin to " tell each other everything," they are hiking for senility. There must be a bit of well-defined reserve. We are told that in matter—in solid steel for instance—the molecules never touch. They never surrender their individuality. We are all molecules of Divinity, and our personality should not be abandoned. Be yourself, let no man be necessary to you—your friend will think more of you if you keep him at a little distance.

Friendship, like credit, is highest where it is not used.

I can understand how a strong man may have a great and abiding affection for a thousand other men, and call them all by name, but how he can regard any one of these men much higher than another and preserve his mental balance, I do not know ∽ ∽

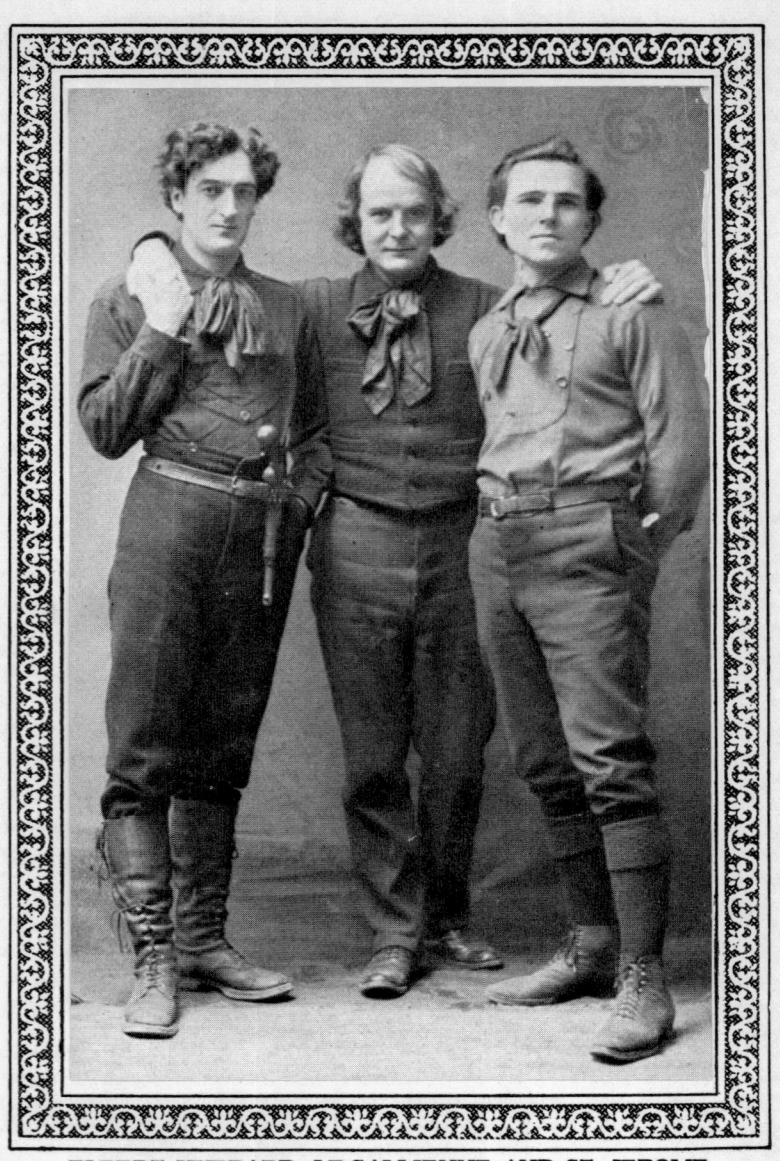

ELBERT HUBBARD, LE GALLIENNE AND ST. JEROME

The Good Fellow

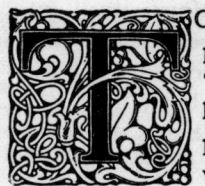OLSTOY somewhere tells of a priest who saw a peasant plowing and asked him this question, " If you knew you were going to die this night, how would you spend the rest of the day? " The peasant thought a moment and answered, " I would plow." A man of the true type, if he had but a day to live, would not change his occupation. Every day he is preparing to live; and men who are prepared to live are prepared to die.

In family life the average man is apt to treat every other woman with more courtesy than he does his wife, and other people's children with more consideration than his own. A man in his home may be an absolute tyrant, and at the same time be known to the world as a " good fellow." Communism has no more use for the tyrant than it has for the good fellow. In family life, usually, a man sees too much of his family and they see too much of him; and society does not see enough of the good fellow with his antique brass, or he would be well squelched.

The good fellow is one who bothers the busy; deals in pretense and hypocrisy; encourages the idle—assuming both virtues and vices. He has not the courage to live his life, and so has neither friends nor foes. His praise and blame are alike futile, and his lavish spending and " treating " are at the expense of some one else—he lives to impress the waiters. Such a one may deceive a society made up of individuals, but he can not deceive a community. There his measure is quickly taken. He does not have to be sent away—he goes. In a community an ounce of loyalty is worth a pound of cleverness.

No coin of conduct is current in a community but sterling honesty—truthfulness alone is legal tender and passes at par. Apologies and explanations are never in order; your life must proclaim itself and must be its own excuse for being. And while all faults are forgiven in the man of perfect candor, the smile that does not spring from the soul will transform itself into a grimace. A community can not be deceived. Only those who deal in deception can be duped. William Penn once asked a man who was much given to drawing the long bow, " Why do you not lie to me? " And the liar answered, " What's the use? "

⁋ In Athens of old the criterion or standard of art sprang from the most competent; so in a community the criterion of conduct is formed by the best. The highest minds fix the standard, and the lesser ones try to adapt themselves to it; but there is an unseen mark which, if they drop below, eliminates them absolutely from the community.

The question may here be asked, " Why may not a special community be formed where the standard of conduct is low, and so make the good fellows, idlers and rogues feel at home? "

And the answer is this: A community is only possible where truth and loyalty abide. Weakness never formed a community and never can. And if it could, the institution would not hold together a day. In weak and vicious people there is no attractive force, no coalescing principle. The weak pull apart—they thwart, retard and impede one another. They are like drowning people—they clutch and strangle one another. A goodly degree of integrity, disinterestedness and unselfishness are demanded even to start a community, and the more of these qualities you can get the more enduring the institution. A partnership of weak men does not give strength. Weakness multiplied by weakness equals naught. Two weak people will not make a strong team. Strength multiplied by strength gives strength. Weak men need a monarch, and defectives need a priest. They want some one to direct—to think for them. But the enlightened co-operate, and in pooling their best in thought and effort they reach a degree of power and excellence that can be obtained in no other way.

Physician's Farewell

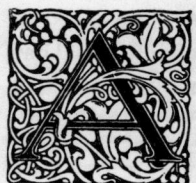PHYSICIAN'S FAREWELL TO HIS PATIENTS: Dr. A. L. Mitchell of East Aurora has issued a printed address to the public telling why he has abandoned his profession. Coming from a highly educated and successful physician it is worthy of more than a passing perusal. I prescribe a portion of it, every two hours, for the elimination of effete matter from the allopath system of the laity—physicians, all save the fledglings, know the truth, already.

I have known the doctor for twenty years. He is a most superior man, one of great intelligence, insight, sympathy, and in point of sincerity, earnestness and purity of purpose I have never known his equal. In soul-worth he is as fine as Balzac's Country Doctor, only Balzac had to create his hero out of the stuff that dreams are made of, while Mitchell is a live man, just turned forty-five, in full possession of his powers.

It is not unusual for patients to say a word of farewell to the doctor. But for a doctor to bid good-bye to his patients is like the resignation of a Democratic office holder, a scene no romancer has ever yet dared picture.

And the beauty of it is, that in this case, none of the patients are mis'ble, for the doctor sails away on a sea of success, dabbling his feet in the warm pedilyvium of love, and the good-will of the patients can be seen from afar, fluttering in the breeze like antiseptic gauze.

Mrs. Mitchell is also an extraordinary individual. Her industry, patience, kindness and desire to serve and benefit are heroic. Time and time and again, at dead of night, I have heard the hoofbeats of the horse of the messenger, and then in what seemed but a few minutes, I could hear the wheels of the doctor's carriage or his sleigh bells as he went away on his errand of mercy. Mrs.

Mitchell never tried to save herself from these night rides, and regardless of season or weather, she has faced the darkness and the storm, often alone, to do what she felt was her duty.

Now this man and his wife have come to the conclusion that medicine is only palliative—that disease springs from wrong thinking, wrong living and fear, and that mankind has thrown the burden of responsibility on the doctor instead of facing it each for himself.

Dr. Mitchell and his wife have abandoned the practice of medicine, but they haven't abandoned the practice of health. I hope and believe that they will come back here and show us how to live. We must learn how to keep well ourselves. The Mitchells will tell us how, and we ought to be willing to pay them five dollars or more in advance every time we consult them. They will give us no medicine, but they will investigate our case and tell us honestly why we suffer, and then it is for us to reform our ways of life and keep well.

It is cheaper to keep well than to be sick; it is cheaper to be sober than drunk; and it is cheaper to be fairly rich than poor. In order to be poor you have to waste an awful lot of time and money. Likewise, you have to persistently disregard and violate the laws of nature in order to destroy your health.

Several of our neighbors have asked, in way of criticism, " If there is nothing in the Science of Medicine, why did n't the Mitchells tell us so ten years ago?"

And the answer is: The Mitchells did n't know it ten years ago. The truth is something that dawns slowly, and instead of finding fault because the Mitchells did n't tell us this before, we ought to be grateful because they have told us now. Says Dr. Mitchell:

The habit of thought, cultivated through the years, has fixed upon the physician a pernicious subserviency—a tendency to do the thing which the other person wishes, regardless of his own personal convictions,—to think and speak and act in harmony with the many—to do the popular thing.

If a physician can practice medicine successfully and not juggle policy and principle, he has accomplished a feat seldom attainable. In fact, I doubt if it is ever done, continuously.

The physician of today sacrifices his self-esteem for the whim and prejudice of his patients. The homeopathic attenuation, the Galenic " dough pill," as well as its ultra-modern successor, the blank tablet, synonyms of the many things that might be classed under the head of " dope," are some of the subterfuges that he uses as reminders, to fix bits of good advice in minds fickle through fear and excess. Of course, I realize that it is an open question as to whether the end justifies the means; but I venture the conclusion that it carries a lasting penalty to both the doctor and his patient.

Much the greater number who come to the physician for medicine are those who do not need it. They are not, strange to say, the people isolated by circumstances, nor those confronted by the only real problems, those of insufficient food and clothing; but rather, from that vast middle class, who are trying to adjust themselves to prosperous appearances, and testing the lesser excesses of luxurious living. It is they who have delegated as many of the functions of both mind and body to its own particular specialist, as is consistent with modern usage,—handing out, if you please, their weaknesses as an æronaut does his ballast, to maintain altitude. These people for the most part, need mental adjustment. They have drawn upon their reserve,—have lost their equilibrium in the universal hurry. Their nerves worn out,—irritated by excesses, perhaps involuntary,—handicapped by several generations of improper breeding,—choked in natural development by wrong environment,—these people seek health in drugs, but never find it. They must retrace their steps over the same road that led to such conditions. There is no other way. No palliative or tonic will solace the ills of indiscretion. Only the unyielding persistence of natural law can be relied upon to bring ultimate comfort and relief; and it must be attained through their own conscious acknowledgement of the power of natural law to swing things back to poise and adjustment.

For a brief space medicine whips up the functions of mind and body, and gives false security against the continuance of weakening influences.

If this rooted evil of applying a drug to every ill were but overcome, much of the fear of disease, as well as its anticipation, would be avoided. Fear is itself but a kind of anticipation, nine-tenths of which never materializes. An instance: A child " takes cold;" the mother becomes anxious; she sees a long or a severe illness, and a possible death ahead. The child's temperature comes up; the mother weakens; the doctor comes, he bolsters his reassurances with Piso's, or something just as good. Acetanalid to bring fever down. A few doses of calomel to aid elimination. All to be followed, under favorable circumstances, by strychnine to restore the equilibrium. Piso's you know, closes up,—calomel opens—acetanalid depresses—and strychnine stimulates. In spite of all the child lives—would have lived anyway. A culpable fear led to what would naturally be considered poor judgment. The mother had delegated one of her weaknesses to a specialist, whose business it was, first to be satisfactory and second to cure. She would demand results that could not come naturally in a few hours. She would ask for changes that appeal to the senses, and the physician, schooled by years of experience, would do his best for the mother and her fears, and then the child ๛ ๛

The physician is, primarily, the product of a demand. He stands for that part of the human economy that feels the need of a prop. You encourage him to overreach himself, often, by expecting to separate cause from effect, and relieve ills in an hour that took a lifetime or longer in the making. Left to his own judgment the doctor would not drug you; but you have forced him to educate himself in those subtle devices that eventually mislead you, and often himself as well, by appearances that stimulate natural processes. He dwells upon drugs, sickness and death through his whole life; and in a measure, his observation of all things and conditions is through the eyes of his own particular calling. Hurry and ambition stimulate the commercial features of his relation to you; and if he has the expected professional spirit, he will act according to the popular medical opinions of the day. All of which latter you can not gainsay; and the issue, which is of personal and vital interest to you, becomes one of drugs and routine.

Unwittingly, you who employ physicians are responsible for these conditions. You do not desire to influence the opinions that you wish to depend upon, but you do it, surely. If you would have a little more faith in natural processes and seek the physician more particularly for his advice, and be willing at heart to follow it, and to pay for it, I am sure you would be happier and healthier.

Mrs. Mitchell has practised medicine for ten years and I for twenty-five, and we have seen all phases of life from grave to gay. We have had the pleasure of seeing our business grow to dimensions greater than any heretofore known in East Aurora; and of noting an appreciation and confidence which was as new to us as it was grateful. We have been happily situated, and fortunately free to work at our best, and all these years we have given our work our undivided attention. There have been few homes in this village and in the country 'round that we have not visited professionally. It has afforded us an opportunity for observation rarely excelled. We have seen sham and pretense laid aside, and human impulse left unguarded. No more critical or serious moments occur in the lives of men than we have witnessed over the incidents of our work. Yet, withal, by degrees over a period of many years, as youth has become cleared of some of its fancies, and medicine for us, of its fetich, we have come to feel a lack of faith in drugs as a cure of disease.

If we have been successful in a professional way, I am convinced that it has been through an ability to restore confidence to the minds of our patients.

The Other Side

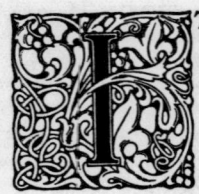T is, of course, very necessary that when you are entrusted with a message you shall deliver it to the right party in the least possible space of time ⁂ ⁂
The man, however, who entrusts another with a message has a duty to perform quite as much as the man who is given one.
There are men who can never get messages carried; and other men there be who inspire messengers with loyalty, fidelity and courage ⁂ ⁂
It is a somewhat curious thing that the most able men are never good teachers. " The great teacher," says Emerson, " is not the man who supplies the most facts, but the one in whose presence we become different people."
Too much individuality repels, overawes, subdues. An overpowering personality is a willopus-wallopus, or a steam-roller that flattens anything and everybody in the vicinity. A great actor seldom surrounds himself with able actors. In fact, a great actor usually reduces the whole company to nullity. In his presence animation subsides, ambition declines, originality takes to the tall uncut, and initiative becomes apologetic.
In the United States there are a few merchants who are discoverers of genius, but most are served by the mediocre, not to mention the timeserver, the hypocrite and the lickspittle.
One great merchant in the United States lives in history, not only because he was a great merchant, but because he discovered to the world fully a half-dozen other great merchants. That is, he took young men, gave them an opportunity, and under his beneficent guiding influence these country boys mentally bloomed and blossomed.
When you expect a messenger to deliver a message it is well not

to hamper him with too many instructions, nor scare him into innocuous desuetude by retailing the dangers that he will encounter, describing for him the punishment he will receive if he fails to " make good."

It is a great man who knows when and how to place reliance in another; to relegate and delegate and keep discipline out of sight. To let one line of figures at the bottom of the balance-sheet tell the tale—this is genius. Of course, if you repose confidence in the wrong man you will rue it, but genius turns on selection. Big men, nowadays, are big because they get others to do their work.

❧ Napoleon said, " I win my battles with my marshals." And then, when he was asked where he got his marshals, he said, " I make them out of mud! "

What he meant was that he took obscure men and lifted them into positions of prominence by throwing responsibility on them.

❧ Note the loyalty and love of Bertrand, who followed his master to Saint Helena, giving up home, religion, family and all of his own private interests that he might serve his master— even refusing to leave his master when he was dead, but remaining at Saint Helena in order that his own dust might be buried in the grave of this man he loved. Any man who can inspire another with such love can not be obliterated by the scratch of a pen or the shrug of the shoulder.

Napoleon certainly had personality; at the same time he did not use it to destroy the personality of others.

Great is the man—supremely great—who does not bestride the narrow world like a colossus and cause other men to run and peep about under his huge legs to find themselves dishonorable graves ❧ ❧

The world is big enough for all of us, and the very good slogan is, " Make room! Make room! " And if you are bound to give an order, let it be this: " Open up that gangway! "

Ben Lindsey has entrusted a thousand boys, each with a message,

and the message he gave them was their commitment-papers.
⁋ These boys carried the message; and out of the thousand a scant half-dozen proved derelict. And just remember that all of these boys belonged to the " criminal class."

Let us here quote Napoleon again, who said: " The criminal class? Ah, yes, I fight my battles with the criminal class! "

To entrust a message to a messenger with the full confidence that he will do naught else but deliver it to the proper person, and this expeditiously, is a fine art that employers would do well to acquire ෴ ෴

A trusted messenger is fine, but a trusting employer is finer still. Suspicion taints the whole fabric of trust. If Ben Lindsey doubted that his boys would go where they were sent, very few of them would ever reach the iron gates and hear their clanging welcome. The secret of Ben Lindsey's success is simple: he believes in his boys. And that is why the boys believe in him.

Ben Lindsey kissing the cheek of a bad boy and sending the lad away to prison alone, unattended, uncoerced, is a finer thing to me than Napoleon's habit of pulling down the head of one of his marshals and kissing the bearded cheek.

" Know thyself! " said Socrates.

" Trust thyself! " said Emerson.

" Trust others! " says Ben Lindsey.

When President McKinley gave that message to Rowan, he trusted Rowan to carry it. There were no instructions, no threats, no implied doubts, no injunctions. Rowan asked no questions; neither did McKinley.

The big man is not the man who wants to live not only his own life but the life of others, but he is great who reposes faith in others, and thus brings out the best there is in them, that which was often before unguessed.

He Used the Synonym

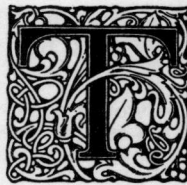HUS it happened several years ago that the Bishop of Ripon journeyed Westward, and fell into the hospitable arms of the Dean of Denver. The servants in the household had been cautioned that the Great Man should be addressed as "My Lord." All thoroughly understood the lesson, including Eph, an American citizen of Afric descent.

The Bishop duly arrived and was shown to his apartment. Eph was told to go up presently and see if there was not something that the Great Man wanted.

Eph tapped at the door and asked if he could be of service. "Yes," said the Bishop, "bring me some shaving water, please."

"Yes, my God!" said Eph, and straightway went and brought a pitcher of ice water.

J. B. Runs Things

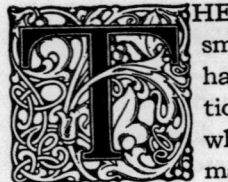THERE was a Jail-Bird, once upon a time, in a small town in the state of Iowa. This J. B. had had all that he wanted, and it was his firm intention if he ever got another chance, he would show what he was made of. Many other J. B.'s have made similar resolves. After he got out almost everybody gave him the Icy Mitt, but finally he Accepted a Position (or as some might say, Found a Job) in a Factory. He started in at four dollars a week, working with the boys, for jail-birds can not afford to be either fastidious or finicky. They have to take whatever offers.

Responsibilities gravitate to the person who can shoulder them, and power flows to the man who knows how.

And so it happened that before the J. B. was in that factory a month the boys were going to him asking him where things were. When they ran out of one kind of work they would ask him what they should do next; and he, knowing the sequence of the work, would advise them. Now, there be employers who are Proud and Overbearing, but others there be who have Common-Sense. And it so happened that the man who owned the factory where the J. B. worked had a modicum of Common-Sense. Seeing that the J. B. knew where things were and what should be done next, and that the J. B. put the work away at night and got it out in the morning, and planned things at home, and picked things up instead of walking over them or kicking them aside, why the Boss encouraged the J. B. and Raised his Wages.

So the J. B. evolved into a Right Hand Man, and in time came to know a deal more about the details of the business than the Boss, and I believe eventually married the daughter of the Boss, inherited his money and became sole owner of the Factory, but of these things I am not certain, so I do not record them. But the little incident I am about to record really happened. One day the Boss saw two girls who worked in the factory coming in with a basket of wild clematis. These girls proceeded to festoon the pillars of the big room with the beautiful plant. " Who told you to do that? " demanded the Boss.

" Why, Mr. So-and-so," said the girls, referring to the J. B.

" Did you send those girls away during working hours after weeds? " asked the Boss shortly after of the J. B.

" Certainly," was the answer. " You see, I noticed those particular girls seemed very white, and not very strong and sort of nervous and worn—they say they have things tough at home—and I just thought I would try to improve their complexions and spirits by giving them a run out in the sunshine."

" Oho, you thought they were getting Prison Pallor, did you? "

" Yes, you guessed it—I was thinking of Prison Pallor."

" And so contrived an excuse to send the girls on a two-mile walk out across the fields? "

" Yes."

" Had Prison Pallor yourself, eh? "

" Yes."

" Used to look into a pocket mirror and thought it was a Ghost? "

" Possibly."

" Never saw the blue sky except through a grating, or when walking lock-step across a stone-paced courtway? "

" You have it."

" Well, look here, J. B., don't stand around here keeping me from work—I wish t' Lord I could find a few more J. B.'s to help me run this shebang. And say, make a little list of the pale, nervous, yellow and scared girls and send them out by turns for clematis whenever the sun shines—don't stand around keeping me from work—don't you think I have anything to do myself? Go on with you! "

His Umps Saves the Day

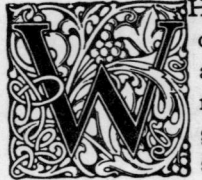HEN I speak well, as I occasionally do, I know a dozen words ahead just exactly how these words are to be expressed. Last week at Pittsburgh I reached a point in my lecture where I usually give a certain quotation, and this quotation was so familiar to me that I neglected to formulate it in my mind before voicing it. In other words I ran right up on it a-tilt, without taking a good look at it, and when I got to it I was looking down in the auditorium at a big hat all covered with nodding roses, the whole as big as a bushel basket. And for the life of me the quotation would not come at my bidding. I grasped for it in mid-air, gasped, coughed—it was no use. The circuit between me and the listeners was broken. The audience was away off there, a goggle-eyed, staring monster, spread out over a hundred feet—just staring at me, little me dressed in black, standing all alone on a big platform.

The room seemed to be teetering up and down, and then it began to swirl ❧ ❧

I dived for my quotation, but brought up the wrong one, when from the back of the room came a stentorian voice, thus: " Two Strikes!" ❧ ❧

There was a grim silence, just as you see a gun fired from a mile away and then hear the report.

Then came a wild burst of applause, and laughter from the audience, and in it I, too, joined. The self-appointed umpire had saved the day.

I seized the quotation firmly by the collar, and all the rest of my speech as well.

And the lesson taught me was this: Don't be too sure.

A Fable

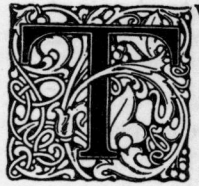TWO sons of Milesia were once delegated to sit up with a corpse, and keep the candles burning.
Towards midnight the whisky, which should have lasted all night, was consumed.
Both men were thirsty and very nervous. Pat proposed that he should go to the saloon next door and work the growler.
"Not on your life!" said Mike, who amended the motion by proposing that Pat should remain with the corpse and he himself go to the saloon for drinks.
"In God's name, I'll never agree to that," says Pat.
Neither one being willing to stay alone with the dead man, and both having promised the priest that they would not leave the corpse, a great thought came to Pat.
The plan was this: They would take the corpse with them.
¶ No sober man would ever have thought of such a thing, but these men were just enough under the "infloonce" to be inventive. Now, the dead man was not very big, and he was dressed in his "best," just as the watchers were.
So they stood the corpse up, clapped a stove-pipe hat on his head and pulled the tile down over his face.
Then one on each side, they half-dragged and half-carried the dead man into the street and into the saloon.
They stood the dead man up against the bar, and he tipped at an angle, not unlike that often taken by convivial parties at the midnight hour.
"Two whiskies!" ordered Pat in a voice of authority.
"Make it three!" shouted Mike, who hadn't quite lost his ability to reason.
Three glasses and the bottle were dexterously shot out by the Dutch barkeeper.

Pat poured a big drink for himself, and Mike poured two—one for himself and one for the corpse.

Pat and Mike gulped the whisky in nervous haste. And just as they were setting down their glasses, a commotion was heard outside, and some one yelled, "Dog-fight!"

And by habit, urged on by their nervous condition, both Mike and Pat shot through the screen-door, leaving the corpse leaning up against the bar, the high hat pulled over his face. In his fine Sunday suit the corpse looked like a man who had been to a party.

"Vell!" said the Dutch bartender.

No response.

"Did n't you hear me already—I said, 'Vell'?"

Still no response.

"So you don't like der visky, eh? You ordered it, and now you von't drink it. And your two dirty Irish chums has run avay and left you to pay already. Vell? All right, you need n't drink, but you vill pay, or my name is not Vilhelm Schneider. You hear me?"

And still no response.

The Dutchman reached for his bung-starter. He took the mallet in one hand and then the other. "Pay up, or I'll schmash your high hat vorse around your ears than it is. Pay up, I said. Ein—svei—trei—!"

And the mallet descended with a thundering whack on the Saint Patrick's Day hat. The corpse toppled, slid, fell. And just as it hit the floor, Pat and Mike came back.

They rushed forward, and stooping in tearful solicitude, cried, "Are you hurt, Felix, are you hurt?" And then in wild wrath they shouted to the Dutchman, "Oh, Oh, Oh! you have killed our Felix!—you have killed him! you have killed him!"

"Vell," shouted back the Dutchman, "the sunovagun pulled a knife on me!"

Moral: Any man who hits another with a bung-starter always says it was in self-defense.

Good Night

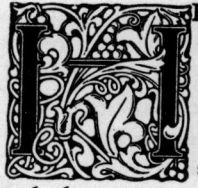ERE is a true story that I have pinched for the benefit of the Hivites, the Moabites, the Hittites and the Parasites: A nice young man in Scranton called on a nice young lady and spent the evening. When he arrived there was not a cloud in the sky, so he carried no umbrella and wore neither goloshes nor mackintosh. At ten o'clock when he arose to go, it was raining cats and dogs; the gutters o'erflowed and if it had been in Johnstown it could properly have been called a Johnstown flood ᛫᛫

"My, my, my!" said the nice young lady, "if you go out in all this storm you will catch your death a' cold!"

"I'm afraid I might!" was the trembling answer.

"Well, I'll tell you what—stay all night; you can have Tom's room, since he's at college. Yes, occupy Tom's room—excuse me a minute and I'll just run up and see if it's in order."

The young lady flew gracefully up the stairs to see that Tom's room was in order. In five minutes she came down to announce that Tom's room was in order but no Charles was in sight. Like old Clangingharp, he had passed out—no one knew where or how. But in a very few moments he appeared, very dripping and out of breath from running, a bundle in a newspaper under his arm.

"Why, Charles, where have you been?" was his greeting.

❡ "Been home after my night shirt," was the reply.

Acquired by Antiquarian

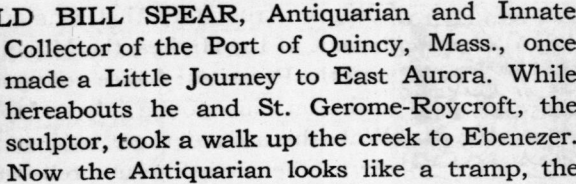OLD BILL SPEAR, Antiquarian and Innate Collector of the Port of Quincy, Mass., once made a Little Journey to East Aurora. While hereabouts he and St. Gerome-Roycroft, the sculptor, took a walk up the creek to Ebenezer. Now the Antiquarian looks like a tramp, the Sculptor dresses like one; and so when this lovely pair applied at a farm house for something to eat, the Good Woman threatened to turn the dog loose. But the Antiquarian flashed up a little silver, however, and after some bargaining the bread and milk were set forth on the kitchen table. As the Innate Collector munched, his eye spied, by the kitchen stove, a beautiful pair of tongs— tongs at least one hundred and fifty years old, all pounded out by hand with the loving marks of the hammer upon them. And the collector's soul yearned within him. But he said nothing. After the meal the travelers shook hands with the Good Woman and went their way.
When out in the road, the saint, who combines in his character something also of the Sinner, remarked, " Did you see those tongs? "
" Which tongs? " asked the Antiquarian.
" Why there was a pair of tongs in that house that would have gladdened your heart—made before the Revolution, I 'll bet. I would have pinched 'em for you but the old woman kept her eye on me all the time."
" Oh, just as much obliged—it really makes no difference. Don't walk so fast, please, I have that pair o' tongs in my trousers' leg and have to take short steps, as I can't bend my knee! "

Every Man to His Job

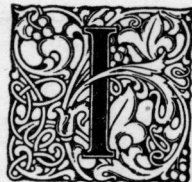T so happened one fine day that Uncle Billy Bushnell, Ali Baba and a hoodlum kid known as Odds Bodkins were laying a new sidewalk in front of the Shop. I was quite particular that the job should be done right. That is, I wanted sand under the walk instead of earth, and I wished the walk to line up properly with the roadway and adjacent walks. Therefore I went out and told " the boys " (all men are boys in East Aurora) to tamp the sand down well and make sure the grade was right. I also availed myself of the opportunity to rub a little good advice and admonition into them while I was at it, as to doing one's tasks well and working for the highest so as to receive the approbation of your Other Self.

As I told them how to do the job I took up a shovel and exemplified my meaning with a few object lessons.

" There! " said I, " d'ye see that? There! That 's the way to do it —see! " ∞ ∞

" Hain't you got nothing to do inside, sonny? " asked Uncle Billy in a tobacco chewer's voice. " 'Cause if you have you better climb right along and do it—we air layin' this 'ere walk, we air! " ∞ ∞

Then Ali Baba took it up, increasing the tone-volume, and disposing of the subject by saying, " That 's all right, John, you better go right along now and 'tend to your own business, an' we will tend to ourn! "

And all the time Odds Bodkins stood by giving me the smile audible ∞ ∞

Diplomatic relations were getting a trifle strained, and I resolved to break off communications at once. I made a hasty run for cover. That night I went out with a lantern and inspected the new sidewalk. It seemed exactly right, in fact the boys did a better job than I could have done. Possibly it is just as well not to bother and badger men who are doing their work, nor confuse them with too many instructions. Anyway, that is the opinion Uncle Billy Bushnell seems to hold.

Titanic Survivor

THE other day I met a man who was on the ill-fated *Titanic*. ⁋ When the boilers burst, and the great ship took her final plunge, my friend felt himself going down into the waters.

Being an experienced swimmer, he involuntarily knew enough not to inhale. He held his breath, but he did a deal of thinking. So down he went, but he knew, too, that soon he would be coming to the top, and it was only a question of being able to hold his breath long enough to escape immediate drowning.

When he felt himself coming to the surface a great joy possessed his soul. As his head came above the water, he reached out his arms, flattened himself on the surface of the wave as nearly as possible, and took in a great big breath.

Then he looked up at the stars, and gratitude filled his mind.
⁋ He was still alive; his senses were intact; he was able to think, to breathe, to realize, to see the shining stars. He felt as one who had been dead, like Lazarus, and returned to earth. He was alive!
⁋ But suddenly there came to him the thought that he could swim for a little while only. The water was icy cold, and he began to look around for deliverance.

About a hundred feet away he saw a floating spar, and it came to him that if he could reach that spar it would indeed be paradise. So he struck out for the spar. It seemed to be floating away from him as he swam, but with great effort he reached it, grasped it with his hands, drew himself up and then sat upon it.

When he felt that it was holding his weight he was relieved. Again he was filled with a great sense of gratitude. And as he sat on that spar, holding on with hands and feet, he looked up at the sky in thankfulness. He was alive; and to know that this spar was holding his weight filled his soul with joy.

But the wind was cold. His frame was chilled, and he knew that it was only a little time that he could hold on.

Just then he saw a boat pulling away at fifty or a hundred yards' distance.

He shouted, and called again and again.

And slowly the boat turned in his direction. It came nearer and nearer, and he knew that if he could once get in that boat and feel that the boat was under him, it would be paradise, indeed.

In a few minutes the wish came to pass, and he was in the boat. He was exhausted, too weak even to lift his hand. But the joy was exquisite: he was with human beings.

So they floated with the tide, and they pulled the oars. After a long time, a flush of pink came into the East, and they knew that day would soon come.

And then they saw a great gray-like form, with many lights, away off in the distance.

They prayed, they wept, they waited—there was nothing else to do.

The *Carpathia* came nearer, and my friend breathed a great prayer that he might be able to climb the side of the ship and lie on the deck. That was all he would ask—simply the privilege of lying flat on the deck, and knowing that the ship was beneath him.

And his prayer was answered. He climbed up the rope ladder and knelt on the deck in thankfulness.

But soon he realized that strength had gone out of him, and he begged that he be placed in the meanest room in the steerage, just so it was a bed and he was covered with blankets.

Some of the mothers and children in the crowded steerage made room for him, and when he was in the bunk, he said to himself, "Surely, this is paradise!" and he closed his eyes in gratitude.

But after an hour or two the crying of the children, the smell of cooking, the presence of so many people began to pall on him. He felt he must get away from this mob.

So he called to a petty officer and begged that he might have a cabin ৯• ৯•

And a bunk was found for him in a cabin.

And here in this cabin he was very happy, and he said, " This is paradise, indeed! " and he rested and thought, and tried to write out telegrams to send to his friends when he reached shore.

⁋ He slept soundly that night, but when he awoke in the morning he realized that the cabin was n't exactly right. And so he asked the steward who came to wait on him if there was not a berth somewhere in a cabin on the upper deck. And the steward said that every bunk was full, except, possibly, one berth in the captain's cabin.

And so my friend took pencil in hand and wrote a letter to the captain of the ship. And this is a copy of the letter:

" Dear Sir:

" This cabin in which I am located is right alongside of the engines. I hear the clank and clash of machinery all the night-time through. I am awakened by the noise and foul air, for this cabin is very small and illy ventilated.

" I understand that you have a vacant bunk in your cabin on the upper deck. Kind sir, please send word by bearer, allowing me to occupy this cabin with you, and I will ever be

" Your sincere friend."

No answer came from the captain.

But the moral of this true story is this. Nobody is ever satisfied with anything after he gets it.

"Days Are As Grass"

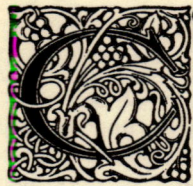COMING up from Hot Springs I met a smooth faced, jaunty little man. He was dressed like a youth, and at first sight, I took him for a young man, but another look convinced me he was sixty, at least. Whether he was born sixty years ago or not really makes no difference, he had lived sixty years. Evidently he had made money, but just how, it would have been indelicate to ask. His short, sharp sentences revealed an intimacy with the ringside and the race-track, and the diamond stud in his scarf told of gains I hoped not ill-gotten ❧ ❧

The little man had gone the pace, and now was paying the penalty ❧ ❧

This was sure, for sprinkled in his sporty talk were remarks about MacFadden, Rest Cure, No Breakfast, Health Foods and Mental Science. These things were new to him, but in them he had now a direct and personal interest. He asked me what I thought of Mary Baker Eddy; and at another time questioned me as to what the test was for uric acid; and then asked if I wore an Electric Belt ❧ ❧

On the second day of the journey we were in the smoking car together. I was reading and he was sitting looking out of the window in an abstracted way, his neat Fedora slightly tilted over one eye.

The train whizzed through a little village. I was conscious that my friend was looking attentively at something out on the landscape ❧ ❧

He turned to me and said, "There is another one of those graveyards!" ❧ ❧

One of the Elect

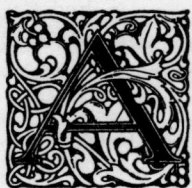
FROWSLED, towsled, greasy and shiny One, in battered dinky derby and tightly buttoned Prince Albert, blew into the Shop the other day and greeted me effusively. He was one of the Elect, he said, temporarily reduced and slightly disfigured by too much contact with a cold and cruel world. He glibly explained these things, although he needed not, for life writes its record on the face, and the record in this case was writ large.

Society was all wrong—the rich were getting richer, the poor poorer—merit was never considered, all things went by favoritism—my friend longed for the Ideal Life. I started to say something, but the Lubricated One shut me off with the gracious wave of a hand unmanicured. "Oh, never mind that," said he, "I anticipate you—you are going to say that the Ideal Life is an iridescent dream, and that all the East Aurora there is is the East Aurora that one carries in his own breast. Truth, truth, shining truth, but you see I brought my East Aurora with me—my heart is right—I believe in the Brotherhood of Man!"

"And you have no money?" I mused aloud, trying to gain time to formulate a Scheme.

"Money—money? Have I money? Why, Comrade, I am a feather! I trust I am in time for the quarterly dividend!"

"Yes," he continued, "and I never could have reached this Haven of Rest—I mean Work—were it not for Col. Smith of Cleveland—A. J.—great fellow, is n't he? He gave me a ticket here. Where 's Ali Baba? I think I 'll have him take me over to the Phalanstery and get a bit of something before I go to work. 'You can take no joy in your tasks if you are on half rations,' William Morris used to say, and wisely say. Ali Baba, he 's the man I want to see!"

"There he is," I exclaimed, "out there on that wagon with the spotted pony, and the load of mail bags." I walked to the door, arm in arm, with my new found friend, and as we reached the steps I pressed a big silver dollar in his palm and called, "Oh, Baba, one moment, please—here is a gentleman going to Buffalo. He wants to catch the four o'clock train!"
Baba reached out a big calloused hand, and gave the fellow a lift to the top of the mail bags.
"Hold on," called the Elect One, "just a second!"
He flashed out one of Dr. Pierce's Ladies' Calendars and the stub of a pencil and began to write most vigorously, just as Richard Mansfield writes a letter on the stage.
"It's the little accommodation, you know—I always keep track of these things—I'll return the amount in a day or two—so long!" ∞ ∞
We shook hands warmly.
"Give my regards to Col. Smith when you see him," I said, as the wagon moved away.
"That I will!" called the passenger astride of the mail bags—"that I will—he's our kind, is the Colonel—so long!" And he lifted the battered derby with a flourish that symboled sincerity, respect, good will, and told of the brotherhood of man. I now hear that the Frowsy One has given a not wholly complimentary lecture on "The Roycrofters as I Found them."

In the Wrong Pew

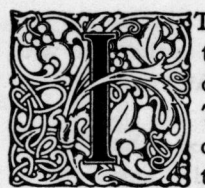IT is a well attested fact that all jokes can be traced back to six originals, evolved in Egypt during the Fourth Dynasty.

This being true, it is the right and moreover the duty of every man to improve on any old joke that he may find lying around loose. For instance, Bernard Shaw tells of a man from Oil City who was visiting a Cathedral in England, and the Oil City man, being affected by the history and atmosphere of the place, knelt in prayer. A zealous and watchful verger happened by and shaking the man by the shoulder said, " Look you, sir, none o' that! If I'd let one do that here, there would soon be folks praying all over the place."

⁋ And now comes that excellent man, Booker Washington, and tells of the new " High Church " that has recently been consecrated at Tuskegee. It seems old Aunt Chloe ventured in to vespers one evening, and hearing others respond, took a hand, too. " Thank God!—Blessed Jesus—Amen! " shouted Aunty, in fine falsetto.

The Chief Warden went softly over and whispered, " Madam, you will please keep order! " Aunty promised, but soon smote the air with a very loud, clear, " Blessed Jesus—dat's so! "

Then the Chief Warden decided on more heroic measures, and going over, said to Aunty, " Madam, what's the matter with you, anyway? " as preliminary to ejecting her.

" Oh, I'se got religion," shrieked Aunty. " Blessed Jesus! I'se got religion! "

" Madam," said the Warden sternly, " Madam, this is no place to get religion! "

Health and Play in North Woods

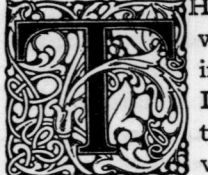THE Reverend W. H. H. Murray, known to the world as "Adirondack Murray," is the man who introduced the Adirondacks to America.

I can remember in the old geography that I used to study—dog-eared and tattered—there was a vast section of the West marked " Terra Incognita "—in other words, " Unknown Land."
Also, the Northern part of New York was included in a circle two hundred miles in diameter duly labeled, " The Adirondack Forest."
This was supposed to be an impenetrable jungle of trees, streams, logs, mountains, into which only the most hardy and hardened pioneers might trust themselves.
Adirondack Murray, however, entered this forest and gave it to the people, as Livingstone and Stanley opened up the Congo.

❡ Forty years ago there were no railroads in New York, North of Utica and Syracuse. Then there came a time when a little timorous right of way and a streak of rust was sent up North from Syracuse. It was a logging-railroad, and it was extended as fast as the timber was cut off. Gradually it extended until it reached the city of Watertown, but it took ten years to get there.

❡ Watertown itself was built around a sawmill that sent its products out to the West by water route, and down to Syracuse by rail
Adirondack Murray taught the world the beauty of the great out-of-doors. He preached the doctrine of fresh air and fresh water, and put us on good terms with the open. You read his Adirondack stories now and you can see the brook-trout with their yellow spots flash in the sun. Also, you can snuff the bacon frying in the pan. Man thrives, is happy, courageous, resourceful, only when he is on good terms with the world of Nature.

Then there comes a time when we perceive the beauties of Nature; then we move with Nature. When we realize the dictum of Emerson that "man is strong only as he takes hold of the forces of Nature," we have intellectually arrived.

There is no doubt at all about it that the evolution of the human race came when man's early ancestor climbed a tree to escape his enemies. Then, to break off a branch and use it as a club was as important a move as the invention of the Gatling Gun.

The animal that has a hoof has no evolution. The animal, however, that reaches up and seizes a branch and lifts its weight into safety, away from the wild beasts, is the one that evolves a brain.

⁋ The tree was man's first home; and men only who love trees, who realize their kinship to Nature and their obligation to the forest, are prosperous, happy and courageous.

Vast fortunes were made in cutting off the timber in the Adirondacks, but now a limit has been placed by the State, so that the Adirondacks are practically a playground for the people for all time. Here the waters run and sing their way joyously to the sea. Here the winds blow, but they do not blow in blizzards, nor attain the velocity that destroys, as they do where they gather a momentum across the prairies.

The land round about—if we may call it land—is simply a mass of bowlders. When you want to start a garden in Wanakena you have to go out somewhere and buy a few carloads of earth. Here the glacier performed her great terpsichorean act—bowlders on bowlders, rocks on rocks, unending geological specimens.

And yet in the crevices and cracks of the rocks the forest-trees found a footing and have lifted their heads high in the air, and bade defiance to the storm. Pine, spruce, elm, oak, ash, hickory, chestnut, hazel—but most of all, silver birch—are here on every hand ❧ ❧

No such thing as miasma is known here. Hay-fever, asthma, can be found by reading about them in the encyclopedias.

It is a marvel to me that people go South for recreation and to build up overtaxed nerves, or to find rest for tired brain, when the bracing atmosphere of the North Woods invites.

In the Southland, beautiful and lovely though it be, there is something lacking. And that one thing that is lacking is what the chemists call " The Oxygen Content."

Now, say within the last two years, cunning science has evolved a plan, sure, absolutely without fail, by which a cubic foot of air can be analyzed and its oxygen content proved. It is exactly the same with water.

The water that flows down past New York City contains an oxygen content of, say, sixty per cent, counting one hundred as the pure article. When we get to fifty per cent, water putrefies, decays and becomes absolute poison. No one now ever thinks of drinking water from the Hudson River. The towns, the villages, the cities, pour their sewage into it from Albany to the Sea. The bottom of the Hudson is coated with a seething, bubbling mass of septic death and dissolution.

Water that runs joyfully over the rocks, moving rapidly, purifies itself as it goes. Only water that is in motion contains a high degree of oxygen content.

Business is a game, and we are all in it. It requires a terrific, unending energy to succeed. But the men who do big things are those who occasionally get away from the mass and find rest and recreation where the winds blow and the soothing waters flow; where the odor of the pines is perpetual, and where Nature supplies everything in the way of health and healing that tired bodies demand.

Farming and Railroading

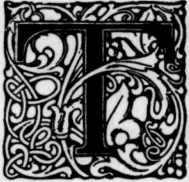HE most important economic interest in the world is agriculture.
Agriculture it is that supplies us the materials with which we are fed and clothed. The very existence of the race turns on the ability of the farmer to produce food.
The next thing in importance is transportation.
This must be so, because it is transportation that takes the thing from the farmer and delivers it at your door.
The article must first be produced; then it must be transported from where it is plentiful to where it is needed.
Distance between food and man is death.
The railroads annihilate distance and make it as though it were naught ∾ ∾
The railroads have but one thing to sell, and that is transportation. They deal in the second most valuable thing in the world. So let this proposition stand: In point of importance farming comes first, and second comes transportation.
The third greatest interest is distribution, or the business of storekeeping. It is storekeeping that builds the cities.
The cities do not produce food and clothing. They store and distribute the necessities of life to the people.
A city is a continuous fair, a big booth, where the people come to buy the things they need. And the railroads are the caravans that carry the things in and out.
Closely associated with storekeeping is manufacture, which takes raw materials and puts these materials together in useful form, so that they can be transported and used by mankind. Manufacturing is assembling.
But always you will note that the value of a thing turns upon its being in a certain place at a certain time.

Food a mile from human bodies has no value, save as it is known that this mile can be bridged. The cost of bridging the mile is added to the cost of the food, and this is the basis of its value, plus the cost of distribution.

The one and only service that a railroad undertakes to supply is to bridge distance.

The unit which the railroad sells is the mile-haul. It carries a man a mile for two cents. It transports a ton of freight a mile for the same sum, or less.

The principal buyers of transportation are the farmers, the storekeepers and the manufacturers.

The railroads are the sellers.

Naturally, questions occasionally arise between buyer and seller as to the proper price for this mile-haul unit.

To settle these questions the Federal Government has provided a special Court, called, " The Interstate Commerce Commission."

And every State has its Railroad Commissioners who look after the interests of shippers.

The judges in the Interstate Commerce Commission are selected and named by the President of the United States, on account of their special fitness by experience and mentality to fill the position ∾ ∾

The Interstate Commerce Commission has a right to enter its protest against any act, rule or rate of the railroads, where it deems the interests of shippers are threatened.

It is the duty of the Interstate Commerce Commission to hear all complaints of shippers, and if rates are too high, the Commission is empowered to say what the legal rate shall be.

The Interstate Commerce Law provides that, before a rate can be advanced, the new or proposed Tariff must be filed with the Commission, and also the change must be advertised in certain specified ways.

For over two years the entire railroad interests of the country have maintained that freight rates were too low to meet safely the expenses and up-keep of the property.

The question has been brought before the country at great length and with many facts and figures. The railroads have issued arguments and statistics, fully setting forth their position.

In April, Nineteen Hundred Ten, twenty-four railroads of the Middle West issued notices of an advance in rates, and duly filed their new tariff-sheets with the Interstate Commerce Commission ❧ ❧

No objection was raised by the Commission, and the rates were to go into effect on June First.

On May Thirty-first, six hours before the new rates were to go into execution, the telegraph flashed the news that a United States Judge at Hannibal, Missouri, had issued an ex-parte injunction restraining the railroads from carrying out their new tariff, on the charge that they were guilty of "conspiracy" and had combined in violation of the Sherman Act.

This action of the Attorney-General was in the form of a war measure, a coup d' état. He had sprung a lawyer's "surprise," and had done it on the advice, or at least with the permission, of the President of the United States. Practically, the President had issued the injunction, not the obscure party in Hannibal, Missouri.

⁋ The Sherman Act is now on trial for its life before the Supreme Court of the United States. Chief Justice Fuller, appreciating the gravity of this situation, hesitated about passing on it, except with a full bench, and until the people could be heard. The Sherman Act was passed twenty years ago and just what it means has never been defined or expressed.

But the President, seizing this tottering statute, hurled it at the second greatest economic and industrial interest in the country.

⁋ To accuse the railroads of this fair country of conscious and deliberate crime is not only an insult to every railroad man, but is also an insult to the intelligence of our time. All railroad-

managers know that they can only prosper as the people prosper who live along their lines.
When you accuse a man of crime you assail his credit.
Credit is the very lifeblood of Commerce; and President Taft and Attorney-General Wickersham have injured the commercial fabric of this country, at home and abroad, to the extent of millions of dollars.
It is a most serious thing when your own Government turns upon you. Especially is it a serious thing when the Chief Executive of the Government usurps the functions of the judiciary and steps over a court which he himself has provided.
I am a farmer and a manufacturer; consequently, I am a shipper. And as such, with the big majority of shippers, I am willing to pay for my mile-haul what the service is worth.
With the advancing trend of prices, the cost of living to a railroad is in the same proportion that it is to the individual.
The railroads have to meet this advance. They have all advanced wages, and they have met the upward tendency of materials without cutting down their proposed improvements. The Pennsylvania's depot and subways in New York, costing three hundred million dollars and more; the Grand Central Station, costing one hundred million; the Bergen Open Cut of the Erie; the palatial Northwestern depot in Chicago; the vast expenditures by the Santa Fé for new stations and double-tracking, only symbol the activity of most of our railroads.
The railroads have no surplus cash—they are all borrowers. Their capital is more than active, and their credit is constantly strained. Last month they borrowed two hundred million dollars in France, to put into improvements here in America. These improvements are for the people—all the people.
The railroads are the greatest consumers of manufactured goods and the greatest employers of labor in America.
When the railroads prosper, we all prosper.

When the railroads cease to expand, and enthusiasm and enterprise are chilled and checked by Government baiting, an injury upon all the people, awful in extent, is invoked which may take years to repair.

Our Government is the people. And the people of this country are not at war with the railroads.

The people own the railroads, make the railroads, work for the railroads, use the railroads.

When a few lawyers at Washington, who accidentally hold transient official positions, by their acts make it appear that the Government is at war with the railroads, or the railroads are at war with the people, they misrepresent us and do us all great harm.

¶ Are we living under the rule of the shyster?

It really looks so.

In hard times thousands of men wander through the city streets, tired and wan, looking for work.

In Nineteen Hundred Seven there was a procession of unemployed in London ten miles long. At the same time the bread-line formed in New York at midnight, and soup-houses were established to ward off dire starvation.

The Government was importuned to lend its assistance that work might be provided, and further panic averted.

Always in times of stress a vast number of people look to the Government for relief. But what shall we say of a Government which makes war on those who are now giving work to millions, and thereby assure us peace and prosperity!

If the men in charge of our Government insist on being Business-Baiters, the bread-line will again form; the hoarse roar of the mob, demanding work or bread, will again be heard; and women and children will be pushed defenseless into the storm.

Business in this country gives work and wage to every one who wants to work. Let business alone!

The problem in good times is to get men to do the work. There then is no problem of the unemployed, because there are no unemployed. The country is safe only when its people are busy. The busy man is the happy man.

Three days after the injunction was issued, a conference was held at the White House between President Taft and his Cabinet, and Ripley of the Santa Fé, Delano of the Wabash, and Winchell of the 'Frisco. The railroad men stated their case in terms not to be misunderstood, a thing they should have been allowed to do before that injunction was issued.

The result was that President Taft said, " If you will withdraw your tariffs, I'll withdraw my injunction—this until my new proposed railroad bill is passed."

The railroad men were absolutely secure in their legal rights, yet they temporarily agreed to this proposition.

President Taft then explained that this was all he issued the injunction for, and " the intents of the action were fully met," thus claiming a victory where no victory was scored.

What the President does not know about railroading would fill a large book. The man is a judge, not an economist, and his entire tendency is to listen to recitals of woe and to sit in judgment. Note his sophomorish cracks out of the box when talking of Post-Office affairs last December!

But just grant that his reasons in this matter were right, here is what he did: He charged the managers of twenty-four railroads with criminal acts " in conspiring to defraud, injure and wrong," and on these charges of criminal acts and intents the injunction was issued, preventing the railroads from doing a thing which they had a perfectly legal right to do, until such a time as Taft could have a law passed extending the scope of the Interstate Commerce Commission. That is, Taft demands obedience to a law which he has merely suggested, and in order to bring about this obedience he assails the character and credit of men engaged in a great and useful undertaking.

It was like arresting a man for murder in order to keep him from going to the theater, and then smiling it off as "one on him." Is it such a small matter to accuse men of crime and hold them up in scorn before the world! Taft reveals the lawyer mind, making charges which can not be sustained, with a dumb, dull indifference to human needs and human suffering. He comes demanding obedience to law, and then resorts to illegal methods to secure an advantage. Commercial distress is nothing, so long as you can score a point in law. Once, the ruler took your life; now, he just destroys your business and makes little-pig sausages of your good name, and smiles. This is what you call fiddling while Rome burns, done up to date.

The Butterflies

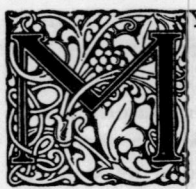MY little girl, 'leven years old going on twelve, has been giving me a few lessons in lepidopterology, which she tells me, and I have no reason to doubt her, for she has never deceived me in anything, is the science of butterflies. I know lots of educated men, but only about one out of a hundred ever heard of lepidoptera. I have always known a little about butterflies but I never imagined they were lepidoptera until last week. I asked the best educated man in East Aurora, the Baptist preacher, if he was a lepidopterologist, and he thought I was calling him bad names.

Among the things my little science teacher has taught me are these: There are more than ten thousand separate and distinct species of butterflies. The life of a butterfly is from three days to three months, but there is one species that migrates, like birds, and this one may live three years. No two butterflies of the same species are exactly alike, and the same species vary much in size. On account of the extremely fragile quality of its body a butterfly usually lives but a few days. A rain-storm always kills many, and collectors in order to get perfect specimens often prefer to breed them ⁂ ⁂

Moths and butterflies are very different. Moths fly at night and butterflies in the daytime. The reason moths fly at night is so to escape the birds—it is a habit. And the reason the whip-poor-will and some other birds fly at night is so to catch the moths—this is a habit, too.

The male butterfly is much more brilliant in color than the female, but the female is much larger. She makes a nest and lays her eggs. These eggs do not hatch out butterflies—bless your soul! They hatch caterpillars. ❡ The caterpillar is a worm. It can not fly; it can not run—it just can crawl. It has lots of legs, it has horns and feelers which are called antennæ, and on the ends of the antennæ sometimes are eyes.

Antennæ are in place of eyes, so to keep from running into things. When Nature got where she could make a good eye she let up on antennæ. The eye is a mirror that reflects things and at the back of the mirror is a telephone to the brain with little nerves for wires, so not only does the eye see but it telephones to the brain what it sees, so you always know whether to run or stay. It took a long time for Nature to make an eye—it was a wonderful invention and God and Gabriel both turned somersaults and walked on their hands when they found the scheme would work. When the caterpillar has been a worm as long as it wants to—and finds out there is nothing in it—it wraps itself in a leaf and makes for itself a cocoon. The silkworm is very particular, so it makes its cocoon of silk instead of calico. It can make silk so well and so much silk, that man, who is a grafter, just steals this silk and fools the worm into making more silk, just as we steal the honey the bee makes, and also as we take advantage of the love of a cow for her calf and steal the milk. Man is the most wonderful grafter of all the works of God. All man gives the silkworm in return for silk is its board. He gives it mulberry leaves and it eats and eats and eats, and spins and spins and spins, making a cocoon, so it can wind itself in the silk and turn into a beautiful moth. But man keeps stealing the silk and fooling the silkworm and after a while it gets discouraged and dies while yet a worm without even having had the fun of being a moth.

Some butterflies are pure white, and there is one kind that is coal black. In this, butterflies differ from men, who are all a kind of slatey gray.

There are some butterflies that are so rare, they are worth a hundred dollars a piece; and some whole species have died out and become extinct within thirty-five years.

Men go from Washington to Borneo just to get butterflies.

Linnæus traveled once over three thousand miles to catch a butterfly ∽ ∽

The most brilliant and beautiful butterflies are brilliant and beautiful only on one side of their wings. The Morpho-cypris butterfly, is a dazzling, brilliant blue, all lined off with tiny lines of gold on one side, and on the other side it is a plain dull dun, a kind of gray-brown. This is so it can fall on the ground when its enemies get after it and never be seen, or it can flatten out on a tree trunk so you would never find it. Then there is the owl butterfly that is very beautiful on one side, and on the other is brown with two black spots that look like the eyes of an owl. When pursued it just stops, turns itself upside down, and there you see the horns and the eyes of an owl, and this often scares the birds half to death.

The most brilliant butterflies are the plainest when their wings are closed and they are in repose. A really wondrous butterfly only flashes in the sunlight and for those it loves, and in this it is like a genius. Most people declare a genius is nothing but a grub. A genius is a man who is plain brown like the earth or a tree-trunk, but he is n't brown all the time or to everybody.

HERE ENDETH "SHORT STORIES AND INDEX," BEING VOLUME FOURTEEN OF THE SELECTED WRITINGS OF ELBERT HUBBARD, GATHERED TOGETHER, PRINTED AND BOUND AS A MEMORIAL TO THEIR BELOVED FOUNDER BY THE ROYCROFTERS AT THEIR SHOPS, WHICH ARE IN EAST AURORA, NEW YORK. MCMXXVIII

INDEX

Abbot, the, X, 67.
Abdul Baha, the servant of God, X, 321; message of, X, 321; in America, X, 326; made a little journey to the International Harvester Company, X, 327; a non-resistant, X, 328; personality of, X, 329; mental attitude of, X, 330.
Abel, XIII, 369.
Abhorrence, XIII, 369.
Ability, man of, VIII, 156; pay envelope and, VIII, 161.
Abnegation, XIII, 370.
Abnormal, XIII, 369.
Abode, XIII, 369.
Abolition, Missouri battleground of idea of, II, 455.
Aborigine, XIII, 370.
About right thinking, VI, 253.
Above the rabble, VII, 233.
Abraham, IX, 113.
Abrasives, II, 203.
Abyss, XIII, 370.
Academic, V, 97; XIII, 369.
Academic mannikins, IV, 97.
Academician, V, 280; and the idealist, V, 293.
Academy of Immortals, IX, 406.
Accidents, utilization of, II, 204; avoidable, IX, 269.
Acheson, Edward G., II, 204; and Edison, II, 206; his patent bought by Westinghouse, II, 209; use of natural gas for making pottery was patent of, II, 209; two great inventions of, II, 211.
Achievement, Emerson on, I, 384; a notable, XIV, 136.
Ackerman, President, VII, 128.
Acquaintance, XIII, 370.
Acquired by antiquarian, XIV, 284.
Act, XIII, 370.
Acting is a most exacting business, XIV, 175.
Actor, art of the, XIV, 157.
Actors, most hazardous life insurance risk, VII, 318; brotherhood among, VII, 320.

Adams, William T., known as "Oliver Optic," II, 159.
Adaptability, II, 27.
Ad-Clubs and salesmanship, VIII, 194; of America, VIII, 322.
Addams, Jane, IX, 31.
Addison and Steele pamphleteers, I, 23; on pin money, I, 448.
Adieu, XIII, 370.
Adios, V, 34.
Ad-Man, I, 195.
Ad-Men, message to, I, 195.
Admiration, XIII, 371.
Admission, XIII, 370.
Adultery, VI, 389.
Advantages and disadvantages, VI, 215.
Adversity, the school of, II, 349.
Advertise, word, traces to the Latin *adverto*, VIII, 385.
Advertiser, a hypnotic, II, 324.
Advertisement, the first, VIII, 42; best, VIII, 385.
Advertisements, fake, I, 189; in *The Menace*, I, 273; medical, IV, 406; how to write, VIII, 102; recipe for good, VIII, 102; some classic, VIII, 104; selling power of, VIII, 138; survival value of, IX, 104.
Advertising, I, 195, 334; IV, 395, 414, 447; VII, 400; VIII, 83, 131, 214; XII, 301; XIII, 369; and salesmanship twin sisters, I, 195; legislative, VIII, 42; the art of, VIII, 101, 105; two reasons for, VIII, 101; all literature is, VIII, 102; a science, VIII, 102; truthful, VIII, 103; of ancient lineage, VIII, 104; reputation built on, VIII, 104; theme of, VIII, 105; value of allusion in, VIII, 106; Bellamy's idea, VIII, 111; Edward Bellamy on, VIII, 131; the science of, VIII, 133; Bunting's book on, VIII, 137; negative, VIII, 170; and auto industry, VIII, 171; wrong tactics in, VIII, 171; old methods of, VIII, 173; dishonest, VIII, 217; tricky, VIII, 217; individuality

i

in, VIII, 324; Elbert Hubbard's ads mark epoch in, in America, VIII, 383; all literature is, XII, 398; the new science of, XIV, 188.
Advertising clubs, IV, 330; of the world, VIII, 214; influence of, VIII, 215.
Advertising copy, VIII, 385; example of, VIII, 107.
Advertising ethics, VIII, 322.
Advertising illustrations, X, 383.
Advertising Man, VIII, 106.
Advice, IV, 468; XIII, 301; to children, X, 238.
Aeronaut, XIII, 369.
Aeroplane, lesson from the, I, 370.
Affinities, III, 225.
Affinity, IV, 28.
Afoot and light-hearted I take to the open road, XII, 147.
Afterward, XIII, 371.
Agamogenesis, I, 309.
Age and achievement, VI, 282.
Agent for the principal, IV, 60.
Agitators, revolutionary, VII, 344.
Agnosticism, bishop of, IX, 335.
Agonies, XII, 157.
Agricultural colleges, I, 412.
Agricultural implements, America leads the world, I, 65.
Agricultural school, I, 188.
Agricultural school instead of dreadnoughts, I, 318.
Agriculture, VIII, 183; XII, 103, 141; basis of world powers, I, 429; VII, 181; Lincoln on, XII, 141.
Agriculturist, XIII, 371.
Agrippina, VI, 297.
Aid, mutual, XIII, 334.
Aims, high, IV, 396.
Air, fresh, VI, 391.
Akron, X, 385.
Alaska, VII, 121; purchase of, VII, 122; the gateway to, VII, 123; copper mines of, VII, 124; need of, IX, 378.
Albany, XIII, 372.
Albert Memorial, VII, 158.
Albertson, Rev. Dr. C. C., IX, 109.
Alcohol, IV, 40.
Alexander the Great, IX, 347.
Alexander of Servia, VII, 265.
Alexander, William C., President Equitable Life Assurance Company, VIII, 161.

Alfalfa, VII, 185; in praise of, VII, 186.
Ali Baba, I, 419; XIII, 261; a collector, VI, 146; hats of, VI, 148; how, got his name, XIII, 266; and his wheelbarrow, XIII, 275; and Rowan, XIII, 297; grumbles, XIII, 300; ideal of, XIII, 304; and Tolstoy, XIII, 304; his respect for the preacher's profession, XIII, 307.
Alienation arose from religious mania, V, 228.
Allen, Floyd, IV, 260.
Allen Grant, on marriage and divorce, IX, 89.
Allen, Sidna, IV, 260.
Alleviation from pain, secret of, IX, 392.
All love we know is man's love, IX, 102.
All stars, X, 18.
Almsgiving, the evil of, I, 359.
Altruism, a form of, VI, 318.
Ambitions, new, I, 367.
America, rich resources of, I, 67; wealth of, I, 68; nation of builders, I, 196; fate of, a prophecy, I, 217; problem of, I, 364; day of, I, 367; duty of, I, 367; the abundance of, I, 368; concerning the early discoverers of, II, 53; true Judaic Zion, IV, 201; and Japan, V, 215; and China, VI, 366; mineral wealth of, VII, 183; ancient civilization of, VII, 193; most needed reform of, VIII, 204; potential riches of, VIII, 205; first locomotive of, VIII, 325; hallowed ark of human life, XII, 97; citizen of, I, 38.
American Academy of Immortals, XIII, 229.
American Bible, an, XII.
American business philosophy, the, VIII, 15.
American businessman, new model of, II, 340.
American clothes, I, 368.
American Commonwealth, Bryce's, IV, 167; V, 298.
American farm machinery, the largest market for, I, 65.
American fashions, IX, 274.
American Federation of Labor, I, 119.
American inventive genius, I, 65.
American leadership, I, 367.
American Legion of Honor, IX, 401

American-made farm-machinery, I, 69.
American manufacturers, inventive genius of, I, 369.
American pamphleteers, I, 24.
American Parthenon, IX, 402.
American philosophy, an, VI, 43; VIII, 19; XII, 399; the, founded on science of economics, VI, 43.
American plan, XIII, 371.
American Renaissance, VII, 276.
American Tinplate Company, X, 341.
American wars and the Du Ponts, II, 240
American women, I, 368.
American writers, recognition of, by England, V, 141.
Americanitis, IX, 88.
Americans are the best shod people on earth, II, 183; tireless energy of, I, 37.
Americus Sum, I, 37.
Amphibian, man an, IV, 81.
Amusement a panacea, VIII, 304.
Anak, a son of, V, 258.
Analysis, habit of, IX, 216.
Anamosa Reformatory, warden of the, IV, 214.
Ananias, XIII, 371.
Ananias Club, XIV, 113.
Ananias Dare, XIV, 16.
Anarchist, I, 52, 70; VI, 131; XIII, 370; Jesus an, VI, 131.
Anarchist community, the, IV, 148.
Anarchistic friends, our, V, 173.
Anarchists and law, V, 173.
Anarchy and free-speech, V, 171.
Ancestor-worship, XIII, 330.
Ancient maxim, an, IX, 213.
Anderson, Judge Albert B., and the Dynamiters, IX, 366.
Anderson, Professor, of Yale, IV, 104.
Angels, IX, 232.
Anger, XIII, 371.
Anglified Americanese, VI, 158.
Anhydrous ammonia, VIII, 181.
Animals, domestication of, IV, 188; IX, 229.
Animation, the businessman's raw stock, I, 347.
Ann Arbor, perfect girl of, IX, 123.
Annas, XI, 68, 71.
Annexation bugaboo, XIV, 181.
Annihilation, V, 227.

Ansted, E. W., X, 246; birthplace of, X, 249.
Anteny over, XIV, 28.
Anthony, Susan B., X, 346; and Doctor Collyer's photograph, X, 347.
Anthropology, Andrew Lang on, V, 92.
Anti-cleric, I, 358.
Antioch College, V, 266; and Peter Cooper, V, 272; tradition of, V, 275.
Antique Tale, an, X, 45.
Anti-trust laws criticized, II, 359.
Anvil Chorus, the, IV, 44.
A. P. A., I, 272.
Aphorism, a popular, V, 209.
Apis mellifica, IX, 140.
Apocrypha, the, III, 459.
Apocryphal, III, 458.
Apologia, I, 252.
Apoplexy, X, 139.
Apostle, XIII, 372.
Apostolic succession, V, 199.
Apparition, a fearful, IV, 316; IX, 411.
Appendenda, VI, 95.
Appendenda vermiformis, VI, 95.
Appendicitis, VI, 95; a fashionable complaint IX, 285.
Appian Way, VII, 395; VIII, 390.
Appius Claudius and the making of the Appian Way, VIII, 390.
Apple country, VII, 97.
Apples, VII, 315.
Apprentice system and Stetson, II, 439.
Aquadag, II, 214
Arcadia, VI, 56.
Arch-skeptic, the, V, 160.
Are you lovable, IX, 284.
Aristocrat, an, VI, 131.
Aristocratical landholders, XII, 120.
Aristophanes and Juvenal, spirit of, IX, 395.
Aristotle, on trees, II, 150; the teacher, IV, 15; and the horse, VI, 17; and Leonardo, horse-lovers, VI, 17; and Alexander the Great, IX, 347; world's first naturalist, X, 356; IV, 255.
Arkansas, VII, 83; and Hot Springs, VII, 83; part of the Louisiana Purchase, VII, 86.
Arliss, George, as the prodigal son, I, 326; and Freddie Welsh, X, 210.
Armies, XII, 371; and navies, I, 318.

Armistices, IV, 396.
Armour, Philip D., II, 216.
Armstrong insurance law, VI, 222.
Army, XIII, 370; a medieval appendenda vermiformis, VIII, 242.
Arnold of Rugby, I, 409.
Arson, XIII, 369.
Art, I, 225; II, 49; IV, 395; V, 142; VIII, 232; XII, 385; XII, 372; egotism soul of, III, 449; second commandment death of, III, 465; suggestive, IV, 122; the price of, IV, 327; nude in, IV, 329; and the camera, V, 196; and impudence, IV, 350; province of, VI, 212; is symbolistic, VI, 51; power in, VI, 53; that wins, VI, 212; sanity in, VI, 213; true test of, IX, 42; Millais criticized for commercializing, X, 380; beautiful, is always a collaboration, XIII, 370; and music, XIV, 104; standard of, in Athens, XIV, 268.
Art of Ad, the, VIII, 401.
Art-collector, XIII, 372.
Artesian Wells, IX, 295.
Arts and crafts as a prophylactic agent, X, 137.
Arthur, King, I, 323.
Artificial life, XI, 385.
Artist, I, 458; VI, 289, 378; religion of the, VI, 378.
Artistic conscience, IV, 112.
Artistic jealousy, I, 107.
Artistic standards, XIII, 361.
Artistic temperament, I, 471; IV, 360; improvidence and the, I, 474; expression of undisciplined mind, I, 475; Satan's, IV, 43.
Aryan race, II, 47.
Asbestos, XIII, 369.
Ascetic, VIII, 323.
Asceticism, IV, 180; IX, 315.
Ashley Tavern in Bloomington, XIV, 30.
Aspasia, X, 343.
Asquith, H. H., and Irish Home Rule, I, 231.
Assassins, IX, 130; secret order of, IX, 130.
Assembly, XIII, 371.
Assets of a country, I, 333.
Astor, John Jacob, IX, 17.
Astuteness, I, 77; VI, 245.
Asylum for the insane, X, 57.
Asylums and madhouses, I, 154; and restraint, X, 58; graded wards, X, 58.
Atheism, calumny of, XII, 104; Emerson on, XII, 220.
Atheist, XIII, 372.
Athens, XIII, 372; and slavery, XIII, 359; art and beauty of, XIII, 360.
Athlete, professional, VI, 333.
Athlete Mex, XIII, 372.
Atlee, Doctor Washington L., X, 361.
Atonement, XIII, 372.
Attention, XIII, 373.
Audience, attitude to, VIII, 302; an, is a woman, X, 127.
Audiences, make-up of, VIII, 315.
Augustus, the Age of, VII, 274.
Aunt Hannah and Uncle Elihu, X, 235.
Aura, the idea of the, IX, 343.
Austin, VII, 400.
Authority, entrenched, V, 168; watches symbol of, VIII, 225; clothed in a little brief, XIII, 300.
Auto, and good roads, I, 385; the Age of the, VII, 74; a great move in behalf of temperance, VII, 79; makes for sanity, VII, 80; effect of, on trade, VII, 81.
Auto industry and advertising, VIII, 171; Mexican athlete in, VIII, 172.
Autobiography, XIII, 371; some, XII, 30.
Automobile, influence of the, VII, 78; evolution of the, VIII, 265.
Automobile accidents, IX, 266.
Automobile business, I, 393.
Automobile clubs and legislation, VII, 78.
Automobile extravagance, VIII, 395.
Automobile waste, XIV, 213.
Automobiles, demand for, VIII, 173.
Average man, the, IV, 231.
Avocation, VI, 334.
Aztecs, I, 73.
Bab, X, 323.
Babies, IX, 72; X, 395; in flats, VII, 57.
Babson, Roger, X, 282; tables of, X, 286; service, X, 285.
Baby, object of admiration, V, 335.
Baby Bonds, first railroad, VIII, 80.
Baby farm, IX, 245.
Babyhood, IV, 315.
Bacchanalian dance, old, XIV, 88.
Bach, Sebastian, and organ music, II, 69.
Bachelors, hypocritical, IX, 188; a word about, IX, 188.

Back, XIII, 373.
Back to the land, VI, 36.
Back to nature, VI, 217.
Bacteria in milk, IV, 243.
Baedeker, VII, 191.
Bagot, Charles, signer of agreement with Canada, I, 160.
Bahais, X, 321.
Baha'u'llah, X, 323.
Baird-North Company, XIV, 94.
Baird-North workers, XIV, 99.
Balivorax, XIII, 373.
Ballot, the power of the, I, 357; smokeless and non-explosive, I, 357.
Balloon, up in a, VII, 236.
Bal-masque, XIII, 373.
Baltimore restaurant, VIII, 347; patrons of the, VIII, 348.
Bank of futurity, I, 76.
Bank president, II, 265.
Banker, business of a, II, 269; modern, II, 269; a progressive, II, 275.
Bankers, I, 65; VIII, 363; X, 101; Ford and, II, 86; and farmers, IV, 365.
Banking, a necessity in economics, I, 334; a symbol of conservatism, II, 266; confidence and, II, 277.
Baptism, XIII, 374; rites of, I, 399; the, of blood, III, 317.
Baptist mathematics, I, 402.
Bar, IV, 69; of justice, IV, 70.
Barb-wire fences and hell, X, 46.
Bard, XIII, 374.
Barn, a modern, VI, 84.
Barn-storming tour, a, VII, 165.
Barns, hygienic, VI, 84.
Barnum, P. T., on humbug, I, 223.
Barr, Marquis, warden of Anamosa Reformatory, IV, 214.
Barretry, IV, 71.
Barrett, Elizabeth, IV, 321.
Barristers, IV, 70; and bribes, IV, 70.
Barron, Clarence, W., X, 216.
Barroom, IV, 69.
Barrowclough, S. L., of Winnipeg Band, II, 120.
Bartenders, V, 374.
Bartlett, Paul, VI, 327.
Barton, Clara, X, 345; a symposium, V, 325; a good psychologist, V, 328; and the clergy, V, 331; childhood of, V, 334; girlhood of, V, 335; her book, V, 335; the early childhood of, V, 335; is an organizer, a systematizer, V, 337; Civil War activities of, V, 337-340; and the International Red Cross of Geneva, V, 340; and the Franco-Prussian War, V, 341; on the battlefield in Europe, V, 342; pleads for the Red Cross, V, 343; first president of the American National Red Cross Society, V, 344; honors to, V, 345; the, Memorial, V, 345; in Cuba, V, 347; at San Juan Hill, V, 347; endurance of, V, 347; her experience in the Spanish-American war, V, 349; in Europe, V, 353; appreciated by the European powers, V, 355; simple needs of, V, 355; incidents in the life of, V, 356; being dead yet lived, V, 358; at her home in Glen Echo, V, 360; tells her most terrible experience, V, 360; tells her most beautiful experience, V, 361-362; her business methods, V, 362; place of, in history, V, 367.
Baseball, indoor, IV, 87; Sunday, IV, 45.
Basic elements of truth, V, 305.
Bass viol, IX, 300.
Bastard, XIII, 373.
Bastile of the brain, IV, 267.
Bath-Sheba, IX, 397.
Batten Agency, George, XIV, 190.
Battle Creek, II, 321.
Battle-cry of 1776, I, 347.
Bean, XIII, 373.
Bearer of glad tidings, X, 30.
Bear dump, the, VII, 39.
Bears, XIII, 175; are like folks, XIII, 175.
Beatitude, XIII, 373.
Beau Brummel, VI, 146.
Beautiful back yards, VII, 138.
Beauty, II, 391; earth and, in *Song of Songs*, III, 460; body and soul, VI, 331; and goodness, VI, 332; of form, VI, 334.
Beavers, the, VII, 32.
Beck, Martin, XIII, 243.
Bedford, Edward Thomas, II, 371, 373; birthplace of, II, 373.
Bee, life of the, VII, 303; IX, 143-144; scouts, IX, 142.
Beecham habit, VI, 330.
Beecher, Henry Ward, " Bibles " of

II, 450; old John Brown and, II, 450.
Beer garden, I, 135.
Bees, VII, 293; IX, 141; XII, 379; and civilization, IX, 141; and Jews alike, IX, 142.
Bee's wax, mystery of, IX, 144.
Beet sugar factories in Michigan, VIII, 291.
Beggar, XIII, 373; paternalism breeds the, I, 286.
Beggar woman, Besant and the, XIII, 234.
Beggars, Italian, VII, 152.
Belgrade, VII, 261.
Belief, a legacy, IX, 110.
Beliefs, Ingersoll on, XII, 166.
Bell, Alexander Graham, VII, 75; inventor of the telephone, II, 301; honors to, II, 311.
Bell system, the, II, 313; ambition of the, II, 315.
Bell Telephone Company, beginning of the, II, 307; first owners of the, II, 308; Western Union suit against the, II, 308; and Western Union agreement, II, 309.
Bells, origin of, VIII, 225.
Ben Greet, V, 379.
Ben Greet Players, V, 379.
Beneficence, X, 30.
Benefit, futile efforts to, XIII, 326.
Benefits, the law of, XII, 242.
Benjamin, the moon-faced, IX, 82.
Bennett, James Gordon, I, 113.
Bennett, Richard, in *Damaged Goods*, I, 326.
Benzine-buggy craze, VII, 77.
Bergen Cut, II, 136.
Berkmann, V, 172.
Bernhardt, Sara, X, 18.
Besant, Sir Walter, XIII, 233; and the beggar, XIII, 233.
Bessemer Process, VIII, 89.
Best, doing our, V, 122.
Best man, VI, 167.
Best society, IV, 468.
Bethel Orphans' Home, I, 338.
Better part, the, VI, 131.
Better pay bribe, VIII, 159.
Better than men, VI, 104.
Betting to beggardom, IV, 358.

Beveridge, VII, 170.
Bible, I, 403; XII, 284; its wealth of literary allusions, I, 359; slavery justified in the, III, 257; most valuable book in the, III, 449; oldest book in the, IV, 121; science and the, V, 3 23; *Book of Mormon*, American sequel to, IX, 64; references to time, IX, 361; definition of, XII, 15; and business, XII, 16; Ingersoll on the, XII, 163; the real, XII, 163.
Biddle, XIII, 373.
Big business, I, 196; VIII, 54; IX, 117; XII, 327; and Germany, I, 63; Henry Ford's genius for, I, 64; Justice Holmes on, I, 64; and trust busting, I, 64; some things, has done, I, 66; and exports, I, 70; on trial, I, 70; and the yellow press, I, 71; National Cash Register Company example of, I, 170; and by-products, I, 196; division of profits and, I, 197; liberal policy toward, II, 382; government and, VIII, 72; fighting, VIII, 81; and climate, VIII, 178; stupidity of, VIII, 221; government attitude towards, VIII, 223; and economy, VIII, 253; and little, VIII, 253; supervision of prize-fights and, X, 203. (See also Business)
Big Five, II, 347; X, 359.
Bigelow, John, IV, 48.
Biggest businessmen borrowers, I, 195.
Bildad's platitudes, IV, 129.
Billings, Cardinal Josh, an authority on the New English, VI, 158.
Billingsgate, VII, 207.
Billingsgate abuse, I, 108.
Bills, repudiated, VI, 142; small, IV, 252.
Biltmore Hotel, X, 372.
Biographies, dull, VI, 181.
Biography, V, 96; XIII, 259; happy lives and, XIII, 265.
Birds, the ecstasy of forest, III, 26; teach initiative, VI, 374; and their young, VI, 374.
Bishop Quayle and Hubbard, V, 151.
Bishop's voice, the, IX, 87.
Bispham, David, XIV, 93, 148.
Blaberino, XIII, 374.
Black, Winifred, on husbands and lobsters, I, 43.

Black Cat, the, XIII, 246.
Black Fast, IV, 177.
Blackfoot foils an ambuscade, III, 83.
Blacksmith teaching Greek history, IX, 84.
Blanket Indians, V, 198.
Blasphemy, VI, 388.
Blazed trail, the, I, 438.
Blind lovers, VI, 231.
Bliss, IV, 437.
Blondin, V, 392.
Bloody Assizes, I, 174.
Bloomin' bacteria, the, IV, 243.
Bloomingdale, XIII, 373.
Blue envelope, I, 111.
Bluff, large oval, I, 427.
Bob-veal, I, 245.
Boehman, John, case of, XIV, 253.
Bogey man, the, V, 261.
Bohemia, XIII, 375.
Bok, Brother, I, 411.
Bond, Carrie Jacobs, VI, 213.
Bonuses, system of, II, 439.
Book agent, III, 435.
Book-learning, IV, 401.
Book lovers, VI, 139.
Book-plates, VI, 106.
Book sales, VI, 136.
Bookish inclination, XII, 30.
Bookmakers, two famous, I, 222; and monks, IV, 145.
Books, IX, 252; favorites of Elbert Hubbard, I, 163; one of the greatest, ever written, I, 380; cheap, III, 436; shoddy, III, 436; when, were religious oracles, III, 459; as to advertising, VI, 136; the joy of well made, VI, 156; subscription, VI, 337; opinions concerning, VI, 339; inscribed, VIII, 127; autographed, VIII, 128; Roycroft, VIII, 128; movies and, compared, VIII, 252; Erasmus authority on, IX, 254; written behind prison bars, XI, 382; Franklin on, XII, 30.
Boone, Daniel, V, 266.
Boost our country, I, 201.
Booty, XIII, 374.
Booze, tobacco and universities, IV, 175.
Boredom, XIII, 374.
Born with his hat on, the man who was, I, 442.
Boss, who is, XIV, 201; the farm, XIV, 202; qualifications of a, XIV, 202.
Boston, booze-bazaar and the red-light district, I, 409; a visit to, VII, 202; the clearing-house of industry, VII, 312; culture, I, 404.
Boston missionaries, VII, 312.
Boston News Bureau, X, 216.
Boston Store, the origin of the, X, 311.
Boswell, James, V, 90.
Bourne, Senator Jonathan, I, 315.
Bow-legs and courage, XI, 107.
Bowery Mission, I, 401.
Bowlder that had grown from a pebble, XIII, 279.
Bowsher, Doctor, I, 287; the celebrated psychologist, IX, 356; dictum of, I, 287.
Boxer movement, VI, 203.
Boxing is a game, X, 207.
Boy, the, from Missouri Valley, I, 82; and man, I, 465; farming and city, IV, 32; a potentiality, IV, 246.
Boy farmers, scientific, IX, 355.
Boylston Professorship of literature and oratory, VI, 48.
Bradlaugh, V, 155.
Bradley-Martin Ball, I, 315.
Brain, IV, 306; XIII, 374; Bastile of the, IV, 267.
Brains, business and, IV, 220; and life insurance, IV, 220.
Brandywine, the battle of, VII, 225.
Brann, V, 283; the iconoclast, X, 271.
Brashear, John A., X, 167.
Bread, XIII, 375; and honey, XIII, 333.
Breakfast foods, II, 321.
Breathing, deep, and health, VI, 391.
Breeds, types and sects, IV, 156.
Brewer, Justice, I, 97.
Bribes, barristers and, IV, 70;
Bridegroom's policy, a, IV, 106.
Bridger, Jim, VII, 66.
Brieux, I, 326.
Bright's Disease, V, 329.
Brisbane, Arthur, salary of, II, 85.
British Columbia, forests of, VII, 350.
British Empire, organization of the, I, 323.
British Parliament restricting the building of ironworks, VIII, 88.
British Sovereignty, VII, 353.
British possessions in North America, VII, 350.

British supremacy in India springs from the work done by Warren Hastings, I, 165.
British worthies denied paradise, VII, 159.
Broadmindedness, IX, 39.
Bronco buster, the, VI, 183.
Brook Farm, IV, 147; XIII, 357.
Brook Farmers, IV, 147.
Brother to the trees, a, II, 143, 147, 153.
Brother's keeper, a, VI, 122.
Brotherhood, Fenian, I, 229; of Consecrated Lives, IV, 447; the Golden Rule, VII, 90; among actors, VII, 320; of man, VIII, 209; world, VIII, 214.
Brown, John, III, 15; VII, 308; Browns and Judsons starting west, III, 19; a day of incidents, III, 22; an emergency well met, III, 36; a vigil with death, III, 48; conform or fight, III, 53; a cattle sale at Zanesville, III, 69; finds friends and foes, III, 72; the deacon does a-wooing go, III, 90; meets trouble, and faces it, III, 96; doctrine of, III, 97; a literary courtship, III, 105; a horse-back ride through the woods, III, 112; runaway slaves, III, 129; hunting fugitive slaves, III, 136; makes a decision, III, 147; Margaret Silverton writes to, III, 177; Jim Slivers disappears, III, 190; a fruitless chase, III, 193; defeat and doubt, but not discouragement, III, 201; hot hopes fade off into mist, III, 206; his Patent Adjustable Nigger Carriage, III, 248; a night-ride to freedom, III, 248; trouble in the church, III, 255; results of mixing sentiment and business, III, 277; family of, III, 279; politics and strife, III, 290; caught in a trap, III, 295; to the rescue, III, 301; and Governor Shannon, III, 324; Governor Shannon's message, III, 327; Shannon's agreement, III, 328; masked peace and smothered embers, III, 330; blockhouse near Osawatomie, III, 331; and Uncle Sam parley, III, 350; and Colonel Brydges, III, 352; compromise effected, III, 361; Captain Carver holds a reception, III, 363; Osawatomie, III, 367; and outdoor life, III, 370; explains his plan, III, 382; Emerson's opinion of, III, 392; the blow is struck, III, 418; the plan had failed, III, 422; Governor Wise met Old Brown of Osawatomie, III, 423; " I am ready," III, 423; address to court, III, 424; bust of, by St. Jerome, V, 74.
Brown Museum, John, V, 73.
Brown, Owen, III, 16.
Browne, Walter, of *Everywoman*, IX, 208.
Browning, Robert, ideal life of, VI, 287; as a wrestler, X, 209.
Bruno, I, 129, 355.
Brush, the evolution of the, XIV, 153; making of the modern, XIV, 153.
Brushes, early, used by the Romans, XIV, 153.
Brushmakers, the world's greatest, XIV, 155.
Bryan, William Jennings, VIII, 377.
Bryce, Ambassador, V, 297; *American Commonwealth* by, IV, 167; V, 298; VII, 347.
Bucephalus, that big black horse, VII, 306.
Buck, Glen, XIV, 191.
Bucke, Dr. Richard Maurice, V, 228; X, 57; death of, X, 63.
Buckle, Thomas Henry, *History of Civilization*, by, I, 380; VI, 308.
Buddha, XI, 23.
Buddhism, VI, 197.
Buddhists and Buddhism, VI, 199.
Buffalo, I, 325; the greatest horse-market in the world, II, 395; growth of, XIV, 135.
Bughouse, XIII, 374.
Building, VII, 395; the most remarkable, in the world, VII, 254.
Bull Moose, VIII, 365.
" Bull-work " of defense, VIII, 369.
Bullied by body, X, 116.
Bum Dukaboor, I, 183.
" Bum Peter Cooper," IV, 63.
Bundling, marital, III, 467.
Burbank, Luther, II, 344; X, 299; citizen of the celestial city of fine minds, II, 347.
Burial, a pioneer, III, 49.
Burke, Old Dan, XIV, 173.

Burke, Edmund, on law and public opinion, I, 68; Extract from *Essay on the Sublime*, VI, 206; and George Washington, X, 361.
Burlington Route, VII, 18.
Burne-Jones, Philip, "The Vampire," by, IV, 67.
Burns, Robert, the lover, IV, 189.
Burpee, Doctor David, X, 361.
Burpee, W. Atlee, X, 356; interests of, X, 364.
Burpee efficiency, X, 363.
Burpee Farm, X, 363.
Burroughs, John, V, 35; heart of youth in, V, 35; in the cabin of, V, 36; memoranda and, V, 37; the most universal man, V, 39; boys and, V, 41; life is a prayer to, V, 41; and Walt Whitman, V, 42; and Thoreau, V, 44.
Burton, Sir Richard, X, 202.
Bush, Benjamin Franklin, II, 289; birthplace of, II, 292.
Business, I, 371, 383; II, 258, 270, 325, 363, 393; IV, 410; VIII, 215; X, 218; XII, 273, 312; XIII, 374; modern, an exacting taskmaster, I, 28; and politics, I, 62; human element in, I, 65; and lawyers, I, 65; crippling, I, 67; effect of gambling on, I, 76; greatest science in the world, I, 102; founded on the thought of reciprocity, I, 133; as a civilizer, 1, 171; and jealousy, I, 173; evolution of, I, 178; is human service, I, 196, 371, 453; newspaper, I, 232; Carnegie on, I, 416; the empire of, I, 416; retail clothing, I, 425; truth in, I, 425; two kinds of men in, II, 18; friendship in modern, II, 34; monopoly in the shoe, II, 183; modern, II, 245; IV, 391; VIII, 22; XII, 404; essential element of success in, II, 258; patience in, II, 259; a, founded on friendship, II, 278; definition of, II, 289; romance in the rise of, the telephone, II, 310; results of mixing sentiment and, III, 277; success in modern, IV, 98; brains and, IV, 220; life insurance and, IV, 221; legal limit of, IV, 225; sentiment and, V, 131; war is, VI, 269; and war, VI, 270; and William Morris, VI, 309; the divinity of, VIII, 22; advent of women into, VIII, 117; science in, VIII, 134; men valuable to, VIII, 156; and finance, VIII, 206; the individual financier and, VIII, 208; the brotherhood of, VIII, 215; self-interest in, VIII, 219; a brain for, VIII, 232; some activities of, VIII, 233; the field of, VIII, 233; loyalty in, VIII, 239; faith in, VIII, 348; public, and bankers, VIII, 372; war helps, IX, 243; demands devotion, IX, 264; will get an armistice in war-time, IX, 289; statistics, X, 285; modern American, X, 342; personality in, X, 412; romance of, XII, 374; bad breaks in, XIV, 185; true index of, XIV, 196; false standards in, IV, 202. (See also Big Business)
Business asset, a, VIII, 294.
Business-baiter, I, 201; X, 335.
Business banquets, VIII, 329.
Business basis, the United States Government on a strictly, I, 315.
Business builder, I, 195; a big, II, 289.
Business cars, II, 296.
Business college, I, 292, 413.
Business combination, an admirable, V, 399.
Business conditions, XIV, 196.
Business consolidation, benefits of, II, 189.
Business correspondence, VI, 54.
Business development, VIII, 87.
Business ethics, VIII, 21.
Business house policies, I, 80.
Business intellectic, VIII, 195.
Businessman, the. XII, 406; XIII, 374; new type of, II, 291; of today, I, 332; new model of American, II, 340; animation of the, I, 347; raw stock of, I, 347; our only scientist, II, 444; what is a, XIII, 236.
Businessmen, II, 363; V, 326; VIII, 25, 65, 217, 232; band of greedy grafters, I, 201; lawyers as, XIII, 331; treatment of, by Canada and the United States, XIV, 120.
Business rivals, VIII, 157.
Business romance, a, VIII, 358.
Business salvation and publicity bureaus, I, 72.
Business success, VIII, 17.
Business supervision, rise of, IX, 379.

ix

Bustard, Doctor, II, 246; VIII, 375.
Busting broncs, VI, 182.
Busy Man's Creed, the, XII, 271.
Butler, XIII, 374.
Butterflies, XIV, 304.
Butt, Major, IX, 16.
Buttons, X, 32.
"Buy a bale of cotton," VI, 31.
Buyer, the, VIII, 165.
Buying, VIII, 83; and selling for cash, X, 312.
Buying mood, the, VIII, 83.
By-products, utilization of by big business, I, 196; utilizing, I, 333.
Bwana Tumbo, I, 418; IV, 207.
Cabin, a, and God's Acre, VII, 271.
Cabinet forecast, a, VIII, 221.
Cady, Doctor, farm of, VII, 178.
Cæsar, Julius, the builder, I, 40; the lawyer, I, 332; road builder, I, 395; father of the corporation, II, 226; and initiative, VII, 306; legions of, VIII, 391; the conqueror, IX, 347; an epileptic, X, 137.
Cæsarian operation, I, 309.
Cafeteria, IX, 317; a picketed, IX, 320.
Caiaphas, XI, 68.
Cain, XIII, 380; wife of, XIII, 273.
Calf raising, I, 249.
California, a land of sunshine, VII, 281, and the Japs, VII, 290.
California Fruit-Growers' Exchange, II, 379; VII, 300.
California Missions, the, VII, 53.
California oranges, VII, 298.
California poppy, the, V, 34.
California railroads, VII, 144.
California Canaan, VII, 162.
Caligula compared with the Kaiser, I, 280.
Calumet and Hecla, the, VII, 362; workers in the, VII, 365; grievances, VII, 380; Grievance Bureau of the, VII, 386.
Calves, to raise, I, 249.
Calvin, John, pamphleteer, I, 22; and human rights, I, 212; his Reign of God, VIII, 16.
Calvinism, IV, 381.
Camp Co-operation, X, 98.
Camp Fire genesis of science, I, 438; modern variants of the, I, 439.

Camp-Meeting impulse, II, 104.
Camp Meetings religious orgies, II, 106.
Cana, XI, 27.
Canada, I, 201; American people covet, II, 180; can feed the world, VII, 333; annexing the United States, VII, 334; the new, VII, 346; some things, has, VII, 351; virgin forests of, VII, 351; water-power of, VII, 351; loyalty of, VII, 352; described by a high-school sophomore, XIV, 113; and United States, some comparison, XIV, 113; and reciprocity, XIV, 180; Richard Rush and Charles Bagot signers of the peace compact with, I, 161; naval forces to be maintained on the Great Lakes according to the peace compact with, I, 161.
Canadian Club at Vancouver, VII, 346; the work of the, VII, 347.
Canadian Clubs, VII, 346.
Canadian Pacific, XIV, 118.
Canadian sentiment toward the United States, II, 178.
Canadians, the, VII, 327.
Cancer, VI, 392; Dr. Tilden's declaration concerning the, I, 142; wrongful eating may cause, I, 142; caused by jealousy, VI, 260.
Candy-shop, antidote for the, IX, 384.
Canned life, IV, 319.
Cannibal, XIII, 375.
Cannon, Uncle Joe, VI, 337; and subscription books, VI, 337; in vode, VIII, 307.
Canonical, III, 458.
Canonization, IX, 405.
Capernaum, XI, 40.
Capital, VI, 406; from savings, I, 39; unutilized, I, 462; and labor, V, 88; IX, 264.
Capital Punishment, IV, 342; opposed by Dukaboor, I, 182; in Michigan, VII, 259.
Captains of industry, X, 129.
Captains of industry, I, 390.
Carbon, three forms of approximately pure, II, 212.
Carborundum, II, 203.
Carelessness, XIII, 375.
Carlisle Indian, I, 139; VII, 210.
Carlyle, was cruel, VI, 352; wife of, VI, 353.

Carlylean phrase, V, 385.
Carnegie, Andrew, and college training, I, 401; *Empire of Business*, by, I, 416; maxim of, II, 425; his beneficent pension fund for teachers, IV, 376; evolution of mind of, IX, 259; liberality of, IX, 375.
Carnegie Institute, the, IV, 324.
Carnegie Library, IX, 260.
Carnival, the, IV, 273.
Carroll, Johnny, V, 161.
Cars, business, II, 296; high-priced, IX, 268.
Carson, Doctor C. H., X, 253; a successful mental healer, X, 258.
Cartoons by Powers, IX, 342; and cartoonists, IX, 342.
Cartridge invented, II, 235.
Casey, John F., X, 370; Company, X, 374.
Cash register as a business civilizer, I, 374.
Cash Register Company, I, 170.
Cassie Chadwick, VIII, 363.
Cast iron, manufacture of, inaugurated in Germany, VIII, 88.
Caste, IX, 334; XIII, 380; a Chinese Wall, I, 219.
Cat farm, VI, 172.
Cat in gloves, XIV, 72.
Cats, VI, 173; civilization and, VI, 172; and success, VI, 342.
Catholic, foolish Protestant suspicions of, I, 271; Protestant lies about, I, 272.
Catholic consistency, IX, 171.
Catholics, hammering, I, 268.
Catholicism, American, XI, 395; Spanish, XI, 395.
Cause and effect, law of, I, 217; IV, 314.
Caves and human happiness, VII, 241.
Celestial, a genuine, V, 189.
Celestial City of Fine Minds, VI, 328.
Celestial midway, XI, 47.
Cellini casting his "Perseus," VI, 289.
Cellos, progenitor of all, II, 68.
Censor, IV, 115.
Census report, a, IV, 243.
Centaur, the, VI, 16.
Centennial Exposition, I, 284.
Cerebellum, XIII, 376.
Chalk, XIII, 376.
Challenge, the, IV, 124.

Chamois-skins, X, 403.
Chance, an order built of, V, 160.
Changing creeds, IV, 254.
Changing styles in garb, VI, 68.
Channing's Symphony of Life, XIII, 281.
Chaperon habit is a bad one, IX, 249.
Chapman, Doctor, IV, 276.
Character, XIII, 329; what is, VIII, 370; four concepts enter into the making of a strong and useful, X, 229; Emerson on, XII, 237, 248; is higher than intellect, XII, 248.
Character building and college, I, 411.
Charitableness, XIII, 285.
Charity, II, 264; IV, 429; XIII, 376; or business—which, VIII, 152.
Charm, IV, 51; of manner, I, 43, 454.
Charming bit of Scotch folk lore, XI, 383.
Charter, perversion of terms to say that a, gives rights, XII, 110.
Chase, Ethan Allen, a tree planter, VII, 298.
Chauffeur, XIII, 376; the convivial, IX, 268.
Chautauqua Circle, the, II, 109.
Chautauqua course, Edison and the, II, 116.
Chautauqua cross between camp-meeting and a country fair, II, 106.
Chautauqua idea, II, 103.
Chautauqua movement, the, II, 114.
Cheap products make cheap men, VI, 155.
Cheap thinking and high kicking, IV, 467.
Cheapness, rage for, III, 435.
Cheek, XIII, 376.
Cheerfulness, IV, 173.
Chef, XIII, 376.
Chicago, motto of, II, 154; thirty-four, railroads of, II, 266; growth of, VIII, 272; first hotel of, VIII, 273; and health, VIII, 276.
Chicago Board of Education, IX, 352.
Chicago Fire, II, 265.
Chicago Tongue, I, 106; XIII, 377; and W. T. Stead, I, 106; the basic principle of, I, 109; devils' bait, I, 109; a ludicro-tragic feature of, I, 112; and Lincoln, I, 113.
Chicken pie socials, VI, 171.
"Chickering," IX, 301.
Child, teaching of the, IV, 384; divinity

xi

of the, V, 116; other mother of the, IV, 139.
Child-garden, VI, 249.
Child labor, VI, 402.
Child slavery, IV, 346; VI, 399.
Childhood, spirit of, XI, 390.
Children, XII, 176; XIII, 375; playgrounds for, IV, 160; give your, liberty, IV, 250; divine bugaboo of, IV, 279; recipe for educating, IV, 455; recipe for having beautiful, IV, 455; law restricting the employment of, VI, 402; Paine on, XII, 116; Emerson on, XII, 195; of drunkards are often temperance fanatics, XIII, 132; sale of, XIII, 315; Ingersoll on rights of, XII, 175.
Chimera, that mystical beast, X, 238.
Chimeric, XIII, 378.
China, I, 201; economics of, I, 201; the case of, IV, 370; women of, interested in the suffrage question, IV, 371; three state religions of, VI, 201; missionaries to, VI, 202; our grievances against, VI, 202; indictment of, VI, 364; pleas for, VI, 365; and America, VI, 366.
Chinaman as a machine, VI, 371.
Chinese, the, VI, 364; Joaquin Miller and the, IV, 24; first came to California in 1849, VI, 366; as servants, VI, 368; and organized labor, VI, 371; made the first paper, VII, 397.
Chinese Gordon, IX, 132.
Chinese labor in California, VI, 367.
Chin-Fly, the, XIII, 253.
Chopin, influence of, V, 142.
Choral societies, XIV, 105.
Christ, bride of, IX, 307; Christianity and the religion of, IV, 200; Christmas presents and, VI, 276; and war, IX, 78; before Pilate, XI, 75.
Christ life, Tolstoy's teaching and the, XI, 59.
Christ spirit, IV, 36.
Christian, XIII, 376.
Christian Science, VI, 163; XII, 317; healing principle in, IV, 321.
Christian Science Monitor, VI, 76.
Christian Scientist, the typical, VI, 165.
" Christian union," V, 144.
Christian Work and Evangelist, I, 126.

Christianity, IV, 157; XII, 286; some definitions, I, 204; essence of, I, 205; founding of, I, 207; paganism part of, I, 208; in the Dark Ages, I, 209; and religion, I, 256; muscular, II, 106; Constantine and, IV, 157; and the religion of Christ, IV, 200; XII, 386; was at first socialistic, XIII, 341.
Christians, primitive, IX, 35; assaults against, IX, 108.
Christmas present business, VI, 276.
Christmas presents, origin of, VI, 276.
Chums, IX, 181; XIII, 375; the danger of, IV, 290; beware of, IV, 447.
Church, XIII, 377; some reasons, uses to claim exemption, I, 130; decline of, I, 210; of England, I, 212; liberty of man and the, I, 213; real enemies of the, I, 298; Tolstoy's criticism of the, I, 353; the ideal, I, 354; as a police system, I, 354; IV, 163; Sunday baseball and the, IV, 46; is a social institution, IV, 164; bulwark of the, VI, 195; reasons, has always sided with slavery, VI, 407; built on mendicancy, IX, 167; sociology of the fallacious, IX, 245; Emerson on, XIII, 211.
Church co-operation, IX, 123.
Church debts, XIII, 127.
Church fairs, VI, 171.
Church-going, VI, 117; and Sabbath-breaking, VI, 380.
Church of the Latter Day Saints, IX, 63.
Church members, VI, 225.
Church membership, V, 331.
Church mendicant, the, I, 355.
Church organizations, II, 263.
Church property, taxation of, Elbert Hubbard's views thereon criticised, I, 126-128; Rabbi Levy favors taxation of, I, 128; the Corsican and, I, 361; value of the untaxed, held in America, I, 364.
Church raffles, I, 364.
Church and school, divorce between, XII, 169.
Church and State, Constitution of the United States on, I, 365; divorce of IX, 169.
Church trials, III, 273.
Church Trust, I, 122.

xii

Church union, VI, 70.
Church unity, VI, 396; XIII, 377.
Church work, excuse for, IV, 96.
Churches, overlapping of, VI, 170; fellowship, X, 148; founded on social feuds, XIV, 216.
Churchianity, X, 148; spielers for, IV, 279.
Churn, patent, XIV, 185.
Cigarettist, the, XIII, 377.
Circumspection, XII, 74.
Circumstance, XIII, 375.
Cities, labor in, I, 430; center of power, VII, 182; problem of feeding, VIII, 143; one of the most beautiful little, in America, IX, 233; and solitude, XI, 393.
Citizen of the world, a, II, 180; the ideal, universal, XIV, 140.
Citizens' Alliance, the, VII, 383.
City, XIII, 377; and country, XIII, 340.
City boys as farmers, VI, 35.
City of Angels, VII, 289.
City of Tagaste, III, 435.
Civic-centers, VII, 103; value of idea of, VII, 104.
Civic pride, a little, VII, 325.
Civic righteousness, IV, 166.
Civil marriage, I, 45.
Civil rights, XII, 111.
Civil War, I, 284; a matter of politics, I, 62; last survivor of great generals of the, VII, 227.
Civilization, I, 147, 225; IV, 282, 392; XIII, 377; business of, I, 44; is an evolution, I, 224; Luther's influence on, I, 297; scrap-heap and, II, 13; symbol of, II, 13; a matter of pipes and wires, II, 14; and steel, II, 14; and railroads, II, 139; shoes mirror the progress of, II, 186; and hardware, II, 358; and cats, VI, 172; history of, VII, 60; America's ancient, VII, 193; inspirers of, VII, 396; printing press glory of, VII, 397; turns on organization, VIII, 17; three processes in, VIII, 93; and cooks, VIII, 130; unit of, IX, 45; great moving mass of survival values, IX, 104; our modern, IX, 127; Ingersoll on, XII, 163, 169; a great system of transfers, XII, 303; tools of, XIV, 152.

Civilized man supported on crutches, XII, 220.
Claim your heritage, IX, 215.
Clan, the, I, 39; chief of the, I, 322; purpose of, IX, 180.
Clan instinct, VI, 27.
Class hatred, I, 30.
Class war, a, VII, 383.
Classes and masses, IX, 333.
Classic garments of our grandmammas, IX, 271.
Classical education, a, IX, 256.
Claudius, Emperor, VI, 296.
Cleopatra, X, 344.
Clergy, the, IV, 403; Ingersoll on the, XII, 172.
Clergyman not champion of unpopular cause, VI, 407.
Clergymen on half rations, VI, 72.
Clergymen's sore throat, IX, 87.
Clerical cough, XI, 139.
Clerical profession, IX, 115.
Cleveland, city of, X, 370; and Tom Johnson's administration, VIII, 30; city of feuds, VIII, 33; diversity of industries of, X, 370.
Cleveland, President and polygamy, IX, 73.
Climate, IV, 117; of Greece and California compared, IV, 117; man and, VII, 313; and progress, VII, 313; and big businessmen, VIII, 178.
Clique, XIII, 376; the menace of the, IV, 291.
Clock, XIII, 377; punching the, IV, 168.
Closed or Open Shop, I, 115.
Clothes, II, 338; American, I, 368.
Clothing, fashion and, I, 368; seasonable, I, 369.
Clover Club, X, 21.
Clover-Clubites, X, 21.
Club, our woman's, XIII, 267.
Clubs, advertising, IV, 330; woman's, IV, 51.
Clydesdales, I, 190.
Coal, I, 435.
Coal Oil Johnny, II, 336.
Coalition between England and America, VII, 353.
Coal-mining in Colorado, VII, 336.
Cobden, Richard on marriages and corn,

I, 333; and the Corn Laws, VIII, 63.
Coffin, XII, 154; XIII, 378.
Cold storage and food products, VIII, 185.
Cold Storage Plants, VIII, 186
Coleridge, Samuel Taylor, and the leisure class, IX, 215; one of the points of, IX, 217; methods of, IX, 217.
Coliseum, IX, 358.
Collateral, best, in the world, II, 35.
Collecting, psychology of, VI, 107.
Collection agencies, XIV, 244.
Collection-agency attorneys, XIV, 244.
Collective enthusiasm, I, 347.
Collector, the, VI, 150; the ex-libris, VI, 106.
Collectors, notable, VI, 108.
College, XII, 289; XIII, 377; medical, I, 312; primary intellectual purpose of the, I, 410; and character building, I, 411; business, I, 413; the curse of, I, 418; David Starr Jordan on value of, II, 461; one thing to recommend, IX, 257.
College Bulletins, IX, 322.
College Coach, IX, 322.
College courses, I, 400.
College degree, I, 400; X, 228; XIII, 378; advantages in, I, 404.
College education, I, 463; Emerson on, XII, 198.
College graduates, successful men not, I, 401; and initiative, IV, 370; and the Hall of Fame, V, 260.
College honors, I, 404.
College Inn, VIII, 275.
College presidents, task of, VI, 319; theses for consideration of, VI, 323.
College Settlement, the, IV, 185.
College training, I, 401; a neutral entity, I, 402.
College youth, dangers to the, I, 408.
Colleges, what is the matter with the, IX, 322; business, I, 292; and red light districts, I, 409; athletics in, I, 419; physical culture in, I, 419; chief error of, VI, 320; graduate physical and mental cripples, X, 227.
Collingwood's Disaster, IX, 240.
Colonel Littlejourneys and blind lovers, VI, 231.

Colquitt, Governor and Texas properties, VII, 404.
Colt, Samuel Pomeroy, II, 26; organized United States Rubber Company, II, 31; a particular trait of, II, 33; ancestry of, II, 42; revises commandments, II, 45.
Colt, Theodora, II, 40.
Colt Farm, the, II, 37.
Colt Memorial School, II, 40.
Colt Museum of Fine Arts, the, II, 40.
Columbia Grafonola, a Little Journey to the home of the, XIV, 142.
Columbia records, making of, XIV, 148.
Columbus, I, 370; V, 31; found no bees in America, IX, 141.
Come lovely and soothing death, XII, 159.
Comedy and tragedy have the same source, III, 445.
Comic, XIII, 378.
Comic Spirit, IX, 108.
Comic Sunday Supplement, IV, 476.
Commandment, second, death of art, III, 465.
Commandments, Colt revises the, II, 45; Germany's ten, VIII, 212; the twelfth, IX, 88.
Commerce, XII, 282, 367; some definitions of, I, 277; and war, I, 277; the incense of, VIII, 85; putting art into, X, 380; embarrassing, XII, 103; Ingersoll on, XII, 180.
Commercial and financial teddy bears, IX, 258.
Commercial progress, VIII, 120.
Commercial sanity, I, 381.
Commercialism, II, 473; IV, 93.
Commercializing art, X, 380.
Commissions, I, 376.
Committee, XIII, 376; of one hundred, IV, 169.
Common law of America founded on common law of England, XIII, 314.
Common People of Ancient Rome, the, by Frank Frost Abbott, XIV, 260.
Commonsense, IV, 333; XIII, 377; gospel of, I, 456; what is, IV, 333; creed of, XII, 310.
Commonsense Culters, IV, 173.
Commonsense living, IX, 127.
Commonsense party, the, IV, 172; basis of, IV, 172.

Commonwealth Avenue, IV, 184.
Communal family group, XIII, 342.
Communal feeding, VI, 57.
Communal idea, XIII, 344; form of monastic impulse, IX, 31.
Communal Life, XIII, 347; about the, IV, 145; best feature of, XIII, 356.
Communion of the Great Spirit, IV, 19.
Communism, XIII, 345; the religious aspect of, IV, 145; applied, IV, 149; an experiment in, VI, 56; as a theory XI, 407; of two, XI, 407; voluntary, XIII, 346; no use for the tyrant, XIII, 349.
Communists and Harmonists, IV, 146.
Community, the Oneida, IV, 146, 248; the Anarchist, IV, 148; of interest, VI, 313.
Commuters, IX, 105.
Companionable, to be, IV, 51.
Companionship, in search of, IX, 383.
Company's store, VII, 342.
Comparison, a, IV, 311.
Compensation, V, 386; Law of, I, 159; 367; VII, 48; for fire and earthquakes, VII, 269.
Competition, I, 196; II, 33; VIII, 50, 124; XIII, 378; the result of, I, 375; and co-operation, IV, 443; destructive, VIII, 51; quality, VIII, 53; unlimited, VIII, 53; wasteful, VIII, 112; of ideas, IX, 337; or emulation, IX, 335; as to, XIV, 215; versus co-operation, XIV, 215.
Competitive stage, VI, 311.
Competitive system, VI, 311.
Complacency, smirking, V, 384.
Compleat Angler, the, VI, 109.
Compliment, XIII, 378.
Comte, Auguste, *Pure Reason*, by, VI, 26.
Concentration, VIII, 159; IX, 181, 389; a habit with Hays, II, 356; to cultivate, IV, 54; and success, VI, 344.
Conception, Immaculate, I, 153, 306.
Concerning Copy, VIII, 385.
Concerning the Dukaboor, I, 179.
Concoction, XIII, 378.
Concordat, the, I, 361.
Concrete, the building material of the future will be, IV, 81; God's, IV, 81.
Conduct, the standard of, IV, 211; culture cream of, IX, 351; community criterion of, XIII, 349.
Conferences, VIII, 193.
Confession must be genuine, VI, 66.
Confessional in letters, VI, 62.
Confidence, II, 277; XIII, 378; and business stability, I, 383; and banking, II, 277; mutual, II, 277; credit basis of, VIII, 204; betrayal of, IX, 213; and health, XIV, 273.
Confirmation, I, 399.
Conforming to usages, XII, 199.
Confucianism, Taoism and Buddhism, VI, 197.
Confucius, VI, 197; XI, 30.
Congress of Hygiene, I, 325.
Connersville, X, 246; man who keyed, X, 248.
Conquering of the Desert, the, VII, 192.
Conscience, X, 33; XIII, 377.
Consciousness, XIII, 379.
Conscription, IV, 254.
Conscription in America, IX, 179.
Consequences, Law of, IX, 34, 40.
Conservation, refrigeration the science of, VIII, 180; the folly of, IX, 377.
Conservation, banking a symbol of, II, 266.
Conservative, I, 225; XIII, 278; definition of, I, 226.
Conservatives, I, 358.
Consistency, foolish, XII, 201.
Consolation, sickroom, IV, 131.
Console, XIII, 378.
Conspicuous American successes, XIV, 228.
Conspicuous consumption, XIII, 317.
Conspicuous leisure, XIII, 317.
Conspicuous waste, IV, 137; XIII, 317.
Constantine, Christianity and, I, 209; IV, 157; if, had embraced Judaism, IV, 200; and the rights of woman, IX, 175.
Constitution, God in the, I, 353; of the United States on church and state, I, 365; party politics and the, II, 360.
Constitution and government, definition of, XII, 113; when a country may boast of its, XII, 117.
Consumption, VI, 392.
Contentment, V, 87.
Continental and Commercial Bank, II, 271.

xv

Contradiction, XIII, 378.
Contrast, VII, 191.
Convenient loaf of brown bread, a, VI, 286.
Conversation, wit of, XII, 47.
Conversion, XIII, 379.
Convictions, personal, XIV, 271.
Convicts, appraisal of, I, 155; two general classes of, IV, 78.
Cooking and theology, XI, 239.
Cooks and civilization, VIII, 130.
Cooper, Peter, and Antioch College, V, 272; land carriage of, VIII, 325; steam engine of, VIII, 325; tea-kettle of, VIII, 328.
Co-operation, I, 70, 222; II, 262; VIII, 175; XIII, 379; of railroad companies, I, 224; solvent of economic evils, I, 334; mutuality and reciprocity, I, 386; rivalry now in, I, 386; and nature, IV, 117; and competition, IV, 443; spirit of, VI, 307; and conspiracy, VIII, 53; what, and right environment can do, XIII, 361.
Co-operative, VI, 311.
Copper workers, prehistoric, VII, 369.
Coquetry, XIII, 378.
Corbett, James J., X, 18; and Marshall Wilder, V, 237.
Corn and Potatoes, X, 352.
Corn Clubs, IX, 354; idea of the, IX, 354.
Corn Laws and Cobden, VIII, 63.
Cornelia, X, 343.
Corner Candy Store, the, IX, 382.
Corner-Grocery Infidel, IX, 120.
Cornishmen, VII, 361.
Corot, VI, 285.
Corporal punishment, IV, 297.
Corporations, I, 223; VIII, 122; rise of, I, 40; definition of, I, 41; big, I, 202; father of, II, 226.
Correspondence School plan, the, II, 198.
Corsican, the, and church property, I, 361.
Corwin, Thomas, X, 23; Ingersoll's tribute to, X, 23; greatest popular orator that America has ever produced, X, 23; birthplace of, X, 24; Wagon Boy Orator, X, 24; Secretary of the Treasury under President Fill-

more, X, 25; quality of, X, 26.
Cosmic bank-balance, X, 163.
Cosmic consciousness, X, 61; IX, 40.
Cosmopolitan city, VII, 325.
Cosmopolitan idea, VIII, 246.
Cosmopolitan radical, V, 193.
Cost, selling at, VIII, 52.
Cotton is king, I, 369; VII, 388; buy a bale of, VI, 31.
Cotton pickers, VII, 390.
Countercheck quarrelsome, the, IX, 160.
Country, assets of a, I, 333; the, an ideal place to bring up children, IV, 89; the calm of the, IV, 422; and city, XIII, 340.
Country lass, IV, 62.
Counts, their origin, I, 41.
County, I, 323.
Courage, I, 366; III, 451; VIII, 46; XIII, 379; mental and moral, I, 366; physical and moral, I, 366; physical and spiritual, I, 366; Dutch, IX, 266.
Courier, IX, 340.
Courtesy, II, 384; XII, 299; XIII, 375; as an asset, I, 451; is catching, I, 453; as an asset, II, 385; Texas, VII, 285.
Courtship, XIII, 13; a literary, III, 105; VI, 190.
Cow and burning barn, I, 241.
Cow talk, I, 240.
Coward, James S., X, 393; early days of, X, 394; customers of, X, 396.
Coward, John M., X, 396.
Coward policy, the, X, 397.
Coward shoe, X, 398.
Cows, six famous breeds of, I, 242; best type of milk breed, I, 242; kindness to, I, 250; care of, VI, 85; healthy VI, 85.
Coxey's present army, I, 53.
Craig Colony for Epileptics, X, 132.
Crane, Stephen, V, 140; reincarnation of Frederick Chopin, V, 141; on hats, VI, 148.
Crapsey, Doctor Algernon, of Rochester, VIII, 335.
Crawford, Capt. Jack, V, 138.
Creation, V, 153; XII, 122.
Creative impulse, II, 333.
Creator, XIII, 380.

Credit, XIII, 380; social letter of, I, 405; basis of confidence, VIII, 204; great game of, VIII, 376; Franklin on, and character, XII, 61.
Creditors, XII, 78.
Credo, VI, 37; XII, 397.
Creed, XIII, 379; of the future, XII, 13.
Creeds, V, 248; metaphors with ankylosis, V, 284; the sum of all the, XII, 171.
Cremona, IX, 301.
Crime, Emerson on, I, 34; every jail is a school of, II, 328; Nietzsche on, IX, 69; statistics of London, VII, 355; statistics of New York City, VII, 355.
Crimes against criminals, IX, 42; permitted to punish crime, IX, 42; and punishment, IV, 345.
Criminal, XIII, 379; reformation and reclamation of the, IV, 215.
Criminal class, VII, 91; XIV, 61.
Criminals, lady, II, 327.
Crisis, the, I, 25; XII, 105.
Critic, Elbert Hubbard's most captious, V, 393.
Criticism, II, 262; XI, 417; XIII, 270; recipe for unkind, II, 18; the Higher, IV, 232; Emerson on, XII, 225.
Critics, XIII, 379; literary, XI, 416.
Cromwell, Oliver, XIII, 379; XIV, 19.
Crooks, a kindergarten for, XIV, 245.
Crop rotation, VII, 367.
Crops, rotation of human, VI, 36.
Crosby, Ernest, rare type of philosophic anarchist, I, 51.
Crosby, Nathan, III, 16; death of, III, 45.
Crown, the, XII, 119.
Crucifixion, XI, 78, 81.
Cruelty, I, 309; to animals, prevention of, I, 310; always irrational, I, 312; refined, VI, 354.
Cry against the Japs, VII, 290; of the Little Peoples, VI, 132.
Cryptogram, IV, 25.
Culture, IV, 408, 440; VII, 48; societies of, I, 363; not a monopoly, IX, 84; and useful work, IX, 84; grace of, IX, 350; cream of conduct, IX, 351; and art, IX, 350.

Cumberland Pike, when devised, I, 25; I, 384.
Cumulative punishment, IV, 305.
Curie, Madame, X, 346.
Curiosity, XIII, 379.
"Curse God and die," IV, 126.
Curvetings of law, X, 168.
Custer, ridge where, fell, VII, 210; characteristics and qualities of, VII, 212; the ambitions of, VII, 213; and General Grant, VII, 213; his viewpoint of the Indian, VII, 213; and Terry, VII, 214; why, failed, VII, 220; disobedience of orders, VII, 216.
Custer Battlefield, VII, 207; a vision of, VII, 211.
Customer, faith in, VIII, 109.
Customers first, VIII, 109.
Czolgosz, who killed McKinley, V, 173.
Dagon, IX, 398.
Dagonic device, a, VIII, 403.
Daily Newspaper, I, 233; in prisons, IV, 77.
Daily Press, rottenness of, I, 237.
Dairy products, VIII, 148.
Dairy sharp, definition of a, I, 247.
Damaged Goods, I, 325.
Damien, Father, X, 132.
Dana and Talmage, V, 181; and the New York *Sun*, V, 183.
Dance of Death, XIV, 90.
Dandelions, XI, 404.
Danes introduced the capital H into England, X, 40.
Danger of exclusive friendships among young women, the, XIV, 263.
Daniels, George H., II, 469; and *Message to Garcia*, I, 252; birthplace of, II, 469.
Daniels, Mark, VII, 45.
Dante and Beatrice, I, 210.
Darest thou now, O soul, XII, 151.
Dark ages, I, 347; status of human race during, I, 348.
Darlington, Doctor, X, 103.
Darrow, Clarence, X, 146; Joaquin Miller and, V, 23; best American exponent of non-resistance, X, 146.
Dartmouth, I, 85.
Dartmouth College case, I, 361.
Darwin, Charles, and Herbert Spencer, IV, 16.
Darwinian Theory, Huxley and Wil-

berforce and the, IX, 227.
Davenport, Iowa, VII, 138.
Davey, John, II, 140; the Clara Barton of trees, II, 148.
David and Uriah, IX, 397.
Davidson, G. Aubrey, and the San Diego idea, VII, 197.
Davis, Gail, XIV, 111.
Davis, James J., X, 168.
Dawn, XIII, 380.
Day dreams, IV, 300.
Day, Mary Anne, III, 233.
Daylight saving, IX, 360.
Days are as grass, XIV, 290.
Dayton Flood, II, 171.
De Quincey, Thomas, IV, 65.
De Soto, VII, 85.
Dead, pity for the, IV, 29, 310.
Dead beat, the, IX, 390.
Dead language, I, 403.
Dead languages, IX, 357; fakery of, I, 421.
Dead Sea fruit, VI, 119.
Deaf and dumb, I, 154.
Deal, a queer, XIII, 152.
Death, IV, 306; IX, 112; XIII, 380; from vaccination, I, 265; a vigil with, III, 48; fear of, IV, 49; King, V, 121; lovely and soothing, V, 124; XII, 159; day of your, XIV, 256.
Death Penalty, the, IV, 342; abolishing the, IV, 343.
Deborah, IX, 82; XIII, 238.
Debs, Eugene V., X, 128; on the New Order, I, 52; and Reynolds, X, 125.
Debt, IV, 162; IV, 465; XIII, 380; Franklin on, XII, 77.
Debts of honor, IX, 390.
Decalogue, XIII, 380.
Decentralization, II, 374.
Decimal system, Jefferson gave us, VII, 87.
Declaration, a, XII, 329.
Declaration of Independence, XII, 81-86; was first issued in pamphlet form, I, 24-25.
Dedham Society for the detection and apprehension of horse thieves, VI, 274.
Definitions, IX, 24.
Degradation, reforming power in, IX, 43.
Delaware, a Little Journey to, VII, 222;

climate of, VII, 223; in history, VII, 224.
Delaware berries, VII, 223.
Delaware farm crops, VII, 223.
Delay adolescence, IX, 256.
Delsarte, XIV, 163.
Demagogue, I, 70; VIII, 59; X, 336; XIII, 380; rule of the, I, 120; claim of the, VII, 341.
Demand and supply, law of, VII, 74.
Democracy, VIII, 237; X, 240; XIII, 381.
Democrat, VI, 131.
Denmark, X, 39.
Dennis, XIII, 381.
Denominationalism, I, 212; XIII, 340.
Denominations, IV, 387; V, 105; VII, 103; IX, 38; founded on personal aversions, IX, 124.
Denouement, the, IV, 135.
Denslow, XIII, 266.
Dental dicta, some, X, 193.
Dental societies, VIII, 43.
Dentist, modern, VIII, 41; success of, VIII, 41.
Dentistry and longevity, XIII, 37; a new science, VIII, 39; gave anesthesia to the world, X, 196; use of gold in, X, 197.
Denver, City of, VII, 49.
Department Store, the, I, 284; girls, I, 285.
Des Moines, VII, 171.
Desdemona and the Moor, VI, 262.
Despotism, XI, 206.
Destiny, IX, 393.
Detectives, a comparison, X, 80.
Detention School, II, 328.
Detroit stores, XIV, 98.
Development, arrested, III, 324.
Devil, XIII, 382; first real estate agent, I, 181.
Devotion and enterprise, IX, 264.
Dewey, V, 62.
Dewey, Prof. John, VI, 218.
Dewey School, VI, 218.
Diamonds by the bushel, II, 212.
Dianism, VI, 110.
Diary, XIII, 381.
Dickens, Charles, characters of, IV, 216; criticism of, IV, 216; painted picture with a broom, IV, 218; and the Jews,

VI, 101; the England of, VI, 160;
Dictated but not read, I, 426.
Dictator, the evolution of a, V, 373; *American Notes*, by, IX, 219.
Dictionary, the development of the, VIII, 404; New Standard, of the English language, VIII, 406; The Standard, IX, 253.
Dictionary habit, the, VIII, 405.
Diet, strong men and, IV, 104; mixed, VII, 163; health and, X, 199.
Dietetic sinner, X, 193.
Dietetics, IX, 228.
Digestion, Nature's plan of, VIII, 47.
Digging, man's first business, VIII, 94.
Diginity, XIII, 381; of judges, VIII, 168.
Diminishing Returns, Law of, I, 115; VIII, 51; IV, 224; VIII, 136; Oliver Wendell Homes apropos of the Law of, I, 116.
Dining Clubs, IX, 219.
Diocletian, the Edict of, I, 348; plan of, I, 348.
Diocletian Edicts, the, XIV, 260.
Diplomacy, VIII, 110; XIII, 381; a little matter of, III, 307; supplemented, by forty-four, III, 324.
Diplomat, XIII, 381.
Diplomats, VIII, 110; and diplomacy, VIII, 369.
Disadvantage, XIII, 382.
Disagreeable girl, the, IV, 353.
Disappointment, XIII, 381.
Disarmament, I, 319; VIII, 240; IX, 117; international, VIII, 241.
Disciple, definition of, VI, 246; VIII, 256.
Discontent, XIII, 382; restless, III, 437.
Discord, XIII, 382.
Discoverie, II, 59.
Discoveries, VII, 397.
Discovery, Sir Humphrey Davy's first, VIII, 235.
Discredit, tales of, IV, 431.
Discussion, right of free, II, 361.
Disease, V, 329; largely a matter of mind, I, 141; result of wrong thinking, I, 143; jealousy a, IV, 186; unnaturalness of, IX, 23; fast as a curative measure in, IX, 313; the devils of, X, 254; fear of, XIV, 272.
Diseases are symptoms, I, 295.

Dishonorable, XIII, 382.
Disinherit, XIII, 382.
Disinterested, XIII, 382.
Disloyalty, penalty for, VIII, 239.
Disorganizers, VIII, 113.
Disraeli, X, 210; V, 154.
Distance a matter of mind, VII, 359.
Diversity, unity in, V, 102; XIII, 336.
Divine, kinship to the, I, 296.
Divine attraction, I, 48.
Divine collection agency, I, 131.
Divine energy, the, IV, 287; XII, 374.
Divine Ones, the, IX, 130.
Divine passion, III, 474.
Divine right, XII, 113; X, 37.
Divine Sara, X, 18.
Divine Transformer, IV, 289.
Divorce, V, 100; IV, 169; IX, 89; XIII, 382; freedom in, I, 44; marriage and, I, 45; VI, 169; heroic remedy, I, 46; should be made easy, IX, 89; theological conventions and, IX, 167; why the church opposes, IX, 171; is the last expedient, IX, 172; scars of, IX, 172; an expedient directed toward moral benefit, IX, 173; unfaithfulness and, IX, 174; theologians discuss, IX, 175.
Divorce laws, uniform, I, 43.
Divorcee, XIII, 382.
Divorcees, IX, 92.
Do brilliant men prefer brilliant women, IV, 50.
Doctor, XIII, 382.
Doctors, IV, 114, 138; V, 283, 333; why Elbert Hubbard criticises, I, 31; and quacks, I, 191; viewpoint of, I, 191; lawyers and businessmen, VIII, 217.
Doctrine of the Atonement, XII, 164.
Dog, yellow, IV, 407; loyalty of the, VI, 105; XIII, 248; not quite so much, VIII, 198.
Dogma, I, 360; XIII, 380; never changes, I, 361; inadequate to stormy present, XII, 137.
Dogmatism, I, 421.
Dogs of the Lord, XIII, 248; of war, IX, 288.
Doherty, Henry L., II, 366; X, 105.
Doherty idea, the, II, 367.
Doherty Public Utility, XIV, 207.
Do it electrically, X, 109.

Dollar, XIII, 381.
"Doll's House," IV, 354.
Domestic cantharides, VI, 301.
Domini Canes, XIII, 248.
Dorcas, Aunt, I, 467.
Dotheboys Hall, I, 246.
Dotted line, on the, VIII, 194.
Double life, immorality of, VI, 45.
Doubter, XIII, 383.
Dowie, Reverend John Alexander, V, 101; VI, 196; a reincarnation of Elijah, V, 101; and Buckley, V, 102; methods of, V, 103; financial schemes of, V, 106; chief asset of, V, 109; address delivered by, at open grave of daughter, V, 110.
Down a Butte copper mine. VII, 146.
Down-and-out Club, graduate of the, I, 401; member of the, XIV, 160.
Doylestown Farm School, the, IV, 32.
Draga Machin, VII, 265.
Drawing, I, 458; growing recognition of, IV, 74.
Drama, the soul of the, XIV, 161.
Dreadnaught, I, 316.
Dreadnaught policy, the, I, 317; XIV, 92.
Dreadnaughts, agricultural schools instead of, I, 318.
Dream, XIII, 383; of John Ball, IX, 380.
Dreamer of the Ghetto, I, 106.
Dress, I, 454; mode in, VI, 67; Franklin on, XII, 77; reform, VI, 68.
Dreyfus, IV, 51.
Drinking, growth of the habit, of, IV, 39.
Drones, IX, 142.
Drugs and stimulants, VI, 41; and disease, X, 156.
Drummond on the Creation, I, 214.
Duchess, XIII, 382.
Ducking-stool, IV, 349.
Duds, psychology of, X, 122.
Dukaboor bishop, I, 179.
Dukaboors, who they are, I, 179-186; and the Canadians, I, 181; Dominion Government and, I, 182; and Mennonites compared, I, 182; characteristics of, I, 185.
Dummy directors, I, 65.
Dun, R. G., XIV, 75.
Dunce-cap, VI, 251.
Du Pont, Doctor Pierre Samuel, and Benjamin Franklin, II, 237.

Du Pont business, expansion of the, VII, 231.
Du Pont Powder Company, VII, 231.
Du Ponts, the, and American wars, II, 240; II, 234.
Du Puy, Louis, V, 163.
Durkin, Jimmie, XIV, 73.
Dustless Highway, I, 384.
Dutch, the world's debt to the, XIV, 103; the, and truth, X, 221.
Dutch bookmakers, two famous, I, 223.
Dutch courage, IX, 266.
Dutchman and the churns, XIV, 185.
Duty, III, 453; XIII, 382.
Dynamiters, IX, 366; trial of, IX, 366; Detective Burns and the, IX, 367; organized labor and the, IX, 367; defense of the, IX, 368.
Dynamiting Times Building, IX, 371.
Dynamo, XIII, 382.
Eagle's aerie, the, VII, 24.
Earning a living, II, 94; VIII, 333; and mental growth, VI, 319.
Earning power, VI, 22.
Earth. XIII, 383; and beauty in *Song of Songs*, III, 460; a mile down in the, VII, 377.
Earthquakes, VII, 268; compensations for, VII, 269.
East Aurora, IV, 89; VI, 72; XIII, 266, 362; farmers, VI, 112.
East India Company, I, 40, 164.
Eat, XIII, 383.
Eating, cancer may be caused by wrongful, I, 142; moderation in, IV, 340; farmhand habit, IX, 285; indiscriminate, IX, 382; between meals, IX, 382; excess in, X, 201.
Ecclesiastes, Book of, III, 444; did Solomon write, III, 447.
E. C. O. girls, the, V, 40.
Economic dogmatism, I, 460.
Economic echoes, I, 332.
Economic freedom, XII, 28; of women, I, 292.
Economic investment, an, I, 287.
Economic misdeeds, I, 175.
Economic waste, VIII, 111.
Economics, II, 377; VI, 92; XII, 401; XIII, 383; of China, I, 201; woozy, I, 315; banking a necessity in, I, 334; science of, II, 169; the greatest

xx

study in the world, II, 377; as a science, VIII, 17; based on falsehood, VIII, 21; a lesson in, VIII, 50; an experiment in, VIII, 144; highest science man has yet discovered, XII, 16.
Economist, farmer is an, II, 241; a great, II, 377.
Economyites, VIII, 147.
Eczema for regulating things, IV, 227.
Eddy, Mary Baker G., X, 345; victim of her philosophy, VI, 165.
Edicts of a President, II, 362.
Edison, Thomas A., and the Chautauqua course, II, 116; and Acheson, II, 206; religion of, VI, 227; mother of, VII, 366; letter from, X, 106; indefatigable, X, 107.
Editor, IX, 325; XIII, 384; the worries of an, VI, 121.
Edkohl, Fra, XIV, 175.
Educate yourself, IX, 337.
Educated, are we, IV, 235.
Educated Englishman, an, X, 31.
Educated fools, IV, 335.
Educated man, II, 335; Socrates' idea of an, V, 257.
Educated men, II, 401.
Educated millionaires, IX, 258.
Educated person, an, VI, 317.
Educating the Indian, I, 138.
Education, an, I, 289; II, 261; IV, 159, 393; V, 85; VII, 125, 397; VIII, 25; IX, 45, 353; XII, 303, 305; XIII, 383; and the Indian, I, 137; and Indian Reservation Schools, I, 137; and books I, 138; for social distinction, I, 219; and superior class, I, 219; in work, I, 220; Emerson's recipe for, of child, I, 291; must be racial, I, 319; object of, I, 397; the object of, IX, 46; is growth, I, 397; primal requisites in, I, 389; the higher, I, 397; IV, 362; fallacy of the higher, I, 403; Herbert Spencer's Essay on, I, 405; argument in favor of the higher, I, 415; wrongs worked by monarchical exclusiveness of the higher, I, 402; essay on, I, 405; monastic methods of, I, 412; the natural, I, 416; of head, hand and heart, I, 456; IV, 74; college, I, 463; as evolution, II, 121; of the Jew, IV, 31; a vital factor in, IV, 74; man's first, IV, 118; second-hand, IV, 142; the government and, IV, 153; a bulwark and defense, IV, 154; the rich need, IV, 230; the new, IV, 234; the ideal, IV, 362; academic, IV, 451; recipe for, of children, IV, 455; is a conquest, V, 128; in Japan, V, 212; science in, VIII, 135; manual training necessary part of every man's, IX, 86; Montessori system of, IX, 135; a classical, IX, 256; is comparative, IX, 352; Emerson on, XII, 214, 231.
Educational campaign, Patterson's, II, 177.
Educational factor, picture shows as, VIII, 250.
Educational systems, IV, 395.
Edward VII, XIV, 53; and United States' firemen, X, 293.
Efficiency, II, 332, 391; things that spell, I, 288; is habit, IX, 248; secret of, IX, 248.
Efficiency engineers, five big, II, 331.
Efficiency schools, I, 286.
Efficient man, the, IX, 248.
Efficient service is price for a living wage, I, 288.
Effort, joy is useful, IV, 268.
Ego, exaggerated, is a primal necessity, I, 33.
Egoism, IX, 396.
Egotism, soul of art, III, 449; in literature, IV, 400.
Egypt, the gift of the Nile, II, 124; wealth of, VII, 181; and honey bees, IX, 141.
Eiffel Tower, VII, 233; cost of, VII, 235; familiarity bred contempt for, VII, 235.
Electric sign, home of the, VII, 130.
Electrical energy, VII, 118.
Electricity, I, 434; VII, 117.
Electrocution, IV, 343.
Eleemosynary institution, an, I, 354.
Elegy, where Gray wrote the, V, 201.
Eleusinian mysteries, I, 398.
Elgin, a Little Journey to, VIII, 225.
Elgin watch industry, rise of, VIII, 228.
Elihu's zeal, IV, 134.
Elimination of the unnecessary, XI, 145.
Eliot, Charles W., V, 308; and college

training, I, 417; an intellectual, V,
309; tribute to, V, 309; on the New
Religion, V, 311; his proclamation, V,
311; on rationalism, V, 313; America's
first citizen, V, 316; his teaching, V,
319.
Eliot, George, and Emerson, VI, 62.
Elk, the, VII, 36; the true, VI, 392.
Elk's banquet in Louisville, VII, 167.
Elk's Creed, the, VI, 293.
Ellis Island, I, 30.
Eloquence, XI, 414.
Emancipated man, XIII, 385.
Emancipation, social, V, 300.
Emerson, Ralph Waldo, XII, 193; on achievement, I, 384; on atheism, XII, 220; on character, XII, 237; 248; on children, XII, 195; on church, XII, 211; on a college education, XII, 198; on consistency, XII, 201; on creed, XII, 215; on crime, I, 34; on criticism, XII, 225; on education, XII, 214, 231; on emotion, XII, 201; *Essay on Friendship* by, XIII, 283; on fops and chagrins, XII, 240; on fortune, XII, 223; on friendship, I, 157; on genius, XII, 193, 249; on government, XII, 246; on greatness, XII, 203; on growth, XII, 210; on immortality of the soul, V, 232; on isolation, XII, 237; on kings, XII, 205; on love, XII, 212; on love and lovers, XII, 242; on man, XII, 208; on the master mind, XII, 209; on nature, XII, 239; on nonconformity XII, 196, 200; on obedience and faith, XII, 211; on party promises, XII, 228; on philanthropy, XII, 198; on poetry, XII, 224; on postal rates, I, 95; on prayer, XII, 215; on property, XII, 222; on reading, XII, 205; on resources, XII, 214; on riches, XII, 241; on self-reliance, XII, 194; on self-trust, XII, 201; on sense and character, XI, 243; on shoes, II, 184; on sickness, XII, 238; on society, XII, 221, 234; on soul and spirit relations, XII, 207; on standards, XII, 213; on success, XII, 214; on sympathy, XII, 241, on theologians, XII, 225; on travel, XII, 217; on trifles, XII, 211; on truth, XII, 249; on usages, XII, 199; on virtues,
XII, 198; on work, XII, 232; recipe for educating child, I, 291; his opinion of John Brown, III, 392; brooking the displeasure of his Alma Mater, IV, 15; and Parker were irrigators, IV, 158; and Shelley, IV, 313; revolutionary essay by, V, 300; an alumnus of Harvard Divinity School, V, 313; Law of Compensation, VII, 48; and the Sherman House, VIII, 271; infidel essays of, XI, 318; turning trickster, XI, 391; our modern Plato, XII, 25; heresy of, XII, 26; philosophy of, XII, 26.
Emigration, Hell and, II, 174.
Emmiline, our, XIII, 249.
Emotion, IV, 286; XII, 256; Emerson on, XII, 201.
Emperor, reverence of Japan for, V, 211.
Emphasis, XIII, 383.
Empire builders, VII, 395.
Employee with enlarged ego, I, 81.
Employer, the generous, V, 129; modern American, VIII, 113.
Employees, to play upon the prejudices of, II, 364; careless, VIII, 114; inefficient, VIII, 114.
Employing agents, VI, 404.
Emporia *Gazette*, V, 119.
Enemies, IV, 383; IX, 190.
Enemy, XIII, 384.
Energetic living, VIII, 336.
Energy, VIII, 54; XII, 257; misapplied, I, 175; supreme, I, 404; man the transformer of, IV, 288; animal, VIII, 54; electrical, VIII, 54.
Engen, Fred, XIV, 123.
Engineer, the, IX, 338.
England, recognition of American writers by, V, 141; the, of Dickens, VI, 150.
English, the, and the Indians, VII, 330.
English authors, ignorance, of, VI, 102.
English language, the, VI, 23.
English monuments, VII, 157.
English philosophers, VI, 185.
English-speaking people, the, VII, 353.
Enlightenment, the age of, IV, 464.
Ennui, XIII, 384.
Enterprise, IX, 264; a great engineering, X, 370.
Enterprises, diversity of, VII, 183.
Entertainment, VII, 398.

Enthusiasm, X, 333; XIII, 384.
Environment, IX, 251; IX, 411.
Envy, III, 44.
Epictetus and Aurelius, I, 294.
Epigram, XIII, 384.
Epilepsy, best authority on, in America, X, 133; and diet, X, 133; and apoplexy, X, 139; environment plays an important part, X, 139; very ancient disorder, X, 141; theories about, X, 141.
Epilogue, IV, 135.
Episcopopagy, I, 299.
Epistle, a pointed, XI, 365.
Epitaph, XIII, 386.
Equal suffrage, IV, 369.
Equality, I, 361.
Equanimity, II, 385.
Equitable, XIII, 384.
Equitable Life Assurance Company, founder of the, VIII, 161, 164.
Equity, I, 365; XIII, 384; a question of, VIII, 26.
Erasmus, as a pamphleteer, I, 22; illegitimate, I, 152; and the *schamp*, IX, 253.
Erie Canal, II, 124.
Erie Railway, II, 125; Goshen to Binghamton, II, 128; reached Elmira, II, 130; Piermont to Dunkirk, II, 130; Piermont to Jersey City, II, 134.
Esprit de corps, XIII, 236.
Essay on Friendship, Emerson's, XIII, 283.
Essay on Silence, X, 402.
Essay on the Sublime, VI, 206.
Esteem and confidence of fellowmen, how to procure, XII, 93.
Esthetic futility, XIII, 322.
Estimating people, XIII, 306.
Eternity, XIII, 384.
Ethical dentist, XII, 394.
Ethical Monism, I, 133.
Ethical Monistic Concept, I, 133.
Ethics, I, 184; the new business, I, 376; the newest theory in, II, 169; of medicine, V, 328; modern business, VIII, 21.
Eton, Harrow and Rugby, IX, 57.
Etruria pottery, XIV, 98.
Eucalyptus, VIII, 315.
Eucharist, XIII, 384.

Eugenics, a suggestion in, IV, 106; the science of, IV, 322; what is, IV, 322; defined by proponent, IV, 323; records, IV, 324.
European, XIII, 386.
European culture, XIV, 226.
Euterpe, X, 343.
Evangelist Torrey, XIV, 76.
Evans, Fanny Riegel, X, 411.
Everybody, XIII, 385.
Every man to his job, XIV, 285.
Everywoman, IX, 199; play of, IX, 200.
Evil, VI, 254; fear of, IX, 386; Ingersoll on existence of, XII, 186.
Evolution, IV, 118, 364; VI, 185; VIII, 86; XII, 349; XIII, 313, 385; an easy lesson in, I, 39; natural, I, 227; social, I, 322; IV, 137; education as, II, 121.
Excesses, XIV, 271.
Excitement, advantages of, IV, 320.
Ex-communication, IV, 163.
Ex-convict, the, I, 154; advice to, I, 158.
Executive, XIII, 386.
Exercise, IV, 423; as an investment, X, 124.
Existence, XIII, 385; tragedy of, IV, 471.
Exodus, the, IX, 394.
Exodus, women of the, IV, 184.
Expectancy, XIII, 384.
Expectation, XIII, 385.
Experience, IV, 475; XIII, 385; sweetest that can come to a man, VI, 63; during Des Moines lecture, VII, 172.
Expert, public-utility, II, 366.
Explanations, IX, 24.
Exploded idea, an, I, 411.
Exploiting the public and prosperity, III, 150.
Explosive powder, invention of, II, 235.
Exposition with a soul, VII, 196.
Exposition grounds, VII, 194.
Express companies, I, 90; VIII, 278.
Express Company, Post Office and, compared, I, 90-99; methods of, VIII, 280.
Expression, VI, 185; XII, 259, 321; XIII, 386; and life, IV, 180; temperament and, IV, 181; we grow through, VI, 240; must equal impression, XII, 259.
Eyeball, XIII, 385.
Eytinge, Louis V., XIV, 60; and mail-

xxiii

order business, XIV, 63.
Fabian, origin of name, VI, 306; a definition of, VI, 307.
Fabian Socialism, I, 30.
Fabius, VI, 306.
Fable, a XIV, 281.
Faces are maps, X, 125.
Fact and fiction, X, 125.
Factory betterment, and Krupps, I, 173.
Factory betterments, first, in America, I, 172; father of all, II, 175.
Factory laws, IV, 347; how regarded by worker and employer, IX, 379.
Factory melancholia, II, 295.
Factory system and Robert Owen, IX, 380.
Fads of successful men, VIII, 125.
Faerie Queen, VI, 339.
Fagin, the Jew, VI, 101.
Failure, IV, 381; IX, 248; XIII, 386; the why of financial, VI, 238.
Failures, sympathy for, IX, 44.
Fair play, II, 403.
Fairbanks, Ex-President, V, 52.
Faith, IX, 325; XIII, 386; and freedom, I, 347; in humanity, II, 163; undaunted, VII, 279; in customer, VIII, 109; in your fellowmen, VIII, 109; and mail-order business, VIII, 348; diluted, IX, 325.
Faithfulness, IV, 110.
Fake, XIII, 386; advertisements, I, 189.
Fakers, theological, I, 423; medical, I. 423; and fakes, I, 423.
Fakery, metaphysics and, I, 421; of dead languages, I, 421.
Fallacious focusing, VI, 30.
Fallen folks, VI, 110.
Falsehood, XII, 403; economics based on, VIII, 21.
False standards in business, IV, 202.
Fame, IV, 382; V, 123; XIII, 386; the hall of, VI, 225.
Famed orange belt, the, VII, 161.
Families, genius and, II, 62.
Family a community, XIII, 342.
Family life in the country, XIII, 334.
Family line, XIII, 386.
Famous Gary dinners, the, II, 24.
Fanaticism, III, 368; XII, 316.
Fane, empty, XIII, 348.
Farm, II, 264; Vail's, II, 317; Brook, IV, 147; hard life on the, XII, 262.
Farm boss, the, XIV, 202.
Farm life, VI, 119; burden of, used to fall upon the women, II, 418.
Farm School of Jews, IV, 31.
Farmer, XIII, 386; the supreme, I, 407; the, an economist, II, 341; Jew as a, IV, 31; as a feeder of men, VII, 188; Jap as a, VII, 291; retired, VIII, 201; hope of the race, IX, 356.
Farmers, Brook, IV, 147.
Farmers, city boys as, VI, 35; Mormons as, VII, 68; millionaire, VIII, 145; retired, VIII, 201; women, XIV, 209.
Farming, I, 333; VII, 181; VIII, 75, 143; and horses, I, 432; scientific, II, 279; IX, 239; the city boy and, IV, 32; in northwestern Ohio and southern Michigan, VII, 185; intensive, VII, 294; co-operative, VIII, 143; dry, X, 353; and railroading, XIV, 297.
Farming implements, I, 432.
Farms, "abandoned," of New England, I, 432.
Farragut, David Glasgow, VII, 133.
Farrell, James, II, 21.
Fashion, XIII, 386; and clothing, I, 368; in letters and things, VI, 67; why does, change, VI, 67; latitude in, IX, 273; the tyranny of, XIV, 212; foreign dictators of, XIV, 213.
Fashions, the future of, IX, 270; Paris and American, IX, 272.
Fast as a curative, IX, 313.
Fast fan, characteristics of the, IX, 315.
Fast train, XIII, 386.
Fasting fans, IX, 313.
Fasts and feasts, IV, 197.
Fasts had rise in India, IX, 314.
Fatalism, IX, 300.
Fate, in the grasp of, III, 222.
Faugeron, M., IV, 326.
Fault-finding, spirit of, I, 60.
Faults, IV, 412.
Favors, mutual, 388.
Fear, I, 294; IV, 306, 442; V, 229; IX, 146; XII, 318, 324; XIII, 386; much of our sickness is caused by, I, 295; a formula of, I, 301; of death, IV, 49; and hell, IV, 161; and hope, IV, 161; and formal religions, IV, 164; tyranny of, IV, 275; and death, IV, 306;

theology fosters, VI, 393; of evil, IX, 386; the only, IX, 386; and investigation, IX, 388.
Feasts, fasts and, IV, 197.
Feathers, XIII, 387.
Federal Steel Company, II, 20.
Feed starving Europe, I, 367.
Fellowmen, faith in, VIII, 109.
Fellowship Churches, X, 148.
Felting, science of, II, 428.
Female jail, II, 327.
Femininity, IV, 407.
Feminist movement, XIII, 387.
Fenian Brotherhood, I, 229.
Ferguson, Charles, XIV, 248; *The University Militant* by, XIV, 248; army of, XIV, 250.
Ferrer, Francisco, V, 167; fall of, V, 170; demonstration, V, 171.
Festivals, II, 103.
Feud, XIII, 387.
Fiction, I, 335.
Field, Gene, as a letter-writer, VI, 267; letters of, VIII, 408.
Field, Marshall, and High School graduate, I, 465; order of, I, 465; merchant prince, IV, 97.
Fiend, the, who leads the orchestra, VII, 320.
Fifth Avenue, XIII, 378.
Fifty years ago, VIII, 163.
Fighting Bob, X, 163.
Filtration plant, a, X, 372.
Final union, I, 228.
Financial panic, insurance against, VIII, 210.
Financiers and business, VIII, 208.
Finery and fashions, XIII, 319.
Fire, secret of the gods, I, 438; father of transportation, I, 439; Greek, II, 235; compensations for, VII, 269.
Fire Insurance, I, 441; germ of, VIII, 152.
Fire Insurance Company, first in United States, I, 441.
Firecracker, IX, 241.
Fires, historic, I, 440.
Fire-places, V, 146.
Fireworks, death toll of, IX, 240; and July Fourth, IX, 240; menace of, IX, 240.
First families, the, I, 216.
First requisite, I, 398; XIII, 387.

Fiscal reform, VIII, 60.
Fish, dead, IV, 432; the, are coming, XIV, 45.
Fish, Honorable, F. P., authority on patent law, X, 103.
Fisher, Carl, I, 390; world-maker, I, 389.
Fiske, John, I, 421.
Five dollars a day, I, 287.
Five-foot Shelf, I, 417.
Fixing on the affirmative, IV, 202.
Fixity, the fallacy of, IV, 286.
Flats, babies in, VII, 57.
Flatterers, paid, IX, 410.
Flattery, Jefferson on, XII, 86.
Flee the disciple, VI, 244.
Fletcher, Horace, I, 147; X, 193; philosophy of, X, 202.
Fletcherism, I, 144, 149; what is, I, 145.
Fletcherize, I, 141; IX, 314; X, 193.
Flimflammers, expert, IV, 276.
Flintlock was invented in Fifteen Hundred Fifteen, II, 235.
Flower, the mission of a, VI, 175.
Flower City, the, I, 395.
Flower seeds and Burpee, X, 362.
Flowers, III, 463; and rose gardens, VII, 293; twigs and blossoms, XI, 403.
Flunkey and the good fellow, IX, 319.
Flunkeyism, IX, 317.
Fly, XIII, 387.
Flynn of Atlanta, VI, 384; attack of, on Fra Elbertus, VI, 383.
Folderol, XIII, 387.
Folk lore, Andrew Lang on, V, 92.
Folks out of focus, VI, 160.
Following the races, IV, 358.
Folly, Franklin on, XII, 76.
Fonetik spelling, IX, 158.
Food, taste is test of quality of, I, 146; and work, I, 148; nature's first, IV, 240; pure, IV, 241; raisin finest, that grows, VII, 163; a fuel and a stimulant, IX, 313; the wrong kind of, IX, 286; selection of, IX, 287; love and life, IX, 344; production of, without increasing our acreage, X, 354.
Food prices, VII, 182.
Food supply and healthy nation, IX, 344.
Foods, breakfast, II, 321.
Foodstuffs, high prices of, VII, 183.
Fool, genius or, XIII, 273; educated, IX, 335.

Football, I, 411; IV, 398; the, table, IV, 104.
Forbearance, XIII, 387.
Forbes of Harvard, XI, 293.
Force, IV, 386; fanaticism and sentiment, III, 368.
Forces, opposition of, IV, 64.
Ford, Henry, II, 85; mfg., methods of, I, 391; income of, II, 85; second largest taxpayer in the United States, II, 85; and bankers, II, 86; and the banker, VIII, 371; ingrowing payroll of, II, 87; the king of standardization, II, 91; general manager of the United States, II, 92; thinks in millions, II, 92; a lover of the great Out-of-Doors, II, 97; motto of, II, 101.
Ford Company and labor, II, 90.
Ford workman, the, II, 101.
Fords and good roads, I, 392.
Forecast, XIII, 387.
Forehead, XIII, 387.
Foremen, how made, VIII, 190.
Forgiveness, XII, 279.
Forgotten freak of nature, a, VII, 240.
Fort Worth, VII, 390.
Fortitude, I, 370; IV, 417; XIII, 388.
Fortresses and castles on the Rhine, IV, 192.
Forum, XIII, 388.
Foster, M. B., XIII, 241.
Foster, Thomas J., II, 195; founding the I. C. S., II, 198; his men, II, 197.
Fourier's prophecy, XIII, 356.
Fox, Charles, I, 364.
Fra, XIII, 387.
Fra Elbertus replies to attack, VI, 384.
Fra Junipero Serra, V, 177; ranks with Saint Benedict, V, 177.
Frame up, XIII, 388.
Franciscan spirit, new, X, 296.
Franklin, Benjamin, X, 386; XIII, 238; on author's satsifaction, XIII, 70; on commerce between nations, XII, 80; on contentment and busyness, XII, 61; on credit and character, XII, 61; on debt, XII, 77; on dress, XII, 77; on folly, XII, 76; on idleness, XII, 73; on industry, XII, 72; on leisure, XII, 73; on pride, XII, 76; on riches and rich, XII, 44; on taxes, XII, 71; on trade, XII, 79; on the treatment of prisoners, IX, 44; on value of time, XII, 72; on vanities, XII, 75; on vice, XII, 74; first Post-Master General in America, I, 95; and the Bible, I, 360; economic break of, I, 461; and investments, I, 462; and money, I, 462; spirit of mirth, persistency, patience, commonsense, IV, 15; a faddist, VIII, 125; best all-round educated man that America has produced, IX, 328; epitaph of, IX, 328; capital of, XII, 17; the typical American, XII, 17; and books, XII, 30; and the *Spectator*, XII, 31; a vegetarian, XII, 32; and the Junto, XII, 34; his rules of health, XII, 35; his state of mind with regard to his principles and morals, XII, 36; Presbyterianism and, XII, 38; the virtues and, XII, 40; observations on reading history, XII, 42; and the Dunkers, XII, 43; epigrams of, XII, 45-69; and wit, XII, 47.
Frat, XIII, 388; menace of the, VII, 128; demolition of the, VII, 129.
Frat idea, I, 399.
Fraternity, I, 361.
Frawley Law, X, 203.
Frederick the Eighth, X, 37.
Free bread, slogan of, VIII, 33.
Free motherhood, I, 306.
Free school, the, IX, 45, 57.
Free society, in a, IV, 149.
Free speech, V, 174; and a free press, II, 360; and anarchy, V, 171.
Free Trade, I, 63; VIII, 64; XII, 103; United States moving toward, I, 63.
Freedom, I, 347; III, 358; V, 73, 220; XIV, 55; in divorce, I, 44; growth of I, 298; Uncle Sam's middle name is, I, 347; love ever fights for, III, 356; battle of, X, 288; Paine on, XII, 105; Greece and, XIII, 361.
French heels, XIII, 320.
French religious trust, death of the, I, 364.
French Revolution, I, 361.
Frey, Charles Daniel, X, 380.
Frey organization, X, 383.
Friend, XIII, 388.
Friendly Inn for worn-out, tired, galled horses, X, 368.
Friends and friendship, IV, 309; IX, 190;

and enemies, X, 109; and money, X, 297.
Friendship, II, 258, 278; III, 184; IV, 309; VII, 305; X, 279; XII, 253, 280; XIII, 388; XIV, 264; in modern business, II, 34; a business founded on, II, 278; the desire for, IV, 28; an ideal, IV, 29; exclusive, IV, 290; the finest, IV, 291; fine art of, VIII, 379; platonic, IX, 91; nothing so hygienic, IX, 193; betrayal of, IX, 213; perfect, X, 41; Essay on, by Emerson, XIII, 283.
Friendships, IX, 191.
Frisco fire, one feature of the, VII, 271.
Froebel, Frederick, VI, 249; XII, 390; and children, I, 153; on drawing, I, 457; and Pestalozzi and the divinity of the child, V, 116.
From the Atlantic to the Pacific, I, 384.
Fruit-Farming, VII, 187.
Fruits and Flowers are primal sex products, VII, 98.
Fry, Elizabeth, I, 154; VII, 304; X, 344.
Fuel, what is the best, I, 435; some comparisons, I, 435; oil as a, I, 435; wood as a, I, 435; kerosene is Nature's own, I, 436; waste of, II, 405 food a, IX, 313.
Fulton, Robert, VIII, 325.
Funeral obsequy, XI, 140.
Furniture and Grand Rapids, IV, 166.
Future Authors, IX, 310.
Future for a bustle, I, 200.
Fuzzy wuzzy fads, VI, 93.
Gabberinos, VIII, 195.
Gable, William F., IV, 99; Traubel's tribute to, IV, 101.
Gabriel, horn of, I, 180.
Gage, Lyman J., VIII, 368.
Gaiety, XIII, 388.
Galilee, XI, 50; meaning of word, XI, 21.
Gallagher, X, 290.
Gallant, XIII, 388.
Gallio, a brother of Seneca, XI, 78.
Gambler, I, 75.
Gambling, I, 76; effect of, on business, I, 76; effect of, on health, I, 76; morality of, I, 76; effect of, on morals, I, 77; code of, III, 167.
Games have survival value, IX, 106.

Game warden, X, 50.
Gang-plows, II, 414.
Gang workers, XIII, 333.
Garb, distinguishable, XIII, 324.
Garcia, General, I, 254; carry a message to, I, 256.
Garcia episode, the, I, 254.
Garcia matter, this, XIII, 297.
Garden of the Gods, XIII, 108.
Gardens, X, 356; playgrounds and, IV, 160; John Wesley and, X, 358; Josiah Wedgwood and, X, 359.
Gardiner, VIII, 21.
Gardner, Fred, IX, 411.
Garibaldi, I, 363.
Garnet the superb, VI, 18.
Garret philosophy, VIII, 18.
Garrulous smiles, VI, 119.
Gary, Elbert H., II, 13; VIII, 378; the great pacificator, II, 15; birthplace of, II, 16; his early life, II, 16; lawyer, II, 17; first mayor of Wheaton, II, 17; a county judge, II, 19; diplomat and financier, II, 19; one of the demos, II, 23; head of the Steel Corporation, II, 24.
Gas, I, 435.
Gasoline by-product, II, 32.
Gates, John W., VIII, 377.
Gautama, XI, 30.
Gaynor, William J., X, 288; the Samuel Adams of our day, X, 288; mental make-up of, X, 289; his assassin, X, 290.
Geers, Ed, VI, 377; X, 65; battles of, X, 66; and trotting records, X, 67; excerpts from his book, X, 69; his epitaph, X, 71.
General Electric Company, I, 286.
Genius, II, 347; VI, 163, 285; VII, 268, 394; X, 347; XII, 193, 271; XIII, 389; penalized, I, 297; the secret of, IV, 25; nature's best use for, IV, 389; Hoosier, V, 54; respect for, VI, 89; what is a, VI, 284; in groups, IX, 336; should never marry, XI, 129; transmitted, XI, 129; Emerson on, XII, 193, 249; what is, XII, 249; or fool, XIII, 273.
Genoa and beggars, VII, 152.
Gent, XIII, 388.
Gentiles, the Jews and the, IV, 199.

Gentility, rottenness of, I, 218.
Gentleman, IV, 144.
Gentlemen, XIII, 388.
Gentleness, I, 453, 408.
Genus buckwheat, the, V, 112.
Genus Loafer Rusticus, XI, 101.
Genus porcher, VI, 264.
George, Henry, I, 120.
George, Kara, VII, 262.
George III, I, 360.
George V, XIV, 53.
George Junior Republic, I, 157.
Germ of both Life and Fire insurance, VIII, 152.
Germans made the first type, VII, 397; and promulgation of music, XIV, 105.
Germany, motto of, I, 64; and Thirty Years' War, I, 280; compulsory military system of, IV, 248; a solidarity, VIII, 212; ten commandments of, VIII, 212.
Get out or Get In Line, I, 57.
Getting old is simply a bad habit, VI, 281.
Getting a start in vaudeville, VII, 317.
Getting together, VIII, 142, 359.
Gettysburg Address, XII, 130.
Ghetto, Dreamer of the, I, 106; first, was at Venice, IV, 198.
Ghetto habit, IV, 31.
Gibbons, Cardinal, I, 362.
Gillette, VII, 208.
Gilman, Charlotte Perkins, XIII, 353.
Girard, Stephen, II, 371; on trees, II, 153.
Girard College, I, 402.
Girls, IV, 381; gifts to, VI, 278.
Give it to him, Tim, XIV, 49.
Giveth, XIII, 388.
Gladstone, I, 229; loyalty of, to England, IV, 112; and Inverness cape, VI, 79.
Glenwood Mission Inn, VII, 296.
Glenwood Tavern, the old, VII, 296.
Glib informer, the, I, 111.
Globe Theater, VII, 158.
Globe-trotting Briton, IX, 17.
Glorious Fourth, the, IX, 240.
Glory, XIII, 388.
Glover, Lyman, VIII, 308; XIV, 175.
Glutton, XIII, 389.
Goblins, IV, 165.
God, XIII, 389; one of the little tragedies of, I, 336-340; in the Constitution, I, 353; an honest, I, 360; champions of, IV, 133; a, a bit out of focus, V, 196; sunsets of, VI, 391; what we microbes think of, IX, 65; word, not in our Constitution, IX, 65; child of, XI, 236; and Satan, XIII, 389.
God save the King, XIV, 53.
Goddess, XIII, 389.
God-like life, the, XI, 34.
Godlove, Lewis, X, 260.
Gods in the chrysalis, XII, 321.
Goethe, Johannes Wolfgang, jealousy of, VI, 259; and Charlotte Von Stein, VI, 259; XI, 399; and his wife, VI, 286.
Going down a mine, VII, 372.
Gold, use of, in dentistry, X, 197.
Golden Gate, VII, 270.
Golden Rule, application of the, XII, 17; in prison, VII, 90; as a working policy, VIII, 109.
Golden Rule Brotherhood, VII, 90.
Goldman, Emma, and the new regime, I, 52; the chief anarch of her time, V, 172.
Goldsmith, Oliver, VII, 82.
Golgotha, XI, 80.
Good, the greatest, IV, 233; doing, XII, 358; doing, by stealth, XIII, 281.
Good cheer, messages of, XI, 350.
Good fellow, the, IX, 405; XIII, 349; XIV, 267.
Good habits, XIII, 389.
Good luck, IV, 400; X, 226; XIII, 389.
Good Night, XIV, 283.
Good old times, I, 67.
Good sense and character make their own forms, XII, 243.
Good sport, XIII, 389.
Good things travel incog., VI, 223.
Good-will, IX, 104; XII, 373; world redeemed by, I, 178; fostered by good roads, I, 308.
Good writing, secret of, X, 85.
Goodrich, Dr. B. F., X, 385; birthplace of, X, 387; and Walt Whitman, X, 389; some early inventions of, X, 391; inventor by prenatal tendency, X, 391.
Goodrich Company, the B. F., VIII, 388.
Goodrich Tire, the, VIII, 389.
Gooseberry Jake, XI, 334.
Goose-dogma, VI, 170.
Gordon at Khartum, IX, 132.

Gore, Senator, of Oklahoma, VI, 33.
Gorky, Maxim, X, 243.
Gossip, XIII, 389; tragic result of, I, 107.
Gotham, III, 439; VII, 326; a city called, III, 439; newspapers of, III, 439.
Gould, Billy, VII, 317.
Gould system, II, 294.
Gourmand, XIII, 389.
Govern, the right to, IV, 350.
Government, VII, 329; XIII, 389; XIV, 71; a dual proposition, II, 93; the, and education, IV, 93, 153; one weak spot in American, IV, 167; the ideal, V, 373; soul stuff in, VII, 394; and big business, VIII, 72; whole art of, XII, 87; Jefferson on, XII, 98; Paine on, XII, 110; legitimate object of, XII, 139.
Government railroad, a, IX, 377.
Gracchi, VIII, 223.
Graduation, I, 464.
Graft, IV, 467; VII, 270; XIII, 389.
Graham, Margaret A., I, 264.
Grammar, IV, 439; XIII, 389.
Granada, I, 356; capital of the world, II, 48.
Grand Canyon of Colorado, X, 186.
Grand Trunk, Railway, II, 352.
Grant, General, I, 237; a grocer, X, 66.
Graphite, II, 212; lubricating, II, 213.
Grass, what is the, XII, 161.
Gratification, love for, VI, 235.
Gratitude, IV, 434; V, 221; XIII, 390; a prayer of, IV, 15.
Gravedigger Dog, XIII, 245.
Gravediggers, the, XIII, 245.
Graves, John Temple, and suffrage, II, 449.
Gravitation, law of, IX, 409; XIII, 344.
Gray, Judge, VII, 228; birthplace of, VII, 228.
Great awakening, X, 98; times of, VII, 274; in England, X, 358.
Great betterment, a, IV, 30.
Great Blonde Beast, IX, 118.
Great Britain's hope now lies in her colonies, VII, 353.
Great compliment, a, IX, 277.
Great engineering enterprise, X, 370.
Great Kentucky revival, II, 104.
Great lawyer, a, II, 229.

Great man, XIII, 390.
Great migrations, VII, 65.
Great milk breeds, I, 244.
Great Obscure, The, IX, 392.
Great Pyramid, the, VII, 233.
Great Reaction, IX, 119.
Great Secret Doctrine, VI, 128.
Great White Way, lure of the, I, 289; VIII, 390.
Great world powers had basis on agriculture, VII, 181.
Greatest book ever written, I, 101.
Greatest good, the, IV, 233.
Greatest horse-general the world has ever seen, X, 66.
Greatest trust in the world, the, II, 93.
Greatness, XII, 203; final proof of, I, 58; woman's, III, 468; secret of, of great men of Athens, XIII, 358.
Gredag, II, 214.
Greece, XIII, 358; grandeur of, II, 48; freedom and, XIII, 361.
Greek fire, II, 235; first used for priestly purposes, II, 235.
Greek tongue, the, IV, 363.
Greeley's advice, V, 308.
Grey Brothers, the, IX, 194; at Roycroft, IX, 195.
Grief, IV, 419; VI, 208; XIII, 390.
Griffith, Colonel Griffith J., and Prison Reform League, IV, 210.
Grind, the, XIII, 18.
Grizzly bear, XIV, 89.
Grocery trade, VIII, 67.
Grosscup, Peter Sterling, X, 266.
Groucherino, XIII, 390.
Grown-up children, IV, 218.
Growth, conditions of, VI, 374.
Grubb, Eugene H., X, 347; the heroic type, X, 348; *The Potato* by, X, 351.
Guelph, Edward, XIV, 53.
Guenther, XIV, 193.
Guesswork, XIII, 389.
Guests, paid, IX, 220; hotel, XIII, 339.
Guggenheim, Benjamin, IX, 19.
Guilt and innocence, IX, 54.
Guinea hens, baby, XIII, 231.
Guineas, the, XIII, 229.
Guinevere, defense of, V, 148.
Gumma, XIII, 390.
Gun gumption, I, 316.
Gutter, XIII, 390.

H, the letter, XI, 148; famous names beginning with the letter, II, 52.
Habit, XII, 291; XIII, 390; men creatures of, I, 141; Study, II, 114, 195; the Ghetto, IV, 31; growth of drinking, IV, 39; of self-confidence, IV, 55; the Health, IV, 341; of analysis, Coleridge's, IX, 216; sleep, X, 121.
Habits rule our lives, I, 398.
Hadley, President, I, 59; a pragmatist, I, 400; of Missouri, X, 268; Kansas product, X, 269; influence of mother's teaching on, X, 270.
Hadley Commission, the, VII, 402.
Hæckel, Ernst, and survival value, IX, 107.
Haggis, XIII, 390.
Hagiology and civilization, IV, 282.
Hair, XIII, 391.
Hale, Edward Everett, X, 145.
Hale, George, world's greatest firefighter, X, 292.
Half-Moon, the crew of the, II, 54; hoists sail, II, 54; first ship to stretch her sails on the Hudson, II, 57.
Hall, Bolton, VI, 121; devotion of, to single tax, I, 51.
Hall, Doctor Stanley, I, 456.
Hall, the, of Fame, VI, 225; IX, 403.
Halley's Comet, IV, 205.
Halsted, Ruth, III, 16.
Hambletonian Ten, VII, 179.
Hamburg Belle, breeder of, II, 375.
Hamilton, VIII, 60.
Hamilton, Alexander, financial methods of, VIII, 204.
Hamlet, Prince of Denmark, one of the greatest advertisements ever written, X, 38.
Hammering Catholics, I, 268.
Hand, XIII, 391.
Handicapped with orders, XIII, 301.
Handicrafts, VI, 91; in the homes, I, 41.
Hanged, when a man is, V, 343.
Hangman's Oak, II, 153.
Hanseatic League, I, 277; a revival of the, VII, 348.
Happiness, I, 49, 397; IX, 32, 105; XI, 387; XII, 165, 329, 405; XIII, 390; key to, IV, 286; man's search for, IX, 33; by appropriation, IX, 34; stages of, IX, 34-38; Ingersoll on, XII, 178;

and health, XII, 290.
Happy habit, I, 397.
Happy lives, VI, 181; and biography, XIII, 265.
Hard Knocks, University of, I, 401; graduates of, VI, 375.
Hardware and civilization, II, 358.
Hard water, IX, 298.
Harmonists and Communists, IV, 146.
Harmony, IV, 402; IX, 181; wisdom of, I, 294; the universal, XIV, 142.
Harmonyites, VIII, 146.
Harper's Ferry, III, 394.
Harrigan and Hart, XIV, 173.
Harris, Henry, IX, 16.
Hart, Dean, I, 33; X, 150; as an unconscious comedian, X, 151; read prayers for rain, X, 152.
Hartford, Connecticut, VII, 171.
Harvard, I, 400; IV, 177; XI, 297; of the West, V, 270; teachers of, VI, 50.
Harvard culture, VI, 322.
Harvard endowment, IV, 177.
Harvard fence, the, VI, 322.
Harvey, Fred, II, 472.
Has-been, XIII, 391.
Hastings, Warren, I, 163; and others, I, 163; and East India Company, I, 164; and British supremacy in India, I, 165; arrest and indictment of, I, 166; honors conferred on, I, 166; private character of, I, 167.
Hastings, by Macaulay, I, 163.
Hat, reveals the mood of the mind, II, 437; and attitude, VI, 79; personality in the, VI, 146.
Hate, I, 34; IV, 397; VI, 253; XIII, 391; *The Menace* fire-brand of, I, 269; and calumny, IX, 192.
Hatred, Marxian socialism and, I, 30; and Labor Unions, I, 124.
Hats, Ali Baba's, VI, 148; Steve Crane on, VI, 148; the matter of, XIII, 289
Hat-Snatcher, the, I, 443.
Hat-Snatching as a fine art, I, 444.
Hatter, the old-time, II, 421.
Hawkins, General Rush C., VI, 104.
Haying time in Scotland, IV, 190.
Hays, Charles M., II, 349; IX, 19; birthplace of, II, 349; declines knighthood, II, 352; *Message to Garcia* and,

II, 354; *Politeness Pays* and, II, 354; concentration a habit with, II, 356.
He digged a pit, IX, 25.
He faces the East, VI, 327.
Head, hand and heart, XIII, 366.
Headgear, personality in, VI, 145.
Headliner, I, 341.
Healing art, incantations big factor in, II, 457.
Health, IV, 411; VIII, 183; XII, 356; effect of gambling on, I, 76; attends mastication, I, 146; and life insurance, IV, 106; key to, IV, 286; ideal of perfect physical, V, 326; Boards of, V, 328; science and, VI, 166; IX, 23; and the woods, VI, 350; and deep breathing, VI, 391; laws of, IX, 250; XII, 268; Manchester Board of, IX, 379; and clean teeth, X, 195; and diet, X, 199; temple of, X, 253; care of, and other matters, XI, 347; recipe for good, XII, 290; and play in North Woods, XIV, 294; and confidence, XIV, 273.
Health Habit, I, 398; IV, 341; VI, 42; XII, 287.
Healy, Patrick J., II, 154; originated the phrase, " everything known in music," II, 162.
Heart, XIII, 390; hunger of the, III, 212; supreme prayer of my, XII, 261; tragedies of the, XII, 335; ache, IX, 139.
Heaven, IV, 394; XIII, 391; what makes, XI, 398.
Hebrew character, VI, 103.
Hegel, the poet-philosopher, IV, 205; was the Holy Eremite of philosophy, IV, 206.
Heine, Heinrich, I, 185; IX, 199; and irony, IV, 258.
Heirs to the past, IV, 129.
Hell, II, 314; IV, 161; XIII, 331, 391; emigration and, II, 174; and Texas, VII, 405; definition of, IX, 106; and barb-wire fences, X, 46.
Help Yourself, I, 79.
Helpers, choosing, XII, 393.
Helta-skelta, XIII, 391.
Hen, XIII, 392.
Henry, the Ate of England, VI, 298.
Hepburn Bill, VIII, 74.

Herald of Freedom, III, 322.
Herbert, Ewing, V, 333.
Hernia, heroic treatment of, by Doctor Hubbard, I, 143.
Herod Antipas, XI, 37.
Herodias, XI, 37.
Heroes, II, 172; on the *Titanic*, IX, 18.
Heroic types, X, 348.
Herren, Doctor, I, 54.
Herreshoff brothers, II, 28.
Herschel, Caroline, X, 345.
Hessians, XIII, 329.
Hieroglyphics, I, 458.
Highbrow, XIII, 391; IV, 333.
High cost of living, I, 429.
Highflyer, XIII, 392.
High-priced cars, IX, 268.
Higher Criticism, the, IV, 232.
Higher Education, the, I, 397.
Hights, the, V, 13.
Hill, Professor Adams Sherman, VI, 46.
Hill, James J., VII, 331.
Hillel, XI, 23.
Hints to salesmen, I, 455; to those that would be rich, XII, 44.
Hiring other folks' help, VIII, 155, 157.
His soul goes marching on, III, 429.
His umps saves the day, XIV, 280.
Historian, recompense of the, XI, 14.
History, VI, 69; XIII, 392; what is, I, 380; great women of, V, 396; women who live in, VI, 181; Delaware in, VII, 224; in little, VIII, 161; five great dates in, X, 97; what is, XI, 13; three epochs in, XII, 91; of the race is a history of war and blood, XII, 354; a little, in tabloid, XIV, 131.
Hive, Spirit of the, VII, 303; XII, 379.
Hobgoblin of little minds, XII, 201.
Hobson, Congressman, I, 315.
Hodge, Doctor J. W., I, 311.
Hohenzollern, William, I, 278; a poseur, I, 279.
Holden, Professor, IX, 354.
Holland, the Schoolmaster of the World, II, 49.
Holmes, Oliver Wendell, X, 15; apropos Law of Diminishing Returns, I, 116; on education of the child, I, 291; funeral of, X, 145.
Holstein, I, 242.
Holy Cross Day, IV, 199.

Holy See, Napoleon's contract with the, I, 361.
Home, IV, 150; XIII, 392; basis of civilization, VI, 35; the unit of civilization, IX, 45; art spirit in the, XIII, 337; music in the, XIV, 107; of the big red apple, VII, 97.
Home industries, II, 184.
Home Rule, Ireland and I, 228; Gladstone and Irish, I, 229; Parnell and Irish, I, 229; and religious differences, I, 230; Ulster and Irish, I, 230; Mr. Asquith and Irish, I, 321.
Home Study, II, 198.
Homecomers' Week and Homecomers' Day, X, 221.
Homer, VII, 400.
Homesickness, XI, 314.
Honest God, an, I, 360.
Honest hypocrites, I, 421.
Honesty, XII, 93, 403; in literature, VI, 64; as a business asset, VIII, 119.
Honey out of the carcass, VIII, 140.
Honey-bees in Egypt, IX, 141.
Honeymoon, XIII, 392.
Honor, professional, IV, 111.
Honor system, VII, 92; success of the, VII, 95.
Honors, I, 166.
Hoodlumism, the rise and progress of, IV, 90; cure for, IV, 91; a carnival of, V, 175; and vaudeville, VIII, 313.
Hooker, General, I, 57.
Hooliganism, IX, 363.
Hoosier, genius, V, 54.
Hoosier, habitat, the, V, 52.
Hope, III, 446; IV, 453; XIII, 392; the Star of, IV, 35; fear and, IV, 161; eternal, VI, 180.
Hopkinson Smith, V, 145.
Horse, partnership with a good, VI, 15.
Horse lovers, VI, 20.
Horseback riding, XIII, 302; and health, VI, 16.
Horse-market, greatest, in the world, II, 395.
Horse-power, VIII, 93.
Horse-racing, I, 77.
Horses, XI, 166; love for, XI, 203.
Hosiery, the consumption of, VIII, 340; and royalty, VIII, 340; and society, VIII, 340; and John Wesley, VIII, 340.

Hostages to fortune, IX, 251.
Hot Springs, VII, 83; Indian relics at, VII, 85; therapeutic value of, VII, 85.
Hotel and restaurant music, I, 476.
Hotel guests, XIII, 339.
Hotel Sherman, Little Journey to the, VIII, 271.
Hotelkeeper's obligation, IX, 219.
Hotels, VII, 296.
Houghton, VII, 364.
Houlton, I, 231.
House, XIII, 392; of Peers, XII, 121.
Household drudgery, XIII, 351.
Hovenden, Tom, V, 73.
How foremen are made, VIII, 190.
How I Found My Brother, VIII, 410; XIV, 27; where and how Elbert Hubbard wrote, VIII, 410.
How to live long, IV, 339.
How to write well, IX, 310.
Howe, Ed, VI, 223.
Howell, J. Frank, X, 72.
Hubbard, Alice, V, 396; X, 345; and economic betterment, V, 398; poise of, V, 401; strongest feature of nature of, V, 402; knowledge and beliefs of, V, 404; the ideal mother, V, 405; winsomeness of, V, 407; a model housekeeper, V, 408.
Hubbard, Elbert, XII, 251; the heart of, I, 13; the *Selected Writings* of, I, 13; passing of, I, 15; his comment after the torpedo struck the *Lusitania*, I, 17; last dramatic act of, as the *Lusitania* was sinking, I, 17; favorite books of, I, 163; first visit of, to Chicago, II, 217; how, became "John." VI, 113; ads of, mark an epoch in advertising in America, VIII, 383; the ad writer, VIII, 383; works of, and East Aurora library, IX, 152; the most positive human force of his time, XII, 27; a businessman and a philosopher, XII, 28; and man's need, XII, 28; first visit of, to Buffalo, XIV, 131; in the soap business, XIV, 131; has a million dollar idea, XIV, 133; in vaudeville, XIV, 157; vaudeville experiences of, XIV, 164.
Hubbard, Elbert and Alice, on board the *Lusitania*, I, 15; philosophers both, I, 18.

xxxii

Hubbard, Gardiner G., II, 302.
Hubbard, Sanford, XIII, 282.
Hubbard, Doctor Silas, treatment of hernia, I, 143.
Hudson, Henry, II, 47; nationality of, II, 51; did he live and die in vain, II, 61.
Hudson Bay Company, VII, 328.
Hudson Bay District, VII, 327.
Hudson River, first ship on the, II, 57.
Huerta, General, V, 377.
Hugged to death by Cassie Chadwick, VIII, 363.
Hugo, Victor, the slogan of, II, 191.
Hulahula, XIV, 89.
Hull House, IV, 185.
Hulswit, Frank T., X, 220; birthplace of, X, 223.
Human Betterment, VII, 278.
Human crops, rotation of, VI, 36.
Human dynamo, XIII, 392.
Human energy, VIII, 334.
Human face, the, IX, 340.
Human felicity, XII, 38.
Human love, XIII, 392.
Human mind, the, IV, 109.
Human nature, IV, 216.
Human outcasts, V, 285.
Human rights, XII, 264.
Human service, I, 397; IX, 291; XII, 393.
Human sympathy, VI, 394.
Humanity, XII, 265; Pascal's view of, I, 284; faith in, II, 163; evolution of, V, 317; keeping well, V, 328; religion of, VII, 310; knowledge of, IX, 165; first factor in the evolution of, XIII, 334.
Humbert King, I, 363.
Humboldt, Alexander, I, 48; and his brother, William Humboldt, IV, 15.
Humbug, V, 269.
Hume, David, IX, 278; influence of, on world, IX, 278.
Humility, XIII, 392.
Humor, IV, 394; XIII, 392; V, 166.
Hunchback's garden, I, 101.
Hundred-Point Man, a, X, 15; XII, 269.
Hundred-pointers, I, 80.
Hunger, first incentive to migration, I, 429; of the heart, III, 212; and rebellion, III, 335.
Huntsman crucible process, VIII, 89.

Husband, XIII, 392.
Husbands, VI, 204; and wives, VI, 205.
Husband-disciple, VI, 245.
Husking Bee, XIII, 272.
Hussey, William G., XIV, 94; idea of, XIV, 95.
Hutchinson, Anne, X, 345; XIV, 94.
Huxley, Thomas, IX, 280; X, 359.
Hyde, Henry B., founder of Equitable Life Assurance Company, VIII, 161.
Hygeia, apostles of, VIII, 258.
Hygiene, Congress of, I, 325.
Hymettus, IX, 141.
Hypatia, I, 294; X, 344.
Hypnotism, II, 327.
Ibsen, I, 335; Norwegian intellectualisms of, IX, 201.
I carry the white man's burden, VIII, 392.
Ice, manufactured, VIII, 186.
I. C. S., II, 198; idea, II, 200; scholarships, II, 201; text-books, II, 202.
Ictinus and Callicrates, XIII, 361.
Idea, materializing an, IV, 386; big, V, 326.
Ideal, XIII, 393.
Ideal education, the, IV, 362.
Ideal life, the, IV, 89; XIII, 393.
Ideal mother, the, I, 354.
Ideal woman, the, IV, 65.
Idealism, IV, 206.
Idealist, V, 279; XIII, 393; the academician and the, V, 293; what is an, tendency, V, 279.
Ideals, V, 282; IX, 82; new, I, 367; live, VII, 309; association of, VIII, 91; the supremacy of, VIII, 245; hunting for, IX, 253.
Idle money, VIII, 207.
Idle rich, I, 28.
Idleness, V, 168; VI, 243; XII, 71; Franklin on, XII, 73.
Idols, II, 323.
Idyllic Association, VI, 59.
Idyl of the Dumping Ground, V, 150.
If, XIII, 393.
Ignoramus, XIII, 393.
Ignorance, II, 262; IX, 215; the, of the rich, IV, 230; a discreet, IV, 427; of English authors, VI, 102; of the citybreds, IX, 345.
I-have-here, IX, 99.
I know I am deathless, XII, 152.

"I'll buy this dog's life," I, 313.
Ill-health and indictment, VI, 332.
Illegitimate, I, 152; XI, 19.
Illegitimates, famous, I, 152.
Illinois, has wonderful soil, X, 72; men of genius of, X, 73.
Illiteracy and postage, IV, 152.
Illuminator, the passing of the, III, 435.
I love my identity, VII, 323.
Imagination, IV, 434; XI, 28; XIII, 393.
Imitation, XIII, 393.
Imitator, XIII, 394.
Immaculate Conception, I, 153, 306; XI, 19.
Immaculate oath, XI, 19.
Immorality, I, 288; bearing of wages on, I, 289.
Immortality, XIII, 394; individual, V, 226; personal, V, 231; Emerson on, of the soul, V, 232.
Imperialism, XIII, 394.
Important things, I, 333.
Impressionism, VI, 69.
Improvidence and the artistic temperament, I, 474.
Impulse, creative, II, 333.
Incantations were a big factor in the healing art, II, 457.
In Colorado, VII, 335.
Incompatibility, VI, 167; IX, 169.
Incompetence, X, 230.
Incompetent witnesses, I, 381.
Independence, XIII, 394; New Declaration of, I, 366, 369.
Indeterminate sentence, I, 154; IV, 209.
India Rubber, II, 29.
Indian, education and, I, 137; the cry of the, for Reservation Schools, I, 138; North American, IV, 17; and sign language, IV, 19; an, council, IV, 18; disposition of, dead, IV, 23; the, farewell, IV, 17.
Indian Reservation School, I, 135.
Indian tribes, Hot Springs neutral ground for all, VII, 86.
Indiana, the hub of the literary zone, X, 339.
Indiana quality, the, V, 56.
Indianapolis Speedway, I, 389.
Indians, love of, for children, I, 136; are our only American poets, IV, 18; Last Council of, IV, 21; the English and the, VII, 330.

Indices expurgati, V, 135.
Indifference, XI, 397.
Indignation, righteous, IX, 36.
Indiscriminate eating, IX, 382.
Individuality, IX, 181; XIV, 188; penalized, I, 297; make way for, X, 336.
Industrial Disputes Conciliation Act, the, VII, 356.
Industrial hara-kari, VIII, 174.
Industrial leaders, VIII, 237.
Industrial league for the promotion of Saskatoon enterprises, XIV, 127.
Industrialism, VIII, 86.
Industries, service to society of consolidated, I, 35; big manufacturers had their rise in home, I, 431; home, II, 184; peaceful, II, 243; Cleveland's diversity of, X, 370.
Industry, IV, 53; XII, 71; effect of vigilance on, I, 28; physical and mental, IV, 55; Boston the clearing-house of, VII, 312; Franklin on, XII, 72.
Inefficiency, things that spell, I, 288.
Inertia, tug of, I, 35; Law of, IX, 377.
Infant factory slaves, VI, 399.
Infant Prodigy, IV, 58.
Infidel, XIII, 308, 394; definition of, IX, 37; Corner Grocery, XIII, 277.
Infidelity, XIII, 395; the new, IX, 120.
Infidels, Ingersoll on, XII, 180.
Infinite, in touch with the, V, 64; strength in the, XI, 325.
Infinite power, IV, 268.
Infusoria, XIII, 395.
Ingalls, John J., VII, 223.
Ingersoll, Robert, XII, 163; on art, IX, 42; on beliefs, XII, 166; on the Bible, XII, 163; on children's rights, XII, 175; on civilization, XII, 163; on civilization and liberty, XII, 169; on the clergy, XII, 172; on the college, I, 404; on commerce, XII, 180; on the Doctrine of Atonement, XII, 164; on existence of evil, XII, 186; on forgiveness of gods, XII, 165; on freedom of thought, XII, 171; on happiness, XII, 178; on infidels, XII, 180; on labor, XII, 185; on liberty, XII, 184; on love of women, XII, 178; on Napoleon, XII, 189; on parsimony, VII, 307; on progress, XII, 182; on religion, XII, 166; on

sacred things, XII, 182; on sectarian colleges, XII, 169; on self-reliance, XII, 179; on true religion, XII, 184; on woman's rights, XII, 175; on worship, XII, 168; and Amiel, V, 195; writings of, and East Aurora library, IX, 149; writings of, tribute to, IX, 153; influence of, IX, 281; appeal of, XII, 24; humorist, iconoclast, and lover of humanity, VII, 24; at the grave of Napoleon, XII, 189; his creed, XII, 190; staunch upholder of the home, XIII, 356.
Ingrate, XIII, 395.
Ingratitude, V, 327; XIII, 395.
Initiative, I, 255; VI, 369; VIII, 190, 233, 235; XII, 313; XIII, 395; men of, II, 172; qualifications of man of, VIII, 236.
Injured wife, IX, 91.
Inkfish, the, VII, 340; the tactics of the, II, 347.
Innovation, most useful, of Nineteenth Century, VI, 249.
Innovations, XII, 272; public opinion against, I, 63.
Inoculating the human body, XIV, 232.
Inoculation by cowpox virus, XIV, 235.
In praise of the potato, IX, 231.
In prison and out, IV, 260.
In re Johannes Brahms, V, 134.
Insane, asylum for the, X, 57; hospitals for the, X, 60.
Insects, some, I have chummed with, XIII, 237.
Insidious, an, lobby, VIII, 224.
Inspiration, IV, 415.
Inspired writers, IX, 396.
Insull, Samuel, X, 102.
Insurance, germ of both fire and life, VIII, 152; life, I, 93; life, policy, VIII, 152; value of life, VIII, 399; actuaries prefer to insure men, XIII, 352.
Insurance-policy, IV, 106.
Insurance risk, women and, XII, 352.
Intellectic, IV, 333; VIII, 195; the danger of the, IV, 336.
Intellectual rights, XII, 111.
Intelligence, XIII, 394.
Intensive farming, VII, 294.
Interdependence, VIII, 87.
Interests, community of, VI, 313; mutuality of, I, 120.

International arbitration, I, 322.
International disarmament, VIII, 241.
Interrupted dentition, terrible effects of, X, 195.
Interstate Commerce Commission, I, 349; and railroads, VIII, 74.
In the Copper Country, VII, 360.
I think I could turn and live with animals, XII, 148.
Intimacy, the strangle-hold of, IV, 290.
Intimation, the, IX, 149.
Intimidation, IV, 398; of Unions, I, 117.
Inventions, II, 235; identical, II, 99; great, XIV, 222.
Inventive genius, American, I, 65.
Inventors, Scotch, as, II, 235.
Investigation, IX, 388; an, V, 351.
Investments, I, 382; XIII, 23; on making, XIV, 211.
Invocation to Man, XII, 252.
Iowa, VII, 170; policy of, VII, 171.
Ireland, Archbishop, I, 361; and clothes, II, 338.
Ireland, "Final Union," I, 228; and Home Rule, I, 228; Pope Adrian sold, I, 231.
Irish, strong men of England, X, 264.
Irish Parliament, I, 228.
Iron workers, ancient, VIII, 88.
Irony, XIII, 395; Heine and, IV, 258.
Irrigation, IV, 120; first attempt at, on the North American continent, VII, 67.
Is it worth the cost, VI, 98.
Islam, five cardinal points of, X, 324.
Isle Royale, VII, 360; Mine, VII, 362.
Is motherhood dishonorable, I, 343.
Issue, XIII, 394.
Italian, beggars, VII, 152; the, Hall disaster, VII, 383.
Italian Renaissance, the, I, 210; VII, 274.
Italy, in sunny, IV, 242; handicap of, VII, 154.
"I would plow," XIV, 267.
I. W. W., I, 70.
Jack Philosophy, I, 29.
Jackson, Andrew, VII, 133.
Jackson Penitentiary, VII, 254.
Jacob, X, 29.
Jail, female, II, 327; every, a school of crime, II, 328.
Jamie, at the House of, VI, 209.

Jap, as a farmer, VII, 291; problem, VII, 290.
Japan, religion in, V, 211; education in, V, 212; a hermit nation, V, 213; military science in, V, 213.
Japanese, some, characteristics, V, 214; characteristics of, VII, 291; are vegetarians, V, 214; in California, VII, 290; cry against, VII, 290.
J. B. runs things, XIV, 278.
Jealous spasm, VI, 257.
Jealousy, XII, 331; and hate, I, 215; a disease, IV, 186; as to, VI, 256; Othello portrayal of, VI, 256; sex, VI, 256; Goethe's, VI, 259; cancer caused by, VI, 260; cure for, VI, 262.
Jefferson, Thomas, XII, 18, 81; on allegiance and protection, XII, 87; on atheism and Christianity, XII, 104; on the Bible, I, 360; on freedom of expression, XII, 97; on freedom of thought, XII, 99; on flattery, XII, 86; on government, XII, 98; on honesty, disinteresteness and good-nature, XII, 93; on international commerce, XII, 103; on Jesus of Nazareth, XII, 102; on judges, XII, 89; on labor, XII, 98; on lawyers, XII, 91; on national morality, XII, 91; on the four pillars of our prosperity, I, 347; on public opinion, XII, 97; on right to self-government, XII, 100; on slavery, III, 236; on treason, I, 310; on tyranny, XII, 90; on ward republic, XII, 101; on Washington, XII, 94; on good roads, I, 384; travel in time of, I, 387; ambition of, II, 342; owned slaves, II, 454; achievements of, VII, 87; gave us the decimal system, VII, 87; invented the moldboard plow, VII, 87; founded our public-school system, VII, 87; and public-school system, IX, 353; prescience of, XII, 19; his First Draft of the Declaration of Independence, XII, 86; review of services of, XII, 92; Character of Washington, by, XII, 96; IV, 296.
Jehovah and Satan, IV, 123.
Jenkins Sons Music Company, J, W., XIV, 102.
Jenner, Doctor, XIV, 232; discovery of, XIV, 230, 233.

Jerome Connor, V, 207.
Jersey City Tunnel, II, 135.
Jersey lightning, XIII, 241.
Jesting, VII, 396.
Jesus, I, 205; taught New Thought, I, 294; had his limitations, II, 322; an anarchist, VI, 131; reincarnated in America, IX, 63; myths and legends of birth of, XI, 17; disagreement as to progenitors of, XI, 18; and Joseph, XI, 21; at adolescence, XI, 25; controlling impulse in life of, XI, 29; and John the Baptist, XI, 35; and Peter, XI, 41; and the Magdelene, XI, 42; pantheism of, XI, 43; philosophy of, XI, 46; Jewish formulæ and, XI, 47; and caste, XI, 51; psychic power of, XI, 53; chief charm of teachings of, XI, 53; an analysis of some of his teachings, XI, 55; some illusions of, XI, 56; priests' attitude toward, XI, 63, 67; friends of, XI, 64; his standing in society, XI, 64; arrest of, XI, 71; of Nazareth, Jefferson on, XII, 102; greatest of all reformers was, XII, 102.
Jew, as a farmer, IV, 31.
Jewelry, the, center of America, XIV, 97.
Jewish farm school, IV, 31.
Jews, I, 356; IV, 197; VI, 93; persecution of the, IV, 30; education of the, IV, 31; the, and the Gentiles, IV, 199; in Great Britain, IV, 348; and bees alike, IX, 142.
Jezebel wore the welter-weight championship belt of Assyria, I, 318.
Jiner instinct, the, VI, 127.
Jiners, the, VI, 127.
Jink-fests, IX, 107.
Jitney, the jump of the, VIII, 264; idea, VIII, 264; service, VIII, 265.
Job, the Book of, IV, 121; oldest book of the Bible, IV, 121; prologue to the Book of, IV, 122; comforters of, IV, 128; confession of, IV, 128; petition of, IV, 130; rejoinders of, IV, 130; his reply to Eliphaz, IV, 129.
John the Baptist, XI, 34; and Salome, XI, 38.
John Barleycorn, IV, 38.
John Dough Proceedings, XIII, 395.
John R. Gentry, X, 67.

Johnson, Samuel, I, 33; VIII, 404; his definition of patriotism, I, 321; does penance, VIII, 35.
Johnson, Tom, VIII, 30.
Johnston, Sally Bush, V, 49.
Joint-Stock Company, I, 223; had its rise in England, II, 226.
Jokes, cheap, IX, 336.
Jones, Buffalo, X, 174; lions lassoed by, X, 176; capturing a rhinoceros, X, 179; subduing zebra, X, 180; feats of, X, 181; birthplace of, X, 183; buffalo and, X, 185.
Jones, Golden Rule, V, 124.
Jones, Milo C., X, 93.
Jones, Samuel M., of Toledo, IV, 37; elected mayor of Toledo four times, V, 127; motto of, V, 130; his passion for purity, V, 132.
Jordan, David Starr, and college trained men, I, 401; and college life, I, 409; on value of college, II, 461.
Joseph and Mary, XI, 18.
Josephine, I, 152.
Josephus, XI, 64.
Journal of Koheleth, the, III, 443.
Journalist, XIII, 395.
Jove, Sons of, IV, 80.
Jovian Society, X, 108.
Joy, VIII, 218; in useful effort, IV, 268; in work, IV, 268; what is the big factor in, VIII, 218.
Joy, Henry B., II, 338; at East Aurora, II, 339.
Joy-rides, IX, 107.
Joy-riding, IX, 266.
Joys, and glooms, IX, 342; of life, the genuine, I, 144.
Judaism, if Constantine had embraced, IV, 200; liberal, IV, 201.
Judas, XI, 70.
Judea, XI, 50.
Judge, XIII, 396; the business of the, IV, 71.
Judges, and litigants, VIII, 169; problem of, X, 266.
Judgeship, X, 266.
Judiciary, a heartless, IV, 36; a word for the, VIII, 167; are the, corrupt, VIII, 168.
Judicious, XIII, 395.
Judson, Jedediah, III, 32.

Junipero, Serra, Bishop Conaty on the life and work of, V, 179.
Junkshops, XIII, 360.
Junto, the, IX, 328; Franklin and, XII, 34.
Junto membership, IX, 330.
Junto prayers, IX, 330.
Junto questions, IX, 328-329.
Jury, XIII, 396.
Just snakes, XIII, 241.
Just water, IX, 294.
Justice, XII, 376; XIII, 396; for the worker, I, 286; a legal fiction, IV, 69; bar of, IV, 70; and law, IV, 72; human and divine, XIV, 252.
Juvenal, and sleep, I, 308.
Juvenile Court, I, 150.
Kabojolism, antithesis of plagiarism is, IV, 57.
Kaiser, Caligula compared with, I, 280.
Kansas, in the Fifties, III, 281; and oysters, VII, 224.
Kansas City, XIV, 103.
Kansas, first legislature, II, 455.
Kant, Immanuel, VII, 141; the great agnostic, IV, 204.
Karenina, Anna, V, 134.
Keats, X, 209.
"Keener," II, 69; XIV, 144.
Keep Your Car, VIII, 393, 396.
Keeping humanity well, V, 328.
Kellogg, Dr., and Charles W. Post, II, 321.
Kellogg Sanatarium, the, II, 321.
Kelmscott House, V, 147.
Kennedy Farm, III, 399.
Kennerly, Mitchell, V, 278; X, 86; XIV, 248; connoisseur of letters, V, 278; who publishes books for love, X, 86.
Kennicott, X, 372.
Kerosene, VIII, 96; the supply of, II, 409.
Kerosene-oil, I, 435.
Kerosene Route, VII, 76.
Kesitah, IV, 135.
Key to health, happiness, wealth, power, success, XII, 256.
Keyhole point of view, VI, 29.
Khartum, Gordon at, IX, 132; siege of, IX, 133.
Kidd, Captain, lineal descendants of, XIII, 329.

xxxvii

Kimball, Kate F., II, 112.
Kindergarten, the, VI, 249; XIII, 396; method in prison, VI, 241; the idea, VI, 250.
Kindness, VI, 392; to animals, I, 250.
King, XIII, 396; Copper, VII, 378; of the Groucherinos, IV, 473.
"King of Ireland," I, 228.
King Lear and Ivan, IV, 315.
Kings, X, 37; the lot of, X, 38; courts and hirelings, XII, 121.
Kingsley, Charles, secret of his success, V, 395.
Kinsmen only in name, III, 386.
Kipling's *Vampire*, IV, 294.
Kirksville School of Osteopathy, II, 463.
Kit Carson, X, 29.
Kite, Bramley, I, 32.
Knighthood, Hays declines, II, 352.
"Knights of Columbus," I, 269, 271.
"Knights of Luther," I, 269.
Knocker, the, IV, 43; I, 112.
Knocking, XIII, 396.
Knock-knees and bow-legs, XI, 107.
Knowledge, I, 406; II, 284; IV, 385, 433; XIII, 396; usefulness criterion of, I, 406; for service, IX, 256; essential foundation of, IX, 114.
Knox, John, I, 212; IX, 278.
Knox's Stock Farm, XIII, 362.
Knoxville, a Little Journey to, VII, 130; great men of, VII, 132.
Koheleth, admonition of, I, 180; a man with a "past," III, 448; lover of letters and, III, 450.
Krauskopf, Rabbi, and Jewish farm school, IV, 31.
Kruppery, IX, 292.
Kruppism, I, 278.
Ku Klux, I, 117; Klan, IX, 131.
Labor, IV, 382; VII, 391; XII, 142; Stephen Reynolds on, I, 54; American Federation of, I, 119; commodity, I, 283; and the cities, I, 430; Ford Company and, II, 90; manual, IV, 140; capital and, V, 88; dignity of, VI, 336; intelligent supervision of, VIII, 235; divinity of, IX, 85; useful, IX, 85; union, IX, 372; Jefferson on, XII, 98; Lincoln on, XII, 143; Ingersoll on, XII, 185.
Labor combination, VII, 337.

Labor Law and South Carolina, VI, 402.
Labor troubles, XIV, 198.
Labor Trust, I, 122.
Labor-Union, and class hatred, I, 124; and injunctions, I, 124; Open Shop and the, I, 118.
Labor-Union meetings, ex-parte, I, 118.
Labor-Union organizers, I, 118.
Labor-Unions, I, 117.
Labouchere, his newspaper, *Truth*, X, 52; unique character, of, X, 52.
Lacteal preachment, a, IV, 237.
Ladies' night, IX, 221.
Lady criminals, II, 327.
Lady of the beautiful hands, IX, 307.
Lafayette on liberty, XII, 107.
La Gioconda, IX, 306.
Lamentation, XII, 149.
Lampton on the subject of travel, VII, 142.
Land, VI, 35; VII, 182; is universal mother, I, 430; the great mother, VII, 182.
Land value in Ohio and Michigan, VII, 184.
Land of Friendship, IX, 399.
Land o' Goshen, VII, 178.
Landis, the family, V, 56; laddies, the five, V, 56.
Lane, Honorable Franklin K., VII, 46.
Lang, Andrew, V, 90; on anthropology and folk lore, V, 92; as a translator, V, 92; as a controversialist, V, 93.
Language, XIII, 398; Indian and sign, IV, 19; the English, VI, 23; of colloquialism, VI, 25; invention in, 25; only a makeshift at best, XIII, 303.
Languages, I, 403; VI, 23; dead, I, 403; IX, 357; growth of, VI, 24; slang and, VI, 24.
Lao-tze, VI, 198.
Large oval bluff, I, 427.
Last Council, IV, 21.
Last, survivor of the great generals, who fought during the Civil War, VII, 227.
Late hours and late suppers, IX, 249.
Late suppers, joy-rides, jink-fests, IX, 107.
Later, XIII, 396.
Latin tongue, the, IV, 362.
Latter Day Saints, the Church of, IX, 63.

Laud, Archbishop, I, 173, 310.
Lauder, Sir Harry, X, 18; characteristics of, X, 20; spontaneous act of, X, 22.
Laundry and soft water, IX, 297.
Laugh of a child, XII, 177.
Laughter, III, 445; IV, 390, 429; XIII, 397.
Launching of a third party, X, 269.
Laundries, and labels, VIII, 255; as testers of shoddy goods, VIII, 261.
Laundry, the modern, VIII, 255; modern, methods, VIII, 257.
Laundrymen, VIII, 258; enemies of, VIII, 258.
Laundrymen's National Association, VIII, 259.
Laurier, Sir Wilfrid, II, 178.
Lauterbach, Edward, XIV, 100; V, 205.
La Verite, IV, 326; described, IV, 327-329.
Law, IV, 307; VI, 314; XIII, 397; is a game, I, 32; Humboldt's epigram, I, 48; Blackstone and Burke on, I, 68; of Pivotal Points, I, 115; of Diminishing Returns, I, 115; IV, 224; VIII, 51; Oliver Wendell Holmes apropos of, of Diminishing Returns, I, 116; of Compensation, I, 159; I, 367; VII, 48; XIII, 263; Chief Justice White and, I, 198; basis of all American, I, 199; Blackstone on interpretation of, I, 199; of Cause and Effect, I, 217; justice and, IV, 72; what is, IV, 307; theology and medicine, VI, 391; of Demand and Supply, VII, 74; of obedience, VII, 221; obedience to, VII, 354; criminal, VIII, 335; of consequences, IX, 34, 40; of Inertia, IX, 377; the curvetings of, X, 168; of primogeniture, XII, 87; of Heredity IX, 397.
Law books, I, 199.
Law-breaker in America, VII, 355.
Law game, I, 32.
Laws, of man, I, 49; vicious, I, 69; for the prevention of cruelty to animals, I, 310; of Nature, II, 456; factory, IV, 347; and will of the Zeitgeist, VIII, 55; institutions and progress, XII, 96; derive force from consent of the living, XII, 123; Paine on repeal of, XII, 123.

Lawyer, XIII, 396; qualifications for, I, 32; the ideal, I, 193; a great, II, 229; a clever, II, 230; the business of the, IV, 70; the best, XIV, 246.
Lawyers, I, 65; IV, 138, 456; VI, 141; VIII, 217; XII, 279; why Elbert Hubbard criticises, I, 31; rogue, I, 31; and business, I, 65; and litigation, I, 192; three kinds of, II, 17; what, thrive on, V, 329; Jefferson on, XII, 91; businessmen, XIII, 331; damage-claim, XIV, 244.
Lazarus, XI, 45.
Learn, XIII, 396.
Leave us alone, IX, 77.
Leaving things to George, VIII, 222.
Le Bon, Gustave, *The Crowd* by, VI, 27.
Lecky's *Map of Life*, I, 238.
Lecture Bureaus, so-called, VI, 115.
Lecture Lyceum, VI, 115.
Lee, Harry (Whitehorse Harry), VII, 320.
Legacy, the, XIII, 13.
Legal exploitation, VIII, 20.
Legal lallapaloosa, I, 32.
Legal marriage, IV, 302.
Legal orphans, I, 344.
Legal profession, XIV, 242.
Le Gallienne, Richard, VI, 65; of the Quest, IV, 65.
Legislation, medical, IV, 114.
Legislators vs. life members, VII, 254.
Legits, and vodes, VII, 321.
Le Grand Passion, VI, 207.
Lehmann, Fred W., X, 280.
Leisure, how to use, II, 199; penalty of, VIII, 202; Franklin on, XII, 73.
Leisure class, IX, 215.
Lentz, John J., X, 42; X, 165.
Lentz, Kate Alexander, X, 42; tribute to, X, 43, 44.
Leonardo da Vinci, IX, 307; XIII, 248; and Aristotle, horse lovers, VI, 17; lover of Nature, X, 357.
Lepidopterology, XIV, 304.
Let Thrift Be Your Ruling Habit, I, 100.
Letter to Hooker, I, 57.
Lettergram of love, VIII, 409.
Letters, on writing, VI, 266; vitalized, VI, 266.
Letter-writers, famous, VI, 267.
Letter-writing, VI, 266; a sample of, VIII, 373.

Levitation, XIII, 398.
Lewis, Alfred Henry, on almsgiving, I, 359.
Lewis and Clark Expedition, I, 139.
Liar, XIII, 397.
Libel, a clumsy, V, 156.
Libelous, XIII, 397.
Libertines, when, turn saints, V, 397.
Liberty, XIII, 397; religious, I, 365; danger to, II, 362; give your children, IV, 250; versus license, V, 171; and license, VIII, 85; and progress, VIII, 85; Ingersoll on, XII, 184; to others, XII, 184.
Liberty, Fraternity, Equality, I, 361.
Liberty Hall, VI, 209.
Liberty Tadd, I, 457.
Librarian, IX, 326.
Library, XIII, 398; Philadelphia Public, IX, 329.
Library loafer, the, IX, 326.
Lichens, the pioneers of vegetation, XI, 412.
Lie, IV, 385; XIII, 397; the Circumstantial, IX, 164; the, Direct, IX, 164.
Life, IV, 314; VIII, 295; IX, 344; XII, 388; XIII, 398; a bank-account, I, 76; the genuine joys of, I, 144; love of, I, 144; long, attends practice of Fletcherism, I, 145; after this, I, 397; luck plays a part in this game of, II, 32; the ideal, IV, 89; expression and, IV, 180; canned, IV, 320; everlasting, IV, 391; a search for power, IV, 394; IX, 178, 183; desire to radiate, IV, 411; dual, IV, 426; what, meant to Elbert Hubbard, V, 391; zest in, VI, 282; lies in the quest, VI, 374; the simple, VII, 29; of the bee, VII, 303; standard of, in The Copper Country, VII, 364; of trade, VIII, 50; a matter of mercury, VIII, 178; love and, IX, 284; optimism applied to, XI, 349; of labor, XII, 73; of leisure, XII, 73; qualities that fit a man for a, of usefulness, XII, 296; preparing for, XII, 307; a voyage, XII, 384; is human service, XII, 393; of man, XIII, 115.
Life insurance, I, 93; VIII, 400; X, 263; health and, IV, 106; and business, IV, 221; as a stabilizer, IV, 221; and poverty, IV, 228; actors most hazardous risk in, VII, 318; germ of, VIII, 152; value of, VIII, 399.
Life Insurance Companies will not insure the lives of married women, XIII, 352.
Life Insurance Policy, VIII, 152; is a commodity, IV, 222.
Lightning, Jersey, XIII, 241.
Li Hung Chang, V, 189.
Like produces like, V, 209.
Lilacs, XII, 153.
Limit, the, VIII, 177.
Lincoln, Abraham, XII, 130; on acquiring property, XII, 140; on agriculture, XII, 141; on labor and its rewards, XII, 143; on men to be trusted, XII, 138; on politicians, XII, 132; on progress in degeneracy, XII, 132; on property, XII, 131; as a letter writer, I, 57; Letter to Hooker, I, 57; speeches of, I, 57; aim of, I, 62; wife of, I, 447; at twelve, IV, 246; man who first suggested as President, X, 174; counselor for country, XII, 21; liberator of men, XII, 21; integrity of, XII, 22; work of, XII, 22; Extract from Inaugural Address, XII, 88; Address at the Dedication of the Gettysburg National Cemetery, November 19, '63, XII, 130; Reply to committee from the religious denominations of Chicago asking, to issue a proclamation of emancipation, XII, 132; Letter to General J. Hooker, XII, 134; Letter to Major-General Hunter, XII, 135; Letter to General G. B. McClellan, XII, 136; Letter to Mrs. Bixby, XII, 137; Address to the Legislature of Ohio, XII, 141.
Lincoln Memorial Highway, the, I, 394; II, 341.
Lincoln, Nancy Hanks, grave of, V, 47.
Lincoln story, a, VII, 225.
Lindsey, Judge, II, 327; XIV, 275; and reform schools, I, 156.
Linguists, IX, 340.
Literature, IV, 397; V, 38, 288; XIII, 387; egotism in, IV, 400; is a gallery of spiritual ideals, V, 84; what is, V, 288; term, in Nobel bequest, V, 289; clearness in, VI, 50; great, VI, 51; and feeling, VI, 54; honesty in, VI, 64;

truth in, VI, 65; two schools of, VI, 69; grown-ups in, VI, 244; all, is advertising, VIII, 102; pure, IX, 252; and advertising, XII, 398; and conformity, XIII, 323.
Litigation, XIII, 398; is war, I, 192.
Little Big Horn, the, IV, 20; VII, 207; Indians' Last Council, at, IV, 21.
Little Corporal, cocked hat of the, VI, 79.
Little Journey, manuscript of the Mozart, II, 138.
Little Journey Cabin, IX, 28.
Little Journeys, Memorial Edition of, I, 13; how it came to be issued, I, 13.
Live, how to, long, IV, 339.
Lives, habits rule our, I, 398; Brotherhood of Consecrated, IV, 447.
Living, XIII, 398; the science of making a, I, 102; high cost of, I, 429; VIII, 282; earning a, II, 94; perfunk, IV, 319; making, a, V, 330; simple, VIII, 379.
Livingston, VII, 21.
Loafer, XIII, 398.
Loan, best collateral for a, VIII, 370.
Loans, XIII, 284.
Lobsters, IV, 381.
Locomotive, America's first, VIII, 325.
Logic, XIII, 398.
London, Jack, I, 27; his treatment of John Barleycorn, IV, 38.
London and "The Plague," I, 262.
Lonely, XIII, 398.
Longevity, IV, 48; and dentistry, VIII, 37.
Lord and Taylor, Little Journey to, VIII, 339; the house of, VIII, 340; growth of, VIII, 343.
Lord of Language, X, 91.
Lords of the Ghostland, the, X, 86.
Lorenz, Doctor, X, 34; his discovery, X 35.
Los Angeles Fellowship, the, X, 147.
Los Angeles Waiters' Union, IX, 317.
Loss, and calamity are great teachers, VII, 279; and gain, XIV, 226.
Loubet, President, I, 363.
Louisiana, VII, 262.
Louisiana Purchase, VII, 124; XII, 19; Arkansas was part of the, VIII, 86.
Love, II, 211; IV, 192, 288, 321, 384, 387, 454; VI, 298; IX, 284, 344; XI, 195; XII, 292, 309, 362, 385; XIII, mutual, I, 48; and marriage, I, 48; III, 219, 466; XII, 337; for wife and child, I, 49; Indians, for children, I, 136; conserve, I, 138; of life, I, 144; happiness and peace tangible assets in running a dairy, I, 250; a manifestation of energy, I, 346; parental, I, 464; nothing but, is sacred, II, 213; gives wisdom, III, 224; ever fights for freedom, III, 356; out-of-door, III, 462; of man and woman, III, 462; of man for woman is as sacred a thing as Christ's love for the church, III, 469; is vital, III, 470; reach heaven through, III, 470; that curious lifestuff, III, 470; a great, IV, 29; itself is a form of Kabojolism, IV, 62; individual, IV, 150; universal, IV, 150; cause of, IV, 148; and poetry, IV, 189; work and, IV, 270; VI, 234; for love's sake, IV, 271; VI, 235; haunting memory of a great, lost, IV, 310; Emerson's essay on, IV, 312; human, IV, 401; platonic, IV, 426; of out-of-doors, V, 43; a flower awakens, VI, 176; where, is, VI, 230; for gratification, VI, 235; for a home and darned stockings, VI, 235; for propagation, VI, 235; and ownership, VI, 237; of Pericles and Aspasia, VI, 282; lettergram of, VIII, 409; is life's great lubricant, IX, 252; and life are synonymous, IX, 284; daughterly, X, 244; children of, XI, 21; is the actinic ray, XI, 385; Emerson on, XII, 212; Emerson on, and lovers, XII, 242; woman's, XII, 334; of friends, XII, 357; courtship and marriage, XIII, 13; and spies, XIV, 14.
Love-atmosphere, XI, 386.
Love instinct, IV, 426.
Love letters, VIII, 129; XI, 379.
Love-making, IV, 189.
Love microbes, VI, 299.
Love-musings, III, 474.
Love-relation, XI, 384.
Lover, the, IV, 28; divine, XII, 147; divine and perfect comrade, XII, 147.
Lovers, III, 43; IV, 386; XIII, 398; and poets, III, 462; all things are of

xli

equal importance to, III, 471; the, in *Song of Songs*, III, 472; the conduct of, IV, 413; great, V, 396; litany of, IX, 334.
Love's demitasse, IV, 449.
Lovey-dovey, to, IV, 405.
Loving, sum of all, I, 294.
Lowell, President, I, 409.
Loyal Order of Moose, X, 165.
Loyal service, II, 442.
Loyalty, I, 48; IV, 109, 111-113; XII, 253; XII, 329; is not a mere matter of brain capacity, IV, 109; Gladstone's to England, IV, 112; to the pack, VI, 27; to religion, VI, 27; of the dog, VI, 105; in business, VIII, 239.
Lubricants, II, 203.
Luck plays a part in this game of life, II, 32; good, IV, 400.
"Lucky dogs," X, 226.
Lumber, VII, 184; camps, VI, 347.
Lunacy, V, 156.
Lusitania, Elbert and Alice Hubbard on board the, I, 15; account of sinking of, by a survivor, I, 15-20; Elbert Hubbard's comment after the torpedo struck the, I, 17; some of the horrors of the sinking of the, I, 19.
Luther, Martin, I, 211.
Macaulay and a literary reputation, I, 407.
MacDonald, John B., X, 262.
Macedonian phalanx, VII, 398.
MacFadden, V, 300.
Machinery, leasing of, II, 188; idle, II, 190; the rise of, VIII, 92.
"Machinery Trust" bugaboo, II, 184.
MacNaughton, James, VII, 362.
Madame Curie, IV, 367.
Madden, John E., I, 77.
Madero, Francisco, V, 376; a Utopian, V, 376.
Mad Mullah, IX, 132.
Madonna of our kind, I, 341.
Maeterlinck, Maurice, VII, 303; XII, 379; and bees, VI, 291.
Magazine-rifle dates to Eighteen Hundred Eighty-six, II, 236.
Magazines, chipmunk, VII, 234; muckraking, VIII, 269.
Magdalene, the, XI, 42.
Magnet cranes, VIII, 293.

Magnetism, personal, II, 355.
Mahdis, IX, 131.
Mahin, XIII, 399.
Maid, a frail and innocent, VI, 339.
Mail carriers, XI, 433.
Mail-order age, a, VIII, 346, 351.
Mail order economy, VIII, 349.
Mail order house, and parcel post, VIII, 350; buyer's faith in, VIII, 350.
Maine, two great crops of, IX, 233; potatoes, IX, 237.
Maines, Elbert Hubbard, XIV, 51.
Maintaining the overhead, I, 442.
Majestic Theater, the, XIV, 159.
Make way for individuality, X, 336.
Make-believe, XIII, 327.
Make-up of the Standard Oil, I, 376.
Making a living, V, 330.
Making good, XIV, 275.
Making picture, IV, 73.
Malley, Anna A., IV, 70.
Malnutrition, IV, 339.
Malthus, argument, of, I, 148; his book, *Essay on Population*, I, 460.
Mammon, XIII, 401.
Mammoth Cave of Kentucky, VII, 240; Daniel Webster at, VII, 240; famous visitors to, VII, 240; Jenny Lind's chair at, VII, 241; Beecher preached at, VII, 243; religious services at, VII, 243; famed Rotunda of, VII, 245; specimens, VII, 242.
Mammoth Hot Springs, VII, 28.
Mammoth Hotel, the, VII, 26.
Man, I, 296; IV, 118; XII, 251, 258; XIII, 399; first weapon of, I, 39; laws of, I, 49; big enough to take orders, I, 84; and boy, I, 465; ingredients that go into the making of a, II, 157; educated, II, 335; proposes but woman disposes, III, 58; an amphibian, IV, 81; nature's partnership with, IV, 118; the average, IV, 231; three things that make a man a, IV, 278; a transformer of energy, IV, 288; vices of an old, IV, 316; a new type of, IV, 333; when a, is hanged, IV, 343; greatest blunder, of, IV, 390; formula for a, IV, 393; strong, IV, 404; of violence, IV, 435; wise, IV, 470; of sorrows, V, 62; XI, 13; a god in the crib, VI, 285; an educated, VI,

317; and climate, VII, 313; prehistoric, VII, 369; greatest blessing of, VIII, 24; primal need of, VIII, 143; enlightened, VIII, 154; rights of, VIII, 360; XII, 91, 108, 112; his search for happiness, IX, 33; the, with the hoe, IX, 97; Pascal's individual, IX, 212; the efficient, IX, 248; sleep required by the average, IX, 249; heroic type of, X, 348; a hundred-point, X, 15; XII, 270; Paine on duty of, XII, 116; Emerson on, XII, 208; creed of the busy, XII, 271; misery of, XII, 347; the patient, XII, 374; city-bred, XIII, 306; the master, XIV, 57.

Man-hater, XIII, 399.
Manholes, XIII, 400.
Man-hunt, the biggest thing today is the, VIII, 368.
Man the lifeboats, IX, 16.
Man-power, VIII, 92.
Management, consolidation of, I, 223.
Manchester Board of Health, IX, 379.
Manchester machinery, XIV, 98.
Mangasarian, V, 240; a rationalist, V, 240; power of, V, 242.
Manhood, XII, 195.
Mania, alienation arose from religious, V, 228, for collecting, XIII, 290.
Manikins, academic, IX, 97.
Manitoba, VII, 332; rich soil of, VII, 330.
Mankind, XIII, 398.
Mann, Horace, V, 266; shipwreck of the hopes of, V, 272; the, memorial, V, 277.
Mann, James R., X, 174.
Mann, Colonel William D'Alton, X, 242.
Manner, charm of, I, 454.
Mansfield, Richard, and music at meals I, 476; his protest against music at, meals, I, 477; *Ivan the Terrible* by, IV, 314.
Manual labor, IV, 140.
Manual training, I, 457; IX, 86; cure for hoodlumism, IV, 91; necessary part of every man's education, IX, 86.
Manufacture of cast iron and steel inaugurated in Germany, VIII, 88.
Manufactured ice, VIII, 186.
Manuscript, IX, 94.
Marble, Tennessee, VII, 131.
Marie, Antoinette, and the Paris mob, VI, 290.

Marital bundling, III, 467.
Marital relations, III, 464.
Mark Twain and Christian Science, VI, 163.
Markham, Edwin, IX, 97; XIII, 294; at Roycroft, IX, 97.
Marquis of Queensbury rules, X, 204.
Marriage, I, 329; III, 463; IX, 251; XIII, 13, 313, 399; make, difficult, I, 30; property-right in, I, 44; XIII, 314; scared rite, I, 44; civil, I, 45; and divorce, I, 45; VI, 169; XI, 89; and obedience, I, 446; and love, I, 48; III, 219, 466; a conception of, I, 329; Richard Cobden on, I, 461; II, 475; six requisites in every happy, IV, 440; and mutuality, VI, 296; and Interstate Commerce Commission, VI, 300; and typewritists, VIII, 118; Church rite of, IX, 169; genius and, XI, 129; and "obey," XII, 338; discontent of, XIII, 354; bond of, XIII, 355; grave of love, IV, 301.
Marriage bond, Robert Louis Stevenson on the, IV, 149.
Marriages, and the village barber, VI, 298.
Married and unmarried women contrasted, I, 152.
Married life, IV, 67.
Married minds, children of, IV, 50.
Marshall, A, A., X, 299.
Marshall, John, I, 361.
Martial spirit, IV, 254.
Martial spirit, XIII, 327.
Martinbeck, Fra, VIII, 314; XIV, 175.
Martyr, XIII, 400.
Martyrdom, XIII, 401; modern, IV, 410.
Martyrs to the cause, IV, 351.
Marx, Karl, VI, 306; fallacies of, I, 461; and Morris, VI, 308.
Marxian, definition of a, VI, 307.
Marxian Socialism, I, 55; IV, 176; weak point in, I, 81; and Fabian Socialism, VI, 306.
Marxian Socialist, I, 52, 332; X, 129.
Marxians want Utopia, VI, 306.
"Mary Elizabeth," X, 411; her candy, V, 399; X, 411.
Mason, Walt, V, 119; his potboilers, V, 120-123.
Mason and Dixon Line, VII, 222.

xliii

Massachusetts' apples, X, 300.
Massachusetts Colony, I, 213.
Master-man, IV, 53; XIII, 400.
Master mind of Pericles, XIII, 358.
Mastership, XIII, 400.
Mastership and the master-man, IV, 65.
Masticate, I, 147.
Mastication and health, I, 147.
Mastication clinic, VIII, 38.
Mate, mental, VI, 248.
Mated mentally, IV, 271.
Materialism, IX, 121; challenge to, V, 291.
Materialist, V, 227.
Maternity, natural, IX, 245.
Mathematics, XIII, 400.
Matrimony, candidates for, should be examined, VI, 300.
Matron's story, I, 338.
Matteawan, XIII, 400.
Matthew and Luke, XI, 18.
Maturity, I, 367.
Mauser manuscript, IX, 100.
Max Muller's *Memories*, V, 407.
Maxim, Hudson, X, 210.
Mayflower stock, XIV, 96.
Mayor, XIII, 399.
Mazeppy Act, the, XIII, 89.
Mazzyanovich, XIII, 282.
McAdoo, William G., VII, 134.
McClellan, John J., VII, 55.
McCutcheons, the, V, 58.
McGillicuddy, Colonel Cornelius, IV, 87.
McKinley, the man who killed, V, 173; Rowan and Garcia, XIII, 297.
McNamaras, guilt of the, IX, 369.
Meat breakfast, VI, 41.
Meat-eating, IV, 340.
Meat supply and refrigeration, VIII, 188.
Mechanical power, I, 433.
Mechanics, romance of, V, 387.
Mediation, X, 80.
Medical advertisements, IV, 406.
Medical college, I, 312.
Medical legislation, IV, 114.
Medical prescriptions in Latin, X, 155.
Medical Trust, I, 352; IV, 472.
Medication, most chronic invalids are suffering from, I, 143.
Medicine, IV, 307; VI, 391; XIII, 293; the schools of, II, 459; the practice of, V, 327; the ethics of, V, 328; and theology system of guesswork, VI, 393; science in, VIII, 134; science of, XIV, 270.
Mediocrity, IX, 412.
Me for Texas, VII, 282.
Meissonier, VI, 152; his tribute to his mother, VI, 154; a collector, VI, 152.
Meissonier's mother, IV, 259.
Melancholia, treatment for, VII, 234.
Melania, the Nun of Tagaste, IX, 307.
Melchizedek, the Order of, XIII, 125; Sons of, XIII, 126.
Melzer, Adolph, X, 366.
Memoranda, Burroughs and, V, 37.
Memory, our only friend, IX, 147.
Men, IV, 218; newspaper, I, 232; some hundred-point, I, 417; two kinds of, in business, II, 18; of initiative, II, 172; educated, II, 401; brilliant, IV, 50; and women, IV, 50; strong, and diet, IV, 104; valuable, IV, 383; dependence upon the supernatural makes weaklings of, V, 251; and land, VI, 35; why, collect things, VI, 151; of power, VIII, 23; fads of successful, VIII, 125; who have really put it over, VIII, 195; our big, how we reward them, VIII, 255; of worth, V, 62; safe, to deal with, X, 15; famous who were epileptics, X, 137; of mark, X, 378; the misfortunes of, XI, 382; honest, appointed judges, XII, 89; Lincoln on, to be trusted, XII, 138; prayers of, XII, 216; trinity of strong, XII, 316; learned, XII, 364; armed, XII, 370; great, XIII, 270; that achieve, XIV, 202.
Menace, The, I, 268; advertisements of, I, 273.
Mendicant Institution, I, 358.
Mennonites and Dukaboors compared, I, 182.
Mental ankylosis, cure for, IX, 356.
Mental attitude, wrong, I, 141; right, IV, 419.
Mental dissolution, XIII, 400.
Mental healer, X, 258.
Mental mate, your, VI, 248.
Mental self-reliance, IX, 341.
Mentality, IX, 286.
Mentally mated, IV, 271.
Menus, IX, 318.

Mephisto, XIII, 400.
Merchant, XII, 366.
Merchant tailoring, fallacies of, I, 423.
Mercy, XIII, 40; and justice, XII, 107.
Merit, IV, 392.
Merry del Val, I, 361.
Message, the, of, *Wisdom and Destiny*, a, to Ad-Men, I, 195.
Message to Garcia, I, 254; XIII, 363; George H. Daniels and the, I, 252; how, came to be written, I, 252; suggested by Bert Hubbard, I, 252; and Rowan, I, 252; and Prince Hilakoff, I, 253; and Japanese, I, 253; and Mikado, I, 253; over forty million copies of, have been printed, I, 253; carried in knapsack of Russian soldiers, I, 253; translated into many languages, I, 253; carry, I, 256; and Hays, II, 354.
Message of Koheleth, IX, 306.
Message to Uncle Sam, I, 62.
Messages, miracle of written, III, 457; of good cheer, XI, 350.
Messalina, VI, 296; lovers of, VI, 297.
Messiah, specimen bricks of the literary, I, 53; at Winnipeg, I, 181; a modern, X, 321.
Messianic instinct, the, VI, 178.
Metal silos, first, VIII, 286.
Metals, transmutation of, II, 36.
Metal-workers, the, VIII, 84.
Metaphysics, I, 301; XI, 54; XIII, 400; and fakery, I, 421; skyey, III, 446.
Metempsychosis, XI, 392.
Mexican athlete and auto industry, VIII, 172.
Mexico, V, 375.
Michelangelo, XII, 359; *Moses* of, VI, 109; statue of, at Roycroft, VI, 327; made brushes of bristles, XIV, 153.
Middleman, XIII, 400; what is a, VIII, 131.
Middlemen, VIII, 144; and parasites, VIII, 130.
Middle West products, II, 268.
Midnight, XIII, 400.
Migration, the first, VII, 181; first, stopped, I, 429; hunger first incentive to, I, 429.
Migrations, causes of, II, 47; six principal, II, 47; from India, II, 47; social, IV, 183; great, VII, 65.
Milan, King, VII, 263.
Militancy, XIII, 401.
Miles City, VII, 20.
Militant methods, IV, 349.
Militant suffragists, IV, 351.
Militarism, IX, 117; XIII, 400; in America, IX, 291.
Military, specialized functions of the, IV, 142.
Military Academy, I, 188.
Military Ideals, IV, 256.
Military science in Japan, V, 213.
Military system, compulsory, of Germany, IV, 248.
Milk, IV, 237; bacteria, in, IV, 243; pure, VI, 84; peddling, IV, 238.
Mill, John Stuart, and Jeremy Bentham, VI, 185.
Millais, Sir John, X, 380.
Millenium, I, 220; VI, 133; XIII, 400; how it will come, I, 220.
Miller, C, W., X, 187.
Miller, Frank, VII, 287; X, 303; master of the Mission Inn, V, 178.
Miller, Isabella D., X, 303.
Miller, Joaquin, V, 13; a poseur, V, 17; his monument to Moses, V, 18; his arrangement for his funeral, V, 19; mother of, V, 21; sanctuary of, V, 23; and the Chinese, V, 24; and Clarence Darrow, V, 24; how, got, his name, V, 25; was Utopian, V, 27; and San Francisco *Overland Monthly*, V, 28; the snakes and, V, 28; and Moses, V, 29.
Miller, Doctor Z. T., XIV, 239.
Millerites, I, 52; and the millennium, I, 180.
Millinery, secondary sexual manifestation, IX, 270; and social status, IX, 270; satisfaction in, IX, 273.
Millionaire, one hundred years ago but one, in America, II, 371.
Millionaire farmers, VIII, 145.
Millionaires, obscure, II, 372; circumscribed, VIII, 222; educated, IX, 258.
Millionaire Socialists, I, 54.
Mills, Benjamin Fay, IV, 277; X, 143; one of the prophets of the better day, X, 143; very handy with the forensic mitts, X, 143; a lover of letters, X, 145.

Milton's pamphlets, I, 23.
Mind, abnormal condition means many ills, I, 141; disease, largely matter of, I, 141; what is, I, 301; the human, IV, 109; peace of, and work, IV, 188; is a dual affair, VI, 99; expression of, XI, 368.
Minds, children of married, IV, 50.
Mine, descent into a, VII, 148; copper, VII, 372; down a copper, VII, 373; a mile deep, VII, 377.
Mineral waters, IX, 296.
Mineral wealth, VII, 121.
Miners' Clubhouse, a, VII, 336.
Minimum wage for both sexes, I, 290; for women, I, 283.
Mining, successful, II, 293.
Ministerial endmen, VI, 116.
Minute, XIII, 401.
Miracle, IV, 392; XIII, 401; of motherhood, I, 153; a modern, II, 134.
Miracles, XI, 13; XII, 158; recorded in *Book of Mormon*, IX, 64, 114.
Miraculous Movies, IX, 134; as an educational factor, IX, 134; endorsed by educators, IX, 136; a power for good, IX, 138.
Mirth, immanent, IX, 146.
Misbranded textiles, VIII, 261.
Misery, XII, 347; and environment, IV, 303.
Mismating, IX, 168.
Mission Inn, the, VII, 54, 286; famous, V, 178.
Missionaries, VI, 202; XIII, 402; Mormon, IV, 248; to China, VI, 202.
Missouri Pacific System, II, 297.
Missouri shibboleth, IX, 388.
Mistakes, VII, 394; VIII, 168; of Moses, XII, 26.
Mistress, XIII, 402.
Mitchell, Dr. A. L., XIV, 269.
Mitchell, Doctor Weir, and disease, V, 329.
Mitre Tavern, IX, 222.
Mix, Melville, X, 159; birthplace of, X, 159; and the Dodge Manufacturing Company, X, 160; as a salesman, X, 160.
Mixed diet, VII, 163.
Moab, IX, 395.
Mob-rule, XI, 79.

Mob-spirit, X, 242; and newspapers, X, 242.
Moderation, XII, 295.
Modern American business, X, 342.
Modern bands, value of, II, 166.
Modern business ethics, VIII, 21.
Modern Messiah, a, X, 321.
Modern miracle, a, II, 134.
Modern prophet, a, X, 321.
Modesty, XIII, 401.
Mohammedanism, X, 324; rank of, in religions, X, 326.
Molly Maguires, I, 117.
Mona Lisa, the, IX, 305; authenticity of, IX, 305; and La Gioconda, IX, 305-307; consummate beauty of, IX, 308.
Monohan, Michael, XIII, 282.
Monarch, a democratic, X, 14.
Monarchist, IV, 407; VI, 131.
Monastery, original intent of the, I, 399.
Monastery Le Trap at Charlestown, IX, 194.
Monasticism, IX, 28; mistake of, IX, 32.
Money, pin, I, 448; Franklin and, I, 462; purchasing power of, II, 259; idle, VIII, 207; and brains, VIII, 222; and friends, VIII, 362; X, 297; value of, XII, 76.
Moneyback guarantee, VIII, 68.
Moneyback plan and price-cutting, VIII, 70.
Moneybacking products, VIII, 68.
Monism, X, 226.
Monmouth, Oregon, VII, 125.
Monkeys, IV, 118; IX, 224.
Monks, bookmakers and, IV, 145.
Monogamy, IX, 68; enforced, IV, 148; voluntary, IV, 149; or polygamy, IX, 66.
Monopolies, VIII, 283.
Monopoly, VIII, 54; in the shoe business, II, 183.
Montessori, Madame, V, 115.
Montessori system, V, 117.
Monticello, IX, 275.
Monument, a national, V, 51.
Mood, the buying, VIII, 83; buying a matter of, VIII, 83.
Moods, XI, 412.
Moral qualities, to be lovable we must have, IX, 286.
Moralist, XIII, 402.

Morality, IV, 281, 428; IX, 76; XIII, 402; of gambling, I, 76; superstition and, I, 204.
Morals, III, 465; XI, 398; effect of gambling on, I, 77.
More babies, more pay, II, 442.
Morgue, XIII, 492.
Mormon, Book of, IV, 60; IX, 63; etymology of word, IX, 60; Book of, an American sequel to the Bible, IX, 64.
Mormon missionaries, IV, 248.
Mormondom a matter of economics, VII, 64.
Mormons, VI, 160; IX, 61; Brigham Young's advice to the, II, 431; instrumental music and choral societies of the, VII, 56; as money-makers, VII, 59; virtues of, VII, 61; as miners, VII, 63; and religious freedom, VII, 66; as farmers, VII, 68; have no paid priests, IX, 72; the matter with, IX, 75.
Morrill, "Golightly," XIV, 87.
Morris, William, influence of, VI, 250; and business, VI, 309; on work, IX, 73.
Morse, VII, 75.
Mortals, the happiest, on earth, IV, 381.
Morton, James J., the boy comic, VIII, 319.
Mosaic code, IV, 31.
Moses, VI, 328; XII, 396; Mistakes of, I, 377; Sunday Closing Laws, IV, 46; the author, IV, 121; Joaquin Miller's monument to, V, 18.
Monsieur De Junk, V, 207.
Moose creed, X, 171.
Morris, William, V, 144.
Most important thing in the world, VIII 333.
Mother, II, 387; the ideal, I, 354; Nature is our, II, 466; who pays, VI, 21; work of, VI, 21; every one should be a landowner, VI, 35; Meissonier's tribute to, VI, 154.
Mother-heart, the, V, 298.
Motherhood, I, 341; XIII, 401; divinity of, I, 150; and love for offspring, I, 150; and race perpetuity, I, 150; effect of, on race, I, 153; miracle of, I, 153; divinity of, I, 248; free, I, 306;
is, dishonorable, I, 343; always great and splendid and heroic, I, 343; we must make, honorable, I, 345; sanctity of, II, 466; holiness of, VI, 410; corner-stone of the home, IX, 75; subsidize, IX, 45; service to State of, IX, 246; of God, XII, 297; sacred, XIII, 321.
Mother Jones, VII, 339; and John D. Rockefeller, Jr., VIII, 141.
Mother-love, I, 138, 240, 305, 464; IV, 403; IX, 246; X, 387; natural, I, 346; in the eagle, I, 465.
Mothers, economic freedom of, I, 151; pensions for, I, 153, 304; IX, 245; friend of, I, 346; making, economically free, VI, 22; Little Other, IX, 356; and sons, X, 386; of men, XII, 390.
Moths and butterflies, XIV, 304.
Motion, IV, 286.
Motive, ulterior, IV, 407.
Motto, V, 265.
Motto of Socrates, IX, 128.
Mouth diseases, VIII, 36.
Movies, and books compared, VIII, 252; the Miraculous, IX, 134; in the home, IX, 136; weekly show at Roycroft, IX, 137; in the churches, IX, 138.
Moving pictures, the, VIII, 250; great educational factors of the time, VIII, 251.
Mozart, humor of, IV, 361; his sense of proportion, IV, 361.
Muckraker, XIII, 401.
Muckraking magazines, VIII, 269.
Muldoon, William, X, 113; I, 427; as Charles the Wrestler in *As You Like It*, X, 115; system of, X, 115; his treatment, X, 117; at home, X, 118; his methods, X, 119; trainer of men, X, 124.
Muldoon's, Chauncey Depew at, X, 120.
Mulford, Prentice, I, 296.
Mummy, XIII, 402; Trust, VIII, 45.
Munsey, XIII, 403.
Murder, refined, IV, 343.
Murder machines and big business, IX, 117.
Murderer, XIII, 402.
Murphy, Elmer R., X, 401.
Murphy maximus, VII, 15.
Murphys, spuds and praties, VI, 81.

xlvii

Music, IV, 398; XIII, 402; hotel and restaurant, I, 476; demands an atmosphere, I, 478; classical, IV, 477; most important thing in, VII, 23; and soul, IX, 209; modern, XIV, 102; the youngest of the arts, XIV, 102; art, and, XIV, 104; in homes, XIV, 107; the beginnings of, XIV, 143.
Music at meals, I, 476; Mission Inn and, I, 477.
Music hungry, IX, 209.
Musical instruments, II, 38; IX, 300.
Musician, accomplished, XIII, 343; a great, is a paradox, XIV, 149.
Mutsuhito, V, 210; imperial pedigree of, V, 210.
Mutual Admiration Society, XIII, 340
Mutual aid, XIII, 334.
Mutual helpfulness, X, 135.
Mutuality, II, 290; VI, 296; VIII, 87; of interests, I, 120; and success, VIII, 346.
Mystic, XIII, 402.
Myth and miracle, XIII, 163.
Nancy, XIII, 403.
Nancy Hanks, V, 46.
Napoleon, I, 322; contract of, with the Holy See, I, 361; and "Marshal Vorwerts," II, 66; character of, VI, 250; recipe of, for peace at home, IX, 288.
Nasmyth's steam hammer, VIII, 89.
Natalie Keschko, VII, 263.
Nation, healthy, and food, IX, 344.
National Cash Register, welfare work of, I, 172.
National Cash Register Company, case of the government against the, II, 173.
National honor, XII, 106.
National Purity Association, VI, 110.
National Reserve Association, VIII, 206.
Nations, life of, I, 216; wealth of, VII, 65.
Natural education, the, I, 416.
Natural maternity, IX, 245.
Natural mother-love, I, 346.
Natural poseur, a, V, 17.
Natural religion, XI, 24.
Natural rights, XII, 111.
Natural thought, I, 295.
Naturalist, world's second great, X, 357.
Nature, I, 49; II, 145; IV, 119, 306, 381; XII, 257, 330, 350; XIII, 403; is prodigal of man, I, 37; equality of, I, 47; forces of, I, 144; is ward of health, I, 146; the divine intelligence, I, 242; ability to mix with, II, 336; Laws of, II, 456; is our mother, II, 466; magic wand of, III, 474; co-operation and, IV, 117; partnership of, with man, IV, 118; in partnership with, IV, 172; human, IV, 216; first food of, IV, 240; an unerring Law of, IV, 296; primal law of, V, 283; man a part of, VI, 249; playground of, VII, 43; a forgotten freak of, VII, 240; own fuel of, VIII, 96; denial of integrity of, X, 48; and polygamy, IX, 68; secret writings of, IX, 340; love of, IX, 345; private secretary of, X, 356; controlling impulses of, XI, 212; man a product of, XI, 218; heart of, XI, 382; the infinite mother, XI, 415; and character of aristocracy, XII, 127; Emerson on, XII, 239; takes no thought of the individual, XIII, 115.
Nature cure, V, 301.
Nature dances, XIV, 88.
Nature study, II, 453; VI, 217.
Navies, XII, 369; armies and, I, 318; Paine on, XII, 122; idea of, for protection of commerce delusive, XII, 122.
Navy portfolio, I, 9.
Nazareth, XI, 15.
Nebulous typothetae, XIII, 403.
Neff House, V, 267.
Neighbor, XIII, 403.
Nervous prostration, IV, 388; IX, 87.
Nesbit, XIII, 403.
Netcher, Charles, X, 307; birthplace of, X, 308; slogan of, X, 312; characteristics, X, 313; humanitarianism of, X, 313.
Netcher, Mrs. Charles, X, 305, 345; business ability of, X, 317; virtues of, X, 318.
New Amsterdam, II, 61.
New Brunswick, IX, 235.
New business ethics, the, I, 376.
New Canada, the, VII, 346.
New Declaration of Independence, the, I, 366, 369.
New England, best products of, VII, 311.
New Englander, VII, 314.

New harmony, V, 58.
New infidelity, the, IX, 120.
New light, a, VIII, 72.
New Orleans, IV, 203.
New Thought, I, 150, 293; IV, 283; IV, 393, 397; XIII, 403; distinguishing feature of, I, 293; expressed by Pythagoras, B. C. 600, I, 293; Jesus taught, I, 294; the new theology is the result of, I, 295; Emerson, Kant, Spinoza and, I, 296.
New type of businessman, the, II, 291.
New way, the, VIII, 67.
New Word, the, by Allen Upward, V, 278; some gems from, V, 285.
New York, XIII, 403; the great distributing center of human beings, VII, 325.
New York Central Railroad, I, 286.
New York City, VII, 325; the marvel of, VII, 326; synonym of sin, VII, 326.
New York Philharmonic organized by William Steinway, II, 80.
New York Subway, X, 262.
New Zealand Board of Equity, IX, 53.
Newcomb vs. Newcomb, I, 446.
News, good, IV, 321.
Newspaper, VIII, 296; as educator, I, 232; daily, I, 233; commuter's "dope," I, 236; villainous daily, I, 238; a fool's, V, 384; a wonderful, VI, 77.
Newspaper advertising, VI. 136.
Newspaper business, I, 232.
Newspaper habit, I, 235.
Newspaper office, XIII, 403; truth in, I, 238.
Newspaper offices, I, 110.
Newspaper owners, X, 243.
Newspaper reporters, I, 234.
Newspaper men, I, 232; and journalists, distinction between, I, 232.
Newspapers, IV, 194; owners of, I, 232; and newspapermen, I, 233; and advertising, I, 234; and circulation, I, 234; are business ventures, I, 234; wax fat on calamity, I, 234; and scandal, I, 235; IV, 194, 235; maw of the, III, 439; record of ephemeral happenings, III, 439; and sweat-shops, III, 439; and mob spirit, X, 242.
Newton's *Principia*, XIII, 344.
Niagara Falls, VII, 106; light, heat and power potentialities, IV, 83; age of the gorge, VII, 106; average potential energy of, VII, 106; first practical use of the power of, VII, 107; construction of power canal, VII, 108; Indians and, VII, 113; real wonder of, VII, 113; a prophecy concerning, VII, 114.
Nicene Creed, I, 206.
Nicholas Nickleby, I, 246.
Nickelodeon, II, 103.
Nielson, J. B., invented introduction of heated blast, VIII, 98.
Nietzsche, Friedrich, XIII, 403; on crime, IX, 69.
Nigger, XIII, 403.
Night, the monotonous noises of the, IX, 29.
Noah's Ark, XIV, 83.
Nobel, Alfred, V, 278; what did, mean, V, 279; method of superiority of, V, 279, 286; wish of mind of, V, 287; madness of, V, 291; was an idealist, V, 294; bequest of, interpreted, V, 285; spirit in, bequest, V, 290; criticism of, bequest, V, 291.
Nobel Prize, I, 320; analyzed, V, 285.
Nobility, Paine on, XII, 127.
No-breakfast plan, IX, 313.
No Enemy But Himself, XI, 87.
Nomination, XIII, 403.
Non-church members, famous, VI, 225-227.
Nonconformist, XII, 196.
Nonconformity, XII, 200.
Non-interference, the doctrine of, VI, 87.
Non-resistance, XI, 31.
Noonan, William T., II, 384; birthplace of, II, 386; B. R. &. P. and, II, 397.
Normal schools, I, 284.
Norris, VII, 33.
Norseman, I, 123.
North, the cities of the, XIV, 120.
Northeast vs. Northwest, VII, 311.
Northern Pacific Railway, VII, 17.
Northern Ohio and Southern Michigan, fertility of, VII, 185; farming in, VII, 185.
Northwestern Territory, the, III, 15.
Nothing, XIII, 403.
No war of aggression, IX, 243.
Number One Hard, VII, 331; XIV, 116.

Nusbaum, Jesse L., VII, 200.
Oath, mummery of the, VI, 228.
Oatmeal and haggis, IX, 374.
Obedience, I, 446; X, 115; XII, 311; XIII, 404; Law of, VII, 221; and law, VII, 354.
Obey, I, 447.
Objectionable literature, IX, 160.
Oblivion, XIII, 404.
Obren, Governor of Servia, VII, 262.
Observations on my reading history, XII, 42.
Obstinacy, XIII, 404.
Obtund, VIII, 42.
O Captain! My Captain, XII, 157.
Ohaine, sunken roadway of, I, 37.
Oil and Tobacco Trust, I, 200.
Oil as fuel, I, 435.
Oildag, II, 214.
Oil engine, principle of the, II, 406.
Oil fields, famous, I, 372; Russian, I, 373; untapped reservoirs, I, 436.
Oil-turn engine, II, 411.
Old age, preparing for, IV, 314; the beauties of, IV, 317.
Old Bach, IX, 188.
Old Betsy, VIII, 394.
Old Butternut, II, 152.
Old Faithful, VII, 35.
Old maid, XIII. 404.
Old prison system, the, VII, 94.
Old Salamander, VII, 134.
Oliver, Joseph D., I, 394.
Oliver expansion, VIII, 60.
Oliver Little Journey, XIV, 138.
Oliver Optic, II, 159.
Oliver plows, I, 394.
Omaha, VII, 175; Burlington Station at, VII, 175; the school system of, VII, 176.
On being " entertained," VI, 209.
On getting old, VI, 281.
One of the elect, XIV, 291.
One-price system, VIII, 217; XII, 365.
Oneida Community, IV, 146, 249; V, 107.
O'neil, Robert, I, 263.
Only Democrat, The, IV, 296.
Only fear, the, IX, 386.
Open air life and physical development, XIII, 263.
Open-hearth system of Martin and Thomas, VIII, 89.

Open Letter to Pope Leo XIII, I, 120.
Open Shop and the Labor Union, I, 118.
Opera, XIII, 404.
Opinion, public, IV, 430; freedom of, XII, 99.
Opinions, IV, 422; diverse, IV, 460.
Opportunism, policy of, VI, 306.
Opportunities, VII, 181.
Opportunity, II, 201; IV, 375; VII, 332, 393; XIII, 404; equality of, IV, 375.
Opposites, IX, 120.
Opposition of forces, IV, 64.
Optimism, XIII, 404; applied to life, XI, 349.
Optimist, IV, 382, 425; XIII, 405.
Oral righteousness, VIII, 35.
Orange habit, VII, 300.
Orange John, V, 297.
Orangemen, I, 230.
Oranges, California, VII, 298.
Orang-Outang, IX, 224.
Orator, VI, 64.
Oratorical grace, V, 139.
Oratory, V, 98; VI, 212; XI, 46; XIII, 405; XIV, 163; secret of, X, 26; and literature compared, XI, 392.
Orchards, apple, X, 300; plowing of, X, 301.
Orchestra leader, VII, 320.
Order of Merit, IX, 404.
Orders, women are willing to accept, IV, 381; on giving, XIII, 300.
Oregon, and gardens, X, 360; the idea, VII, 125; teachers of, VII, 126.
Organ recitals at Salt Lake City, VII, 55.
Organization, I, 70; VI, 91; VII, 398; VIII, 110; XIV, 189; rise of modern, I, 41; skill in, II, 168; test of, II, 380; daffy on, VIII, 194; the first necessity in, VIII, 235.
Organizations, work for big, I, 70; church, II, 263; gregarious, VI, 127;
Organize, the ability to, XIV, 205.
Organized religion, XIII, 404.
Organized society greatest of all bribers, IX, 406.
Organizers, IV, 389.
Organs, cottage, XIV, 105.
Orient, XIII, 405.
Oriental, the guileless, V, 190.
Oriental imagination, X, 325.
Origin of Species, VI, 185; X, 407.

Original mysteries, X, 89.
Orphan asylum and the hospital indictments of our mode of life, IX, 247.
Orphans, legal, I, 344.
Orphans' homes, I, 343.
Orpheum Theater in Seattle, VIII, 315.
Orpheus, dimity divinity of, IV, 63.
Orthodontia, VIII, 38.
Orthodox, advisers, VIII, 322.
Orthodox clergy, XII, 172.
Orthodoxy, V, 284; XII, 165; XIII, 405; Ingersoll on, XII, 165.
Osborne, Thomas Mott, VII, 90; work of, at Sing Sing, VII, 94.
O'Shea, Felix, XIV, 192.
Ossining, VII, 90.
Osteopathy, II, 460; beginning of the science of, II, 452; science of, II, 460; the secret of, II, 464.
Othello portrayal of jealousy, VI, 256.
Other side, the, XIV, 275.
Our Brothers in Bonds, IV, 76.
Our flag, IV, 368.
Outdoor life, IX, 345; John Brown and, III, 370.
Outdoor sleeping-rooms, VI, 41.
Outdoor teaching, VIII, 86.
Out-of-doors, love of, V, 43; teaching, IV, 235.
Out-of-doors life, XII, 314.
Over-eating, IX, 285; ills come from, IV, 339.
Overhead, maintaining the, I, 442.
Overlapping of churches, VI, 170.
Overproduction, VI, 367.
Over-soul, XI, 313; Emerson's, V, 232.
Owen, Robert, IX, 379; the world's first businessman, V, 59; and factory system, IX, 380; product factory idea of, X, 359.
Owenites were practically free lovers, X, 60.
Oysters, Kansas and, VII, 224.
Ozarks, VII, 84.
Package goods, VIII, 69.
Paderewski, V, 66.
Paganism, I, 208.
Pain, XIII, 405; secret of alleviation from, IX, 392.
Paine, Thomas, IX, 279; XII, 105; on basis of religions, XII, 109; on being ruled by precedent, XII, 108; on British Constitution, XII, 115; on charters, XII, 110; on children, XII, 112; on civil government, XII, 121; on constitution and government, XII, 117; on dukes and counts, XII, 126; on duty of man, XII, 116; on freedom, XII, 105; on French Constitution, XII, 125; on government, XII, 110; on landed interest, XII, 120; on national honor, XII, 106; on navies, XII, 122; on nobility, XII, 127; on normal government, XII, 124; on peace, XII, 106; on rebellion, XII, 118; on reforms, XII, 116; on religions and man, XII, 109; on repeal of laws, XII, 123; on representative government, XII, 114; on rights of man, XII, 111; on spirit of liberty, XII, 107; on superstition, XII, 106; on taxation, XII, 118; on Washington, XIII, 128; on Washington, XIII, 128; pamphlets of, I, 25; lecture, VII, 303; mother of, VII, 305; religion of, VII, 305; influence of, IX, 280; and liberty, XII, 20; love of liberty, XII, 27.
Painstaking, IV, 357.
Painters, the despair of, IX, 305.
Palestine, IX, 393.
Palisades, the, II, 56.
Pamphilus, I, 21.
Pamphlet, an arsenal of arguments, I, 21; the vogue of the, I, 21; weapon of thinker, I, 21; and advertising booklet compared, I, 22; the revival of the, I, 25.
Pamphleteers, touch history at a thousand points, I, 21; Puritans as, I, 22; famous preachers as, I, 23.
Pamphlets, and pamphleteers, I, 21; and printing, I, 21; Puritans and, I, 22; ban on, I, 23; Milton's, I, 23; noted collections of, I, 23; of Sam Adams, I, 245; of Dean Swift, I, 24; arsenals from which the plain people got their ammunition, I, 25; Franklin's opinion of the, of Paine, I, 25.
Panama Canal, VII, 197, 272.
Panama World's Exposition, VII, 273.
Panics, II, 278; VIII, 205.
Pantheism, and Jesus, XI, 43.
Pantheon, IX, 401.
Paper, Chinese made the first, VII, 397.

Papers, daily in prisons, IV, 77.
Paradise, II, 314; V, 264; XIII, 406.
Paradox, one great universal, IX, 294.
Paranoia, IX, 385; and the psychologist, IX, 385.
Paranoiac, X, 16; XIII, 269.
Parasites, VIII, 130.
Parasitic class, VIII, 335.
Parcel Post, the, I, 90; John Wanamaker's opinion of, I, 91.
Parents, IV, 415; incompatible, I, 49; tyranny in, I, 50.
Paris from a balloon, VII, 236.
Parker, Theodore, V, 308.
Parnell, Charles Stewart, I, 229; death of, I, 229.
Parody, IV, 446; XIII, 405.
Parsimony, Robert Ingersoll on, VII, 307.
Parsons, qualifications for, I, 33.
Parsons, John E., II, 226.
Parthenon, secret of the, XIII, 361.
Parvenu, XIII, 405.
Pascal, I, 284; his view of humanity, I, 284; his individual man, IX, 212;
Passing of the Doctor, X, 173.
Passion, war and, II, 64; the Divine, III, 474; the limit of the grand, V, 401.
Passover, Feast of the, XI, 46.
Past, heirs, to the, IV, 129.
Pasteboard Proclivities, I, 75.
Pastoral calls, I, 33, 422; the business of, I, 422.
Pastoral stage, VI, 311.
Pastorless churches, IX, 123.
Paternalism, I, 286; breeds the beggar, I, 286.
Patience, IV, 182, 441; the virtue of, II, 163; in business, II, 259; wins, IV, 84.
Patriotism, I, 321; XII, 23.
Patterson, John H., II, 171; educational campaign of, II, 177.
Patton, Doctor, V, 80; and David Swing, V, 82.
Paul, XI, 57; founding of Christianity by, I, 207; and Plutarch, V, 95; and Christianity, XI, 57; zeal of, XI, 58.
Paul, Jean, son of Anak, V, 258.
Pauline Judaism, XI, 58.
Pay, VIII, 113; as you go, VI, 141.
Pay-envelope, I, 121.
Peace, IX, 81; XII, 80, 326, 372; XIII, 406; war and, I, 159; universal, I, 324; an advocate of, II, 179; Paine on, XII, 106; reigned, XIII, 31.
Peace ambassador to the Nations, I, 321.
Peace compact with Canada, I, 161.
Peace picnic, a, IX, 116.
Peace, Poise and Power, VIII, 410.
Peace problem, the, I, 315.
Peace recipe, IV, 255.
Peanut policies, VIII, 353.
Peanut-stands are individualistic, I, 79.
Pedagogic weaning time, IX, 323.
Pedagogs, the mote-blind, VI, 217.
Pedagogy, XII, 303; an opinion on, I, 190; and poverty, IV, 409.
Pedal peace, X, 398.
Pedant, XIII, 406.
Pegasus, I, 190.
Penalties, immunity from, on the acceptance of the creed, I, 131; sins and, IX, 35.
Penalty of leisure, VIII, 202.
Penance of Dr. Johnson, VIII, 35.
Penitentiaries, IX, 47.
Penn, William, I, 442; VII, 225.
Pen-name, that, V, 52.
Pennsylvania Railroad, I, 286.
Penologist, proposition confronting the, VI, 241.
Penology, the modern school of, IV, 210.
Pensions, about, IV, 374; for mothers, I, 304.
Pentecost, Hugh, V, 304.
People, literary, IV, 381; happy, V, 117; who travel by the Gorge Route, VIII, 230; estimating, XIII, 306; the common, XIV, 259.
Pepys, Samuel, VI, 66.
Perception, XII, 208.
Perceptions, voluntary and involuntary, XII, 206.
Percherons, I, 190.
Percussion-cap invented about Eighteen Hundred Thirty-three, II, 235.
Perfect gentleman, X, 31.
Perfect girl, the, IX, 125.
Perfection, IX, 126.
Performer, XIII, 406.
Perfume, XIII, 405.
Pericles, XIII, 406; and Phidias, IV, 15; age of, V, 255; VII, 274; Aspasia and Socrates, V, 256; love of, and Aspasia at eighty-five, VI, 282; the

world's master builder, VII, 274;
life of, a search for talent, XIII, 359.
Periodicals, VIII, 269.
Perkins, Oliver H., VII, 172.
Perlmutter and Potash, I, 426.
Perpetuity of the race, I, 304.
Perry, Commodore, I, 160; famous message of, I, 160.
Persecution, religious, III, 33; of the Jews, IV, 30.
Perseus, VI, 289.
Persian lambs, XIII, 238.
Personal experience, a, I, 419.
Personal magnetism, II, 355.
Personal property, rights of, I, 65.
Personality, II, 163, 165, 179; XIII, 286; and hats, VI, 145; in business, X, 412.
Pertinent questions, VI, 272.
Pessimist, IV, 442; XIII, 406.
Pessimistic-optimist, VI, 132.
Peter, XI, 71.
Pew, in the wrong, XIV, 293.
Phalansterie, XIII, 365.
Phantasy, a, IX, 29.
Pharisee, XIII, 410.
Phidias, V, 255; age of, XIV, 79.
Philadelphia, first telephone in, X, 364.
Philadelphia Centennial Exposition, I, 371; VII, 276.
Philanthropy, II, 259; Emerson on, XII, 198.
Philistia, question submitted to, IX, 26.
Philistine, the, XIII, 266, 419.
Philistine, a term of reproach, VIII, 67; XIII, 410.
Philistines, Society of, IX, 392.
Phillipine Magazine, the, XIII, 268.
Phillips, Wendell, business of, V, 308.
Philological appendenda, VI, 96.
Philosopher, XIII, 410.
Philosophers, English, VI, 185; are above the frivolous, XIII, 116.
Philosopher's stone, XII, 78.
Philosophic thinking, IX, 103.
Philosophy, XIII, 405; Jack, I, 29; an avocation, VI, 43; natural, VI, 43; the mystics in, IV, 368; Garret, VIII, 18; pragmatic, VIII, 130.
Phonograph, V, 122.
Photography, V, 195.
Physical culture, IX, 250; in colleges, I, 419; in universities, VI, 323; as a business, VI, 333.
Physical development, open air life and, XIII, 263.
Physical disability, IX, 250; efficiency, IX, 126.
Physician's Farewell, XIV, 269.
Piano, the soul of a man, II, 62.
Pickett of Iowa, VII, 166.
Picture shows as educational factor, VIII, 250.
Picture-story, the, VIII, 252.
Piety, XIII, 406.
Pig-pen Pete, XIII, 227.
Pin money, Addison on, I, 448.
Pine grove, II, 140.
Pioneer days, a night alone in the woods, III, 63.
Pio Nono, I, 363.
Pious hold-ups, VI, 279.
Pirate, respectable, XIII, 329.
Pirates, modern, VIII, 284.
Pirie MacDonald, V, 195.
Pivotal Points, Law of, I, 115.
Placer-mining, XIV, 121.
Plagiarism, antithesis of, IV, 57; and kabojolism, IV, 57.
Plague, the, I, 262.
Plain women, XIII, 132.
Planet, XIII, 407.
Plantin Musee, II, 50.
Plantin Print-Shop, II, 50.
Plantins, the, II, 49.
Platonic love, IV, 426; XIII, 407.
Play, XIII, 497; a, out-of-doors, V, 378.
Play-actors, the, XIV, 161.
Play ball, IV, 87.
Playgrounds, Seattle school, IV, 159; and gardens, IV, 160.
Playing second fiddle, VI, 87.
Plays, American, IX, 201; problem, IX, 201.
Plea, for the cow and the calf, I, 250; of the vivisector, I, 311.
Please be seated, XIV, 41.
Pliny the Elder, X, 357.
Plotters, I, 114.
Plows, Oliver, I, 394.
Plutarch, V, 95; and Paul, V, 95; literature's tribute to, V, 97; some nuggets from, V, 97; style of, V, 98.
Plutocrat, VI, 131.

Plymouth Rocks, XI, 121.
Pocahontas, XIII, 329.
Pocket, XIII, 406.
Poe, Edgar Allen, IX, 100.
Poem, *Song of Songs*, a, III, 460; greatest ever written by an American, V, 13.
Poems Ali Baba loves, XIII, 292.
Poet, XIII, 406; a, by prenatal tendency, V, 26; professional, VI, 335.
Poetic eczema, XI, 137.
Poetic prose, XI, 377.
Poetry, IV, 189; XIII, 407; love and, IV, 189; that has in it meat for men, IV, 294.
Poets, and religion, I, 422; laurel for, V, 72.
Poets " Corner," VII, 157.
Point of view, the, VI, 26.
Poise, IV, 430; V, 394; XII, 378; XIV, 57; and power, VI, 328; IX, 338.
Poisons, a selection from Alfred Russel Wallace's list of, I, 262; as remedies, I, 262; toxins and vaccines, I, 263.
Poker-face, I, 77.
Poker player, I, 75; a scientific liar, I, 77.
Police, XIII, 407.
Police duty, I, 320.
Policy, XIII, 407; is formulated conduct, VIII, 295.
Politeness, XIII, 407; insincere, VIII, 110.
Politeness Pays, and Hays, II, 354.
Political economy, peculiar, XI, 45.
Political mathematics, X, 284.
Politician, parasitic, VII, 392.
Politicians, XII, 142; XIII, 406; and their opinions, VIII, 224; I have known, VIII, 309; and potatoes, IX, 233; Lincoln on, XII, 132.
Politics, party, and the constitution, II, 360; and headgear, VI, 79.
Polygamous husbands, IX, 71.
Polygamy, IX, 67, 188; XIII, 409; the matter of, VII, 71; in nature, IX, 68; and children, IX, 69; and crime, IX, 69; Spencer on, IX, 69; Cleveland and, IX, 73.
Pompeii and Herculaneum, XIV, 153.
Pontius Pilate, XI, 72, 76.
Poor, rights of the, V, 216.
Poor man's club, the, IX, 353.
Pope, the, I, 209; once had temporal power, I, 231.

Pope Adrian sold Ireland, I, 231.
Pope Leo the Thirteenth, I, 360; designates Church's real enemies, I, 298.
Pope Pius the Tenth, I, 360.
Popular fallacies, VI, 30.
Popular standards, XII, 213.
Popularity, XIII, 410.
Populism, I, 197; Sherman act a sop to, I, 197.
Populist, I, 71.
Porifirio Diaz, V, 373.
Poses, IV, 254.
Posey, Colonel, V, 51.
Postage, IV, 152.
Postivity and Pragmatism, I, 301.
Postnuptial agreement, IV, 107.
Post Office, and Express Companies compared, I, 90-99; Life Insurance and Savings Banks and the, I, 93.
Post Office system, VIII, 73; rise of the, I, 94; our best example of applied socialism, VI, 310.
Posthumous publications, III, 443.
Postponement, XIII, 408.
Potato, raising of seed, IX, 236; cultivation of, IX, 236; as a food-staple, IX, 238; Irish, IX, 237; in Ireland, IX, 238.
Potato, The, by Eugene H. Grubb, X, 351.
Potato crops, IX, 234.
Potato Hill and Paradise, VI, 223.
Potato-parer, skilled, XIII, 343.
Potato-raising, four great, districts in America, IX, 235.
Potato seed, IX, 236.
Potato yield in Ireland, IX, 238.
Potatoes, transplanted, VI, 81; Maine, IX, 237.
Potter, Reverend Asa, V, 199.
Potter's field, V, 67.
Poverty, XI, 195; life-insurance and, IV, 228; pedagogy and, IV, 409; is only a comparative term, X, 388.
Powder, invention of explosive, II, 234; smokeless, II, 236.
Powder Trust, II, 242.
Power, IV, 192; XII, 112; tragedy of unrestrained, I, 35; and peace, secrets of, I, 294; money is the measure of, I, 382; waste of, II, 405; setting your brake against the, IV, 227; infinite, IV, 268; source of, IV, 462; early, uses,

VII, 107; cities center of, VII, 182; men of, VIII, 23; life a search for, IX, 178,183; the, of time, IX, 360.
Powers, the cartoonist, IX, 342.
Practical life, sordidness of, V, 165.
Practical politics, XIII, 407.
Pragmatic philosophy, VIII, 130; XII, 301.
Pragmatism, I, 301; XII, 301.
Pragmatists, a community of, VII, 70.
Prairie schooners, I, 385, 430.
Pratt, Silas G., II, 156.
Praxiteles, XIII, 361.
Prayer, IV, 399; XIII, 407; a, III, 475; a, of gratitude, IV, 15; and the Turks, V, 253; Emerson on, XII, 215.
"Prayer," a true story, V, 244.
Preacher, IV, 421; XIII, 407; burden of thought of the, III, 452; salaries, of, VI, 170.
Preachers, V, 330; why Elbert Hubbard criticizes, I, 31; as builders of make-believe tepees, VI, 321; sincerity of, VI, 321; half-portion, X, 148.
Precedent, IV, 384.
Predaceous real estate dealers, VI, 380.
Predatory rich, I, 34.
Prehistoric miners, VII, 370.
Premium publicity, VIII, 138.
Preoccupation, XIII, 15.
Preparedness, I, 281; war, I, 160.
Presbrey Company, Frank, XIV, 189.
Presbyterian Church, founding of, I, 212.
Presbyterian churches, pastorless, IX, 123.
Presbyterian geography, I, 402.
Preserve, the prexie of the, XIII, 227.
President, edicts of a, II, 362.
Press, the, VIII, 295; licensing of, by Queen Mary, I, 23; yellow, I, 70; Lecky on the anonymous, I, 238; free, II, 360; business of the muckraking, VII, 341.
Pretense, IX, 262.
Prevention of cruelty to animals, I, 310.
Prexie of the preserve, the, XIII, 227.
Price-cutting, fallacy of, VIII, 58; and money-back plan, VIII, 70.
Price regulation and Diocletian, I, 348.
Prickett, Walter S., VII, 367; ranch of, VII, 367.
Pride, VII, 399; XII, 76; a little civic, VII, 325; Franklin on, XII, 76.
Priest, the prerogatives of the, IV, 138; is a vicarious soldier, IV, 141; and actors extra-hazardous risks, VII, 318; is society's walking delegate, XII, 349; is the mysterious agent of Deity, XIII, 316.
Priestcraft, I, 361.
Priesthood, professional, V, 105.
Priestly office, XIII, 315.
Priest-ridden, VI, 408.
Priests, XII, 348; and Italy, VII, 154; paid, and Mormons, IX, 72.
Prig, XIII, 407.
Primitive Christians, IX, 35.
Primitive mining methods, VII, 369.
Primogeniture, XII, 127; Law of, XII, 87.
Principle, XIII, 408.
Principles, not persons, V, 128.
Printers, once all, were licensed by the state, IV, 115.
Printing, I, 21; medium of expression, I, 21; the miracle of all time, I, 21; pamphlets and, I, 21.
Printing press, dedication of first, by Gutenberg, I, 211; glory of civilization, VII, 397.
Prison, XIII, 408; of the future, I, 157; in, and out, I, 260; kindergarten method in, VI, 241; the Golden Rule in, VII, 90; old, system, VII, 94; a cemetery, IX, 47; a, with a soul, XIV, 61.
Prison handwork, VI, 242.
Prison industry, VI, 238.
Prison pallor, XIV, 279.
Prison Reform League, IV, 210.
Prison system, VII, 93.
Prisoners, mail for, IV, 77; jury of, VII, 95; Benjamin Franklin on the treatment of, IX, 44.
Prisons, penitentiaries and reformatories, I, 154; silent system in, IV, 76; daily papers in, IV, 77; political and ecclesiastical, XI, 382.
Private and public schools, IX, 56.
Prize-fighting, X, 203.
Probation system, II, 329.
Prodigality, XII, 71.
Producers, XII, 306.
Production and transportation, VII, 74.
Productive power, I, 286.

lv

Professional priesthood, XI, 32.
Professions, freeing the, V, 331; the learned, VI, 391.
Profits, VIII, 53.
Progress, VII, 395; XII, 351, 395; XIII, 408; a definition of, I, 260; and evolution, I, 225; greatest single obstacle to, II, 260; is a continual readjustment, II, 380; path of, V, 73; spiritual influence and, V, 86; climate and, VII, 313; statesmen and, VII, 394; the deadliest foe of, VIII, 242; Ingersoll on, XII, 182.
Progressive, XIII, 408; what a, is, X, 269.
Progressives, the, X, 269.
Proletariat, IV, 333.
Prolific writer, a, V, 91.
Promotion of Christianity among the Jews, VI, 93.
Propagation, VII, 396; love for, VI, 235.
Property, XII, 131, 140; confiscation of private, I, 383; Lincoln on, XII, 131; reliance on, XII, 222.
Property-right in marriage, XIII, 314.
Prophet, a modern, X, 321.
Prophets, XIII, 410.
Prophylactics, science of, VIII, 46.
Proportion, sense of, IV, 361.
Proposal, III, 228; with the feet, XI, 370.
Prosecutor, XIII, 408.
Pro-slavery persecution, III, 297.
Prosperity, II, 295; XIII, 409; four pillars of, I, 347; follows the railroad, X, 337; basis of, XIV, 120.
Protestant religion traces a pedigree to Rome, I, 270.
Protestantism, XIII, 408.
Protestants and the monastic idea, IX, 31.
Providence, City of, XIV, 94; named for obvious reasons, II, 27.
Provincial, the, VII, 141.
Provincialism, IX, 389.
Prynne, Hester, X, 243.
Psychology, XIII, 409; a little study in, VI, 382; science of, VIII, 269.
Ptomaine poisoning, I, 146.
Public, exploiting the, and prosperity, III, 150; rights of the, VIII, 281.
Public libraries, XI, 326; parent of American, IX, 329.
Public opinion, I, 44, 199; IV, 192, 430; XIII, 409; a silent but invincible force, VII, 356; a molder of, X, 275.
Public partnerships, II, 368.
Public playgrounds, IV, 159.
Public school, IX, 56; in England, IX, 57.
Public school system, Jefferson founded our, VII, 87.
Public speaking, V, 394.
Public utilities, VIII, 73.
Public-utility expert, II, 366.
Public-utility policy, modern, II, 370.
Publicist, puritanic, VIII, 323.
Publicity, VIII, 45; XIII, 395; is the great panacea, II, 382; by default, VIII, 221; the great disinfectant, VIII, 244.
Publisher, XIII, 406.
Publishers, X, 85.
Puget Sound, VII, 413.
Pullman, George M., VI, 215; training of, VI, 216.
Pumice-stone, X, 401.
Punching the clock, IV, 168.
Pundit Lalana, VI, 201.
Punishment, XIII, 409; reform and, IV, 35; the, fits the crime, IV, 128; dogma of endless, has become repugnant to humanity, V, 229.
Punishments, Constitution of the United States forbids strange and unusual, I, 310; deferred, IV, 161.
Punster, IV, 469.
Pure-fabric campaign, VIII, 261.
Pure-fabric Law, VIII, 262.
Pure-food Law, VIII, 261.
Pure-food propaganda, VIII, 262.
Pure white mare, XI, 392.
Purgatory, II, 314; IX, 210; XIII, 409.
Puritans, I, 22; IX, 35; and pamphlets, I, 22; as pamphleteers, I, 22.
Purity, XIII, 410.
Purpled ease, I, 27.
Putting art into commerce, X, 380.
Pyle, Howard, last picture painted by, VII, 229.
Pyle, Doctor Walter, VII, 164.
Pyramids of Egypt, VII, 399.
Quack, what is a, I, 191.
Quacks, I, 191; a dissertation on, I, 191.
Quaker Oats, Elbert Hubbard fined for advertising, VI, 295.
Quakers, embarrassments that the, suffered, XII, 43.

Qualities, XII, 296.
Quarrel, the, XIII, 245.
Queen of the porch, VI, 264.
Queensware Wedgwood product, II, 422.
Question, a, do you know, IX, 102.
Question of equity, a, VIII, 26.
Questionnaire, a, IV, 235.
Quieting qualms, III, 158.
Quintette, celebrated, VI, 296.
Quip Modest, the, IX, 150.
Quitter, the, XIV, 218.
Rabbi Levy favors taxation of church property, I, 128.
Race, the march of the, I, 216; perpetuity of the, I, 304; the new, VI, 161; has passed through several economic stages, VIII, 359.
Race between gray horse and teakettle, VIII, 328.
Race horse, visit to grave of, VII, 179.
Race horses, some famous, VII, 179.
Race problem, XIII, 410.
Race suicide, XI, 66.
Races, following the, IV, 358.
Radiate, XII, 261.
Radicals, I, 358.
Radium, IV, 367.
Railroad, II, 139; New York Central, I, 286; Pennsylvania, I, 286; first, constructed in America, II, 124; Erie, II, 125-134; spirit of the successful, II, 138; Grank Trunk, II, 352; a unique, II, 394; a friendly, VII, 18; a government, IX, 377; prosperity follows the, IX, 337; and the station loafers, XI, 99.
Railroad-builder, Canada supplied the United States our greatest, II, 349.
Railroad-builders, a trinity of, II, 349.
Railroad companies, co-operation of, I, 224.
Railroad facilities, VII, 400.
Railroad interest of Canada, VII, 333.
Railroadman, what constitutes a good, I, 452.
Railroadmen, IX, 363.
Railroad passes, I, 376.
Railroad property, trespassing on, IX, 363.
Railroad prosperity, II, 266.
Railroad publicity-bureaus, X, 337.
Railroad regulation, VII, 404.

Railroad Rates, IX, 297.
Railroad-station, a unique, VII, 22.
Railroad trespasser, the, IX, 362.
Railroads, XIII, 411; of America, I, 175; and combinations of capital, I, 223; and civilization, II, 139; thirty-four, of Chicago, II, 266; liberal policy toward, II, 382; and socialism, VI, 315; California, VII, 144; Texas and, VII, 400; need of, in Texas, VII, 406; and Interstate Commerce Commission, VIII, 174; semi-public property. 362; state opposition to, IX, 363; greatest factor in wealth-producing, X, 76.
Rain, IX, 294.
Rainbow tints, XI, 415.
Raisin is the finest food that grows, VII, 163.
Raisin Country, the, VII, 161.
Raisin-fed bacon, VII, 162.
Raisins, famous dietitians on, VII, 164; and longevity, VII, 164.
Raleigh, Sir Walter, XIV, 13; expedition of, discovered iron in this country in Sixteen Hundred Eight, VIII, 88.
Rampolla, Cardinal, I, 360, 364.
Ranchman, definition of a, I, 246.
Rapp, George, V, 59; VIII, 146.
Rapp Colony, the, V, 59.
Rappites, the, V, 59; are celibates, V, 60.
Rationalism, IX, 102-103; Pres. Eliot on, V, 313.
Rationalist, IX, 121.
Rattlesnake Pete, VII, 137; XI, 336.
Raymond, the Great, XIV, 83; and the pigs, XIV, 84.
Reaction, XI, 380; we grow by, XI, 380.
Read, Opie, VII, 83; IX, 190.
Reading, IX, 252; of good books has survival value, IX, 106; value of, IX, 26; Emerson on, XII, 205.
Real estate, IV, 438; in the South, II, 298.
Real-estate boomer, the, XIV, 122.
Reason, VI, 26; XIII, 411; first stage of, IX, 34.
Reason the church has always sided with slavery, VI, 407.
Reasonings are expressions of character, V, 161.
Rebates, I, 376.

Rebec, IX, 300.
Rebellion, hunger and, III, 335; Paine on, XII, 118.
Rebels, XII, 386; from religion, IV, 158; famous, X, 331.
Receptive mood, XI, 390.
Receptive souls, XI, 405.
Recipe, XIII, 410.
Recipe for peace, IV, 255.
Reciprocity, II, 200; XII, 267; XIII, 410.
Reckless drivers, IX, 268.
Recreation, religion and, IV, 45.
Rector, H. M., Governor of Arkansas, VII, 88.
Red Badge of Courage, the, V, 140.
Red Cross, International, of Geneva, V, 340; Clara Barton pleads for the, V, 343.
Red light, IV, 443.
Red light district and colleges, I, 409.
Red One, the, IX, 29.
Red Socialist, I, 70.
Redeemer, XIII, 411.
Reed, Hon. Thomas Brackett, XIV, 100.
Reedy, William Marion, VII, 323; X, 271; on Talmadge, V, 185; birthplace of, X, 271; education of, X, 271; biggest man in Missouri, X, 272; his paper, X, 272; philosophy of, X, 273; an anomalous, X, 274; the stylist, X, 274; bigness of, X, 275; reincarnation of Ernest Renan, X, 277; and punishment, IV, 35.
Reform, dress, VI, 68; a projected, VI, 72; fiscal, VIII, 60; America's most needed, VIII, 204; Paine on, XII, 116.
Reform School at Jeffersonville, I, 154.
Reform Schools must go, I, 156.
Reformation in degradation, IX, 43.
Reformer, XIII, 411.
Reformers, I, 225; IV, 230, 394; VIII, 123; social, I, 51.
Reforming the Reformers, I, 89.
Refrigerated transportation, VIII, 188.
Refrigeration, etymology of, VIII, 179; is the science of conservation, VIII, 180; the birth of mechanical, VIII, 181; boon to farmer, VIII, 184; and transportation, VIII, 185; uses of, VIII, 187; and meat supply, VIII, 188.
Refrigeration, cold storage, and ice-making, VIII, 177.

Refrigeration machinery, VIII, 181.
Region, XIII, 411.
Regrets, IV, 390.
Reid, Daniel Gray, X, 339.
Reign of God in Geneva, I, 174.
Reign of Terror, I, 174.
Relations, proper, II, 263.
Relationship, the highest earthly, IV, 309.
Relaxation, XIII, 410.
Reliance, XII, 210.
Relief service, organized, V, 341.
Religion, IV, 158; V, 104; XII, 264; XIII, 411; Protestant, traces pedigree to Rome, I, 270; Christianity and, I, 356; and recreation, IV, 45; rebels from, IV, 158; a formal, IV, 414; V, 106; VI, 379; XII, 342; formal, and fear, IV, 164; in Japan, V, 211; the new, V, 311; rational, V, 320; loyalty to, VI, 27; natural, VI, 378; formalized, VI, 379; Thomas Paine's, VII, 305; of humanity, VII, 310; XII, 181; XII. 274; an American, XII, 16; Paine on basis of, XII, 109; denominations of, XII, 115; Ingersoll on, XII, 166; Ingersoll on true, XII, 184; work, study, health and love constitute, XII, 291; and superstition, XII, 400; faith in, VI, 200.
Religions, seven great, I, 204; birth and resurrection of, I, 208; multiplication of, I, 208; three state, of China, VI, 201; national, XII, 115.
Religious belief a personal matter, IX, 155.
Religious denominations, XII, 352.
Religious emotion, tidal wave of, II, 104.
Religious founders poets, I, 422.
Religious freedom, XII, 87; and the Mormons, VII, 66.
Religious graft, the advance agents of, IV, 276.
Religious impressions, XII, 37.
Religious institutions in America, over forty-five thousand, I, 364.
Religious intolerance, I, 270.
Religious liberty, I, 365; IX, 277.
Religious mania, alienation arose from, V, 228.
Religious movements, X, 323.
Religious nature and sex nature closely akin, VI, 179.

Religious opinions, diversity of, XII, 114.
Religious organization, VI, 43.
Religious persecution, III, 33.
Religious rancor, I, 230; XI, 65.
Religious revival, the, IV, 273.
Religious systems, XII, 344.
Religious Trust, I, 352, 407; in France, I, 364.
Remarkable engineering feat, a, X, 374.
Rembrandt's *The Christ at Emmaus*, IV, 27.
Remington, Frederick, " Bronco Buster," VI, 183.
Remittance man, I, 414, 464; VI, 318.
Remittance men, VI, 318.
Remorse, IV, 391; XIII, 412.
Renan, and truth, I, 222; reincarnated, X, 277.
Renan's *History of the Apostles*, XIII, 341.
Reno, VII, 215.
Reno's charge had failed, VII, 216.
Renunciation, XIII, 411; Tolstoy's great doctrine of, V, 65.
Repartee, XIII, 411.
Reply churlish, the, IX, 156.
Report on yourself, a, XIV, 207.
Reproach, " Philistine " a term of, VIII, 67.
Reproof valiant, the, IX, 152.
Republic, the, ideal, XII, 372.
Republican, I, 358; government, XII, 98.
Republicanism, American, XIII, 346; French, XIII, 346.
Reputation, II, 472; XIII, 412; a literary, I, 407; built on advertising, VIII, 104.
Requisites, VI, 47.
Reservation School is a kindergarten, I, 138.
Residuum, the great undissolved, IX, 333.
Resignation, III, 445; XIII, 411.
Resistance, X, 147.
Respectability, XIII, 313, 412; hike for, IV, 392; through vicarious virtue, XIII, 330.
Respectable Class, Conspicuous Waste among the, IV, 137.
Respectable mendicants, IV, 335.
Responsibility, II, 261; XIII, 279.
Rest through change of work, VI, 348.
Resurrection, XIII, 412.
Retail grocer, VIII, 67.
Retired farmers, VIII, 201.

Retort courteous, the, IX, 151.
Revenge, VII, 399; and punishment, VI, 240.
Reversed haberdashery, I, 33.
Reversion to type, VI, 60.
Revival, basic element of the, IV, 274.
Revival of the pamphlet, the, I, 25.
Revivalists, IX, 282.
Revolutions, XII, 123.
Reward, XII, 253; of service, VI, 312.
Rewarding our big men, VIII, 255.
Rewards and punishment, I, 132; deferred, IV, 161.
Reynolds, George M., II, 265; birthplace of, II, 273.
Reynolds, Sir Joshua, V, 199; his clerical ancestry, V, 199.
Reynolds, Stephen Marion, X, 125; Red House of, X, 126.
Rhetoric, VI, 46; rules of, XI, 49; IX, 311.
Rhine, taking a trip up the, XII, 353.
Rhode Island, II, 26; as a sanctuary, I, 213.
Rhodes, James H., and Company, X, 402.
Riah, VI, 102.
Rich, idle, I, 28; the, need education, IV, 230; ignorance of the, IV, 230; what is, XII, 241; grade of the newly, XIII, 337.
Richard of the Quest, VI, 211.
Richelieu, I, 41.
Riches, Job's, IV, 123; rot of, V, 88; potential, of America, VIII, 205.
Ricker, Marilla, V, 216; XIV, 70.
Riding a hobby, II, 375.
Riding three horses, I, 188.
Right thinking, IX, 385; XI, 403.
Righteous indignation, XIII, 412.
Righteousness, IV, 233, 393; XIII, 412; oral, VIII, 35.
Rights, women's, IV, 348; of man, XIV, 21.
Riley, James Whitcomb, VI, 376.
Rivalry and strife, XII, 356.
Riverside, VII, 295; Ad-club, VII, 53.
Road-builders, I, 395; some, I, 390.
Roadmaking, science of, I, 385.
Roads, state, I, 387; Rockefeller on, II, 257.
Roads, good, I, 384; II, 264; VIII, 292;

Jefferson and, I, 384; and toll gates, I, 384; and the auto, I, 385; foster good will, I, 388; as monuments, I, 388; big men who sponsor, I, 390; and " Fords," I, 392; automobile's influence in making of, I, 393.
Roadways, the evolution of, VIII, 391.
Roanoke Island, XIV, 17.
Robert, J., X, 67.
Rochester, II, 396.
Rock Island Company, the, X, 342.
Rockefeller, John D., II, 245; VI, 88; VIII, 375; Ida Tarbell's pictures of, I, 378; Alma Mater of. I, 401; a joker, II, 248; jokes of, II, 249; early days of, II, 252; some characteristics of, II, 253; the world's greatest businessman, II, 253; genius of, II, 254; on roads, II, 257; selections from writings of, II, 258; and Colorado strike, VII, 338.
Rockefeller, Jr., and Mother Jones, VIII, 141.
Rockefeller fuel, II, 32.
Rockies, mineral wealth of the, VII, 49.
Rocky Mountains, summer morning in the, XIII, 103.
Rodney, Cæsar, VII, 225.
Rogers, H. H., II, 254; VI, 88.
Rogue clients, I, 31.
Rogue lawyers, I, 31.
Rogues, I, 31; governed by, VI, 133; and the piano business, XIV, 110.
Roman, the supreme type of road-builder, VII, 78.
Roman augurs, X, 282.
Roman Catholic Church, founding of, I, 209.
Roman legions, VII, 398.
Roman sports, X, 208.
Romance, XIII, 412.
Romantic passion, VI, 300.
Romeike habit, IV, 63.
Room to turn in, V, 32.
Roosevelt, Theodore, I, 320; II, 282; XIII, 412; as a peace ambassador, I, 321; as world's first chief of police, I, 321.
Root, Elihu, II, 281; birthplace of, II, 283; parents of, II, 283; a great lawyer, II, 284; Secretary of War, II, 285; United States attorney, II, 285; Secretary of State, II, 286; masterly work at the Chicago Convention, II, 286.
Rostand's rooster, I, 406.
Rotarians, the, VII, 139; and beautiful back yards, VII, 138.
Rotary Club, X, 19; of Davenport, VII, 138.
Rotation of human crops, VI, 36.
Rothschild, Letizia, X, 345.
Rothschild's acumen, II, 68.
Rottenness of gentility, I, 218.
Rousseau, Jean Jacques, *Confessions* of, VI, 62.
" Route of the Great Big Baked Potato," VII, 15.
Rowan, Major Andrew S., I, 254; X, 54; XIII, 296; at Roycroft, X, 54; reward voted down, X, 55.
Rowdyism, V, 175.
Royal Literary Fund, V, 289.
Royalist, I, 358.
Royalty, XIV, 54; inter-relationship of, X, 30.
Roycroft, XIII, 410; building of, VI, 112; statue of Michelangelo at, VI, 327; environment of, VIII, 158; Edwin Markham at, IX, 97; weekly movies at, IX, 137; Grey Brothers at, IX, 195.
Roycroft books, VIII, 128.
Roycroft Chapel, XIII, 365.
Roycroft christening, a, XIV, 51.
Roycroft Dictionary, XIII, 369-426.
Roycroft Farm, XIII, 227.
Roycroft Guinea-Garage, IV, 221.
Roycroft Phalansterie, XIII, 365.
Roycroft reds, XIV, 85.
Roycroft Shop, I, 289; V, 395; VI, 327; IX, 84; XIII, 267, 365.
Roycroft Suggestion No. 79, IV, 458.
Roycroft Trademark, the, VIII, 403.
Roycrofted man, a, VIII, 361.
Roycrofters, the, V, 394; XIII, 362; motto of, XIII, 362; started Eighteen Hundred Ninety-five, XIII, 362; a corporation, XIII, 364; endeavor of, XIII, 361.
Rubber, the Age of, II, 29; Colt and, II, 31.
Rubber stamp, I, 426.
Rubber stamped signatures, I, 427.

Rubber tire made the automobile possible, VIII, 389.
Rudimentary muscles, VI, 96.
Rudolph and Sammy, IX, 28.
Ruins, XIII, 412.
Rule of the best, the, IV, 171.
Rule of the Demagogue, I, 120.
Rule of Three, by, VI, 46.
Rule of the worst, the, IV, 167.
Rule Six, I, 269.
Rules, of health and long life, and to preserve from malignant fevers, and sickness in general, XII, 35; to find out a fit measure of meat and drink, XII, 36.
Rumely, Dr. Edward A., II, 412.
Rupert, the Red One, IX, 29.
Rural Deestrick, underground vocabulary of the, IV, 89.
Rush, Richard, I, 160.
Ruskin, John, his description of Turner's painting, the *Old Temeraire*, IV, 17; reply to begging appeal, VI, 279; and baked beans, XI, 328.
Russia, one man that, feared, V, 62; the greatest thinker in, XIII, 327.
Russian oilfields, I, 373.
Rust, the Tyrant of the, II, 350.
Rustic, XIII, 306.
Rysdyk's Hambletonian, VII, 179.
Sabbath, VI, 304.
Sabbath-keeping and church going, VI, 380.
Sabine women, XIII, 313.
Sabines, XIII, 321.
Sacajawea, statue to, I, 139.
Sacred birds of Minerva, XI, 394.
Sacred shrines, IX, 275.
Sacred soil, XIII, 412.
Sacrilege, XIII, 412.
Safety, in sanity, I, 381; and sanity, VIII, 399.
Saffron journals, I, 197.
Sage plants, V, 72.
Sailing craft, II, 28.
Saint, XIII, 412; the only, VI, 243.
Saint Benedict, V, 176.
Saint Bernard Brotherhood, VII, 286.
Saint Bernard Brothers and their dogs, VII, 287.
Saint Cecelia, IX, 307.
Saint Francis, the modern Sons of, VII, 53.
Saint Francis Hotel, X, 296.
Saint Paul, City of, VII, 19.
Saintship, XIII, 413; sin way to, IX, 332.
Salem witchcraft insanity, I, 108.
Salesman, I, 455; America's greatest, II, 375.
Salesmanship, VIII, 83; as an indoor sport, VIII, 193; and advertising twin sisters, I, 195; Ad clubs and, VIII, 194; success in, VIII, 194; science of, X, 225.
Salesmen, hints to, I, 455.
Saliva, VIII, 47.
Salome and John the Baptist, XI, 38.
Saloon, XIII, 413; the poor man's club, IX, 353.
Salt and Hogs, IX, 299.
Salt Lake City, VII, 56; Back Yard Association in, VII, 58.
Saltus, Edgar, V, 278; X, 83; *The Lords of the Ghostland*, by, X, 86.
Salvation, VI, 273; XIII, 413; the secret of, IV, 318.
Sam, XIV, 38.
Samaria, XI, 50.
Samurai spirit, V, 212.
Sanatorium, XIII, 413.
San Diego, a Little Journey to, VII, 191; Exposition, VII, 194; atmosphere of, VII, 196; idea, VII, 197; IX, 409.
San Francisco, and the Fair, VII, 268; the, fire, VII, 269.
San Joaquin Valley, VII, 161, 281; productiveness of, VII, 161.
San Pedro, IX, 409.
Sanitarium, the Kellogg, II, 321.
Sanity, VIII, 399; XIII, 412; usefulness test of, X, 58.
Santa Barbara, IX, 410.
Sappho, X, 343.
Sartor Resartus, XIII, 324.
Saskatoon, XIV, 113.
Satan, IV, 123; artistic temperament of, IV, 43; fall of, IV, 44; Mr., and his band of knockers, IV, 44.
Satirist, XIII, 413.
Saturday Evening Post, VIII, 83.
Savagery, single file is, IV, 52.
Savages, XIII, 413.
Savannah, the, VII, 75.
Savings from capital, I, 39.
Savings Bank, IV, 402.

Saving-Bank Habit, I, 87.
Saviors, XII, 377; with pompadours, I, 89; Thoreau on, of the world, II, 169; IX, 395.
Sawdust trail, the, IX, 211.
Sawyer, Tom, X, 339.
Sayles, Reverend Mr., XIII, 296.
Scandal, IX, 93, XIII, 413; newspapers and, IV, 194.
Scandal mongers, I, 110.
Scene of horrors, a, IV, 126.
Schaffner from Chicago, XIII, 239.
Schamp, definition of, IX, 254.
Schilling, August, X, 295; motto of, X, 298.
Schlatter, Francis, VI, 179.
Schliemann, Heinrich, XIV, 78; discoveries of, XIV, 79.
Schœllkopf, Jacob F., one of the world's greatest workers, VII, 115.
Scholar, XIII, 413.
School, XIII, 413; Indian Reservation, I, 135, 138; of the department store, I, 285; Colt Memorial, II, 40; the correspondence, plan, II, 198; detention, II, 328; of adversity, II, 249; the Doylestion Farm, IV, 32; the ungraded, V, 115; at disposal of people, VII, 102; a, experiment, VIII, 37; public, IX, 56.
Schoolhouse, II, 139; a national bulwark, IV, 153.
Schoolma'ams make great mothers, VII, 366.
Schools, IX, 46; normal, I, 284; of efficiency, I, 286; technical, I, 412; free, IX, 45, 57; private and public, IX, 57; public and private, a differentiation, IX, 57; private, IX, 58; charity, IX, 59; out-of-doors, IX, 359.
School system of Omaha, VII, 176.
School teachers and teaching, VI, 219.
School teaching, IV, 139.
Science, XIII, 414; strange experiments in name of, I, 309; and human misery, I, 359; of roadmaking, I, 385; camp-fire genesis of, I, 438; of economics, II, 169; is bankrupt, IV, 367; and the Bible, V, 323; and health, VI, 166; IX, 23; of theology, VI, 272; definition of, VIII, 15; and belief, VIII, 16; in prophylactics, VIII, 46; in business, VIII, 134; in medicine, VIII, 134; in education, VIII, 135; the reverence of, IX, 121; foes to, IX, 171; holy trinity of, XII, 178.
Scientific farming, II, 279.
Scientist, businessman our only, II, 444; task of the, XI, 14.
Scotch, I, 404; XIII, 414; own the world, I, 228; as inventors, II, 235; some characteristics of the, IX, 375.
Scotch folk lore, charming bit of, XI, 383.
Scotland, IX, 374.
Scottish customs at haying time, IV, 190.
Scourge of vice, IX, 25.
Scrap-heap, part it plays in civilization, II, 13.
Sea Captain, Trollope's story of, I, 446.
Seaman, Allen B., X, 231; will of, X, 232.
Seaman and Van Sickle of Denver, V, 160.
Searle, Fred, V, 164.
Sears, Richard W., VIII, 358.
Season sales, X, 316.
Seattle, feature of the city of, IV, 159; school playgrounds of, IV, 159.
Seclusion, IX, 196.
Secondhand thought, IV, 284.
Secor, John A., and Doctor Edward A. Rumely, II, 405; his idea of the oil-engine, II, 407; grandfather of, was an engineer in the employ of Robert Fulton, II, 411.
Secret, XIII, 413; of keeping well, VI, 41.
Secret societies, I, 399; excuse for, IV, 96; product of savagery, VI, 128; criticism of, VI, 129; and sex separation, VI, 129.
Secretary of State, II, 286
Secrets, I, 399; IV, 466.
Sectarian zealots, I, 268.
See America First, VII, 48.
Seed-bag of Europe, the, VII, 396.
Seed corn and wealth, IX, 355.
Seer, the, V, 160; XIII, 404.
Selected Writings are Elbert Hubbard at his best, I, 14.
Selectmen, the, I, 468.
Self-complacency, XIII, 322.
Self-confidence, the habit of, IV, 55.

Self-control, XIII, 414.
Self-effacement, VI, 87.
Self-exploitation, one great sin, X, 46.
Self-government, right of, XII, 100.
Self-help, V, 247.
Self-interest, enlightened, I, 218; II, 388.
Self-justification, I, 33.
Self-preservation, IV, 321; IX, 215.
Self-protection, XIII, 415; is the first law of life, VI, 26.
Self-reliance, IV, 248, 410; XII, 214; XIII, 413; developing, IV, 250; and women, VI, 205; Ingersoll on, XII, 179; Emerson on, XII, 194.
Self-respect, I, 49; IX, 248.
Self-trust, Emerson on, XII, 201.
Selfridge store, the, IV, 221.
Selling at cost, VIII, 52.
Selling magazine, the, VIII, 269.
Sells-Floto Circus, IX, 223.
Sense of values, I, 459.
Sensitiveness, literary, IV, 360.
Sensuality and asceticism, IX, 315.
Sentiment, III, 368; and business, V, 131; world is ruled by, IX, 291.
Separation, the act of, I, 363.
Sergeant, the, VI, 361; a beneficent tyrant, VI, 362.
Sermon, abolish the, VI, 117.
Servant-girl problem, XIII, 338.
Servants in common, VIII, 294.
Servia, a Little Journey to, VII, 260; Cæsar and, VII, 260; fertile valleys of, VII, 260; the story of the Court of, VII, 263.
Service, II, 290; VIII, 241; undivided, I, 60; reward of, I, 332; human, I, 397; genuine, II, 261; loyal, II, 442; rewarded, VI, 313; devoted, VII, 220; cheerful, XIII, 277.
Servility, XIII, 414.
Serving God on Sunday, VI, 303.
Seton, Ernest Thompson, X, 47.
Seven hag sisters, VIII, 83.
Seward, William H., VII, 122.
Sewing Circle, IX, 192.
Sewing-machines and knitting-machines as emancipators, IV, 476.
Sex, III, 463; IV, 382.
Sex impulse, IV, 150.
Sex jealousy, VI, 256.
Sex question, the, IV, 147.

Schopenhauer, mother of, X, 240.
Schumann, Clara, V, 137.
Scientific fasting, V, 302.
Scripture history, IX, 112.
Shaker Colony at Sonyea, X, 133.
Shakespeare, and the Jews, IV, 30; used twenty-five thousand words, VI, 24; monument to, VII, 159.
Shakespeare and Lawyers, V, 202.
Sham confession, VI, 66.
Shannon, Governor, message of, III, 327.
Shaw, and the Golden Rule, VII, 94.
Sheeny, XIII, 414.
Sheep in Texas, VII, 284.
Sheep-man, VII, 284.
Sheffield cutlery, XIV, 98.
Sheldon, Arthur F., X, 225.
Sheldonism, X, 225.
Sheridan's Theater, X, 276.
Sherman Act, I, 71, 197; VIII, 267; XIII, 414; effect of the, VIII, 57.
Sherman House and Emerson, VIII, 271.
Shield of Achilles, I, 217.
Shillalah, divinity of the, I, 318.
Shoal, XIII, 414.
Shoddy goods, laundries as testers of, VIII, 260.
Shoemaker, Tolstoy's story of the, II, 182.
Shoes, Emerson on, II, 184; made by machinery, II, 186; mirror the progress of civilization, II, 186.
Shonts, Theodore P., XIV, 49.
Shouldering the blame, XIV, 220
Shrine of Our Lady, XI, 396.
Shulamite, home of the, XI, 15.
Shylock, V, 203.
Sickman, IV, 47; a rascal, IX, 284; XIII, 271.
Sickness, a disgrace, VI, 330; Emerson on, XII, 238.
Sickroom consolation, IV, 131.
Silence, XIII, 414; Essay on, X, 412.
Silent system, the, IV, 76; VII, 257.
Silkworm, XIV, 306.
Silos, VIII, 286.
Silver Arrow, the, XIV, 13.
Silverton, "Kuhnel," III, 70.
Silverton, Margaret, III, 77.
Simeon Stylites, IX, 184.
Simmons, E. C., II, 358.
Simon the Cyrenian, XI, 80.

Simple Life, the, VII, 29.
Simplon Pass, VII, 286.
Simplicity, VI, 212.
Simpson, Jerry, the sockless candidate, VIII, 339.
Sin, VI, 239, 273; IX, 332; XII, 286; XIII, 414; immunity from the penalties of, I, 131; the unpardonable, IV, 252, 382; VI, 143; what is, VI, 388; the only, VI, 390; New York City synonym of, VII, 326; besetting, IX, 262; benefits and advantages of, IV, 299, IX, 332; way to saintship, IX, 332.
Sincerity, XIII, 414.
Sinclair, Upton, I, 54.
Sing Sing, Mayor of the City of, VII, 90; cells of, VII, 92; a, census, XIV, 176.
Single Tax, I, 150; Bolton Hall and, I, 51.
Sins, that admit of no palliation, VI, 388; and penalties, IX, 35.
Six best sellers, I, 335.
Skirt, XIII, 320; short, IX, 271; means servility, XIII, 320.
Skunk expert, a, XIII, 238.
Skunks, XIII, 237.
Sky-scraper, VIII, 53.
Slab-Sides, V, 35.
Slang, king of, X, 21.
Slave, XIII, 415.
Slavery, and slave owners, III, 235; Jefferson on, III, 236; justified in Bible, III, 257; child, IV, 346; VI, 399; reason church has always sided with, VI, 407; and organized religion, VIII, 16; Athens and, XIII, 359.
Slave-stealing and horse-stealing, III, 197.
Slaves, Thomas Jefferson owned, II, 454; runaway, III, 329; hunting fugitive, III, 136.
Slavocracy, a relic of, III, 375.
Sleep, and exercise for health, IX, 249; required by the average man, IX, 249.
Sleepy Hollow Cemetery, IX, 309; X, 48.
Slivers, III, 73.
Sloth, XII, 71.
Smack, XIII, 415.
Smallpox, XIV, 237.
Smile, I, 324.
Smirking complacency, V, 384.

Smith, Adam, I, 287.
Smith, Donald A., VII, 331.
Smith, Joseph, IV, 60; IX, 61.
Smokeless and non-explosive ballot, I, 357.
Smokeless powder, II, 236.
Smooth lawn with terra-cotta dogs, VI, 61.
Smudge, Smut, Smith and Smoot, VI, 355.
Smugglers, IX, 362.
Smugness, XIII, 322.
Snake Drug Store, X, 295.
Snake in Paradise, XIII, 241.
Sober, XIII, 414.
Social Centers, IX, 352.
Social dead-line, IV, 183.
Social evolution, I, 322; IV, 137; a very interesting phenomenon in, IX, 258.
Social letter of credit, I, 405.
Social migrations, IV, 183.
Social play-actors, XIII, 323.
Social Problems, Society for the Study of, XI, 87.
Social reformers, queer phases among, I, 51.
Social Seven, XIII, 338.
Social status, show his, in his hat, II, 437.
Social Washington, I, 46.
Socialism, I, 42, 359; V, 305; VI, 155; IX, 372; XIII, 415; Fabian, I, 30; Marxian, I, 55; IV, 176; Marxian, and class hatred, I, 30; grievance of, I, 56; and evolution, I, 227; and cheap products, VI, 155; Marxian and Fabian, VI, 306; post office system our best example of applied, VI, 310; as an ideal theory, VII, 343; this beautiful dream of, XIV, 262; Christian XIV, 263.
Socialist, XIII, 415; the Red, I, 70; Marxian, I, 52, 332; X, 129.
Socialistic colony at Washington, VII, 230.
Socialistic unionism, I, 71.
Socialists, Jack London's views of, I, 29; fifty-seven varieties of, I, 52; millionaire, I, 54; lukewarm, I, 55; refuse communion to, I, 363.
Societies of culture, I, 363.
Society, III, 436; V, 300; XIII, 415; welfare of, I, 292; in a free, IV, 149;

of sanctified fists, VI, 195; common interests of, XII, 112; never advances, XII, 219; cornerstone of, is the family, XIII, 339.
Society for Electrical Development, X, 98.
Society's Ishmaelites, XI, 90.
Sociology, I, 303; IX, 165; XIII, 416.
Socrates, I, 129, 294; V, 255; his idea of an educated man, V, 257; motto of, IX, 128.
Socratic question, V, 256.
Soft water, X, 372.
Soil, kinship with, IX, 345.
Soldier, VI, 363.
Soldiers, greenhorn, IX, 292; and preachers, XIII, 316.
Solferino, at the battle of, V, 342.
Solitude, IV, 311; XIII, 416; soothing evangel of, XI, 397.
Some big broods, II, 62.
Some big potato yields, X, 352.
Some mocked, some believed, IX, 82.
Some things I saw, VII, 51.
Somnambulism, X, 137.
Song of myself, XII, 23.
Song of Songs, the, III, 457; fanciful interpretation of, III, 461; opinion on, III, 461.
Sonnets, some, VI, 189.
Sophomore of the Sun, V, 184.
Sorcerer, XIII, 416.
Sorcery, XIII, 416.
Sorehead, XIII, 416.
Sorrow, IV, 466; XIII, 415; respite of, found in work, III, 49.
Sorrows, the Man of, XI, 13.
Soul, XI, 413; XII, 149; Emerson on immortality of the, V, 232; the, of woman, VI, 182; immortality of, VII, 309; the evolutions of a, X, 254; relations of the, to the Divine Spirit, XII, 207; good in the, XII, 387.
Spanish Missions, VII, 192.
Spare Room, The, X, 236.
Spartans, a school of, IV, 176.
Spaulding on Evidence, VI, 28.
Spare-room, horrors of the, VI, 209.
Speaking, public, V, 394.
Special-student plan, IV, 250.
Specialist, XIII, 416.
Specialists, VIII, 40.

Specialization, XIII, 416.
Specialties, selling power of, VIII, 138.
Specious, XIII, 416.
Speech, II, 345; liberty of, II, 361; free, V, 174.
Speedway, Indianapolis, I, 389.
Spencer, Herbert, I, 319; VI, 338; X, 357, 359; visit of, to America, I, 304; on education, I, 405; on polygamy, IX, 69.
Sphinx, with stony lips, III, 458; and the clergy, X, 154.
Spinoza, Baruch, IV, 15.
Spinsterhood, XIII, 416; is an achievement, I, 152.
Spirit of the Hive, VII, 303; XII, 379.
Spiritual assets, XII, 355.
Spiritual influence and progress, V, 86.
Spiritual technique, VIII, 155.
Spiritual things, XI, 87.
Spiritualism, V, 230; IX, 62.
Sponge, the life-story of the, X, 408.
Sponges, X, 401.
Sport, the, XIII, 17.
Spratling, William P., X, 132, 201; his book on *Epilepsy and its Treatment*, X, 134.
Spring, the, XII, 154; in the desert, VII, 137.
Spud, superbus, VII, 16.
Square Deal, the, I, 379.
Squaw's story, I, 135.
St. Helena, IX, 403.
St. Matthew, IX, 396.
St. Pauls, IX, 401.
Stage, pastoral, VI, 311.
Stage managers, VIII, 316.
Stage telephone, I, 356.
Stall stuff, XIII, 416.
Standard Knitting Company of Knoxville, VII, 131.
Standard Oil Company, I, 372; X, 270; some assets of, I, 373; reasons for success of, I, 375; assailants of, I, 377, Ida Tarbell and the, I, 378; and its obligations, I, 379; dissolution of, VIII, 56.
Standards, new, I, 367.
Standing together, VIII, 212.
Stange, Ottomar, the man who built the Connecticut Avenue bridge in Washington, X, 377.

Stanley Park, Vancouver, VII, 349.
Star, XIII, 416.
Startling fact, a, IV, 240.
Starvation, XIII, 417.
State, I, 323; XI, 410; Constitution of United States on church and, I, 365; divorce of church and, IX, 169.
State supervision of Trusts, VIII, 267.
Statesman, Thomas Brackett Reed's definition of a, II, 281; and progress, VII, 394.
Statistics, the Science of, X, 283.
Statute, XIII, 418.
Stead, William T., I, 106.
Stealth, doing good by, XIII, 281.
Steam engine revolutionized business, I, 432.
Steam power, rise of, I, 432; and Watt, VIII, 94.
Steam traction-engine, I, 435.
Steamship, first to cross the Atlantic, VII, 75.
Stearns, Lou, IX, 232.
Stedman, Edmund Clarence, XIII, 272.
Steel, civilization and, II, 14; some uses of, II, 14; manufacture of, inaugurated in Germany, VIII, 88; processes in making of, VIII, 89.
Steel Corporation, I, 200.
Steel Trust suit, the, VIII, 355.
Steinmetz, Doctor Charles P., VIII, 366; X, 97; great modern mechanical prophet, X, 100; practical joker, X, 102.
Steinway, Henry E., birthplace of, II, 63; love-piano of, II, 71.
Steinway, first, piano made in America bought by Peter Cooper, II, 76
Steinway Grand, the first, II, 72.
Steinways, the, II, 62.
Stenographer, I, 427.
Stephenson's "Rocket," VIII, 325.
Stern facts, IV, 350.
Stetson, John B., II, 421; life story of, told in tabloid, II, 421; birthplace of, II, 423; loses fortune, II, 426; demonstrated felting of fur, II, 429; made a hat out of felt, II, 430; growth of, enterprise, II, 435; faith of, II, 436; apprentice system and, II, 439; builds hospital, II, 441; was one of the great organizers of the world, II, 445.

Stetson, has passed into the current coin of expression, II, 423; how, was first made, II, 430.
Stetsons, first order for, II, 433; my, in my hand, VIII, 389.
Stevenson, J. W., VIII, 145.
Stevenson, Robert Louis, on marriage bond, IV, 149.
Stewart, A. T., I, 284; business palace of, VIII, 163; greatest merchant in his day, X, 305.
Still, Abram, first Methodist preacher in Northwestern Missouri, II, 453.
Still, Andrew Taylor, II, 450; patients of, II, 462; students of, II, 463.
Still, Doctor Charles E., II, 462.
Stillwell, Arthur E., X, 333; a scout of civilization, X, 334; creator, organizer, builder, X, 335.
Stimulant, food a, IX, 313.
Stinginess, VI, 279.
Stock market, XIII, 34; miracle, XIII, 35.
Stockings, when, were a luxury, VIII, 339.
Stoeckel, Carl, V, 72.
Stoke-Pogis churchyard, where Gray wrote the *Elegy*, V, 201.
Stone, Melville E., writer, businessman, diplomat, X, 175.
Stone was first weapon, I, 39.
Stones, do, grow, XIII, 279.
Stradivarius, IX, 301.
Stranger, passing, XII, 148.
Straus, Mr. and Mrs., IX, 19.
Street-fair, a, IV, 273.
Strength of any nation lies in its middle class, II, 95.
Strenuous days, V, 27.
Strife, politics and, II, 290; physical, IX, 179.
Strike, the most successful, is a defeat, IV, 85.
Striking policy leads to defeat, XIV, 212.
Striving for effect is fruitless, XI, 429.
Strong man, XIII, 418.
Studio, XIII, 416.
Stud-poker, I, 78.
Study, Home, II, 198; short courses of, VII, 102.
Study Habit, I, 398; II, 114, 195.
Study in Syphilis, a, I, 325.
Stupidity, II, 387; XIII, 417.

Stuyvesant, Governor Peter, VII, 224.
Style, XIII, 417.
Subconsciousness, VI, 98.
Subscription books, VI, 337; and Speaker Cannon, VI, 337.
Subsidiary, XIII, 417.
Subsidize motherhood, IX, 245.
Success, II, 260; IV, 393, 437, 457; IX, 248; VI, 340; XII, 321; XIII, 418; essential element of, in business, II, 258; in modern business, IV, 98; the measure of, VI, 21; penalties of, VI, 119; sorrows of, VI, 119; degrees of, VI, 340; and cats, VI, 342; result of mental attitude, VI, 343; most natural thing in the world, VI, 343; and concentration, VI, 344; what is, VIII, 19; pathway to, VIII, 120; in salesmanship, VIII, 194; danger of uninterrupted, VIII, 223; only secret of, X, 278; Emerson on, XII, 214; the secret of, XII, 321; open sesame to, XII, 323.
Successful man, a, VIII, 19.
Successful vaccination, I, 259.
Succor State, II, 448.
Suction, XIII, 418.
Suffering, IV, 475.
Suffrage, John Temple Graves and, II, 449; China's women interested in the question of, IV, 371; equal, IV, 369; XII, 389; woman, V, 333.
Suffragette, America's first, XIV, 94.
Suffragists, militant, IV, 351.
Sugar beet cultivation in Michigan, VII, 187.
Sugar beets, VIII, 290.
Suggestion, VII, 393.
Suggestive Art, IV, 122.
Suicide, XI, 417.
Sun, XIII, 417; every, has its satellites, XIII, 19.
Sun worshipers, XI, 409.
Sunday, Billy, IV, 277; XI, 212; XIII, 373; world's great expert on the unknowable, IX, 229.
Sunday the People's Day, IV, 45.
Sunday baseball and the church, IV, 46.
Sunday laws, VI, 304.
Sunday work, VI, 305.
Sunken rock, the, VIII, 19.
Sunset Cross, V, 178.

Superficial omniscence, V, 91.
Superfluous, Pan-American Society for abolition of, VI, 97.
Superintendent of public schools in the City of Chicago, II, 446.
Superior Class, the, I, 216; VI, 186; IX, 77; XIII, 318; the menace of, I, 218; a burden, I, 219; remedy for, I, 220; the insignia of the, IV, 140; tyranny of, VI, 187; distinguishing features of badge of the, XIII, 324.
Superior Copper Country, VII, 360.
Supernatural, I, 302; XIII, 418.
Superstition, V, 97; VI, 44; XII, 112; XIII, 417; and morality, I, 204; Paine on, XII, 106; tainted with, VII, 308.
Supervision, I, 287; II, 15; VIII, 235; cost of, VIII, 112, 365; problem of, VIII, 115.
Supply and Demand, I, 350.
Supreme Energy, I, 404.
Supreme Farmer, I, 407.
Supreme Intelligence, IX, 290.
Supremely great, equipment of, XI, 22.
Sure reasons Churches use to claim tax exemption, I, 130.
Surgery, XIII, 417.
Survival value, I, 104; IX, 104.
Sutherland, Senator, XIV, 252.
Swear not at all, VI, 228.
Swear-word, a polite Baptist, VII, 178.
Sweat shops, VI, 408; newspapers and, III, 439.
Swift, the Dante of satirists, IV, 258.
Swing, David, V, 78; birthplace of, V. 78; on personality, V, 80; and Savonarola, V, 81; trial of, V, 83; a taste of the quality of, V, 84; epigrams from the sermons of, V, 97
Switzerland, example of, VII, 155.
Sword of Gideon, remember the, III, 358.
Syllogistic catch and toss, III, 469.
Symbolism, VI, 52.
Sympathy, IV, 389, 421; IX, 139; XII, 252, 377; XIII, 418; XIV, 57; Emerson on, XII, 241; knowledge and poise, XII, 377.
Synonym, he used the, XIV, 277.
Syphilis in its relation to marriage, I, 325.
System, II, 351; Gould, II, 294; probation II, 329; painstaking show of, VI, 53;

lxvii

and success, XIV, 204.
Tabernacles and mausoleums, IX, 324.
Tableau vivant a, XIII, 119.
Tacitus, X, 283; the Weisenheimer, X, 282; prognostications of, X, 283.
Tadd's pupils, I, 457.
Taft, I, 321.
Taftian, XIII, 419.
Tagaste, III, 435.
Tailors, the old-time custom, I, 424.
Tait, Dr. Lawson, I, 311.
Talk, XIII, 419.
Talks French like a cow, VI, 264.
Talleyrand on words, III, 444.
Talmage, A. A., II, 350.
Talmage, T. DeWitt, V, 181; indictment of, by New York *Sun*, V, 181; his plea for tenderness, V, 182; posterity's verdict concerning, V, 185; Reedy on, V, 185.
Tall Alcalde, the, V, 33.
Tantrum, the, IV, 315
Tao, VI, 198.
Taoism, VI, 197.
Tapley, Mark, III, 445.
Tarbell, Ida, I, 375; VII, 332; her picture of John D. Rockefeller, I, 378; history of Standard Oil by, I, 380.
Tariff, protective, VIII, 66.
Tariff walls, I, 69.
Tariffs, VIII, 61.
Taste is test of quality of food, I, 146.
Taurus, I, 75
Tax, Single, I, 150.
Taxation, VII, 329; of church property, I, 126; without representation, I, 365; Paine on, XII, 118.
Taxes XII, 70; Franklin on, XII, 71.
Taxicab habit, VIII, 197.
Taylor, Bayard, VII, 226; one of the most cultured men of the time, VII, 227.
Teach, the way to, IV, 75.
Teacher, IV, 139; XII, 339; XIII, 419; efficient, VI, 410; of teachers, V, 309; a., of teachers, X, 272; profession of a, XIII, 307.
Teachers, I, 225; VI, 319; Mr. Carnegie's beneficent pension-fund for, IV, 376; Harvard's, VI, 50; and teaching, VI, 410; better paid, VI, 411.
Teaching XII, 288; the, profession, IV, 138; out-of-doors, IV, 235; object of, IV, 435; things out of season, IX, 256; and teachers, XII, 339; profession of, XII, 342.
Techincal Schools, I. 412.
Teeth, care of the, X, 194.
Telegony, IV, 369.
Telegrams, X, 401.
Telephone, coinage of, II, 303; and Dom Pedro, II, 305; inventor of the, II, 307; democratic, VIII, 79; first, in Philadelphia, X, 364.
Telephone business, romance in the rise of the, II, 310.
Telephone Companies, rival, VIII, 76
"Telephone Ear," the, I, 148.
Telephone-girls, the first, II, 319.
Temperament, and expression, IV, 181; the artistic, IV, 360.
Tempest in a Village Teapot, a, IX, 149.
Temple, the, IX, 47; XIII, 419; commercial air of the, XI, 48; of health, X, 253.
"Ten-thousand-dollar-man," the, VIII, 197.
Tennessee marble, VII, 131.
Tent Cities, VII, 338.
Tenth Legion, I, 40.
Terry, General, VII, 213.
Test of the tub, VIII, 261.
Tetanus germs, I, 260.
Teufelsdrockh, Herr, XIII, 305.
Texas, sheep in, VII, 284; prosperity in, VII, 388; tour of, VII, 388; a prairie country, VII, 391; needs great men, VII, 393; and railroads, VII, 400; need of railroads in, VII, 406; courtesy, VII, 285; Siftings, VII, 388; steer, VII, 390.
Thackeray, I, 458.
"Thanking you in advance," I, 427.
Thanksgiving, XIII, 419.
That boy from the "Patch," IV, 246.
That Corsican boy, IV, 246.
That Mousetrap, VIII, 407.
Thayer, John B., IX, 19.
The, XIII, 420.
Theater atmosphere, VIII, 316.
Themistocles, VII, 398.
Theologian, I, 299; true type of, IX, 167.
Theologians, V, 283; XII, 225; discuss divorce, IX, 175.
Theological appendendæ, VI, 96; XI, 146.

Theological Seminary, XIII, 419.
Theology, IV, 307, 420; VI, 391; XII, 318; XIII, 420; and law, IV, 307; science of, VI, 272; fosters fear, VI, 393; vs. social science, IX, 165; and cooking, XI, 239.
The-scene-changes, XIII, 419.
Thing that lives in History, VIII, 221.
Things, impossible, IV, 459; of most value, VI, 21.
Thinker, XIII, 420; pamphlet weapon of the, I, 21.
Thinking, disease result of wrong, I, 143; right, VI, 253; IX, 385; XI, 402; philosophic, IX, 103; habit of pure, XI, 29.
Thirteen Colonies, I, 360.
This love-piano, II, 71.
Thompson-Seton, XIII, 228.
Thoreau, XI, 362; his place in heart of humanity, IX, 308; obscurity of, IX, 308.
Thorwaldsen, carvings of, XI, 393; his *Night* and *Morning*, XI, 393.
Thought, XIII, 420; natural, I, 295; freedom of, II, 27; second-hand, IV, 284; High Priestess of Free, in America, V, 224; impaired, VI, 254; is the thing, IX, 308; right expression of, XI, 406; Ingersoll on freedom of, XII, 171.
Thoughts of Mother, IV, 259.
Thousand-dollar Draft, X, 367.
Thousand miles for a dollar, VIII, 360.
Thread, needle and gown race, VI, 161.
Three Cent Fares, VIII, 29.
Three Presidents assassinated, VII, 353.
Three requisites of writing, IX, 311.
Thrift, I, 100; habit of, I, 100; Adam Smith's wonderful book on the subject, I, 100; Let, Be Your Ruling Habit, I, 100; as taught by a hunchback teacher, I, 101-102; implies industry, I, 102; Ben Franklin is our greatest example of, I, 104; leads to habit of writing, I, 104.
Through Arkansas on a mule, VII, 83.
Thumb Hotel bear, VII, 40.
Thwing, I, 399; on higher education, I, 410.
Tidal wave of religious emotion, II, 104.
Tightwadity, XIII, 419.

Tilden, Dr. J. H., I, 142; X, 154.
Time, IX, 360; XIII, 420; and money, I, 400; masters of, VIII, 153; power of, VIII, 226; puzzle to philosophers, VIII, 226; power of, IX, 360; Bible references to, IX, 361; right use of, IX, 361; Franklin on the value of, XII, 72; amplitude of, XII, 152; of great awakening, VII, 274.
Time and Chance, III, 15.
Time-clock, the, VIII, 294.
Time Service, VIII, 293.
Tingley, Katherine, I, 314.
Tinplate Industry, the, X, 341.
Tipping, VIII, 347.
Tips, IX, 318.
Titanic, the, IX, 15; heroes on the, IX, 18; sinking of the, IX, 19; survivor, XIV, 287.
Title, XIII, 421.
Titles, XII, 125.
Titus, Emperor, VII, 15.
Toads, XIII, 239.
Tobacco, XIII, 89, booze; and universities, IV, 175.
Tobacco Trust, I, 198.
Today, XIII, 420.
Togo, Admiral, II, 334; V, 112.
Toledo, VII, 187.
Tolerance, XIII, 420.
To live long, keep busy, IV, 48.
Toll gates and good roads, I, 384.
Tolstoy, Leo, I, 353; IV, 181; XI, 59; XIII, 304, his criticism of the church, I, 353; on education, I, 420; opinion of, I, 420; his story of the shoemaker, II, 182; Baba and, XIII, 304.
Toma, Mrs., case of, IV, 265.
Tomb, XIII, 420.
Tommy goes to war, VI, 39.
Tomorrow, XIII, 419.
Tongues, forbidden, IX, 357.
Top-notcher, XIII, 421; XIV, 184.
To raise calves, I, 249.
Torrey, Doctor, and his theological rough-riders, IV, 281; V, 153.
Torrigiano's hammer, VI, 328.
Total depravity, IX, 210; XIII, 421; dogma of, IX, 211.
To the Businessmen of America, VIII, 204.
Tourist, VII, 143; and dining car, VII, 144.

Towards Democracy, by Edward Carpenter, IX, 338.
Town Topics, VI, 155.
Trade, XII, 80; free, I, 63; truth in, I, 371; IV, 330; effect of auto on, VII, 81; trickery in, VIII, 20; the life of, VIII, 50; Franklin on, XII, 79.
Trade-guilds, I, 121; the old, IV, 223.
Trade Paper, the, VIII, 295; possibilities of, VIII, 297; value of, VIII, 297.
Trade-unionism, I, 71.
Tradition, XIII, 421.
Tragedies, one of God's little, I, 336-340.
Tragedy, V, 96; of existence, IV, 471.
Train wrecking, IX, 364.
Trainer of men, X, 124.
Traits, IV, 26.
Tramping, XI, 93.
Tramps, why of, XI, 97; philosophy of, XI, 208.
Transcendentalism and "Beecher Bibles," III, 391.
Transmutation of metals, II, 36.
Transplanted products, I, 228.
Transportation, I, 349, 433; VII, 74; VIII, 75, 143; fire father of, I, 439; and commerce are Siamese twins, II, 124; and labor, VII, 391; and refrigeration, VIII, 185; refrigerated, VIII, 188; evolution in, VIII, 264; efficient, IX, 378.
Trappists, IV, 180.
Travel, VII, 141; X, 393; in Jefferson's time, I, 387; the benefits of, IV, 249; in pioneer days, VI, 311; the value of, VII, 141; Lampton on, VII, 142; vacation, VII, 145; Emerson on, XII, 217.
Traveling, XII, 218.
Traveling Man, experiences as a, VIII, 289.
Traveling tourist, VII, 143.
Traveling salesman two ways for a, to make money, II, 394.
Tree-butchers, II, 144.
Trees, XII, 325; brothers to the, II, 143; man's kinship to, II, 143; wanton destruction of, II, 144; a Brother to the, II, 147, 153; Aristotle, Pliny and Linnæus on, II, 150; Stephen Girard on, II, 153.
Tree-surgeon, John Davey a, II, 148.

Tree-surgery, the father of, II, 147.
Trespassers and trespassing, IX, 362.
Trespassing on railroad property, IX, 363.
Tribe, a collection of clans, I, 39.
Trickery in trade, VIII, 20; XII, 402.
Trinity of man, woman and child, I, 49.
Trip up the Rhine, IX, 178.
Trollope's story of a Sea Captain, I, 446.
Trotters, famous, X, 67.
Trouble, XIII, 421; recipe for, IV, 437.
Trousers, XIII, 320.
Trumpet, XIII, 421.
Trust, the, I, 226; church, I, 122; labor, I, 122; tobacco, I, 198; oil and tobacco, I, 200; world's greatest, I, 351; extravagant claims of the, I, 352; medical, I, 352; IV, 472; the religious, I, 352, 407; church, as a police system, I, 354; religious, in France, I, 364; death of French religious, I, 364; the greatest, in the world, II, 93; machinery, II, 184; father of the, II, 227; powder, II, 242; possible evil in the, VI, 92; mummy, VIII, 45; and economy, VIII, 352.
Trust Busting, I, 351; big business and, I, 64; is an error, II, 378.
Trust problem, the, VIII, 352.
Trust thyself, XII, 194.
Trusts, I, 351; good and evil of, I, 351; represent a phase of human evolution, I, 351; religious and medical, I, 352; must be supervised, II, 228; Dr. Van Hise on, II, 378; supervision of, VIII, 267; the crushing of the, X, 270.
Truth, the, IV, 326, 427; XII, 394; XIII, 421; is the new virtue, I, 48; recognition of, I, 178; in newspaper office, I, 238; in trade, I, 371; IV, 330; in business, I, 425; is a matter of perspective, love of, V, 322; about keeping well, VI, 41; discovery of, VIII, 21; and convention, IX, 176; and the Dutch, X, 221; is relative, XII, 15; Emerson on, XII, 249.
Truths held by Ali Baba, XIII, 304.
Truth-telling, VI, 26.
Tuberculosis, I, 142; XIV, 237; care of, I, 142.
Tufts College, IX, 322.
Tug of inertia, I, 35.

Tulare, town of, VII, 161.
Turkey Trot, XIV, 89.
Turks and prayer, V, 253.
Turner, J, K., X, 77.
Turner-man, X, 81.
Turnpikes, network, of, I, 385.
Tuskegee, I, 401; X, 227.
Tutorship, private, IX, 56.
Tuxedo, the gravy-scarred, IX, 316.
Twenty greatest women, X, 343.
Twenty-six Broadway, II, 372.
Twilight Club in New York, I, 304.
Two Letters, IX, 108.
Tyburn Tree, I, 34.
Tyndall, John, X, 359.
Type effects, X, 216.
Typewriter, the, IX, 136.
Typewriting machine, the first, VIII, 117.
Typewritists as wives, VIII, 118.
Typical college scenes, XI, 339.
Typical debate described, XI, 343.
Typical educated person, the, VI, 318.
Typical secondhand thought, a, IV, 283.
Tyranny, II, 228; the, of the senses, IV, 354; Jefferson on, XII, 90.
Ubiquitous legit, the, VII, 321.
Ulster, I, 229.
Uncle Joe and Aunt Melinda, XIV, 43.
Underbreathing, IX, 286.
Underground Railway, the, III, 236.
Understanding, XII, 373.
Underwood, F. D., I, 408; II, 124; birthplace of, II, 133.
Unemployment and war, IX, 289.
Unfaithfulness, IX, 174.
Uniform Divorce Laws, I, 43; demand for, I, 45.
Uniforms, XIII, 325.
Union, final, 228; church, VI, 70; Los Angeles Waiters', IX, 317; and representative government, XII, 98.
Unionism, II, 325; VII, 383; and the American workman, I, 71; socialistic, I, 71; and intimidation, I, 117; attitude of, to production, wages and shorter hours, I, 121; diluting danger of, X, 79.
Union labor, IX, 372; XIII, 422.
Union problem, the, VII, 380.
Unions, Labor, I, 116.
Unique service, a, X, 285.
Unitarianism, rebels from, IV, 158.
Unitarians, X, 145.
United Brotherhood, VII, 353.
United Mine Workers, VII, 336; and Rockefellers, VII, 338; and socialism, VII, 343.
United States of America, XIII, 422; Henry Ford, general manager of, II, 92; Canada annexing the, VII, 334; banking system of, VIII, 206.
United States Rubber Company, the, II, 31.
United States Steel Corporation, I, 286; II, 13, 21; defense of, VIII, 355; famous dinners of, VIII, 355.
Unity in diversity, V, 102; XIII, 336.
Universal Movement, a, IV, 370.
Universal peace, I, 324.
Universe, the one unethical thing in the, IV, 435.
Universities, the rise of, I, 398; booze, tobacco and, IV, 175; physical culture in, VI, 323.
University, XIII, 322; of Hard Knocks, I, 401; of Wisconsin, I, 415; of Michigan, 415; a democratic, II, 377; of Valparaiso, IV, 175; of Valparaiso a school of Spartans, IV, 176; graduates of the, of Hard Knocks, VI, 375; of the future, VI, 377; a self-supporting, XIII, 357.
University Clubs, I, 498.
University militant, IX, 348; XII, 263; XIV, 248; program of, IX, 348.
University students, XIII, 16.
Unloyalty, IV, 109.
Unpardonable sin, the, IV, 252; VI, 143; XIII, 422.
Unpublished letter of Byron, IX, 145.
Unrequited, XIII, 422.
Unutilized capital, I, 462.
Uplifter, the, XIV, 91.
Up-to-date, XIII, 421.
Usage, XIII, 422.
Useful Institution, a, VI, 274.
Usefulness, XII, 296.
Utah, agriculture in, VII, 58; wealth of, VII, 62.
Utah Hotel, VII, 63.
Utopia, I, 29, 55; IV, 182; X, 130; XIII, 422; autocrats who play at, I, 29; and American working man, I, 55; Marxians want, VI, 306; trails to, X, 238.

Utopian, XIII, 442.
Vacation, XIII, 422.
Vacations, benefit of, VIII, 230; on, VIII, 230; the man who needs, VIII, 230.
Vacation travel, VII, 145.
Vaccination, XIV, 230; about, I, 259; a disease, I, 259; successful, I, 259; failure of, I, 260; deaths from, I, 260; statistics, I, 260; tetanus following, I, 260; as a prophylactic, I, 261; case of Robert O'Neil, I, 263; case of Margaret A. Graham, I, 263; case of Reverend H. W. Burwell's daughter, I, 265; deaths from, I, 265; Justice Vaughan on, I, 266; compulsory, IV, 115.
Vaccine, introduced into the United States, XIV, 234.
Vaccines, toxins and poisons, I, 263.
Vaccine virus, I, 259.
Vacillation, XIII, 423.
Vagabonds, XI, 92.
Vail, Theodore, N., II, 301; " the Monte Cristo of communication," II, 312; farm of, II, 317; a great economist, II, 319; date of death, VIII, 78.
Vale of Tears, the, IX, 114.
Values, sense of, I, 459.
Vampire, IV, 65, 293.
Vampire, Kipling's, IV, 294.
Van, Billy B., VII, 320; X, 21.
Vancouver, an eminently cosmopolitan city, VII, 348; climate of, VII, 349.
Vancouver Canadian Club, VII, 348.
Vanderlip, Frank A., VIII, 367; X, 99.
Van Hise, President Charles R., I, 62, 415; II, 377.
Van Horne, Sir William, VII, 334, 356; VIII, 377.
Vanities, Franklin on, XII, 75.
Vanity, XII, 76.
Variety-theater, VIII, 312.
Vaudeville, I, 341; XIII, 423; modern, VII, 316; getting a start in, VII, 317; the intensity of the work in, VII, 319; an incident at St. Louis, VII, 323; my lady, VIII, 301; rewards in, VIII, 303; a business proposition, VIII, 304; essence of, VIII, 305; two great things in, VIII, 306; and hoodlumism, VIII, 313; why, is so successful, IX, 199; a venture in, XIV, 157; an experiment in, XIV, 158; literary feller in, XIV, 160; vital thing in, XIV, 163; Scylla and Charybdis of professional, XIV, 165; ordeal of first, appearance, XIV, 168.
Vaudeville audience, VIII, 301.
Vaudeville pace, XIV, 158.
Vaudeville performers, VIII, 307.
Vaughan, Judge, I, 133, 266; on vaccination, I, 266.
Vegetation, IX, 295.
Vegetarian, IX, 126; XII, 32.
Vegetarians, Japanese are, V, 214.
Venice, VII, 152; the art center, XIV, 102.
Venom, XIII, 423.
Venomous snakes in America, XIII, 242.
Veracity, XIII, 423.
Veritism, VI, 69.
Vice, V, 126; scourge of, IX, 25; Franklin on, XII, 74; of the inability to say no, XII, 331.
Vicious, XIII, 422.
Viciousness exemplified, I, 174.
Victory, XIII, 423; at the expense of truth is dearly bought, VII, 277.
View, a larger, V, 321.
Vigilance, effort of, on industry, I, 28; eternal, VIII, 239.
Vile, XIII, 423.
Villainous daily newspaper, I, 238.
Vincent, Doctor George E., II, 103.
Vincent, John H., II, 103; X, 228; helped organize the Sunday School Union, II, 107.
Vincent, Warden, VII, 256.
Vindication, XIII, 423.
Violence, man of, IV, 435.
Violin and Piano, IX, 301.
Violin has a soul, XI, 113.
Virginia, XIV, 16.
Virginia mountaineers, II, 542.
Virtue, IV, 432; the, of patience, II, 163; the new, IV, 329; the vices of, VIII, 322; period of, IX, 34.
Virtues, XII, 198; old-fashioned, IV, 440; with their precepts, XII, 40.
Virus of fear, XIV, 231.
Vivisection, I, 308; IV, 402; XIII, 422; Doctor Lawson Tait, the eminent surgeon, gives his opinion on, I, 311;

how Elbert Hubbard came to cut the class on, I, 312.
Vivisector, the plea of the, I, 311; consciousness of, blunted, I, 314.
Vocabulary, bill-of-fare, VI, 24; a working VI, 24.
Vodes, legits and, VII, 321.
Voice, XII, 383; is the index of the soul, V, 132.
Volta and Galvani, IV, 15.
Voltaire, IX, 277; influence of on world, IX, 278.
Von Stein, Charlotte, XI, 399.
Vulpius, Christine, VI, 259.
Wadsworth, XIII, 423.
Wages, Doctor Bowsher on basis of, I, 287; and immorality, I, 289; and supervision, II, 16.
Wagner, II, 73.
Wagon Boy Orator, X, 24.
Wagon-springs, X, 249.
Wahceta, XIV, 19.
Waiting, the weariness of, III, 182.
Waldorf-Astoria, VIII, 347.
Walker, John Brisben, VIII, 246; and world peace, VIII, 248.
Walking Delegate, I, 117; II, 326; IV, 404.
Wallace, Alfred Russel, I, 262; and civilization, VI, 16; and monkeys, IX, 224.
Walton, Gentle Izaak, XIII, 78.
Wanamaker, John, I, 91; Sunday School of, IV, 94; five objections of, to the Parcel-Post, VIII, 278.
Wanted—great men, VII, 392.
War, IV, 192, 410; V, 317; VI, 38, 220; VIII, 242; IX, 77, 179; XII, 110, 370; XIII, 424; and peace, I, 159; of 1812, I, 160; educating men to, I, 218; some causes of, I, 218; as a corrective for industrial jealousy, I, 277; and commerce, I, 277; wastefulness of, I, 277; and passion, II, 64; a robber, IV, 194; women's part in, V, 325; is business, VI, 269; and business, VI, 270; a class, VII, 383; incentive to, VIII, 243; tools of, VIII, 243; in literature, VIII, 245; and romance, VIII, 245; and sophistic apologists, IX, 116; world of, IX, 116; manufacture of, weapons by private corporations, IX, 117; modern IX, 118; an anachronism, IX, 243;

helps business, IX, 243; gods of, IX, 288; means new adjustments, IX, 288; and unemployment, IX, 289; and politicians, IX, 289; XII, 368; aftermath of, XII, 101; and bloodshed, XII, 354; moral equivalent of, IV, 257.
War Lord, pen picture of, I, 278.
War Lord spirit, I, 159.
War preparedness, I, 160.
Ward, Professor Edward J., VII, 104.
Warrior, XIII, 424.
Wars, Du Ponts and American, II, 240.
Warwick slang, VI, 191.
Washington, VII, 123.
Washington, Booker, I, 157; and the color line, VI, 242.
Washington, George, and clothing, I, 368; self-reliance of, at Valley Forge, XIV, 229.
Waste, XII, 318; conspicuous, IV, 137; vicarious, IV, 141; the elimination of, VIII, 111.
Wastefulness, III, 348.
Watch and Ward Society, V, 166.
Watches, first made by Swiss, VIII, 225; first wearers of, VIII, 225; symbol of authority, VIII, 225; Aaron Dennison and, VIII, 227.
Water, VII, 118; X, 371; XII, 325; value of, IV, 82; has a great affinity for electricity, X, 371; soft, X, 372; filtration of, X, 372; purification plants, X, 374.
Water-softening, X, 372.
Water wagons, noble fleet of, V, 121.
Waterhouse, Professor, XIV, 234.
Waterloo, I, 37.
Waters, healing, VII, 85.
Watson, James E., V, 53.
Watson, Thomas A., II, 304.
Watt and steam power, VIII, 94.
Waves, XIII, 423.
Wawdsworths, the, VI, 160.
W. C. T. U., VII, 328.
We, XIII, 424.
Wealth, I, 39; IV, 428; XIII, 424; what constitutes the, of the world, I, 39; and wheat, I, 429; Adam Smith defines, II, 289; four factors in production of, VI, 369; the, of nations, VII, 65; four sources of, VII, 121, 183; mineral, VII, 121; of Egypt, VII, 181; what is the

lxxiii

one thing in the evolution of, VIII, 218; to get, X, 76.
Weapons, stone first, I, 39.
Weapons, evolution of, I, 40.
Webster, Daniel, at Mammoth Cave, VII, 240.
" We call no man master," I, 123.
Wedding, a pioneer, III, 17.
Wedgwood, Josiah, II, 147, 422; X, 359.
Wedgwood, Sarah, X, 345.
Wedgwood ware, X, 359.
We grow by reaction, XI, 380.
Weir, Harold M., XIV, 127.
Welfare work, II, 193; and National Cash Register Company, I, 172; real V, 129.
Well-doing, IX, 335.
Wellington Mausoleum, VII, 157.
Wells, IX, 295.
Welsh, Freddie, X, 203; at Roycroft, X, 204; book-lover, X, 209.
Welsh, Jeannie, VI, 352.
Welsh variety of the *lepus cuniculus*, XI, 339.
Wesley, John, I, 34, 132; II, 421; X, 358; went barefoot, II, 182; and flowers, II, 422; *Journal* of, V, 391.
Wesley, spirit of, IX, 109.
Wesley, Susannah, X, 344.
Western big-heartedness, VII, 97.
Western Reserve, VII, 360.
Western Union Company, organized, II, 305; and Bell Telephone Company, II, 308.
Westinghouse, George, I, 408; invented the air-brake, II, 410.
Westminster Confession, IX, 111.
What builds a city, IX, 409.
What this country needs most, I, 347.
Wheat, VII, 181; and wealth, I, 429; northward march of, XIV, 114; a grain of, XIV, 117.
Wheat Country, VII, 19.
Wheat-growing, XIV, 121.
Wheat producing districts, XIV, 116.
Wheelbarrow is the symbol of industry, XIII, 275.
Where Gush the Geysers, VIII, 386.
Whipping post, the, IX, 43.
Whiskers, II, 447.
Whisky, XIII, 424.
Whistler, James McNeill, I, 459; X, 243, 382.

White, Chief Justice, I, 199.
White, Will Allen, and Walt Mason, V, 119.
White child, first, born in America, XIV, 17.
White Cross Library, I, 296.
White Doe, XIV, 19.
White Hyacinths, III, 471; V, 391.
White Mileposts, VII, 274.
White Plague, Great, II, 427.
White Rat, VIII, 307.
Whitlock, Brand, *Turn of the Balance* by, IV, 209.
Whitman, Charles S., XIV, 66.
Whitman, Walt, I, 132, 242; XII, 22, 147.
Whittaker, Superintendent, and reform schools, I, 156.
Who Lifted the Lid Off of Hell, I, 277..
Who's Who, I, 410.
Why a man marries, IX, 91.
Why don't they eat cake, VI, 290.
Why I am a Philistine, IX, 392.
Why I ride horseback, VI, 15.
Why men collect things, VI, 151.
Why women write, IV, 300.
Widener, George, IX, 19.
Widows, about, VI, 204; and appetite, VI, 204; happiest mortals on earth are, VI, 204; and hope, VI, 204; emotions of, XI, 206.
Wife, IV, 141; XIII, 424; meaning of word, I, 431; injured, IX, 91; and children hostages to fortune, IX, 251; right to "reprove" a refractory, XIII, 315.
Wilcox, Honorable Benjamin M., VII, 123.
Wilder, Marshall P., V, 235; X, 22, 140; and James J. Corbett, V, 237; at the court of King Edward VII, V, 238.
Wilderisms, V, 235.
Williams, Roger, XIV, 94.
Willys, John North, II, 331.
Willys-Overland Company, secret of, II, 333.
Wilmington, VII, 223; greatest enterprise of, VII, 231; peak system of, VII, 230.
Wilmot, W. D., XIV, 91.
Wilson, General James Harrison, VII, 227.
Wilson, Woodrow, epitaph of, IX, 292.

Wilted Hyacinths, VI, 175.
Wine, XIII, 424.
Winners, the, XIV, 188.
Winnipeg, VII, 52, 327.
Winnipeg, Lake, VII, 327.
Winnipeg Band, II, 120.
Winslow, Sidney W., II, 182.
Wireless boys, IX, 193.
Wisconsin Idea, the, VII, 101.
Wilson products, X, 73.
Wisdom, IV, 399; XIII, 423; XIV, 57; love gives, III, 224.
Wisdom and Destiny, the message of, X, 166.
Wise guy, the, XIII, 240.
Wise man, XIII, 424.
Wisest fool in Christendom, X, 37.
Wit, XIII, 424.
Wives, brilliant, IV, 52; importunate, VI, 287; jealous, VI, 287; stupid, VI, 288; plural, VII, 71.
Woe, family, VI, 286; domestic, VI, 287.
Wollstonecraft, Mary, X, 344.
Woman, IX, 410; XII, 308; XIII, 424; the, and the law, I, 467; burden of farm-life used to fall upon the, II, 418; man proposes but, disposes, III, 58; work of, III, 59; XI, 217; greatness of, VIII, 468; Sam Jones and the erring, IV, 37; clubs of, IV, 51; the, who understands, IV, 66; position of, in England, IV, 348; rights of, IV, 348, 349; the new, IV, 383; a side-issue, IV, 436; is the worst enemy of her sex, V, 234; part of, in war, V, 325; when, was discovered, V, 299; the soul of, VI, 182; self-reliance and, VI, 205; a chattel, IX, 173; who makes a "mistake," IX, 245; in the business world, X, 305; administrative ability of, X, 306; and truth in the world of trade, X, 306; womanly, XI, 210; sphere of, XI, 342, 345; Ingersoll on rights of, XII, 175; love of, XII, 334; freedom of, XII, 391; a natural conservator, XIV, 71.
Woman Suffrage, V, 333.
Women, IV, 50; gossipy, I, 107; married and unmarried, contrasted, I, 152; minimum wage for, I, 283; economic freedom of, I, 292; American, I, 368; make good physicians, II, 434; are more heroic than men, III, 269; virtuous, III, 464; of the Exodus, IV, 184; earnest, IV, 185; young, with ambitions, IV, 424; club house for overworked, V, 127; and war, V, 333; can, go to war, V, 338; great, of history, V, 396; wooden, VI, 179; who live in history, VI, 181; advent of, into business, VIII, 117; twenty greatest, X, 343; lack literary, analytical power, XI, 321; peculiar power of, XI, 389; Ingersoll on love of, XII, 178; plain, XIII, 132; Sabine, XIII, 313; and insurance risk, XIII, 352; wage-earning, wealth-producing, XIII, 352.
Woman who did, the, X, 239.
Wonder, genius has, IV, 366.
Woodcraft, II, 143.
Wood silo, VIII, 286.
Woods, to the, VI, 347; miracle of the, XII, 158.
Woozy economics, I, 315.
Word, the last, I, 15.
Words, XIII, 425; Talleyrand on, III, 444; woozy on, X, 91.
Wordsworth, William, XIII, 425; terror to his friends, IX, 100.
Work, II, 261, 365; IV, 427; VIII, 381; XII, 277; XIII, 425; and food, I, 148; college education in, I, 220; makes for happiness and contentment, I, 300; sorrow's respite found in, III, 49; peace of mind and, IV, 188; love and power, IV, 192; joy in, IV, 268; and love, IV, 270; VI, 254; a blessing, VI, 234; brain, VI, 281; on Sunday, VI, 381; and service, VIII, 294; William Morris on, IX, 73; culture and useful, IX, 84; menial, X, 247; and health, XII, 14; Emerson on, XII, 232; is for the worker, XII, 362; and the Bible, XII, 363; pick your men to do the, XII, 393.
Work Habit, I, 398.
Worker, justice for the, I, 286; cheerful, IV, 84; XII, 375.
Workers, one of the world's great, II, 354; gang, XIII, 333.
Working bee and bedbug, IV, 393.
Workman, the Ford, II, 101.
World, reformation of the, I, 292; peace of, I, 322; will be redeemed, IV, 471;

of war, IX, 116; has been instructed by its kings, XII, 205.
World Brotherhood, VIII, 214.
World-builders, my brave, V, 33.
World conquerors, IX, 347.
World Federation, I, 281; a necessity, I, 281.
World peace, J. Brisben Walker and, VIII, 248.
World vision, VIII, 245.
World's Congress, VIII, 245.
World's Fair, first, in America, VII, 275.
World's first Chief of Police, I, 321.
World's fruit supply, X, 301.
World's greatest business statistician, X, 284.
World's greatest question, VIII, 241.
World's greatest Trust, I, 351.
World's most valuable secret, IV, 286.
World's six educated men, X, 357.
Worlds to conquer, IX, 347.
Worms, XIII, 425.
Worries, IV, 393.
Worry, XIII, 425.
Worship, Ingersoll on. XII, 168; the god Terminus, XII, 395.
Worshiping at a shrine, IV, 439.
Wrestler, X, 209.
Wright, Wilbur, V, 386.
Wrigley, XIV, 191.
Write, to, well, V, 393.
Writers, America's two most significant, V, 144.
Writing, thrift leads to habit of, I, 104; three requisites in correct, VI, 46; example of good, VIII, 107; the secret of good, X, 85.
Wu Ting Fang, V, 189; and Ireland, I, 228; youth of, V, 190; witticisms of, V, 192; built the first railroad in China, V, 194.
Xantippe, VI, 300; XIII, 13; compensations of a, VI, 301.
Xenophon's *Memorable Things of Socrates*, XII, 33.
Yagerites, land of the, VIII, 289.
Yakima Valley, VII, 97, 315.
Yale, I, 85, 400.
Yale spirit, the, I, 59.
" Yankee Invasion," I, 69.

Yankee Trick, I, 244.
Yellow Journals, I, 235.
Yellow Press, I, 70; and big business, I, 71.
Yellow Springs, first white man to locate, V, 266; distinguished visitors at, V, 269.
Yellow Springs Tavern, V, 274.
Yellowstone Park, VII, 24; VIII, 386; a Little Journey to the, VII, 15; bear and cubs in, VII, 29; beavers at work in, VII, 32; geysers in, VII, 33; elk in, VII, 37; feeding of elk, VII, 38; beautiful camping grounds, VII, 44.
Yeoman, Captain, of Fort Dodge, VII, 169.
Yesterday, XIII, 425.
Yokel, VII, 48.
Yoshihito, V, 214.
Youmans, Edward L., VI, 338.
Young, Brigham, IX, 61; his practical advice, VII, 183.
Young, Ella Flagg, II, 446; X, 306, 345.
Young, James Carleton, VIII, 125.
Your duty, XIII, 425.
Yours, XIII, 425.
Yours for the Revolution, I, 51; VI, 35.
Youth, IX, 145; XI, 387; XII, 156; as saviors, X, 311; instruction of, XII, 121.
Zacchæus, XI, 67.
Zangwill, Israel, I, 106; V, 240; child of the Ghetto, IV, 197; *Dreams of the Ghetto*, VI, 28.
Zeal, XIII, 426; hectic religious, I, 269.
Zebedee, XI, 41.
Zeitgeist, I, 68, 319; VIII, 103; XII, 380; XIII, 426; laws and will of the, VIII, 55.
Zephyr, XIII, 426.
Zero, XIII, 425.
Zeus, XIII, 426.
Zigzag, XIII, 426.
Zionists, XII, 324.
Zodiac, XIII, 425.
Zola, IX, 118.
Zone, XIII, 426.
Zophar, the malice of, IV, 130.
Zueblin, Professor, IV, 93.

INDEX TO ILLUSTRATIONS

Vol. 1

	PAGE
Elbert Hubbard	2
Roycroft Shop	5
Elbert Hubbard II	12
First Roycroft Shop (*facing*)	152
Chapel (*facing*)	312

Vol. II

Elbert Hubbard at Press	4
Elbert H. Gary	12
Henry Ford	84
Hubbard, Rockefeller and Bustard	244

Vol. III

Elbert Hubbard on board the *Lusitania*	6
John Brown	14
John Brown's Fort and Cottage	104
Kennedy Farm near Harper's Ferry	200

Vol. IV

Elbert Hubbard—The Speaker	4
Rostrum from which Elbert Hubbard gave his last talk at Roycroft	13
Roycroft Chapel	195
Monticello—Elbert Hubbard's Residence	337
John Brown on Way to Execution	426

Vol. V

Elbert Hubbard—The Farmer	4
Joaquin Miller	12
Wu Ting Fang	188
Alice Hubbard	390

Vol. VI

	PAGE
Elbert Hubbard and Garnet	4
"Is He Sincere?"	14
Ed Howe	222
Michelangelo and Paul Bartlett	326

Vol. VII

Elbert Hubbard in Vaudeville	4
On My Way	12
Elbert Hubbard and Captain Jack Crawford	99
The Custer Battlefield	206
Elbert Hubbard at the Grave of Tom Paine	302

Vol. VIII

Elbert Hubbard and Elbert Hubbard II	4
Leather Worker	14
Every Knock a Boost	100
Elbert Hubbard, Ali Baba and Eleanor Douglas	200
Copper Craftsman	300

Vol. IX

Elbert Hubbard, The Publicist	4
The Titanic and Her Captain	14
The Man With The Hoe	96
Everywoman	198
Mona Lisa	304

Vol. X

Elbert Hubbard, Lynette, Dr. Silas Hubbard and Elbert Hubbard II	4
Grandmother Hubbard and Elbert Hubbard III	14
Dr. Charles P. Steinmetz and Elbert Hubbard	96
Horace Fletcher	192
Abdul Baha	320

Vol. XI

	PAGE
Elbert Hubbard—The Sage of East Aurora	4
The Christ—The Man of Sorrows	12
Oliver Wendell Holmes	287
Walden Pond	355

Vol. XII

Elbert Hubbard—The Philistine	4
Lincoln—The Children's Statue	12
Walt Whitman	146
Ralph Waldo Emerson	192

Vol. XIII

Elbert Hubbard—The Fra	4
Buster Brown	12
Pig Pen Pete, Pygmalion and the Pigs	226
Ali Baba and the Kiddies	258

Vol. XIV

Elbert Hubbard—The Play Boy of East Aurora	4
Hubbard, Reedy, Norvell, Strauss and Miriam	12
Elbert Hubbard and The Great Raymond	82
Le Gallienne, St. Jerome and Hubbard	266